*The*

# GUARDSMAN

# *The* GUARDSMAN

The Olympic Peninsula series #2

## Cat Treadgold

The Guardsman
ISBN: 979-8-9877363-2-6 (Trade Paperback)

Library of Congress Control Number: 2023908990

Any references to historical events, real people, or real places are used fictitiously. Names of restaurants and companies central to the plot are products of the author's imagination.

Cover design by Gemma Rakia @gemmarakia
Interior design by Cat Treadgold
Anacortes, Washington
cat@CatTreadgold.com
www.CatTreadgold.com

Printed in the United States of America

---

ALSO BY THE AUTHOR

THE OLYMPIC PENINSULA SERIES

The Silent Woodsman
The Guardsman
The Magic Man
The Changed Man
The Fallen Man

BEYOND THE OLYMPIC PENINSULA SERIES

Mister Movie Star

Coming Soon...
Miz Country Goddess
Mister Heartbreaker

# CONTENTS

# AUTHOR'S NOTE

———◆———

Almost every summer of my childhood, my family traveled to the Olympic Peninsula after the summer term of the University of Washington ended and my professor father was finally free to take a vacation. We bypassed Port Townsend, until one day my parents agreed to drive through, just to prove to me it was nothing but a ghost town of decrepit buildings. No wonder I became obsessed with the place as an adult. After Port Townsend experienced a glorious revival, I began to visit as often as I could. My opera quartet performed a few times at the Upstage, which closed several years ago, while staying at Lizzie's, which I believe is now a private residence.

My husband Jeff can't handle constant cloud cover and endless drizzle, so we winter in Arizona, summer in Seattle. Although my visits to Port Townsend are less frequent than I'd like, I travel there often in my mind.

Those hoping to find a dead-on snapshot of the beloved Victorian town of my childhood will be disappointed. For instance … the kind of estate overlooking the Strait of Juan de Fuca Teresa chose for the O'Connell Compound may or may not exist, but if so, it is in Sequim. Near Port Townsend, it wouldn't have beach access.

Much of this story is not entirely plausible, though I tried to keep one foot in reality. My definition of escapist fiction is that it takes you to a place where everyone is beautiful "and the skies are not cloudy all day."

My sister Laura and friend Karin were my earliest readers, and their feedback was invaluable. In my sister's case, I think she read every draft. Karin was my main feedback for the audiobook version. My dear friends Tina and Anna came along at a later stage to offer suggestions and support.

Thank you, from the bottom of my heart. My husband Jeff is my loving, supportive rock, and a source of endless inspiration and insight into the male psyche.

*The Silent Woodsman* was originally a standalone. But from the moment I finished the first draft in 2018, I knew that Liam couldn't be dead and I wasn't ready to say goodbye to Joe and Ali. Then the other brothers began to emerge to tell me their stories. My imaginary Olympic Peninsula and the company of the O'Connells—my improbable family of kind, well meaning, too beautiful for their own good, troubled rich people—along with the resilient Ryan twins et al. have served as beacons of light in dark times. I hope readers will suspend disbelief and enjoy the ride into fantasyland.

If you eagerly await Book Three, thank you, thank you, thank you! Please post reviews on GoodReads and Amazon and help me spread the word on social media. For more information, including my social media links, go to www.CatTreadgold.com.

# PART I

# CHAPTER 1

———•———

IT WAS SEVEN IN THE morning, too early for Teresa O'Connell, who was a "drag yourself out of bed at eight and wake up over the course of two strong coffees" kind of gal. Nor had she been sleeping well. In Seattle it was four in the afternoon. Very confusing. Though the visit to Jerusalem was three days in, she still felt walloped by jetlag. Fortunately, according to the hotel's receptionist, the David Citadel Hotel was only a seven-minute drive from the Mahane Yehuda market. She could complete her fool's errand in under an hour, allowing her to return in plenty of time before the group departed on the tour of the Old City and the Western Wall at nine thirty. If her bear hunt proved to be a wild goose chase, she'd take a moment to savor an espresso at the Café Rafa over a copy of the *Jerusalem Post*.

The moment she slid into the backseat, Teresa regretted hailing her own cab. The driver was young and intense and openly ogling her. Start with Omar Sharif, thicken the neck and eyebrows, shrink the eyes and bring them closer together and you had this guy. Or maybe it was just the oily smile that repelled her. "Hello," she said, "do you speak English?"

"Yes," he replied and continued in a thick accent, "I can take you where you need to go, believe me." His caterpillar brows did a little mating dance.

"I certainly hope so." She kept the tone of her slightly husky voice tart and no-nonsense. "I happen to know that the Mahane Yehuda market—the *shuk*, I think you call it—is only seven minutes away. Please take me there, directly. Café Rafa."

His laugh was a nasty chortle. "I know better café. This one too common for Sharon Stone. I like you in *Basic Instinct*."

1

She chuckled in spite of herself. She bore scant resemblance to that actress other than the blonde chignon. If only she'd worn a scarf and a caftan to conceal the rest of her, instead of the white capris and robin's-egg-blue silk blouse. She fastened the top buttons, even though the neckline was hardly plunging to begin with.

"You go on secret mission?" he snickered.

She rolled her eyes. "Listen, if you don't say another word until we arrive, I'll triple your fare."

With a tight grin, he mimed zipping his lip. She couldn't get out of the car fast enough, tripping on the cobblestones in her high-heeled sandals, but not before she was out of earshot of his lechy laughter. Why couldn't he have been a nice old guy? If the object of her search didn't materialize and she didn't like the look of the café, she could have just hopped back in and let herself be rushed back to the safety of her luxury hotel. She was the last person you'd mistake for a femme fatale. She wasn't out to seduce anyone. She was a comfort and safety girl, not a risk taker.

She scanned the café's terrace. Her watch read eight o'clock. This man, Sagiv Zaslow, worked as a security guard for a bank and reportedly bought an espresso here every morning. The detective recommended by the American embassy had been poking about for months now, armed only with a high school yearbook photograph of Liam and a few grainy Polaroids. He'd welcomed the assignment, which came with a generous monthly stipend. It was agreed he'd search for a year. Two months ago, he'd run across this man, and the lead was the most promising so far. Teresa had always wanted to see Jerusalem, and her parish, Church of the Sacred Heart, just happened to be organizing a tour at the end of April. Not that she attended Mass except on Easter and Christmas Eve.

*Good Lord.* Was that him? How could it not be? In profile, he was a dead ringer for Duncan, who had discovered he had a daughter who had a missing twin brother a year and a half ago. Longish, straight raven-black hair parted at the side and falling across his forehead like a horse's forelock, slightly aquiline nose, full lips, golden skin. As if sensing eyes boring into him, he whipped his head around to meet her gaze. She gasped. The newly revealed cheek and brow were freckled with purplish shrapnel scars the size of raindrops that didn't detract from his startling good looks. Rather, they gave him a dashing, piratical air. The only person she knew with eyes like that was her sister-in-law.

"Ali," she whispered.

His hostile cobalt-blue eyes widened in confusion. Such an unusual color.

Deeper set than Ali's and unmarred by the explosion that had supposedly killed him three years and four months earlier.

The detective, Ephraim Haddad, had been convinced that the man he had confronted here was Liam, though he hadn't admitted to being Ali's brother or followed up with Ephraim after pocketing his card. So Teresa had concluded it had been a false lead. Now she had no doubt that, against all odds, she was looking at Liam. He reminded her of a jungle cat, a panther maybe, with that smooth, shiny black pelt. Afraid of nothing but wary. Or simply determined to be left alone.

Unaccountably shy, she averted her eyes, slipped inside the café, and ordered a double espresso. The stout middle-aged woman at the counter tried not to stare as she gulped it down. "I'll take another," she said. "Still adjusting to the time difference."

"Ah," was all the woman said.

Girding her loins, she took the cup outside. The man had gone back to reading his newspaper. She was not cut out for this. She wanted to go home. It would have been different if he weren't so outrageously handsome. She hovered next to his table, as if waiting for him to vacate it. There was an unoccupied table next to his, so she sat down.

He looked up from his paper. "If you prefer this view, you can join me," he said in American-accented English. "I don't bite."

"I wasn't …" she sputtered. "I mean, that's not why …. Oh hell." She took a seat across from him, spilling coffee on her blouse.

He offered her a napkin. She was embarrassed beyond belief. "Thank you," she muttered, blotting the stain too hard and popping the top button of her blouse. He leaned down to pick it up at the same time she did, and they knocked heads.

His deep, easy laugh calmed her fears. "Who *are* you?" he asked, as if convinced he was the target of a practical joke.

She was still recovering her dignity, but his laugh was so genuine that it was difficult to take offense. "I'm Teresa. Teresa O'Connell. You?"

"Sagiv Zaslow." His lips quivered with amusement. "Sorry about your blouse."

"Not your fault. Silk isn't the best travel fabric."

"And tourists usually wear more comfortable shoes. Sorry, couldn't help but notice."

She had planned to wear flats, but on the slim chance he turned out to be the object of her search, she'd wanted to look her best. "Your name doesn't sound very American."

"I'm not American."

"Now if you'd told me your name was Liam …."

He grew still. "That's not a name you just pull out of the air. In Israel, anyway." He folded his hands in front of him, waiting for her to continue. They were large, graceful hands with long, tapered fingers. The backs bore more faint shrapnel scars. His skin was a golden shade similar to Ali's, only darker. Must be all the sun here.

"I've been looking for Liam. His sister married my brother."

He didn't answer immediately. Finally, he said, "Ah yes, I met their detective. I've been mulling over what to do. Now, I suppose, you've decided it for me." He might have been making harmless small talk.

"How long have you known about Ali and Joe?"

"Ever since news of their wedding hit the press. This isn't some remote island, you know. We have Wi-Fi and everything. I saw the stories online. But I'd let go of all that." He stared off into the distance.

"Wow, just wow. That must be some story. They thought you didn't return because you'd forgotten who you are."

He exhaled a long, weary breath. "I know who I am. It's true that I don't remember the day of the terrorist attack or the month after, when I was in an induced coma. All I know is, we were at a café. I assume I left my coat on the back of a chair while I went in search of a WC. Did Ali get my message?"

"The toy soldier? Yes. Was there supposed to be a note included in the package you sent? She's never stopped believing you were alive. Said you always told her to 'soldier on.' "

He nodded in a self-satisfied way. "I knew she'd 'get' it—didn't think a note was necessary. After I emerged from the coma and got my bearings, I wanted to send her a message so she wouldn't worry. She's my twin, you know." He paused, and his gaze seemed to turn inward. "She's had a rough couple of years. I'm sorry for that." He abruptly directed his laser-like gaze back at Teresa, and her breath hitched. "Where are my sister and her new husband now?"

Still breathless, she replied, "In Paris, renting an apartment on the Left Bank."

She reminded herself to keep breathing from her diaphragm, the way she did in yoga class. His blindingly white grin didn't help. A tooth even winked at her in the sunlight like in a toothpaste ad. Observing that it was a gold canine, she wondered if his teeth had been damaged in the explosion.

"Paris," he marveled. "Nice. He's a good guy?"

"The best." She cleared her throat. "What have you been doing all this time? After the swelling went down, why weren't you identified?"

His full lips quirked. "So many questions. Someone did identify me, only as the wrong person. My mother—*adopted* mother. Her real son died in that same attack. No remains, just a scorched piece of ID and remnants of a sock with a pattern she recognized. He didn't look much like me, not really. When Maya moved me into her home after all the months in a private hospital then rehab, I saw photographs. I believe he was shorter. Similar coloring and blue eyes—ordinary blue, unlike mine." Rather than bragging, he appeared to take the unusual color of his eyes for granted.

"Why didn't you set them straight?"

His grin grew more forced, as if his patience was wearing thin. "I took a liking to Maya, and I was curious to see how it would all play out."

"Ali has missed you terribly. Come home with me."

"I have a life here," he said quietly.

"A wife? Children?"

"No."

Either the caffeine was kicking in, or the admission had delivered a shot of adrenaline.

She waited for him to continue until the silence started to take on an impermeable texture. Finally she blurted out, "A visit, not a lifetime. We'll pay for it. Money is no object for us."

*Whoops*, that sounded like boasting. If it was money he wanted, he would have contacted Ali and Joe ages ago.

"I don't need money."

*Oh, Jeez.* He did sound offended. You'd think she'd offered to pay for his sexual services. The thought made her cheeks flame.

He was taking in his surroundings as if memorizing them. "It's time for me to leave in any case. I may have outstayed my welcome." Meeting her gaze again, he asked, "When will they be back in the States?"

"Not sure. Ali's seven months' pregnant."

He blinked rapidly, absorbing this surprising news. "I'm going to be an uncle." He must have noticed the way her gaze wandered to the scars on his hands, because he explained, "They flew up to protect my eyes." He raised his forearms as if to prove he had no weapon and wiggled his fingers. "I still have all my digits, see? My other extremities too." He waggled his eyebrows. Heat crawled up her neck and into her cheeks. "I appreciate you coming to find me," he said then, all levity gone from his voice. "You must be close to your brother to care so much about his wife's happiness." He shook her hand

and held it a beat too long before letting go. "I'll need a few weeks to wrap things up here. I'll see you in Seattle, Teresa O'Connell."

"Let me know when you're in town," she said, handing him one of her embossed calling cards with her contact information. With a delighted grin, he placed it ostentatiously in the front pocket of his guard uniform.

He stood, and so did she. He towered over her, but it wasn't just his height—he looked to be around six-two, like Joe. With his powerful muscles, he might have been a linebacker. Larger than life. She swallowed hard, and he inclined his head in a courtly bow.

* * *

Liam wasn't sure why he'd dropped the ruse so readily. He'd been prepared to keep it up indefinitely, or at least until the universe gave him a sign. He guessed this was it. This angel from heaven. *Damn*, but his sister had married into a good-looking family. Teresa could have been a film star—she had that expensive, sculpted, put-together-by-a-stylist image. Then, when she'd revealed a self-deprecating, quirky side he'd never have guessed from the polished exterior, his perception of her shifted. More Meg Ryan than Kim Basinger. Adorable and totally intriguing. Cable TV in Israel offered a lot of pirated movies—subtitled, not dubbed—he wouldn't have gone out of his way to see in the States. Growing up, Liam and Ali hadn't been to a lot of movies or even watched commercial TV, except at Ali's friend Becca's house. While bedridden, in between learning rudimentary Hebrew and Arabic, he'd humored Maya by keeping her company when her favorite movies were broadcast.

After finally regaining consciousness, Liam had recovered slowly over the course of several months in a private hospital, falsely identified by the rich widow of a high-placed diplomat as her son. He'd had a lot of time to think, and the retrospective of his life thus far disgusted him. His belligerence, womanizing, determination to shield his poor sister from guys like him. Really, the world would be better off without him, particularly the female half. For that first month, his face had been swollen and his features distorted, or so he was told. By the time he woke from the coma, he was recognizable enough. That was when his alleged mother whisked him away. Maya knew he wasn't her son. She'd had a task for him, one he'd completed, and after that she had succumbed to the cancer that had eaten away at her for years.

Now he was free to do as he liked. Only he didn't know what that was. So far he'd resisted the women who flapped into his path like bats with faulty radar. He'd laughed long and hard at Madeline Kahn in *Blazing Saddles*.

"I'm tired of being admired" might as well be his theme song. Until he saw Teresa, and suddenly he surged with new energy.

Her timing was perfect. There was nothing to hold him here, nothing to stop him from answering the siren's call.

After helping Teresa hail a cab back to her hotel, he grinned like a fool. He couldn't wait to see what happened next.

# CHAPTER 2

———◆———

"April in Paris" was playing in a loop in Ali's head, this being the month of April in the city of Paris, though the reality fell short of the idyllic setting described in Vernon Duke's song. Rain, gloom, no blossoming chestnut trees outside her window. Come to think of it, the sentiment of the song wasn't exactly jubilant. The lyricist must have been depressed too. At least the morning sickness that had plagued her first trimester had passed.

At first she'd been buoyed by the news that her brother Liam had been found, but when this Sagiv Zaslow hadn't followed up with the detective, she'd reluctantly concluded that he was, by some cruel twist of fate, Liam's doppelgänger. The detective told them he believed Sagiv didn't know who he was. Ali couldn't buy into that theory. If so, he would never have sent her the toy soldier. No, Sagiv Zaslow was simply another American pretending to be Israeli who bore an uncanny resemblance to Liam. Improbable as that was, the alternative was too horrible. She couldn't accept the hard truth that her only sibling—the twin whose mission it had been to keep her safe during their precarious childhood—no longer wanted anything to do with her.

Ali was trying to read *Crime and Punishment*, but her mind kept wandering. Her life was so easy now, she felt compelled to read bulky, classic tomes to keep her brain from turning to mush. Would it be cheating to opt for the abridged version? Who was going to quiz her, shame her for taking a shortcut? Maybe she'd switch to *War and Peace*. She'd read it in high school and thought that, minus the war parts, it might be even more entertaining than *Anna Karenina*. *Crime and Punishment* was more engrossing than it had any right to be, considering that it was the story of a desperately poor man who

8

kills an evil old woman for her money and then feels really, really bad about it. It was just so … loooong.

Ali had the kind of life most people could only fantasize about, so why wasn't she blissful? It didn't help that she looked and moved like a landed manatee. Joe denied it, of course, and he seemed sincere. She was always either too hot or too cold and uncomfortable overall. Nothing she ate settled quite right.

Her French accent, learned from her Peace-Corps-volunteer foster parents, didn't go over well here, though she kept trying to improve it. She longed to fire the tutor Joe had so generously found for her, a beaky, prunish woman named Madame Crespin whose perpetually turned-down mouth grew more sour at Ali's efforts. She would make Ali repeat the same phrases over and over, eventually closing her eyes as if praying for strength. For instance, the lyrics from the children's song: "*Sur le pont d'Avignon l'on y danse tous en rond.*" The French "u" and the nasal "on" continued to bedevil her. If only she weren't so self-conscious …. At this point she was more or less fluent, had no trouble getting her point across. Could even defend Americans when she heard them accused of being superficial and clueless compared to the rest of the world. Though most of the time she didn't bother. She and Joe socialized with other ex-pats—former celebrities she'd never heard of—and she hadn't hit it off with any of them. They were Joe's friends, not hers, and she could tell they had no idea why he'd done something as crazy as marry a naïve, rather ordinary woman whose main attraction seemed to be that she was pretty—or had been before the pregnancy—and inspired his most famous song, "Babe in the Woods." Why, she was even woefully uninformed when they discussed country music!

Most days, Joe went to the music studio he rented to compose, claiming he didn't want to disturb her or the neighbors. His voice was still rough, but he never complained or moaned that his touring days were behind him because of ongoing vocal-cord-damage issues. The guy had been a country music god, and now he was just an anonymous American in Paris with a giant brioche of a wife.

Ali was also trying to learn French cooking. Because she had never been much good at American cooking, this venture wasn't any more successful than her efforts to acquire a Parisian accent.

Becca had visited for two weeks in February—without her master-chef husband, Jean-Louis, who couldn't leave his two restaurants—and her best friend's presence had shed a romantic light on her surroundings. They'd had a blast doing the classic touristy activities, starting with securing coveted seats at Michelin-starred restaurants. The Eiffel Tower, naturally, the major museums as well as the quirkier ones, the cemeteries, the parks. None of it new to Becca, who had traveled to Paris several times with her family. They'd walked the entire city several times over, despite it being winter. After Becca left, Ali fell into a major funk of loneliness, a state she didn't dare reveal to Joe, who had every right to believe that he had transported his bride to paradise. Then, in early March, her sister-in-law Teresa breezed in and raised her spirits again for a few weeks. As they all watched *Breakfast at Tiffany's* together on the VCR, Ali told Teresa that she was the human equivalent of Tiffany's—when she was around, nothing bad could happen. Teresa promised her they'd do some power shopping after Ali got her figure back, which created an awkward moment as Ali compared her own blob-like form to Teresa's Pilates and yoga-sculpted perfection. But heck, who could possibly stay slim when carrying twins?

After Teresa left, Ali was plunged into an even deeper depression. Joe was the one who had needed to escape the media circus, not her. She'd loved Paris at first, before the snobbishness of the people and the oppressiveness of the mostly gray skies of winter started to weigh her down. Visiting here was one thing. She'd be happy to come again after the twins were born and at least five years old. Right now, she just wanted to go home to Seattle, Becca, Teresa, and her birth father Duncan, whom she'd met for the first time on Halloween of 1996, almost a year and a half ago. He was a recently retired commercial deep-sea diver. Ever since Becca's wedding, he'd been dating a friend of Becca's mom, a stylish and garrulous forty-something gamine named Laurie.

Would Joe and Ali ever be able to go home? He insisted they were still in danger of being hounded by the tabloids. She thought he just didn't want to be reminded of everything he had lost because of his vocal woes.

She checked her watch. One fifteen. If she was going to arrive at the Marché Monge before it closed, she'd better get a move on. Dinner was several hours away, and she'd just had lunch—a simple *salade niçoise*. Parisians ate dinner at eight or later, and Joe and she compromised by eating at seven. He didn't ask that she cook at all—in fact, he'd offered to hire a chef—but she'd insisted. It passed the time.

She would never be Julia Child, but tonight she was going to make coq au vin if it killed her. Julia Child's recipe looked straightforward enough; Ali might not make a complete hash of it. She waddled down the three flights of stairs to the market to buy more ingredients. The vendors had started warming to her, finally. Took them long enough. The rental apartment was located in Saint-Germain-des-Prés, and one of her favorite things to do was stroll around the Jardin des Plantes and the Luxembourg Gardens.

She wandered too long in the botanical gardens while hefting her groceries, and by the time she reached the apartment building, she was winded. The three flights of stairs left her exhausted, so she sank into the couch and huffed and puffed for a while. Finally, she dragged herself into the kitchen, where the chicken was marinating in red wine and broth.

As she fried the bacon and cut up the vegetables and mushrooms, she listened to a CD of Ravel's orchestral works that usually relaxed her. Whenever Joe came in while it was playing, he would joke, "All Ravel, all the time" or ask her if she really thought it was the right time to listen to "Pavane for a Dead Princess." Semi-serious, she told him not to ruin it for her by endowing it with some ominous meaning. He was more of a Brahms guy when it came to classical music, but mostly he listened to guitarists. She enjoyed the Spanish guitar classics, the ultra-modern stuff less so and certainly not the freeform jazz that for her had no discernible patterns. Joe never played country music for enjoyment, at least not in her presence. Joe had introduced her to the songs of Shania Twain, Garth Brooks, and Tim McGraw—along with the "classic" country hits of Willie Nelson, Dolly Parton, and Johnny Cash. And she'd continued to educate herself about the genre on her own. And of course the four CDs Joe had recorded as "Joe Bob Blade." Her husband was so good that it made her more painfully aware of what he had lost. She suspected he had abandoned all hope of ever having healthy vocal cords again.

At the sound of her husband's footsteps outside the door and the key turning in the lock, her heart soared. He was sunshine in the flesh, a glowing presence radiating positivity and love. He came up behind her while she stood at the stove and wrapped her in his warmth, rocking her gently, breathing in the scent of her neck and peppering it with feathery kisses. She relaxed against him, savoring his aura—his woodsy, manly essence. The man always smelled wonderful. Even when he perspired, he only got salty.

"When you're here, everything is beautiful," she said, releasing a pitiful sigh.

He tilted her face so he could look into her eyes. "What's wrong?" he said with real concern. "Hard day?"

She hadn't meant to complain. Hers was the pampered life of an *odalisque*, only with the freedom to go where she pleased and spend from a bottomless wallet. What could be better than that? And yet ....

Joe sniffed the air like a Bloodhound on the scent. "Bacon! Are we having breakfast for dinner?" The prospect seemed to cheer him. Joe had never been picky about food, which made him wonderfully tolerant of her less successful forays into gourmet territory.

"No, silly, we're having coq au vin."

"Cocoa van? Bacon *and* hot chocolate?"

He was teasing, of course. She gave him a comic scowl. "Chicken in wine."

He nodded. "Oh, *coq*." Coming from his mouth, the word definitely had a naughty twist. He pressed his crotch against her leg to make his point. He was definitely hard. She couldn't imagine how she still had such an effect on him when she resembled hardly at all the woman he'd fallen in love with.

She giggled. "Careful, or I'll sic Madame Crespin on you."

He shrugged out of his winter coat and headed for the closet, singing, "We'll be eating coq au vin" to the tune of "Do you know the muffin man" in his painfully scratchy voice.

"That's one elaborate recipe," he called out. "You've been busy."

She forced a laugh. "The days can be long," she admitted.

He wisely refrained from urging her—as he usually did, in the gentlest way—to work on more sketches for her children's book featuring a gang of whimsical creatures living in the Hoh Rain Forest: Beverly Bigfoot, Bunty the Banana Slug, Otto the River Otter, Grady the Gray Wolf—even after Joe explained that no wolves remained on the Olympic Peninsula because the hunters put them all down. Recalling the Pacific Northwest just made her homesick. It was also odd doing sketches for a motley crew with no context. She needed a collaborator, because try as she might, every story line she came up with too closely resembled *Charlotte's Web* or *The Wind in the Willows* set in the Hoh Rain Forest.

The creatures she drew here reflected her dark mood. They all wore disgruntled expressions, as if as unhappy to be in Paris as she was. Homer the Hedgehog looked doleful enough to roll himself into the Seine. When Joe asked to see her sketches, she declared none of them worth keeping, and he knew better than to force the issue.

They'd discussed her possible future as a website designer. Her work on Joe's website had earned high praise. But its completion hadn't attracted new clients for her services. That would require hustling, and in her current role as the outermost Russian nesting doll, she wasn't up for that. Not to mention that she wasn't socializing with potential clients here in Paris.

"What are you thinking?" he said. "I just saw an entire saga cross your face."

"Only that you are perfect, and I have nothing to complain about." She looked up at the face swooned over by countless fans—the curly chestnut-brown hair, the subtly cleft chin, the fathomless chocolate-brown eyes. Was he really hers? Then she added, "Okay, I was also thinking that I look like a Russian nesting doll. The outside one."

He laughed. "Are you still reading *Crime and Punishment*? Give yourself a break. If you're looking for a good wallow and are bent on Russian literature, try Chekov. Or Tolstoy. A lot less depressing."

Her face fell. "Am I wallowing? That's so ungrateful of me."

He drew her into his arms and kissed her soundly, reminding her all over again of that first time. Even now that they were married and she was inflated to twice her normal size, his kisses hadn't lost the intensity and yearning that left her breathless.

He gazed down at her, his eyes shimmering with love. "I don't need you to be grateful. I know this is hard on you. The pregnancy, being an ex-pat. I can lose myself in my work. You must feel like a caged bird. Do you regret marrying me?"

She smiled and touched his cheek. "Not for a moment. I'll adjust."

" 'Every dream-man fades in the cold gray dawn,' " he said, quoting the song he wrote about her.

She nuzzled his chest. "Not you, never you."


AFTER DINNER THEY LOUNGED ON the couch, facing each other. Ali leafed through a magazine as Joe rubbed her feet. His unfocused stare told her he was deep in thought, working out a lyric or a musical phrase. She'd switched to French *Cosmopolitan* as a break from Russian angst and a means of working on her contemporary French slang.

She waved the magazine in front of his eyes, pulling him back to the present. "Have you noticed that the French cover models are way less busty than the American ones?"

He chuckled. "The French appreciate smaller breasts. You know, any more than a champagne-glass full is … *superflu*."

She smiled at his French accent, which made the word for "superfluous" sound like a life-threatening virus. Her own bosoms had ballooned along with the rest of her body. *More like a margarita glass*, she thought. *Or a vase.*

He sat up and leaned over to kiss the cleavage revealed by her V-necked blouse. "Yours are my favorite … at any size."

She leaned into him so that she was encircled in his arms, her head resting against his chest. "You always say the right thing."

Swerving out of what he had to know was dangerous territory, he asked, "Why don't we go to a movie tomorrow? Is it okay if it's American and a *version originale*?" Movies in English with French subtitles were labeled V.O., which meant Original Version—not dubbed into French.

His accent was worse than hers and his French just passable, but none of the Parisians made one of their signature sour faces at him when he used it. Such was the power of his charisma.

"*Ça roule!*" she chirped.

"Translation?"

"Something like 'Yeah, baby!' or 'Sure thing!' What do you want to see? I walked by a theater playing *The Wedding Singer* today." His face crumpled. *Stupid suggestion*, she thought. No stories about singers. Before he could respond, she said, "*Gods and Monsters*? It got good reviews." *No, no*, her brain protested. *Too depressing!* A dying filmmaker crushing on his handsome young gardener. *Ugh*. Too bad only the biggest blockbusters and quirkiest independent films made it to Paris. She could have used a modest, reassuring rom com like *You've Got Mail*, which they'd already seen. There were French movies like that, but she had to see them on her own, because Joe's comprehension wasn't up to French language films with no subtitles. They finally agreed on *Primary Colors*. Great cast, but a movie about politics would never be her first choice.

What went unsaid was that they both had to work at remaining positive in their exile. As much as they appreciated Parisian culture, the luxury of their circumstances, and the anonymity, Paris wasn't home. Ali pictured the primitive cabin in the Hoh Rain Forest that seemed to be Joe's ultimate retreat. She had always dreamed of settling somewhere on the Olympic Peninsula, preferably Port Townsend, with its New Age vibe and Victorian architecture. But she loved it all, really: Sol Duc Hot Springs, Hurricane Ridge, Lake Crescent, Lake Quinault, Kalaloch. Rugged cliffs and crashing waves, driftwood for miles, craggy, sky-piercing trees, everything coated in glistening green moss and lichen ….

He brushed a lock of hair from her eyes. "You have that dreamy look again."

"I was thinking about the cabin in the woods. Do you miss it?"

"You want our twins to be born there?" He gave her the impish smile she loved.

"Hah! But they could be born near there. Maybe in Port Townsend?"

He nodded, was silent for a long moment. "I'm ready to go home too. The tourists are about to arrive. It's going to get hot. You'll be more comfortable in a cooler climate. And I'll worry about you traveling when your due date gets closer."

She gave him a tender kiss on the lips. "You've thought about this too. You will always be my dream-man, even in the 'cold gray dawn' of the Pacific Northwest."

The phone rang, and he disappeared into the bedroom to answer it. She went back to her *Cosmopolitan*, thinking that she needed to find reading material less grim than *Crime and Punishment* but more absorbing than this piece of fluff, entertaining as it was. After she realized Joe had been on the phone for over twenty minutes, she started to worry. He wasn't a phone talker. That meant he was doing a lot of listening.

She had a feeling that their lives were about to change again.

# CHAPTER 3

———•———

"You said you were going to tell me about the conversation with your brother," Paul complained to Teresa after the plane was at cruising altitude.

"Oh course," Teresa said brightly, unbuckling her seatbelt. "But first I'm going to visit the powder room. Be right back."

She should have been totally upfront with Paul. He was her fiancé, after all. But something had shifted for her when she met Liam. He made her heart beat too fast, reminding her of the intensity of her high-school crush on Kilo. It worried her. A lot. She'd had her doubts before; now she was sure she didn't want to get married, ever, least of all to Paul. Liam seemed so ... complete. He didn't need anyone. She needed too much. And she wasn't getting it from Paul. Well, the wedding was eons away. A lot could change between now and then. She might even fall in love with Paul all over again. *Or you could come to despise him.* Where had that come from? Paul was so ... likeable. *A regular good old boy,* the nasty voice added. He was everything her mother—and father, may he rest in peace—had always wanted for her. Princeton undergrad with a degree from the Woodrow Wilson School. A master's degree in business from Harvard. He'd been in Joe's class at Seattle Prep and had once visited the house. She'd been twelve, Paul eighteen, which was hard to stomach if you believed his interest in her started then. It wasn't until Paul was named CEO of an import/export company in Seattle that they met again and started dating. It seemed like a natural fit, especially to her mother. And she thought she'd evolved beyond relationships that tore you apart and made you lose your appetite and turn moony. No more exotic, troubled rebels without causes. No more Kilos.

Back from the restroom, Teresa took her time getting settled. Paul had taken the window seat, of course. Why "of course"? Why didn't he offer it to her? Oh well, did she care? It was colder next to the window. But easier to doze. She never really slept on airplanes, even during long trips. Paul seemed absorbed in *The Economist*, and she had little desire to engage him in conversation. She yawned. Maybe she *could* take a nap. They were in business class, not first class, though they could well afford it. That meant extra leg room and little luxuries like champagne, but you couldn't lie down completely. Paul didn't like to waste money on things like luxury flight accommodations. She kind of agreed with him there, except that this was a really long flight. On United, you didn't transfer until San Francisco.

Come to think of it, there wasn't much they agreed on nowadays.

Teresa had just reclined her seat and closed her eyes when Paul put down his magazine. "I get that you want to get married in June, but why can't it be *this* June? Why does it have to be *next* June? I'm eager to see you sign your name *Teresa O'Connell Andrews*." He said the name in a weird announcer's voice and mimed writing it in large cursive letters on the seat in front of him. She somehow refrained from reaching out to mime erasing it.

She supposed Teresa Andrews wasn't any worse than Teresa O'Connell. An exotic last name would have been nice. Something Russian. Or French. Le Mieux. The Best. Teresa Le Mieux. She liked it. Or if she was going for simple, how about Ryan? A good, honest name. Then Ali and she could be sisters-in-law twice over. *Yeah, like anyone could be happily married to a broody womanizer like Liam.* Not that she'd seen that side of him. She was recalling what Ali had told her.

She rested a placating hand on her fiancé's sleave. "We've discussed this, Paul. Mom still feels cheated for having to endure Joe's intimate ceremony at that old hotel on Willapa Bay, and Joe won't agree to a religious do-over in a church, even with twin daughters on the way. That means we're stuck. Big Church wedding for us. That takes time and planning. All the desirable venues are booked through 1998 and beyond. We were lucky to get this date."

"Why do we need a *desirable* venue? What about August? I'm sure we can find something acceptable. Your mother's backyard would be more luxurious than half the commercial venues. The weather is way more reliable in August or September. And who says we have to wait to get married? Let's marry secretly then go through the gauntlet in a church later. Why do you have to be the good little girl?"

*Good question*, she thought. *I am, almost always, the good little girl. Not in this case. I'm really just hoping that by then I'll stop doubting the wisdom of marrying you at all.*

She patted his arm, which was hogging *her* armrest. "I thought you wanted to hear about my conversation with Joe?"

"All right." He folded his hands in his lap expectantly, awaiting the executive summary. She could imagine how intimidating it would be to face him in board meetings.

*He has a pleasant face*, she thought. *Wide green eyes that tilt up at the corners when he smiles. Somehow red hair doesn't suit him. Maybe it's the shade of red. Caroty. He's too ruddy. Is that from the drinking? He'd make a dandy Og."* She smiled, picturing the leprechaun in *Finian's Rainbow.* The tune from *Finian's Rainbow*, "Something Sort of Grandish," played in her head. She shook it off and concentrated on the conversation at hand.

"Joe was shocked, of course. How could he not be? But after everything Ali had told him about Liam, Joe was glad to hear that he's not itching to hop on a plane and punch his lights out for impregnating his sister."

Paul snickered. "Overprotective, is he?"

"He used to be, at least when they were both in high school, according to Ali. Now he seems … calm. He knows about Ali and Joe from the internet, and he doesn't appear concerned."

Paul threw up his hands. He was not a patient man. He wanted her to cut to the chase. "So, where has Liam been all this time since the terrorist attack? How come his coat got shredded while he was more or less intact? I thought the café was basically wiped out."

Teresa had told him the bare minimum about her meeting with Liam. Paul hadn't shown much interest until now. She raised both palms. "Hold your horses. I'm not sure. It's a weird story, and he's not a talker. He gave me bits of information, not enough for a complete picture. Not even half a picture." She paused. "First, he doesn't recall the explosion, not even the hours leading up to it. He assumes he left his coat on the chair while he went to find a WC. When he came to, he was in the hospital with shrapnel wounds over half his body. His face was swollen beyond recognition. Or so they tell him. He was unconscious for a while. They induced a coma."

Paul cocked his head, more curious than concerned. "He's horribly scarred?"

Teresa pictured Liam. Nothing horrible about him. He might have looked too pretty without the scars. "No," she said aloud. "The scars are faint. At least on his face. I haven't seen—"

Fortunately, Paul interrupted her. "How long was he in the coma?"

"A month or so."

"He had amnesia?" Paul broke into a jaw-breaking yawn.

Her enthusiasm for the story was clearly not translating for Paul. Thinking he might be jealous, she tried to flatten her delivery as if relating a newspaper story. "No. A woman who had lost her own son in the explosion claimed to be his mother and was paying top dollar for his care. He liked her. Ali told me she and Liam lost their real mother when they were five, and none of their foster parents were very affectionate. So when this woman Maya claimed him, he decided to play along and see what happened."

"Then …?"

"Oh, I don't know. Maya died from cancer. Whatever ties he had to her family in Israel appear to be broken. As I said, he's vague on the details."

"What was he doing when you found him?"

"Security guard for a bank."

Paul's smug expression told her he was no longer jealous of Liam. Too socially insignificant to be a threat.

She took the proffered champagne flutes from a stewardess passing by with a tray.

Paul drained his flute quickly, like it was medicine rather than a treat to be savored. "Helluva weird story. Can he just up and leave his job like that?" He eyed her glass as if weighing the wisdom of asking her for it.

"He did say he'd overstayed his welcome." She sipped her champagne, partly to lay claim to it. "In any case, he's not returning to the States right away. He has some wrapping up to do."

"What did Joe say when you told him?"

"They'd already decided to come home so the babies can be born in the States. He wants to buy a place in the Port Townsend area. It will need to have a guest cottage or two in case Liam wants to crash there while he re-acclimates."

Paul was staring out the window, frowning, even though there was nothing to see but clouds. "Why Port Townsend? That's where old hippies and minor artists go to retire. A floating bridge and a ferry ride away from civilization."

"Our whole family *adores* that area. A lot of Seattle's historic buildings were torn down in the name of progress. Port Townsend is the closest thing we have to Brigadoon, the city time forgot. For that, we have the railroad to thank for passing it by."

"It's *charming*, I guess." Her internal translator heard "charming" as "twee."

The champagne did nothing to dispel the grumpy mood that had settled over Teresa. "*I* think so," she said, folding her own hands primly in her lap. She was wearing a flared Norma Kamali black-and-white polka-dot dress that cost a fortune. A dress approved by her mother, like so much of her wardrobe. Not for the first time, she felt as if she was acting in some movie she had no interest in seeing herself.

"After we get back, I'm going to Port Townsend to find the perfect house for them."

"Why would you—" He cut himself off. "Surely he can hire a real estate agent for that."

"I volunteered." Her pointed look dared him to challenge her further. "I need a project. I'm sure Mother is plotting to draw me into her latest charity endeavor. It's the perfect time to get away."

"I'd come with you, but I'm expected in Toronto."

"Yes, I know." She kept her voice neutral, though she wanted to add, *Yay!* The word echoed so loudly in her head, she was afraid he could hear it.

They both dozed for a while, and when he woke, she was playing with her engagement ring.

"Please don't take it off," he said.

"This won't work." She hadn't known she was going to say it.

"I've pushed you too hard," he moaned.

"That's not it." She wished he'd keep his voice low. "We're not well suited."

"Don't make a decision right now," he pleaded. "Keep the ring. Help Joe out. I'm going to Toronto anyway. We'll take a break. Maybe you'll miss me. I love you."

She kept the ring on. "You won't contact me for the next month? Not by phone or email?"

"Cross my breaking heart," he said in a dramatic whisper.

She turned away so he couldn't see her roll her eyes. "Okay." It was easier not to argue.

"You won't tell your mother?"

"No," she said, happy to keep *that* promise.

# CHAPTER 4

---

It was May fifteenth, and Teresa was sitting alone in the backyard of her childhood home on Capitol Hill, lounging on the swing that graced the wraparound porch. Her mother lived there alone now, with cook and handyman Rostand nearby in the carriage house. The towering privacy hedge prevented curious gawkers from disrupting Teresa's musings. It worked both ways. She couldn't watch them either. She liked observing people and their dogs, which was one of the reasons she enjoyed meeting friends to walk around Green Lake. It was the closest thing Seattle had to a Parisian grand boulevard.

To her, the 1924 half-timbered Tudor revival house was too ostentatious. Still, it was the site of her enjoyably sheltered childhood, where she'd grown up surrounded by all four of her adoring and adorable older brothers. The sheltered part ended when she was just shy of fourteen and their father had died, splintering the family in ways that would only become apparent later.

The eldest, Edward—a priest who presided over a large parish in Philadelphia—had turned into a bit of a prig. More than a bit. Surprisingly, considering how wild he'd been in his youth. He was thirty-six now and wouldn't marry unless he left the Church. Had he ever been in love? She might never know.

Joe's twin Jake was all work and no play. Unless you counted fine dining and collecting good bottles of wine as play, which he obviously did. And dating women as if they were books you checked out of the library then returned before their due dates, the only option a three-week renewal. Nothing smacking of permanence. In high school, he'd been a track star, played in a band, and wrote short stories, some of which were published in major literary magazines that catered to lovers of suspense/thriller fiction. He still jogged, but the other pursuits had long since been abandoned. To be fair, being the CEO of Big Paul's Outfitters—the family business—didn't leave much time for writing or playing music. BPO had just opened a new store and offices in Oakland, California, where he spent most of his time now. Was there a woman there, one he hadn't already tired of? Jake had briefly dated Ali, who initially believed he was Joe. It was an honest mistake. They were dead ringers if you couldn't see their jawlines, and Joe had sported a heavy beard at his and Ali's first encounter in that primitive cabin in the woods. Now that Joe and Ali were married, Jake was experiencing a life crisis. Couldn't call it *mid*life, him being only thirty-one.

David was an itinerant doctor in Africa. His calling put him in harm's way and drove their mother crazy. It worried Teresa too. She just couldn't imagine that kind of sacrifice. His infrequent letters and emails were dry and devoid of joy, as if hardship had added decades to his thirty-four years. David, dauntingly tall with eye-catching auburn hair, had always been the most outgoing of the family, with the sunniest disposition. Teresa prayed that the life he'd chosen hadn't crushed his spirit.

As far as she knew, Joe was the only one who was truly happy, and that happiness had been hard-won. In the persona of "Joe Bob Blade," he'd been a huge country music star, but his performing career had been cut short. Like Teresa, he now had a perpetually husky voice, despite two surgeries for nodes. What was the cause? Hard to say. Nothing wrong with his technique. Their father's chain smoking had left them both with a sensitivity to cigarette smoke and other environmental allergies. They'd both been diagnosed with acid reflux, but meds and changes in diet made little difference. Voice therapy had helped. Teresa had stopped worrying about it. She didn't sing, and people thought her breathy speaking voice was sexy. She had wanted to be a musician too—a classical pianist—but, unwilling to stand up to her parents, she'd ended up going to Sarah Lawrence instead of Juilliard. Until recently, she'd accompanied dance classes at Cornish Conservatory for fun. When asked to commit to a more regular schedule, she'd reluctantly quit. Her university degree was in Creative Writing. That would have been great if she'd wanted to be a novelist. She didn't. And socialites didn't become concert pianists.

"Teresa?" She started at the musical lilt of her mother's voice and cool hand on her bare shoulder. "How was the trip?"

Teresa rose to give her mother as much of a hug as she'd accept. Carrie didn't look old enough to have a thirty-six-year-old son. Teresa's birthday was only a month away. She would be twenty-seven, on a steady march toward the big three-oh. At sixty years old, her mother might be mistaken for Teresa's sister. Her remarkably youthful appearance was made possible by all the anti-aging resources money could buy, including surgery, fillers, and peels. Was that Teresa's destiny too, to be preserved in amber? She was already getting weary of the upkeep required to maintain that perfect weave of light-blonde shades. She thought her real hair color might still be blonde—a darker shade—and she was toying with the idea of growing it out. *Ah, to be liberated from all this.*

"The trip?" her mother repeated with her tight smile. "You seem to be somewhere else today."

"Oh, *glorious.* I love being immersed in history while staying in a luxury hotel. All the local color in the marketplaces, the gorgeous mix of ethnicities. Palm trees, sun, massive stone walls. A fascinating array of humankind."

Her mother's laugh was decorous and melodic. "You sound like David Attenborough. Or an advertisement for the Hilton. How was Paul? Did *he* appreciate all the history?"

"He appreciated all the nightlife. He went out on the town almost every evening—without me."

"You didn't share a room?" Carrie quirked an eyebrow.

"You know we didn't. The Catholics don't like it when unmarried people share rooms."

"You didn't even want to?"

Teresa gave her head a decisive shake. "Nope. Paul stopped by my room in the wee hours after barhopping. I told him to go sleep it off. I'm not sure he remembered what he'd done the next day."

"Oh, dear. I hope he doesn't have a problem."

Teresa stared at her French manicure. Still perfect. Paul definitely had a "problem," but Teresa wouldn't be the one to drive that fact home to her mother. "Mom, are you encouraging your unmarried daughter to engage in premarital sex?"

Carrie's smooth brow creased slightly. "A person should at least *want* to sleep with her fiancé. That's all I'm saying."

Time to change the subject. "So … Joe told you the news about Ali's brother?"

Carrie cleared her throat and sat down next to Teresa, first brushing the seat and checking it for dirt and bird droppings—a precaution Teresa had not thought to take.

Her mother laced her fingers together on her lap. "Yes. That is one strange story."

Teresa raised her eyebrows. "You don't believe it? You think Liam made it up?"

"It's just that, whatever the facts, there is too much left unexplained. It worries me." She frowned. "He sounds like trouble."

"I met him. He seems okay to me. Taciturn, yes. But not like a person with something to hide. More like someone who values his privacy."

"I hope he doesn't make trouble for Ali and Joe. I gather he was quite overprotective when he and Ali were growing up."

Teresa felt an odd need to defend Liam. "He had to be. They were foster children, and their foster parents—well-meaning as they were—never warmed to them."

"Thank goodness they cared about education. Ali is surprisingly sophisticated and well-informed for a former foster child."

*Yes, thank goodness for that,* Teresa thought. *Better to be well-educated and gently reared than cherished and loved.* Her mother could be so dense. What if Joe had married Rina Bakersfield, his one-time fiancée and fellow country-music icon? Carrie would have had a cow, as they used to say on the playground. Rina was far too colorful a personality for their well-heeled Catholic clan. Ali didn't fit in either, but at least she wasn't an embarrassment.

"What is the timeline?" Carrie asked. "You know, when is everyone arriving in Seattle?"

"Ali and Joe are coming on Saturday. The sale on the Port Townsend place closes tomorrow. I've authorized some repairs and remodeling."

Carrie's eyes widened with shock. "That was fast. Doesn't Ali want to weigh in on the décor?"

"She said not. She trusts my taste."

Shock turned to vexation. "What about Liam?"

"He's already here."

Carrie looked around in alarm.

"Not *here*, here," Teresa corrected herself. "He's in town."

"Why did no one let me know?"

"Me, I'm letting you know." Teresa kept her voice low and calm so that Carrie's wouldn't rise further. Her mother hated being kept out of the loop. "He didn't let anyone know. I got the phone call earlier today. He left a message. Very brief. 'Hello, Teresa, this is Liam. I arrived in town this morning.'"

"That's all? How do we reach him?"

"He left a cell phone number. He's staying at a motel on Aurora."

"My God," Carrie muttered, a rare instance of taking the Lord's name in vain. "I hope it's not one that rents by the hour." Aurora Avenue North—part of SR-99, once the state's main north-south highway—was one long strip mall lined with motels, warehouse stores, car and porn-related businesses, and frequented by many working girls.

"If so, I'm sure he'll take precautions against disease."

"Teresa!"

"Mom, I don't mean he's going to visit prostitutes. I just hope the bathrooms are clean. Jeez."

Carrie patted her hair, even laughed a little to acknowledge the humor in the situation. In a neutral voice, she asked, "He's going to live with Joe and Ali in Port Townsend?"

"That's the plan. If he agrees. It would give him time to figure out what's next."

"What do you all see in the Olympic Peninsula?" Carrie huffed. "You'd think Ali would want to be near the best hospitals for the birth."

"I guess we all have wonderful memories of summer vacations there. Before we got so damn rich."

Carrie gave her a vexed look. Teresa knew she didn't understand why all the children didn't just enjoy their privileged circumstances rather than insisting on rocking the boat. Starting with Edward, although you could hardly argue with a religious vocation. Only Jake seemed to have embraced their family business and profited from their exalted social ties. He was Carrie's least favorite, which was why he tried so hard to please her.

"Shall we have a big family dinner on Saturday night to welcome everyone home?" Teresa proposed. "Rostand can whip up something appropriately low brow, like macaroni and cheese." Seeing her mother's face, she raised a hand and said, "Just kidding. How about Copper River Salmon? Cedar-planked. With roasted new potatoes and a big Caesar Salad."

# CHAPTER 5

ALI CAST AN ADMIRING GLANCE around Carrie's spacious backyard, a vast expanse of emerald-green lawn that looked so soft and cushy that you wanted to lie down and roll in it. A rose garden with at least thirty varieties bordered one side. A trellis thick with purple clematis shaded the tiled terrace where a table was set for ten. Next to it was a small pond fed by a Romanesque fountain presided over by stone cherubim and fish, their mouths forming spouts. At least the cherubim weren't peeing, as they did in so many European fountains. Carrie was too proper for that.

It was a curious setting for a family reunion of foster children raised in austere circumstances and the birth father who had surfaced only recently. Ali had basically stepped through a magic portal when Joe had asked her to marry him. But her bright, shiny new life's one dull edge had been her brother's absence. Now he was about to saunter back into their lives as if returning from an extended vacation. If he'd been sufficiently aware to send the toy soldier after he woke up from the coma, why hadn't he included a note? What had he been doing for three years and four months in a country where he didn't know the language? He wasn't even Jewish. Or hadn't been. For all Ali knew he would be wearing a broad black hat, those odd side curls—what were they called?—and a full beard. Nah, that was a particular type of extreme Judaism you were born into, and Teresa hadn't reported anything like that. Still, what did Ali know about her brother now? Next to nothing. Liam had told Teresa that he preferred his first contact with his sister and brother-in-law to be in person, ruling out phone exchanges.

Before the others arrived, there would be a quiet reunion between Ali and Liam. Soon after, they would be joined by Duncan, his girlfriend Laurie, Joe, Teresa's former fiancé Paul—Teresa had hinted at a breakup—Ali's best friend Becca and her husband Jean-Louis. Carrie had it all scheduled like hour-long therapy appointments. Ali and Liam reunion: three thirty. Duncan added to the mix: four thirty, cocktails and hors d'oeuvres: five thirty, dinner: six thirty. It was now three forty-five, and Ali was still waiting. She had described Liam to Joe as her "soul mate." That was the twin thing. In a sense they'd been too close, especially as children, less so as teenagers, when he'd taken it upon himself to keep her safe, nipping any possible romance in the bud. That had been his superpower. Call him Captain Stink-Eye. After high school, Liam finally left her alone to see what she'd been missing. Not his fault that while attending the University of Washington, she'd been drawn to two equally jerky men from opposite sides of the tracks: Trip, a rich preppie who dropped her when his Waspy parents found her wanting, and Luis, a scholarship student like her who turned out to be a bit of a stalker. Liam *did* intervene then, but only because she asked him to. Because both men had been indifferent lovers, she'd sworn off relationships—that is, until she met Joe. While her best friend Becca was at Princeton and doing summer internships, Ali and Liam grew close again, hiking and camping together.

After Liam was presumed dead in the terrorist attack, Ali had hiked into the Hoh Rain Forest to hold a little ceremony for him, stayed too late, and met Joe, who was holed up in that remote cabin in the woods recovering from vocal node surgery. Unable to talk, Joe had had to rely on one small pad of notepaper to write his side of the conversation. Now he was her one and only. That would not have been possible without Liam's fierce guardianship.

"Alf!" a voice called out.

For a moment Ali was so choked up, she couldn't speak. Liam was so beautiful. The scars on his cheek and forehead were more pronounced than Teresa had led her to believe, but not at all disfiguring. They seemed to heighten the perfection of the rest of his face, like the beauty patches women wore hundreds of years ago. They had the same coloring—black hair, blue eyes, and honey-colored skin—but otherwise Liam strongly resembled their father, and she, their mother, Duncan insisted. The soft androgyny that had provided the sheep's clothing to Liam's inner wolfishness was gone. He'd bulked up with muscle, and his beautifully bronzed face appeared sculpted in stone. His piercing, deep-set blue eyes had a new watchfulness, and his full lips formed a harder line. Ali hoped he'd share the stories behind these changes. She wouldn't bank on it.

Despite her paralysis, Liam came right up to her, lifted her from the chair, and enfolded her in his long, muscular arms. Then he just held her in a warm hug. They both started to cry, which led to laughter and more tears of joy. Finally, they collapsed into a pair of teak Adirondack chairs, exhausted.

"You look … amazing," she finally said. "Can I say you're a sight for sore eyes? My God, I can't believe you're finally home. I *knew* you were alive, even before you sent me the toy soldier."

Liam smiled, and the hard lines of his mouth relaxed. The grin gave her a glimpse of the beautiful, androgynous teenager. The mischief-maker who had driven their foster parents to despair. Ali's calming presence had kept his shenanigans from going too far or resulting in serious consequences. *She'd* done as she was told, but not with a smile. At eighteen, the twins had parted ways with their foster parents forever. No one said, "Good riddance," but it was understood that George and Emily were off to rejoin the Peace Corps, their job of raising two solid citizens "as best they could" complete. Now they were dead, and she would have to be the one to tell her brother. Would he care? The only thing *she* felt was guilt for not caring.

"You're … glowing," Liam said with a laugh.

"Don't mince words. I'm a cow. A beached whale. Every cliché used to describe every pregnant woman ever. Thank God it's almost over."

He slapped the arms of the chair in disbelief. "Twins! Like us."

"And Joe and his brother Jake," Ali said. She pointed to her swollen belly. "These are twin girls."

He nodded solemnly. "Watch out, world."

"Can I ask you something?"

He looked wary. "Shoot."

"Why didn't you bring the medicine bag?"

He gave her a blank look. "Huh?"

"To Jerusalem. You always wore it. It was supposed to keep you safe."

Liam chuckled. "That ratty old thing. I stayed safe without it, didn't I? Ultimately. Do you think I actually believed in that crap?"

She felt the heat suffuse her cheeks. "Uh, yeah. I took it with me into the rain forest. Thought it would help me commune with you."

"You *what*?" He cocked his head. Then he nodded, as if finally solving a puzzle. "That was in March of 1995, yes?"

Her mouth dropped open in surprise. "Yes."

"I knew you were in trouble. I also knew I could do nothing about it—that you'd have to save yourself. I worried … a lot. But I had my own battles to occupy me."

"I heard you," she said simply, tears staining her cheeks.

"There was another time …" he began. "A man attacked you."

She nodded. "You told me to fight. I got away. That's a story for another time, okay?"

"Sure." Liam shrugged. Of course he'd respect her need to fill in the blanks in her own time. She'd have to do the same for him. "What happened to the medicine bag? Do you still have it?"

She stared at the ground. "I gave it to Joe," she confessed.

Liam chuckled. "Did it work for him?"

Ali thought back. In a sense, it had. It hadn't healed him, but when she saw him wearing it—much, much, later—she'd realized what the gift meant to him. "Sort of," she said, smiling shyly at the memory.

"I'm almost afraid to ask. Did you sell my Harley?"

"It's still around." She took hold of his hand. "I couldn't find the keys or the title. Not that I would have sold it." *Hmm. Where was the Harley?* They'd been storing it here, but she hadn't seen it in a while. No need to go into that now. It wouldn't surprise her to hear that Carrie had found a way to sell it just to get it out of her garage.

Liam brightened. "You never found the safe deposit box key?"

"I didn't even know you had a safe deposit box."

More infectious laughter. *My God, he's beautiful when he laughs*, Ali thought. *What woman could resist that?* She went on, "You were never declared dead, you know. In Washington, when there's no body, a person has to be missing seven years for that to happen. I've got your stuff from the Renton house, what there is of it. You still have a bank account. Remnants of your passport and wallet. They were in the pocket of your motorcycle jacket, which didn't survive."

"Yeah, I figured. I don't remember that day at all. I was told brain injuries prevent you from turning the short-term memory of the incident that caused the injury into long-term. I must have taken off my jacket and gone to use the bathroom. Or payphone, or something. Anyway, being on the edges of the blast zone saved my life." He acted unaccountably blasé about it all.

"What about these threads?" She fingered the fine material of his sports coat. "You're quite the European dandy."

He looked down at his ensemble. "I suppose. When in Rome …. In Israel, men pay more attention to fashion. Designer jeans, a slimmer silhouette."

"It suits you." She nodded approvingly at the fitted black jeans, leather boots, and tailored sports coat. Only the black T-shirt could have belonged to the old Liam.

He gave her hand a squeeze. "Tell me about you. How you met your husband."

She told him the story of her hike into the Hoh Rain Forest and how it had led her to the cabin in the woods.

"Yeah, I knew about Joe Bob Blade and the cabin from the news feeds. I just didn't get why you'd wander in the woods with no established trail. You could get lost in a grocery store, for Pete's sake."

"You'd have been proud of me. I had a solid method. I wasn't lost, just stayed too long. The sun was going down, and the weather had turned nasty."

His aspect darkened, reminding her of the old Liam. "Why do you think I worried so much about you? That's some foolish shit."

Ali became aware of a presence on the terrace. Realizing he'd been detected, Duncan stepped out. He looked like a reluctant guest on a game show, a bit stiff and considering retreat. She rose to give him a big hug. "Dad, this is your son, Liam. Liam, your dad, Duncan Walsh."

"Call me anything you like," Duncan rushed to say.

"Let's start with Duncan, then," Liam said.

Ali's heart sank. *It'll take time,*" she reminded herself. *Liam is naturally suspicious. He doesn't just let people in on anyone's say-so—even mine.*

"I see the resemblance," her twin continued. "It's hard to deny. How did you locate Ali?"

"Through a photo in the newspaper," Duncan explained. "I did the math. She looked so much like her mother at that age."

"Dad is a retired commercial deep-sea diver," Ali blurted out.

"Cool. I've done some diving."

"You have?" Ali asked.

"In Israel. Not a lot." Liam made a vague gesture.

She almost said, *What else have you been up to?!* But she sensed that Liam was a little like a stray dog. You didn't force closeness or he'd run away.

In the silence that followed, Liam didn't look the least bit uncomfortable. Duncan was waiting for permission. Ali couldn't stand it.

"Liam," she began, unable to stop the question, "why didn't you send a note, a letter, anything? Pick up the phone? The toy soldier was proof enough for me, but everyone kept trying to explain it away, insisting you couldn't possibly be alive." Darn, she had meant to work up to that. Well, no point in holding back now. "Then, when the detective confronted you in Jerusalem, you didn't own up to being you, even though you knew Joe and I had hired him to find you."

He had a faraway look in his eyes. "By the time I had fully recovered, I didn't see the point of trying to pick up where my old life left off."

They waited for him to elaborate.

"Look," he said finally, "I can see you both have a million questions. There'll be time for that. Ali, you of all people should understand. It wasn't like I had much of a life to come home to. And I had never been out of the country before."

She nodded. *What about me? Why didn't you want to come home to me?* she wanted to ask.

Duncan settled into the third Adirondack chair. "After all Ali has told me, I'm thrilled to finally meet you. I was so sorry to hear about your foster parents."

Deathly calm, Liam riveted his gaze on Ali. *Uh-oh,* she thought. *He's way too used to hearing bad news.* Of course their father would assume she'd already told him.

"I'm sorry," she said. "I wasn't sure how to weave it into our conversation. Not long after I met Joe, I was notified that George and Emily had been killed in a motorcycle accident in Botswana."

Liam's response surprised her. In a bland voice, as if referring to mere acquaintances, he asked, "How did they react to the news that I was missing?"

She shook her head at the unfairness of it all. "They didn't know. I wrote them, which is how their Peace Corps colleague knew how to reach me."

Now her brother was fixated on the rose garden as if he'd never seen a rose. "What was *your* reaction?" When she didn't answer immediately, he clarified, "Not to *my* disappearance, to their deaths."

There was no point in lying to her brother. "I was sorry I couldn't feel more," she admitted.

"Yes," he said. "I'm grateful, of course. They were never mean to us, exactly, and they gave us plenty of life tools. But I feel nothing. I can't help it. Other than sorry, because that's a hell of a way to die, and they were good people in many ways."

In the murky silence that followed, Duncan cleared his throat and asked, "Will you go back to Israel?"

"No," Liam replied, easily throwing off the pall of the last several minutes. "I'd already overstayed my welcome."

As Becca used to say, her brother was "one tough dude."

"Joe and I just bought a place in Port Townsend," Ali said, knowing he would not elaborate on that last comment. "We're hoping you'll live with us until you have a plan."

Liam's disconcerting gaze traveled to her face. "In the same house?"

"We have a guest cottage. Cottages." *Ugh.* That sounded like bragging. "Teresa found it for us. We've only seen pictures. We'll be driving there in a few days. Joe is totally on board with the idea."

"I can help with maintenance," Liam said. "As you recall, I'm pretty handy."

"You don't want to try to get your job at Boeing back? Liam was a machinist," she added for her dad's benefit.

"You think they held it for me?" It was a rhetorical question. "No. I have many useful skills, and I picked up a few more in Israel. I'd like to see what else is out there for me."

"Makes sense," Duncan said.

* * *

HER MOTHER HAD BEEN RIGHT to get the more intimate reunion over with before the rest of them arrived, Teresa thought. Although Liam, Duncan, and Ali weren't exactly singing "Kumbaya" and forming a prayer circle, they looked mostly at ease in one another's presence. There was even some joking around, judging from the occasional laughter. As usual, Carrie's cook and general factotum Rostand silently attended to everyone's needs. He'd been in the family's employ for ten years and preferred to keep a professional distance. Though he knew enough about the family to do serious damage, he didn't seem the type to feed the hungry tabloid machine in exchange for a nest egg. He lived in the carriage house above the garage, made a comfortable salary, and had mostly light duties. Not a job to throw away casually. In his early forties, Rostand was a French Algerian with impeccable manners. Teresa hoped he had friends in the area. She had no idea what he did on his day off. None of their business, of course.

When Teresa had first caught sight of Liam, she was glad he wasn't aware of her presence. That way she could observe him much longer than politeness allowed. He looked so … expensive. And fashionable. At their first meeting in Jerusalem, he'd been dressed in his security guard uniform. Now he looked like a celebrity gigolo. *If he weren't so beautiful, would you still think of sex for hire?* she admonished herself. She'd known lots of Eurotrash. That term didn't describe Liam. He was scary, though, in a delightful way.

Joe was sitting at the end of the table with Ali to his right. All eyes were on Liam, seated between Ali and Duncan. His girlfriend Laurie sat across the table next to Jean-Louis and Becca. Laurie was talking a blue streak, something about a trip she'd taken to Montana. She was usually a chatterbox, even more so when uncomfortable. Good for Duncan—he wasn't trying to rein her in. Seizing on a rare lull in the conversation, Ali asked Jean-Louis about the new Bellevue branch of La Fête Sauvage—French for "The Wild Feast." The fare at the high-end eatery centered around wild game and fish and local organic produce. Its popularity had soared in the past year, keeping Becca and her celebrity chef husband crazy busy. Teresa wished they would hire more help so best friends Becca and Ali could see more of each other. Paris and the pregnancy had left Ali feeling sad and isolated. Would Port Townsend provide enough stimulation? Teresa had her doubts. Now she wished she'd found them something closer to the main town—the drive took about twenty minutes—but on short notice, it had been difficult to locate a spread with beach access, guest cabins, and enough acreage to meet Joe's privacy needs.

Teresa envied the rapport between burly Jean-Louis and petite but curvy Becca. He was Québécois, a dark-skinned descendant of fur traders with more than a drop of Aboriginal blood, and she was the exotically beautiful child of olive-skinned Russian-Jewish parents whose own parents had made a fortune in real estate. They were finishing each other's sentences without being annoyed by the habit. Did that kind of closeness ever last? All Teresa knew was, she and Paul had never had it. She hadn't told her mother the wedding was off, and she was in no hurry to do so. Paul was sitting next to Carrie, who presided over the other end of the table. The two were deep in conversation. Though they did spare a glance every so often, neither seemed interested in conversing with Liam, the Prodigal Son. Paul made no effort to engage Laurie, who sat on the other side of him. That was the problem with these large gatherings. The group inevitably split into factions. Teresa was content to observe.

*If you like him so much, why don't you marry him?* she thought as she noted how her mother doted on Paul. *Behave*, she admonished herself. *What are you, ten?*

"What will *you* do?" The question was addressed to her.

She turned to Duncan. "Huh?"

"Everyone seems to be congregating in Port Townsend. What are your plans?"

She blinked, rendered speechless by the question. Her immediate goal had been to find a place for Ali and Joe. Now the summer yawned before her, dauntingly free of fun. She'd be dodging Paul—at least until he left for Toronto—evading her mother's questions about the wedding, and getting pulled into more charity work. *Yuck.*

She arranged the lettuce on her plate as if creating a collage. "You know, I really have no idea."

"You should come to Port Townsend too," Ali said, leaning back to talk to her. "I need someone to help me through the birth and the weeks after."

"Won't you have a doula or something?" Teresa asked. "And a nanny?"

Ali paused. "We haven't thought that far ahead."

"It's a no brainer," Joe said. "You're coming with us, at least until the babies are a few weeks old. Did you get us a grand piano, like I asked?"

"Of course."

"Then you won't be bored, will you?"

"A piano?" Liam asked, turning his dazzling smile on her.

With a gulp, Teresa said, "I play a little."

Paul chortled. That was the word that came to mind. A vaguely demented laugh. His face was flushed. Dang, just how much wine had he imbibed after the two martinis he'd downed at the start of the evening? Why hadn't he protested the calls for her to go to Port Townsend? The answer was, he was too far gone. Also, she knew he had plans to spend the next few months in Toronto on business. Ridiculously overconfident, her erstwhile fiancé didn't doubt for a moment that the wedding would be back on as soon as she got over this current "phase" of rebellion.

* * *

FOR ONCE, LIAM WAS GRATEFUL for the prattling of a lively woman. He understood Ali's vague annoyance with Laurie but guessed it had more to do with wishing for a greater share of their father's attention. *Their father.* What a concept. He liked the man instinctively while knowing better than to trust his first impressions.

Relieved of the need to talk, Liam could observe. He was not going to satisfy their justifiable curiosity. God forbid he should tell them the whole story. Would they believe it? He'd mastered the art of deflecting questions with questions of his own. Laurie was quick to take the bait. Seeing their Northwest-casual attire—in Paul's case, more like Northeast-casual, with his Polo shirt and chinos—he wished he hadn't defaulted to his Israeli dress clothes. He might as well have been wearing a zoot suit. Joe wore jeans with crocodile cowboy boots and a button-down shirt. In Port Townsend Liam could opt for comfort over couture. He felt an instant connection to his new brother-in-law, abandoning his usual wariness. All he needed to know could be found in the new couple's eyes. Joe gazed at Ali as if he couldn't believe his luck. And, despite the advanced pregnancy, Ali had never looked so beautiful and happy.

Whenever he thought he could get away with it, Liam stole a glance at Teresa, who, he couldn't help but notice, was mostly quiet, with an expression that said, "little lost girl." She stirred all his protective instincts along with the baser ones. He didn't normally go for princesses. Her pasty-faced fiancé was chatting up her mother—an upper-crust society type he was all too familiar with. What did Teresa see in this guy, Paul? He was already hammered. Liam supposed he was a successful businessman with the right bloodlines. A woman like Teresa would need those qualifications. Although not once had she regarded her fiancé with the barest hint of fondness. She seemed more interested in pushing food around on her plate. Her mother looked far more smitten. No accounting for tastes. But now, Liam would be living next door to Teresa, a constant temptation. *She won't bother to tempt the likes of you,* he told himself, but then one of his glances met hers, and their eyes locked. He knew that look. A bolt of lust shot through him. Thank God he was seated.

*She wants you too. So what? Nothing good can come of that.* The Pauls and Carries would never get their snoots out of the air, even if Teresa did deign to lower herself to Liam's level. The best-case scenario would be a tawdry, secretive, guilty affair. Wasn't he done with those?

Even in casual clothing—*especially* in casual clothing—Teresa scrambled his brains. Her elegant curves, framed in designer jeans, and the creamy flesh he detected beneath the filmy blouse open to reveal a scant inch of cleavage had him close to slavering. His fingers itched to touch her hair, which fell in soft, loose curls to her shoulders. He gulped and tried to concentrate on the conversation in his immediate vicinity. Laurie was talking about real estate in Port Townsend—something about rising prices.

Dessert was served. Fresh strawberries for Teresa and Carrie and strawberry shortcake with whipped cream for everyone else. He watched as Teresa cut her strawberries into small bites. She was shorter than Ali— he guessed five-foot-six—and not much more than a hundred pounds, with a petite build. He saw the way her mother, equally slender, tracked every morsel that went into her daughter's mouth. Did Teresa really think she couldn't indulge in even a few bites of shortcake? Then he saw her reach for the whipped cream with a distinct air of defiance and grinned.

Ali caught his eye. "Are you having fun? It's nice to see you smile."

He chuckled. "Life is just one surprise after another."

"Don't I know it."

Rostand had turned the heat lamps on, along with the fairy lights that snaked through the clematis and wisteria.

His movements slow and deliberate as those of a man fifty years older, Paul headed toward the house, where he was received by Rostand. Liam hoped they had a guest room to accommodate him. They could hardly let him drive.

Liam scowled. The guy must have serious bedroom skills. He couldn't imagine what else would bind a woman like Teresa to such a putz. Though the bonds must be tenuous. Why else would she agree to relocate, even temporarily, to Port Townsend?

# CHAPTER 6

———◆———

Teresa's arms were shaking. Plank pose would be the death of her. She tried to clear her mind, but it kept racing back to Kilo. *Kilo, when I was young, I used to call your name ….* Wait, that was Shilo. And he'd—she'd?—been Neil Diamond's imaginary friend, if her memory of that moldy oldie so beloved of her mother was reliable. She'd figured Kilo had been enhanced by her imagination in all the years since they'd parted ways. However, reality didn't disappoint. In the flesh, he looked better than ever. More solid, less ethereal.

"If things become too intense, find your resting position," Kilo told the class. She wasn't going to fold that easily. Thank God they shifted gradually into standing warrior, which gave her a clear view of Kilo. In this class, everyone went for the most challenging versions of the poses. She had, too, at first, but it was Friday, her fifth class this week.

How did Kilo feel about her presence? The Monday class had been the first time they'd seen each other since that night in the motel, and that final farewell had been weird, to say the least. Her brother Edward—not a priest then—had almost put Kilo in the hospital.

She couldn't help comparing Kilo with Liam. There were too many similarities. Liam was a couple of inches taller, but at six feet, no one would describe Kilo as short. Their hair was almost identical, straight and blue black, on the long side with endearingly floppy bangs. Liam's had some curl, or maybe they were cowlicks. Kilo had a dancer's rather than a warrior's body. Smoother muscle. Obviously ballet hadn't panned out. Or he'd had an injury. He was so exotic looking, with his vaguely Asian features and

37

androgynous beauty. Native Hawaiian and Japanese on his father's side with a Eurasian mother, raising him alone. They'd met at Cornish College of the Arts, where she'd been taking piano lessons, and he was a scholarship student in the dance program. She'd been in her senior year at Holy Names Academy, a Catholic girl's school. Teresa had never dated, and Kilo was so *other*. She had wanted to be a concert pianist. No career in the arts was acceptable in the world according to Carrie. She didn't know what had happened after they'd parted ways—or, more accurately, been torn apart. Being a dancer couldn't pay much. Kilo was probably doing way better as the owner of a tony yoga studio.

They were holding a balance position. Kilo touched her shoulders to steady her, and she almost lost it. Was he singling her out? Nah, he was touching everyone. That's what yoga teachers did.

She was fairly sure the entire class, both young and old, had a thing for him, including the pretty blonde Britney Spears-wannabe receptionist, Jessica. Kilo was beautiful, and he had this Zen thing going on. Who wouldn't want some of that? She suspected at least part of it was a façade. That first day, when he'd realized who she was, he'd dropped the mask for a moment, revealing the vulnerable though effortlessly charming boy from her senior year. She'd seen him interact with his peers at Cornish, who were from various departments—musicians, dancers, singers. Someone like Kilo might have been bullied, but not him. He was so darn nice to everyone, a natural leader. Weirdly secure and devil-may-care for a seventeen-year-old. Even then, you felt as if he knew the secrets of the universe. And he had gravitated toward *her* ….

"Your other right," she heard him say, and realized he was addressing her. She was facing the wrong direction. How humiliating. *Concentrate, darn you*. She corrected her pose.

After that first class, he had given her a warm but dispassionate hug, as if greeting a long-lost student. No one would suspect their star-crossed history.

"How have you been?" he asked.

"Oh, you know." She made a vague gesture.

He tried again. "What are you doing in Port Townsend?"

"My sister-in-law is very pregnant. And fighting depression. She and Joe just moved here. I'm her head cheerleader."

Kilo nodded, breaking into a dazzlingly white Pepsodent smile. Veneers, obviously. His teeth had been kind of a mess back then. No money for an orthodontist.

He tapped her ring finger. "Congratulations!"

"Oh." She looked down at the engagement ring in dismay. She really should have taken it off. It was too flashy, and she'd already decided not to marry Paul. It was just easier to keep wearing it. Men didn't hit on her as much. Not that there were many single men in Port Townsend, especially young ones. One local shopkeeper had described the culture to her as "Venusian." Was that even a word? Worshipers of Venus? A lot of divorced and widowed women, mostly older. The few jobs for young people were in the hospitality and service industries, so the retirees were gradually taking over, upping the cost of living and driving the working-class population to move ever farther away.

"Teresa, are you engaged?"

He'd been waiting for an explanation. She looked up, embarrassed. "Um, sort of …" she muttered. "We'll see."

"That's interesting," he said. She wondered what he meant by that. Everything he said to her had an ironic edge. Was he still hurting over what had happened between them all those years ago?

"Shall we get coffee?" he asked with another flash of pearly whites.

"Today?" She checked her watch. Ten forty-five. Of course. The class had ended at ten thirty, and they were alone.

"I teach again at eleven thirty, so it will have to be a quick one."

A quick one … A quickie? *Get your mind out of the gutter*. Had she said yes? "I guess so."

He laid a hand casually on the small of her back to guide her out of the room. "There's a coffee shop next door."

Kilo's yoga studio was located on Lawrence Street. Most of the businesses that catered to locals were located uptown, above the bluff from Water Street, the "downtown" area where the tourists congregated.

"Your studio is gorgeous," she gushed.

"I hired someone to give it the full treatment. I'm glad you approve."

She wriggled into her cropped sweater. "Judging by your huge following, it works for everyone."

He laughed. Did it sound predatory? *Weird*.

At the café, she ordered a decaf latte with nonfat milk. He ordered a giant mocha.

"Still rocking that fast metabolism, I see."

He laughed again. A curiously dry heh-heh. "And you're still maintaining the social X-ray thing."

"I'm not all that thin." She didn't appreciate the Tom Wolfe reference.

"You're *very* thin. Almost too thin. Though that's not possible with your set, is it?"

Was he being a jerk about her background? He was entitled, she supposed, given how her family had treated him. He changed the subject before she could reply. "So, explain what you meant earlier. Are you engaged or not?"

"For now."

"For now," he repeated in a mocking tone.

"You?" she said, aiming for nonchalance.

"No. Not in my wheelhouse."

He gave her a long, measuring look. She couldn't help but feel judged.

"What happened to ballet?" she asked, searching for a safer conversational gambit.

"What happened to classical piano?" he responded with a placid smile. "You know what they say about dreams and broken-winged birds."

"I'm not sure that I do."

"It's bullshit, anyway. Most dreams deserve to die. Doesn't mean we don't get to fly anymore. My life is exactly how I like it." She heard a challenge in there somewhere. He checked his watch. "Damn. I'd better go back. Please say you're going to be a regular now, at least for as long as you're here." For the first time she thought she detected a sexual heat. He touched her hand.

She let his fingers linger. She liked it. He was spiritual *and* carnal. *Dangerous combination*, she thought. But no, surely not. He was a yoga teacher. Didn't they have it all together spiritually? Anyway, he removed his hand quickly enough to make her doubt any carnal intent.

"I don't think I'll be able to get in. Today I lucked out. You had a cancellation."

Kilo nodded, matter of fact. "This is my most popular class, so I make people pay for two weeks of sessions whether they show up or not, with no refunds. Don't worry. You're in. Guaranteed." He stood. "It's great to see you, Teresa. You look amazing, as always." He kissed both her cheeks with quick impersonal pecks, European style, and left her standing there, wondering what had just happened.

That had been the first class. Four classes later, and he still hadn't repeated the invitation to coffee, darn it. Or had she imagined the sparks between them? Why else would he go out of his way to secure her a spot? So confusing. And so intriguing.

After class he actually blew her a kiss. He didn't do that to anyone else. "See you Monday!"

Teresa reveled in the smell of sea air and dense foliage as her bike bumped along a gravel road not far from the O'Connell compound. She was far from fit enough to pedal her bike up and down the many hills between Ali and Joe's new place and town, so she'd driven home from yoga class to fetch her Trek 520 touring bike and was getting a little aerobic exercise exploring the immediate area. This part of Port Townsend, with all its unpaved side roads, was better suited to mountain bikes than her hybrid. The houses here were not Victorians, though most had a certain backwoods charm or at least strived to fit in. She passed American Craftsmans, Greek Revivals, and a few mobile homes, mostly well maintained. In Seattle, she hadn't ridden a bike for ages, despite there being some scenic paved trails. The Burke Gilman was too crowded with runners training for marathons, meandering families, and serious bikers. In her yoga class here, she'd heard talk of a bike trail linking Port Townsend with Forks by way of Sequim and Port Angeles, converting the railroad tracks to a paved path as they had with the Burke-Gilman, but that plan was still in its infancy. In the meanwhile, bicyclists competed with cars and trucks for the roads.

Here on the Peninsula, Teresa felt delightfully removed from Carrie and her influence. She never wanted to go home to her townhome, even with its ultra-desirable Madison Park location and unimpeded view of Lake Washington.

The primitive road she traveled having dead-ended, she returned to the paved street and headed in the direction of the compound. Hearing a rumbling behind her, she slowed and coasted as close to the gravel shoulder as possible. The car didn't pass. Peering over her shoulder, she saw an ancient pickup. The driver—baseball cap pulled low—revved the motor and bucked forward. In the blink of an eye, she was cast into a ditch with a heavy thud. She managed to lift her head enough to squint at the license plate as the truck disappeared in a cloud of exhaust. The numbers and letters were too filthy to read.

She lay there for what seemed like an hour but was probably more like ten minutes, staring up into the branches of a giant Douglas Fir tree. Why hadn't the driver stopped? Was it possible he hadn't seen her? He'd slowed down then sped up. Would a man in a truck like that be on his cell phone? Unlikely. Maybe reaching down to insert a new mix tape or change the channel to some misogynistic talk radio celebrity who encouraged women to bare their breasts to other drivers.

She rose to her feet, moving gingerly, and brushed off the fir needles and dirt. She was still in one piece, though if she had injured herself, she'd be more likely to feel the damage tomorrow when the bruises started blossoming and the aches and pains set in. She didn't think she'd sprained, pulled, or broken anything. The bike didn't look so hot. It was oddly twisted, in need of a bike chiropractor. She rolled her shoulders experimentally. All fine. Her yoga pants were snagged and bloody from a skinned knee, and her arm had a long scrape. Everything superficial.

She checked her cell phone. No service. *Ugh*. She'd have to walk the bike home. It wasn't far, but she was moving slowly.

Twenty minutes later she parked the bike in front of the guest cottage where she's been staying. Her yoga pants were ruined; her cropped sweatshirt was bloodstained but intact. It was one o'clock, and she was hungry. Rather than forage for a real lunch in the main house where Ali would fuss over her, she opted for an energy bar. Unable to stop shivering, she drew the hottest bath she could stand and soaked for a good half hour, gently cleansing her abrasions with a washcloth. She found first aid supplies in the bathroom cabinet.

# CHAPTER 7

---•---

WHEN TERESA EMERGED FROM THE cottage clad in a powder-blue floral-patterned sundress, a retro cashmere sweater, and sandals, she felt almost herself again. Ali was seated on the terrace next to the propane firepit—the spot with the best view of the Strait of Juan de Fuca and Victoria, British Columbia. As she walked down the hill to join her sister-in-law, Teresa debated whether to mention what had happened. Best not to make a big deal of it. Ali had enough on her plate, with her due date only weeks away. If the subject came up naturally in conversation, fine, but Teresa wasn't going to go all drama-queen on her. It was simply an accident. She'd been unlucky enough to get in the way of some distracted jerk in a big fat hurry.

"Hi, Ali!" she said cheerily as she approached.

"Teresa!" Ali waved, and her face lit up. "Come keep me company." She pointed up the hill, where Liam was wielding a large ax. "That man is an animal. He's been chopping wood for an hour now with no signs of tiring."

After helping herself to a glass of lemonade from the pitcher, Teresa sat on the lawn chair next to Ali. Liam's blue and black flannel shirt and black T had been tossed aside, leaving him clothed in nothing but low-rise Levis and work boots. Teresa couldn't help but stare at his broad shoulders, glistening chest, and bulging pecs and biceps. From this distance, she couldn't see the shrapnel scars that marred his right side, but Liam wasn't self-conscious about his body and often paraded around shirtless. She already knew he wore those scars better than any man had a right to. Automaton-like, he was fully concentrated on the task at hand. If aware of his admiring audience, he didn't let on.

Ali was remarkable. Only occasionally did she complain about feeling bloated and miserable. Teresa, hyperconscious of her own figure, couldn't imagine what it must be like to carry twins. At least the weather was partly cloudy and cool, not unusual for late June, with temperatures in the low sixties and a briny breeze wafting off the water.

Teresa was proud to have found the perfect place for Ali and Joe. Price being no object, she'd chosen a three-story mansion on ten acres of land at the end of a mile-long gravel road with four hundred feet of private beach and a panoramic view. The construction only dated back to 1990, but the design was retro, with bay windows, cedar siding, and rows of sash windows. Ali had dubbed it the "Sea Captain's House," though few sea captains could have afforded such luxury. According to the realtor, it had been built by an amateur musician born into wealth who had tired of the isolation and cool climate and moved back to California. The barn-like freestanding music studio and separate gym had clinched the deal, as well as the three guest cottages.

Ali flashed Teresa a knowing smile. "My brother's an eyeful, right?"

Teresa groaned. "I'm that obvious?"

"Even I can't stop staring at him. He's packed on twenty pounds of muscle since he left for Israel. I'd love to know the full story. But he's not telling. A man of mystery, he is."

Teresa kicked off her sandals and sat with her knees tucked against her chest. "I'd stand in line for that, but he's not taking tickets. The less he talks, the more fantastical the tale in my head gets. I now have him drafted by Mossad and trained in their most elite camps to be an assassin."

Ali wrinkled her nose. "Do they do that?"

"Only on hokey TV shows, I think." Teresa drew in a deep breath. "God, it's beautiful here. I hope you don't mind, but I'm never leaving."

"You are welcome to stay forever," Ali said happily. "I'd love the company. Joe is holed up in his studio all day long."

Teresa whistled. "Wow, he is *really* disciplined. He spends all that time playing the guitar and composing?"

"There's a lot more to being Joe Bob Blade than that. Calls with his agent Linc and frequent phone consultations with Hank, his personal assistant in Nashville. Hank sifts through his fan mail—sharing the highlights and sending out signed headshots. He also fields PR opportunities, requests from charity organizations, stuff like that." Ali heaved a long-suffering sigh. "Joe only tears himself away to work out in the gym or go hiking with Liam. He will always need lots of space. Not too different from Hercu-Liam there." She jutted her chin in Liam's direction. "Oof!" Her hands flew to her belly.

"The girls are active today. I'll have to sign them up for kickboxing. They'll be naturals."

"I wish I had those skills," Teresa said. "Some men need a lesson in manners."

"You don't mean Liam, I hope."

As if hearing his name—only possible if he had the auditory acuity of an owl—Liam paused in his chopping to look at them. He stared, unsmiling, for a disconcerting moment before his gaze shifted out to sea.

"No, not Liam." Teresa paused. Darn it, she hadn't meant to bring up the accident. Clearly she needed to get it off her chest. "No, I mean the guy who drove my bike off the road just now. If I hadn't landed in the soft dirt of the ditch, I might have broken something." She lifted the skirt of her blue sundress to show Ali her scraped leg and pushed up the sleeve of her sweater to reveal the swath of gauze wrapped around her forearm. "Damn! It bled through and stained my sweater."

Ali strained to look. "Jeez, that looks bad. Did you get the license plate number?"

"Beat-up old pickup truck. Yellow and rusty. Plates too dirty to read." She rewrapped the bandage and pulled up her sleeve to cover it once more.

Ali was bug-eyed with indignation. "This isn't backwoods Georgia. Stuff like that shouldn't happen here. The guy didn't stop?"

"He just sped up." Ali was leaning forward, so tense Teresa thought she might topple out of the lawn chair. "Don't upset yourself. It's nothing. Some guy in a hurry. He probably didn't even see me."

Ali sat back in her chair, huffing and puffing. "I don't think there's any room left in there for my lungs. I sometimes have trouble catching my breath at all."

Jutting a thumb at Liam, Teresa let loose a stagey sigh. "If Big Paul's Outfitters ever needs a stand-in for Big Paul, I'm going to nominate Liam. He'd make a dandy Paul Bunyan."

Ali cocked her head. "Nah, I don't see him in TV commercials. He does have acting experience, though—in high school drama. They cast him as Romeo. He was no Leonardo diCaprio but credible. Totally charismatic, and so good-looking that some Hollywood agent tried to recruit him—said he could make him a movie star. He wasn't interested. Not vain enough. He's a very private person, I think."

Without taking her eyes off Liam, Teresa asked, "Why did he do drama, then? To meet girls?"

Ali shrugged. "Girls threw themselves at him. It required effort to keep them at bay." She paused. "I think he had a thing for his teacher." At Teresa's shocked reaction, she amended, "Not that kind of 'thing.' His drama teacher was a man. He was always looking for father figures. The guy was part Navajo, and they were close enough that he gave him a medicine bag to wear around his neck. Joe has it now."

Teresa stood up to stretch her sore legs. "How did it end up with Joe?"

Ali's expression turned dreamy. "It was at the end of that first adventure in the woods. Before Joe led me back to the place where I'd parked my car, he gave me a stanza he later included in that song, 'Babe in the Woods,' and I gave him the medicine bag, which I hoped would get him through his coming ordeal. *He* got through it, but his voice didn't."

Deflated, Teresa slumped back down in the lawn chair. She didn't like to think of Joe's aborted career. Without the vocal troubles, nothing could have stopped him. It just wasn't fair. "Which lyrics are you talking about?"

Ali recited:

> The Fates, it seems, have played us both for laughs
> They stole my voice and snatched your other half
> But, darlin' girl, your courage is profound
> Whatever's lost can turn up safe and sound.

"Wow, just wow," Teresa said. "I'd forgotten about that verse."

"Once I heard those lyrics, I realized what it was—a message for me, personally. Remember, the song ends with, 'Please don't keep me waiting for too long.' It nearly was just that—too long. If not for that Sully's compilation that played while I was working, I might never have heard it."

"Not *too* long," Teresa said, "maybe just long enough. And besides, you still would have run into Joe at the fundraiser."

"At least by then I knew who he was. Otherwise, I might have had a heart attack."

"You *did* faint, as I recall."

Teresa was still watching Liam, wishing a gorgeous man would write *her* a song. But romantic gestures like that didn't happen to her. *Not true*, a voice in her head reminded her. *Kilo dedicated that performance at Cornish to you. It was the most incredible thing you'd ever experienced. Could that guy ever dance!*

Ali was still reminiscing. "The second time I visited Joe at the cabin, he was wearing the medicine bag. After that I was putty in his hands." She snorted a laugh. "Funny, I thought that battered little leather bag filled with herbs and an arrowhead meant something to Liam. He claims not. Says he never believed in it. It was supposed to keep him safe, and he left it at home. I was sure it would have made a difference if he'd brought it with him to Israel." She shook her head. "I'm still trying to wrap my brain around those lost years. He seems different, as if he got replaced by a golem. Isn't that a Jewish thing? I guess that happens to all of us as we get older. We change, I mean. Sometimes for the better, sometimes not." For a few minutes, the sound of crashing waves and screaming seagulls filled the silence. "He read a lot of books about Native Americans when he was a teenager," Ali went on. "His favorite movie was *Little Big Man*. I think he fantasized about getting kidnapped by Indians and living the warrior's life. Our foster parents had us awfully regimented."

"I can just picture him in—" Teresa began.

"A loin cloth?" Ali finished.

They both dissolved into laughter. "Oh no, I'm gonna pee my pants!" Ali lumbered to her feet.

As she waddled into the house, clutching her belly, Liam approached. Suddenly glued to her lawn chair, Teresa fought the urge to follow Ali. Liam had put his flannel shirt back on, but it wasn't buttoned. She didn't think there was any guile in his display of hard chest and six-pack abs. He seemed to regard her as a sister, if indeed he even realized she was a woman.

"Anything to drink here?" he asked, casually scratching his flat belly. She followed his fingers to the light dusting of black hair that traveled in a slim V down from his chest and disappeared into his worn, clinging jeans. What was that wonderful smell? She surreptitiously breathed him in, trying not to look like a dog scenting bacon. Notes of leather, baking bread, and clean exertion. Even his sweat was sexy.

The sun reappeared from behind a large cloud. Teresa squinted and shielded her eyes. She pointed to the wicker table. "There's lemonade in the pitcher if you don't mind a few drowned bugs."

"What happened to your sleeve? Looks like blood."

She glanced down at her sleeve as if noticing it for the first time. "Oh, that. It's nothing."

Liam looked skeptical. "If you say so."

"Could you hand me my hat?"

He picked up the lacy white sunhat from the table and dropped it on her head. She was startled by the casual rudeness of the gesture.

"Hey! My hair."

"Oh, sorry. Are you attending a soiree later? You can probably summon some field mice and sparrows to repair the damage. There are a lot of both populating these parts. Though not the magic kind."

"Like in a Disney movie," she said dryly. She was being teased, not insulted. As if they were in grade school. Well, what did you expect from a heathen? She didn't like being called a princess, even if he hadn't said it flat out. Tired of the physical intimidation of his giant shadow looming over her, she stood and smoothed out her skirt. She might as well have stayed seated. It was even more obvious that he could immobilize her with one hand if the mood struck him.

"Okay, wise guy, whatever you think of me, at least I'm an open book. You? You're like … like … the Dead Sea Scrolls or something." Her hands flailed and her cheeks burned.

Throwing back his head, he let out a full-throated war whoop of a laugh.

Hands on her hips, she demanded, "What's so funny?"

" 'The Dead Sea Scrolls,' " he repeated, wiping his eyes with the back of his hand. "Which part? The Hebrew Bible, a calendar, astrological stuff? Maybe you mean the section that points to buried treasure."

She felt like an idiot. "Okay, you know something about them."

"I learned a few things while I was … away. *Ehyeh 'ăšer 'ehyeh.*"

"Translation?"

"I yam what I yam," he said in Popeye's voice, squinting one eye so she wouldn't miss the reference. He watched her curiously for a moment then added, "Actually, I am *who* I am. It's Yahweh … never mind. Too complicated. A little poetic license. Moving right along"—he paused, looked away—"I owe you an apology."

She didn't know how to respond. She did feel offended but wasn't sure why. Not quickly enough, she replied, "Don't be ridiculous."

"You and me," he said flatly, "are from different worlds. I don't mean Israel and the States or Mars and Venus. You're from—I don't know—Mount Olympus, and I'm from … the tar pits. I have no idea how to talk to you."

Now she was disappointed. She smoothed her hair and took extra care placing her sunhat on her head. "I know you don't want to talk about Israel. So, you prevaricate."

He gave her a sidelong look. "I'm not evading the subject. You all seem to think there's some great mystery to me. The truth is pretty pedestrian. You'd be destined for disappointment."

"Try me."

"*Try* you?" Ali said. She had appeared out of nowhere. Teresa shook herself. What was that snake in *The Jungle Book*? Kaa had nothing on Liam.

Teresa was quick to explain. "Liam claims that the tale of his lost years would bore us to tears."

Ali eased herself back into the lawn chair before saying, "I won't be bored if it rhymes. I love a good epic poem."

With their laughter, the tension dissipated. Liam poured himself a tall glass of lemonade, fishing out the fruit flies before taking a long drink. When Teresa sat again, genteelly crossing her legs, Liam sat as well, powerful thighs spread. "By the way, Alf, I fixed the plumbing in my guest cottage. I'm counting on you guys to come up with more chores. I hate being a moocher."

Ali narrowed her eyes. "You are a pest, but you're hardly a moocher. And stop calling me 'Alf.' Especially now that I look like him. Other than the huge snout and body hair, that is." Liam opened his mouth to protest, but she cut him off. "You know we don't expect you to work. If you want to go roaming around in search of things to do, that would be cool, but I don't have a list." She nodded at Teresa. "What about your cabin?"

Teresa wished she could come up with something. Especially if it prompted Liam to remove his shirt in her presence. She shook her head. "He's welcome to check it out. It's all pretty state of the art."

He slapped his thighs and stood up. "All right, then. If I can't find stuff to do here, I'm going to check out the local resources. I'll be back by dinner. Can I pick up anything? Maybe kill and field dress one of those pesky deer that have been trying to break into the vegetable garden?"

"Ugh. I don't want to eat Bambi or his mother. That's got to be bad juju when you're expecting."

"That's okay. I'd have to use a knife, and that would be messy." Liam grinned. "Unless you have any hunting rifles lying around."

"I suppose you'd have no problem using one of those?" Teresa said wryly. "How do you kill a deer with a knife, anyway?"

He withdrew a wicked-looking combat knife from a sheath strapped to his calf and threw it, hitting a stump halfway across the field, dead center.

Both women gasped.

Ali giggled. "You'd better mosey along, Big Paul," she said with a wave of dismissal. "Off you go, in search of adventure!"

With a hearty laugh, Liam strutted over to retrieve the knife. After using it to salute them, he tramped off to the guest cottage on the farthermost edge of the property.

"You know," Teresa said, "the family business was originally called Big Dan's, after Daniel Boone."

In her reedy little voice, Ali sang, " 'Daniel Boone was a man, was a biiiig man ....' Why did they change it?"

"The old TV show got it wrong. The historical Daniel Boone was only five feet eight. Someone pointed that out to Da before he finalized his plans. Big in other ways, maybe. His personality, for instance." She realized she was still staring off in her brother-in-law's direction and gave her head a little shake, as if to clear it.

Ali grinned at Teresa. "Liam likes you. He's showing off."

Teresa avoided her eyes. "My mother says he's bad news."

"Your mother," Ali said, swatting ineffectually at a fly, "is most definitely right."

"Besides, he doesn't see me as a woman. Mostly he's convinced I'm a spoiled brat."

Ali seemed to weigh her words. "As a rule, Liam doesn't like rich people. That doesn't mean he's not attracted to you."

"Just the same, I'm not going there."

In the distance, Liam was starting up his Harley.

"I'm so glad I could get it back."

Teresa looked up. "What?"

"His motorcycle. After I moved out of the North Bend rental, Joe parked it at Carrie's. She got tired of seeing it there, so when Jake offered to get rid of it, she said yes. She didn't believe Liam was still alive, and neither did Jake. He sold it to someone at Big Paul's."

"I thought you didn't have the title or the keys."

Ali made a face. "They had keys made. As for the title, Jake pulled some strings. Joe tried to explain it to me. He reported that it was a 'barn find,' whatever that means. At least when Liam resurfaced, Jake did the right thing and got it back."

"That was nice of him."

Ali scowled. "I'm sure he only did it for Carrie's sake."

"Don't be too hard on Jake. Your circumstances were very odd. You dated him because he looked like Joe, and he pursued you to get back at Joe for stealing his girlfriends, or something like that. In actuality, Jake can be a great guy. He's going through a rough time right now."

"I'm sorry." Ali rose laboriously to her feet. "He's your brother. We make a lot of allowances for them, don't we?" She hugged Teresa, who met her halfway. "I'm dead tired. Excuse me while I trundle off to take a nap."

Teresa retreated to her own cabin to read. She wanted to finish her JD Robb novel now, so it wouldn't keep her up all night.

A noise outside Teresa's cabin roused her from a deep sleep. Bushes rustling and footsteps. Her watch read five o'clock. Maybe the plot of her book was making her paranoid, but she didn't want to take any chances. She grabbed the walking stick she had found along the road and opened the door slowly.

Liam jumped back, arms in the air. "Mercy!" he said with a grin.

She clutched her chest. "You scared me half to death."

"Does what happened to your arm have something to do with that?" He drew a line in the air from the raw scrape to her twisted bicycle.

She felt as if she'd been caught in a lie. She wasn't sure why she felt guilty. How was it any of Liam's business?

She folded her arms defensively. "Why are you here?"

His shrug held a hint of annoyance. "You said to stop by. In case anything needed fixing." He flicked his fingers at the bike. "I'd say *that* qualifies."

"Can you fix it?"

"I can try. It might not look as good as new. Which is too bad. Because it *is* new, isn't it? Somewhere around a thousand bucks?"

Did she need to answer? She kept silent.

"Thought so." Was there censure in his tone? Not necessarily. "High end but not top of the line. Did you hit a tree?"

She tried to recall. "You know, I'm not sure. It all happened so fast. I can't even say why I crashed, since he didn't hit me. I landed in a ditch."

Liam's eyes narrowed. "Who's 'he'?"

"A guy ran me off the road. I don't think he saw me."

Liam full lips twisted as if he didn't buy her explanation. "Did you lose consciousness?"

Had she? Why was there a little blank spot in her memory? "No."

"He came just close enough to unbalance you." Liam squatted down to get a better look. He fell to one knee, fully absorbed in his analysis. Was he coming up with a plan on how to fix the bike? Or trying to picture the accident?

"Okay." He stood and brushed the dirt off his knee. "This will give me something to do. See you at dinner." He wheeled the bike away toward his cabin.

"Thank you!" she called after him. He waved over his shoulder without turning around.

* * *

LIAM WOULDN'T HAVE TO WORRY about temptation, because if he kept acting like an asshole, Teresa was going to hate his guts. He shook his head, wishing he was taking *her* back to his cabin rather than her fancy-schmancy bike. Teresa was used to the best of everything, so how could she be so nice and down to earth? He had no reason to conclude she was a spoiled brat other than his own prejudices. Annoying her with his teasing was a lot safer than letting her get too close. She was beginning to star in his dreams almost every night, and they were definitely X-rated. Today he'd stopped by Kelpies for a beer, and the cute waitress had given him her number. He considered following up, but Kelpies was the best pub in town, with a fun turn-of-the-century vibe and a fantastic view of the bay from the patio, and there was no way in hell that obvious little number would provide more than a few nights' amusement. If he wanted something like that, he'd have to go to Port Angeles, where his antics wouldn't bite him in the ass later on. Maybe it would come to that, just not yet.

He admired the mechanics of the bike. Fixing it would be no problem. Had the guy in the truck really been distracted? His gut told him no. Like it or not, he seemed to have tuned into Teresa's wavelength. As she described the accident, he recalled the moment of alarm when he'd known something wasn't right with her. The timing was too eerily perfect. Ali and he had that connection. If he discussed the premonition with his sister, she'd take it seriously; she'd also know right away that he had a crush on Teresa, and she'd worry. He couldn't do that to her with the twins coming so soon.

So much for using this time in Port Townsend to clear his head.

# CHAPTER 8

---

The four of them celebrated a quiet fourth of July at the compound. The only public fireworks display was off a barge in Port Hadlock, and no one wanted to brave the crowds. They lit the gas firepit, Liam grilled salmon, Joe fussed over Ali, and Teresa made lame small talk that distracted no one.

The next day, Joe and Ali decided to return to Seattle so the twins could be born in the safest environment possible. Teresa, Joe, and their other siblings had all been born at Nordic Hospital, and Carrie had found them a top-rated female obstetrician there. When Teresa proposed going with them, they wouldn't hear of it.

Liam had already headed off for parts unknown, leaving the three of them to sit around the kitchen island prior to Ali and Joe hitting the road. "You stay here and mind the fort," Joe told Teresa as he stood to refill his mug with coffee. "Someone needs to keep Liam out of trouble."

Teresa knew he was teasing but still rose to the bait. "Are you kidding me?" She popped up and leaned forward, bracing herself against the granite island. "Who even knows what he's doing this very minute?"

With a sly smile, Joe began to load the dishwasher. They hadn't lived in each other's pockets like this since he graduated high school. Teresa was surprised to find him so unspoiled and normal, starting with chore sharing. No one had to bug anyone to "do their part." Between the four of them, servants were unnecessary, other than a weekly maid service. The house was too big to manage without help, especially with one of them hugely pregnant. The grounds were mostly beach, lawn, and tall evergreens, and Liam enjoyed riding around on the John Deere garden tractor. So far, the fenced-in vegetable garden was modest, and mostly Ali's domain.

Joe was scraping egg yolk off a plate before loading it. "You're the only one who's gotten into trouble so far," he told Teresa. "Maybe we should ask Liam to keep track of you."

"I'm fine," she pouted.

"If you say so. It sounded like a hit-and-run to me. A near-hit. Anyway, I worry about you biking to yoga."

"I didn't bike there. Too many hills. I was just riding around the area."

Ali had been watching them from her seat at the island, a mischievous smile on her face. "Maybe we should worry about the yoga teacher."

Teresa made a mental note to stop talking to her sister-in-law about Kilo. She might as well have emailed her a detailed description and copied Joe. They shared everything.

Teresa handed Joe her empty cup and spoke slowly as if English were his second language. "He's a *yoga* teacher. By definition more evolved than the rest of us."

Now both Joe and Ali were grinning like idiots. Joe used the empty cup to toast her. "If you say so. Though with your history, it's a little more complicated than that, I'd say."

Joe helped Ali to her feet. "Uh, Teresa? We're going to hit the road. You'll be the first to know when Ali delivers. Then we're going to come back here and let you and Liam take over the midnight feedings." Ali glared at him. "Just kidding, sweetie. When all this is over, I'll write a song about it … a really happy song."

Sore and scabby from the bike accident, Teresa had skipped the previous week of yoga, using one of the elliptical trainers in the compact detached gym located over by the cabins. It also contained two treadmills, two stationary bikes, a vintage NordicTrack, and a large-screen TV fed by satellite. Not that she watched it much. She preferred to listen to books on tape using the portable cassette player. Right now, she was highly entertained by *Cold Mountain*, even though it was heavier going than her usual fare. The narrator was perfect, with a weary Southern lilt that brought the melancholy story to life.

Fourth of July being a Saturday, there was no yoga to distract her on this sunny Sunday. Joe and Ali had just left, and here she was, twiddling her thumbs again. After playing the grand piano in the living room for an hour, Teresa positioned her lawn chair on the perfect spot above the bluff to appreciate the view, then cracked the spine on yet another romantic suspense novel. She felt both guilty and relieved to be left behind while Ali and Joe ushered new humans into the world. She did wonder where Liam was off to. He was gone most days, and she missed him. Not to mention she was bored. He made life a lot more interesting.

*Idle hands are the devil's workshop* …. Wasn't that what Ali and Liam's foster parents always said?

She needed a purpose other than yoga, playing piano, and reading popular fiction, darn it.

She read until her vision began to blur, then headed to the kitchen to scavenge lunch. No shortage of delicious leftovers, as usual. Liam did love to experiment. She measured out a half cup of chicken salad—any more than that would constitute a splurge. All the mayonnaise and raisins made it richer than her usual fare.

It being another cloudless day, she returned to her excellent vantage point and read some more. The book was addictive, so she kept returning to it. Finally, stiff and restless, she decided to stretch her legs. She descended the trail to the beach, but it was high tide, and she couldn't go far. There was only one other house along the gravel road leading into the compound, and it appeared to be unoccupied. None of them had ever seen the owner or owners, and on only one weekend had a car been parked there, presumably by ghosts. There wasn't much to see on the paths that threaded around the grounds, which were bordered by a thick tree canopy and purple and yellow wildflowers. Chipmunks and squirrels. She kept encountering the same doe and two fawns who weren't the least bit shy. As she ambled, she wondered about dinner. Would Liam come home? Where was he? Maybe she should go shopping. The boutiques in town would be closed soon. They were starting to buy inventory with her in mind. Soon they'd be financially dependent on her.

When, for the second time, she reached the end of the gravel road where it intersected with Hastings Avenue, her thoughts turned to Kilo. Was he enlightened? She'd love to be enlightened, always the calming force in any situation. Death would have no meaning because you had already found Nirvana on earth. She was just a spoiled rich girl with anxieties she hadn't earned and no purpose in life. She didn't even have her own charities—they were her mother's. She should really find her own causes. Ali and Joe had recently started a charity for young men and women aging out of foster homes. Ali had designed the website. Keeping Ali company during the last weeks of her pregnancy had provided a purpose. Once her sister-in-law returned, Teresa could help with the twins. But wouldn't they have a nanny for that?

Covering for the nanny while she took her break was her destiny? *Enjoy this*, she told herself. *Life will plunge you into some other adventure soon enough, present other challenges. Bask in this island of calm.*

At six o'clock, Liam was still not home. She wasn't hungry. Maybe she'd just skip dinner. She returned to her new favorite spot overlooking the ocean. At this time of day, she could forgo the extra application of sunscreen. Book in hand, she plopped down on the lawn chair.

A sickening *craaaack*, the chair collapsed, and she toppled over, gravity sucking her toward the bluff. She scrabbled to gain purchase, a root or sapling. No such luck. Just as she was about to complete her slow-motion but seemingly inexorable slide over the ledge, she grabbed onto a root and dangled.

Her heart threatened to thump out of her chest; her scream, strangled in her throat, sounded like an amorous feline's yowl. She clutched at the root, her only lifeline. Would it hold? Was this the end? She still hadn't found her purpose in life. Fate was too cruel. Could she survive the fall? She didn't dare look down. How far to the beach, thirty feet? Her sandals slipped off and clattered as they hit the rocks below. *Damn*, she loved those sandals. Her feet shuffled around, scattering loose rock as she probed the ledge for a toehold. Then she heard Liam's melodic baritone voice calling her name, soothing and calm, as if trying to lure a scared animal out of its hiding place.

"Here!" she squeaked out.

He must have seen the whole thing because he was above her in a flash. He squatted down to assess the situation. "Can you hang in there for a few minutes?" he asked in the polite voice of an operator asking her to hold. She thought of that iconic poster of the cat hanging by its claws. "That root looks sturdy enough."

She nodded jerkily, too terrified to speak. Several minutes ticked by before he appeared again, and she must have been holding her breath because she gasped at the sight of him. Lying on his stomach, he scooted his upper body over the ledge until she was within reach. He extended his long arms to grip her under the armpits.

"I have you," he said in a low, husky voice. In one swift motion, he hoisted her up, rolled onto his back, and pulled her onto his chest—effortlessly, as if she weighed no more than a stuffed animal. Still holding her tight against his body, he scrambled to higher ground.

He had anchored himself by tying one end of a rope around his waist and another to a tree.

Despite her terror, she couldn't help but appreciate the sheer strength of him, the hardness of his muscles and satin texture of his bare arms. The dark hairs on his smooth, tanned skin. A heady whiff of pine-scented soap told her he'd come fresh from the shower. His perspiration smelled like fresh biscuits. She wanted to bury her face in his chest and rub up against him like a cat.

"Are you okay?" His hot breath singed her scalp. Neither of them moved. *My God.* Through his jeans, she felt stirring against her waist. It had to be his cock. Was he as turned on as she was? He was the first to move. Peering from side to side, he said dryly, "You can let go now. As long as you can get to your feet without falling over."

Realizing that she held him in a death grip, she relaxed her fingers. Her head resting on his bare chest felt ... amazing. Still unsteady—fear spiked with lust would do that to you—she moved slowly to her knees then began to crawl up the slope.

"I'm here if you trip," he assured her, "but hang onto the rope."

He waited until she was on level ground again then climbed the short distance to join her.

"That was a close one." The customary teasing note was absent from Liam's voice. She tried not to stare at the obvious bulge in his jeans, a condition that didn't seem to embarrass him.

Still reeling, she held a hand to her forehead. "I'm not sure what happened." She gave her sundress a few tentative swipes. No use. It was a filthy mess. "I've been lounging on that chair off and on all day. Why did it pick that moment to break?"

"Why does anything break when it does?" he said as he climbed up the slope and untied the rope. "It works until it doesn't." He inspected the broken chair. "This was left by the former owners?" He examined it further. "It broke here. Funny. It has an expensive look to it. Must be defective." He peered up at her. "You seem accident prone lately." Again, no irony. Just stating the facts. "Why don't you get cleaned up? I'll make us dinner. Already fired up the grill."

"Where did you find the rope?"

"It was holding up that bucket over there." He pointed to the porch. Teresa recognized the bucket as Ali's basil supply. Dangling it outside the kitchen window kept it out of reach of the deer. "Good thing I always have my knife handy."

She gulped. "Yes. Good thing."

Silence. He stared at her intently, his eyes an even more arresting shade of blue than usual.

"What's for dinner?" She sounded so chipper. No one would guess she had just escaped being dashed on the rocks below like a seagull's shellfish snack.

"Fried oysters." Did she detect a hint of his usual mischief? "I hope you like oysters."

"I usually eat them raw." Even to her ears, the statement sounded suggestive in her subtly husky voice.

He grinned, then turned and walked toward the house.


AN HOUR LATER, SHOWERED AND changed into another sundress—the sandals she had lost would have worked perfectly with it—she walked over to the main house. Liam whistled as he tossed the salad. The oysters were breaded and perfectly pan-fried. Teresa's mouth watered, and not just over the oysters.

He didn't look up immediately. "Do you think this is enough food? The salad is full of stuff. I hope you're not allergic to nuts."

"Nope, no dietary restrictions."

"You look as though you restrict your diet a lot." The lazy slide of his eyes over every part of her made it clear that, skinny or just right, he liked what he saw.

"I get it. You think I'm too thin."

His full lips curved into a slight smile. "No judgment. if you don't go around feeling deprived all the time. One of the great pleasures of life is eating—as long as you don't overdo it."

She cocked her head. "Aye, there's the rub."

"No rub," he grinned, "just breading." Seeing her bemused expression, he added, "Give me some credit. Shakespeare."

"I didn't—"

"It's okay. It's true I didn't go to college. University, anyway. Junior college wouldn't count in your circle." Seeing her open her mouth to protest, he raised a palm to stop her. "Again, it's okay. I'm not ashamed of my educational credentials." He poured her a glass of wine. "Have a seat. Take a load off. Well, not much of a load."

She took a long sip of wine.

"Close call today. I do think you would have survived. Might have been banged up, though."

She didn't appreciate him playing down the severity of her ordeal. "Thirty feet?"

"I'd say twelve, maybe fifteen. There were other roots to grab onto, and there was another ledge a few feet down. Chances are it wouldn't have been a free fall." Seeing another protest forming, he said, "It's important to put things into perspective."

After taking another sip of wine, she decided it wasn't worth arguing. "It's not like getting blown up by terrorists, you mean." She instantly regretted treating his life-shattering event so offhandedly. "Oh God, I'm sorry. That was uncalled for. What you went through—"

"Relax. Like I said before, I don't really recall what happened. It did turn my life upside down. The friend I was traveling with died." He was silent for a moment, staring out the window. Just when she thought he might be fighting tears, he turned to look at her, his eyes nearly cobalt blue and sparkling with mischief. His voice was deadpan. "It might have been fun to watch Ali's Cinderella story unfold."

*What if Liam had been there?* Teresa thought. He might have lost all patience with Joe's shilly-shallying and ruined the whole thing.

He drank from his wine glass. "This is nice. We'll have to thank Joe for letting us dip into his private reserve."

"We're a couple of moochers, I guess."

He narrowed his eyes. "Speak for yourself. I intend to earn my keep one way or another." He gave her another appreciative onceover. "Nice dress."

"Uh, thanks." She was pleased that he'd noticed. This particular shade of pale pink suited her coloring, and she liked the lace details on the skirt.

"You look like something out of a forties movie." From his heavy-lidded scrutiny, he might well be picturing her in some compromising position.

She needed to veer him away from a conversational thread that seemed disconcertingly personal. "Ali said you were in the drama club in high school. I would have pictured you more on the football team."

He chuckled. "I played Romeo, which was kind of a hoot, and George Gibbs in *Our Town*. I would have been more at home as Danny in *Grease*, but my singing could make hardened criminals beg for mercy."

"No football?"

Releasing a sigh of resignation, he said, "George and Emily didn't approve of violent sports, and besides, they'd already filled up my free time with volunteer work. I was lucky they let me do the plays."

"Ali told me they died in a motorcycle accident."

His expression grew solemn, but there was no emotion in his voice when he replied, "Yep. It's one of the leading causes of death in the Peace Corps, I read somewhere."

Teresa raised her eyebrows. Ali had told her they had never bonded.

Unlike Ali, Liam didn't seem inclined to take the blame for that. "You have a motorcycle," she pointed out.

He smiled. "Yeah. It's nice to have the Harley back. Although if I return to Seattle, I'll probably sell it."

"Because you need the money?"

He gave her a sidelong look. "Because I'm not a cat. I don't have nine lives. Anyway, I'd rather have a car. Or a pickup truck."

During dinner, they chatted about the Olympic Peninsula, finding common ground in their love for the area. His treasured memories were all about hiking and camping trips, being one with the elements and the savage beauty of untouched places. Hers were with grand old lodges, serene crater lakes, burbling waterfalls, and nature hikes. Still, for once he didn't tease her.

"What's the Catholic Church like here—did you attend Mass this morning?" he asked in all seriousness as he put the leftovers away and loaded the dishwasher.

"You're kidding, right? We're Catholics, but it's more cultural at this point. I did go on that Church tour to Jerusalem, but mostly because it was an excuse to follow up on that tip from the investigator. I haven't been to Mass in … ages." She was surprised to realize that she couldn't recall the last time. Had it been Easter? No, Christmas. The midnight service. *Bad girl.* "Are you Jewish now?"

He moved over to the picture windows to watch the last of the sunset. "What gave you that idea?"

"I guess because you spoke in Hebrew."

"I did learn some Hebrew, enough to get by. I certainly didn't convert to Judaism. You know, for many Israelis it's largely cultural too. At least my family."

"Your *family*?"

"The people who took me in. I have no family here except Ali." She noticed he didn't include Duncan. He turned to her. "So, what are you doing tomorrow?"

"I'm not sure. What about you?"

"I'm meeting a friend at Fort Worden. Will you go to yoga?"

They were standing a few feet apart. Too close. How she longed to just fall right into him.

"Not till Tuesday," she whispered, as if the question had been far more intimate. "The teacher is out of town for a long holiday weekend. Why do you ask?"

"I thought I'd give it a try," he said. "They say it's good for flexibility."

Was he serious? She wasn't sure how to react. Did she really want him and Kilo in the same room? Why did that matter? "I'm not sure they can fit you in," she said, seeing that he didn't crack a smile. "The class usually has a waitlist."

"Not a problem. I tell you what—we'll go separately. I don't want to cramp your style. If they're full up, I won't make a fuss."

"Okay, well …." She stood and shifted from foot to foot like an awkward ten-year-old with a crush. "Guess I'll turn in. Thanks for, um, saving my life."

"I don't think—"

"I know, I know … I wouldn't have died. At the very least you saved me from an extended hospital stay. Or painful plastic surgery." She felt stupid for adding that. If she'd had his shrapnel scars, she'd have done anything to fix them. For such a great-looking man with scars that spanned, however faintly, half his body, he didn't seem the slightest bit self-conscious. As a woman— admittedly a vain one—she envied that nonchalance.

"Good night," he said, still seated, leaning back, powerful arms folded comfortably across his chest. No rising to acknowledge her exit. "Maybe I'll see you tomorrow. Tuesday for sure."

"That will be nice." She had to get out of there—fast. She started backing out the door. "Good night."

"Sweet dreams!" he called after her in an amusing singsong.

* * *

LIAM CHUCKLED TO HIMSELF AS he put away the leftovers and loaded the dishwasher. Teresa was so goddamned cute. He'd never thought of himself as having a playful side, but she seemed to bring it out in him. He loved to tease her, even knowing it was a dangerous game.

She'd tried to help with cleanup, but he preferred to do it himself, his way. His main failing, he supposed, was always wanting to be in control, to do *everything* his way.

His peace of mind had been hard won. Before the terrorist attack, Liam had seen himself as an "angry young man," the kind glorified by Kingsley Amis in the '50s. He wasn't yet thirty, and yet he might as well be sixty. During his recovery, he dreamed of a monastic existence surrounded by the natural landscapes he loved. The path he'd stumbled onto in Israel, through no fault of his own, led to more turmoil and risk. Now here was Teresa, infiltrating his sleep and disturbing his waking hours. She was not part of the plan, not a restful kind of woman. Joe and Ali seemed to be throwing them together. *They don't know you at all*, he told himself with irritation. Honesty goaded him to add, *How could they, when you won't let them in?* Maybe he should just leave, retreat to his own isolated cabin in the wilderness. But then who would watch over Teresa?

He and his sister had only obliquely discussed the psychic current between them. Anyone who heard random small voices of warning could tell you they resisted a direct summons. Maybe true psychics had it all figured out. Not him, though he was more tuned in than most. Yet, how did you tell the difference between simple anxiety or an excess of caution and a genuine premonition? Only in retrospect, that's how. The bike "accident" had left him concerned for Teresa's welfare. Perhaps that explained how he'd known the precise moment she'd needed him today. Perhaps.

*Damn.* As he made his way back to his cabin, buffeted by gusts of wind and breathing deep of the fresh sea air, he popped open a can of beer and took a long drink. Today had been a close call. Not Teresa's tumble—he didn't believe she'd been in mortal danger—but the escalation of intimacy. How was he going to resist jumping her bones when she kept giving him those sheep's eyes, kept needing to be rescued? He'd never wanted anyone the way he wanted this woman, but he was certain that if they acted on this … whatever *this* was, they would combust in a way that would burn not only them but everyone around them. Hadn't they warned her away from him? Her own mother, surely. Seeing himself through Carrie's eyes, he might as well be wearing an eyepatch and raising the Jolly Roger flag. He knew all too well that some girls sought out the bad boys. Trouble is, he wasn't that bad. Oh, he was dangerous enough, if you threatened someone he loved or had sworn to protect. Or if you were some bimbo who caught him at a weak moment.

Teresa was no bimbo. He'd used plenty of women in his time—he wasn't proud of it—and he was damned if he was going to let himself be used by some rich girl looking to reenact *Lady Chatterley's Lover*.

# CHAPTER 9

Teresa discounted Liam's reassurances that she would have survived the fall. She slept poorly, picturing her mangled body and face, a long recovery in rehab or learning to live with paralysis, like poor Christopher Reeve.

She'd always been lucky, or so she thought. Had her luck run out?

It was almost eight when she awoke, and nearly nine when she wandered over to the main house. Normally she would have stayed in the cabin and made use of the Mr. Coffee and minifridge. Only she hoped Liam might still be around. No, his Harley was gone, and the house was quiet. In the end, she must have slept like a log because that loud motor was hard to miss.

She helped herself to a bowl of cereal. With yet another unscheduled day yawning before her, she considered her options. More shopping? She could use a new pair of sandals to replace the ones lost in her tumble. That could wait. She hadn't explored Fort Worden for years. It was only a short drive away, so the distance should be manageable by foot. She wasn't psychologically ready to ride her bike, even though Liam said it was fixed, and she wasn't in good enough shape to pedal up all those hills.

*An Officer and a Gentleman* had been filmed in Fort Worden. The former Army base had loads of atmosphere. The American-Craftsman-style buildings had been spiffed up but not beyond imagining their original purpose, and you could roam the driftwood-lined beaches or walk to the lighthouse. She liked to imagine life in a far simpler era, one that required commitment to hearth and home, before rampant frivolity, even if it had been a terrible time for women. *Stop it*, she told herself. *I don't need to censor my thoughts. It's my fantasy, after all*. With the world her oyster—those oysters last night had been delicious—why was she fantasizing about being the pampered wife of an officer protecting his country in comfortable quarters at the turn of the century? Especially if the officer looked like Liam ….

Oh, and Liam had said he was meeting a friend at Fort Worden. Maybe their paths would cross.

Though the predicted high was in the upper 70s, it was rarely hot at the beach, so Teresa dressed in jeans and a sweater. About an hour into her walk, she wished she'd taken the car. The route wasn't particularly scenic—just a tree-lined main road where everyone drove too fast. Two hours had passed when she finally arrived, feet throbbing. She had to have traveled over six miles. *Darn.* She was tired and overheated, had already drunk her entire bottle of water and was still thirsty. Could she take a bus back? She hadn't seen one. There weren't any cafés at Fort Worden. She thought she recalled a supply store near the beach campground where she could pick up a snack and more water.

Fort Worden had been situated perfectly for defending the Pacific Coast during the two world wars, so it still had empty coastal defense batteries to explore. The base had closed in 1953. Since 1973, it had been a state park. Teresa had been to many tropical paradises. She didn't know why she was so fond of the Pacific Northwest's gray-sand beaches. You couldn't swim here; the water was freezing. As a child she'd jumped the waves at Kalaloch, more intrepid then and in the company of her brothers. The rocks were slick with red and green seaweed, looking like everything from bullwhips to plastic wrap to spaghetti. Rialto Beach was reputed to have the best driftwood, but for Teresa's family, Kalaloch with its '50s-era scribed-log lodge and cabins was the preferred vacation spot. There you could walk along the beach logs for miles, rarely touching the sand. You couldn't do that at Fort Worden, but there was enough driftwood that you ran across the occasional primitive fort. Here you wandered along the shore, gazing at barges, fishing vessels, and pleasure boats and keeping an eye out for herons, who were common but difficult to spot. They could stand completely still for long periods while on the hunt for fish.

No herons today, just seagulls and crows. The beach offered some seaweed, though mostly in dry, dead tangles, and the scant driftwood was leaning atop large rocks. She wondered if a storm had taken most of it out to sea. The water was a bleak gray blue. As she walked on the dry sand and broken shells, sand fleas scattered at her feet, and her tennis shoes started to fill up. After knocking the detritus out of her shoes, she headed down to where the sand was firm and wet and found a few pieces of sea glass and more dead crabs. Not much of visual interest farther inland unless you were a fan of eel grass. The few other walkers were dressed in rain gear and towed along by dogs.

Teresa wasn't far from the lighthouse when she felt the first raindrop. Why hadn't she brought a waterproof jacket? Now she'd have to walk all the way back to Joe and Ali's place in the rain. Rain in the Pacific Northwest rarely came in intense showers that stopped after ten minutes. More like a light drizzle that lasted for hours. She shouldn't have trusted the forecast. She stopped at the Cable House Canteen and bought an energy bar and a large bottle of water. Outside, the rain was getting serious, falling in sheets. The plastic ponchos were sold out.

Leaving the beach, she headed back to the former military base, finding the decorative white anchor that marked the beginning of the paved side street where the commanding officers' mansions were located. Painted a pinkish white with gray trim, they featured inviting front porches on either side. Stone stairs were built into the grassy slopes below. She caught sight of Liam's Harley parked next to a house identified with a discreet, black-lettered placard that read "Col. Norbert S. Byrne." The door was open. Did she dare bother Liam? It was almost three. Too early to beg a ride back to the compound? She balked. There were so many reasons she didn't want to do this, starting with the need to explain why she'd walked all the way here alone on today of all days. Why else except on the chance of seeing him? He might not be done with his current task; then he would feel compelled to leave early and resent her for disrupting his schedule. What if he were visiting a woman? She hadn't considered that possibility.

For several minutes she just stood there in the gently soaking rain, trying to shield her hair with her sweater. Disheartened, she turned to go.

"Teresa?"

She jumped and swiveled about to face him. "Oh! You scared me."

"What are you doing here? Is everything okay?" He didn't sound annoyed, just concerned.

"I saw your Harley. At least I thought it was yours. I wasn't sure."

His smile encouraged her to continue, but he didn't speak. She was starting to realize that a lot of Liam's strategies involved waiting to see how things played out without coaxing them one way or the other. Unlike her, he was comfortable with silence. Though clearly a man of action, he would rarely proceed without giving a situation major forethought.

"I was going to see if I could bum a ride. But you're too busy. I won't disturb you."

"Where's your car? Did the engine stall? Or did you ride your bike?"

"I walked." It sounded so foolish said aloud, she hung her head. If she walked home, she would have traveled fourteen miles on foot today. In simple, canvas Keds. In general, she wasn't much of a walker, certainly not a hiker.

Liam didn't spare her. He threw back his head and laughed.

She was mortified. And she knew she must look like a drowned rat—if rats wore makeup. She wiped beneath her eyes in case her smudge-proof mascara hadn't lived up to the hype.

"Come on in," he said, unaccountably pleased. "I'm helping out my new friend Peter. He's a groundskeeper here. We're working on a project."

She walked up the stairs onto the porch and ventured into the house. Peter shook her hand and introduced himself. Then he handed her a towel. He was an older man with a bald pate—what little hair he had was gathered in a straggly ponytail—a grizzled goatee, and merry, crinkly blue eyes.

"You left your rain jacket at home, I see. The weather here is unpredictable. We're just finishing up. Liam can fix anything."

That didn't surprise her somehow.

"Peter, I'll see you tomorrow afternoon," Liam said. "I have a yoga class in the morning."

Peter looked as if Liam had told him he'd be donning a tutu and dancing in *Swan Lake*. "Really?" was all he could say, mouth agape.

"It's a total mind-body workout," Liam said, eyes twinkling. "Or so I hear."

"If you say so." Peter seemed to suspect Liam was joking but wasn't quite ready to call him on it.

After helping Teresa into his motorcycle jacket—so huge and heavy on her small frame she almost toppled over—Liam herded her out the door and back into the driving rain. "Later," he called out over his shoulder to Peter.

Teresa fingered the buttery-soft leather of the jacket and the silky lining. She couldn't see the label, but she could swear it was St. Laurent, which put it in the four-thousand-dollar range. How could Liam afford such a garment? Was it a gift? According to Ali, Liam's motorcycle jacket had been incinerated in the terrorist attack in Jerusalem, so naturally he'd needed a replacement. Why one this fancy? She recalled how expensively he'd been dressed at that first dinner at her mother's house. In Port Townsend, she'd never seen him in anything but worn jeans, a T-shirt, a flannel shirt, and work boots. Except when he wore hiking gear.

Liam handed Teresa a spare helmet. "Safety first," he said, donning his own helmet. He hopped on. "Put your arms around my waist and hold on tight."

Teresa did as she was told, only a thin, damp black T-shirt between her long fingers and his bulging six-pack. The jacket was unzipped, and her breasts pressed against the rippling muscles of his back. Closing her eyes, she breathed in his now familiar, devastatingly potent masculine scent, telling herself to resist the quagmire of desire that was sucking her down into its beguiling depths. In what TV series had someone said, "Resistance is futile"? Probably more than one. It was so true. With a huge sigh, she snuggled against Liam and held on for dear life.

* * *

ALI COULDN'T BELIEVE SHE STILL hadn't gone into labor. Did pregnant women ever just burst like overripe tomatoes? Perhaps she'd be the first. She was so eager to get this ordeal over with. But then what? She'd be caring for two babies at once. Carrie had hired a nanny she assured them was old enough not to be a temptation to Joe and young enough to handle the babies.

Youthful looking as Carrie was, she had some odd ideas more typical of an older age group. It had never occurred to Ali that Joe would be tempted by a young nanny. Should it? She hadn't seen him so much as glance at another woman since they'd been together. Even after she'd turned into a giant blowfish. When it came right down to it, they hadn't known each other long. The year and seven months between their first and second meetings didn't count.

She and Joe were sitting in the backyard of the Capitol Hill mansion while Carrie deadheaded roses. "Joe, when was the last time you checked in with Liam and Teresa?" she said casually.

"Around dinnertime yesterday. Liam was cooking oysters."

Carrie stopped clipping, her brows knit in consternation. "Dinner for two?"

Joe took a long sip of iced tea. "Why not?"

"You know your sister. When it comes to men, she doesn't have the sense God gave little geese."

Joe shrugged. "Not my concern. She's an adult."

Ali bit her tongue. She'd almost said, *When Liam's around, lock up your daughters.*

Carrie put down the clippers and tore off her gardening gloves as if having just discovered they were Hammacher Schlemmer knockoffs. "Has he ever explained how he spent the last few years? After he recovered from the explosion, of course."

"Not really," Joe said. "I figured he'd tell us when he was ready. Mom, you need to cool out about Liam. He's our guest, and he's got a good head on his shoulders. He's not going to do something stupid like have a fling with Teresa. He's only staying with us until he finds his footing."

"When will that be, do you suppose?" Carrie had given up on the roses and was standing with her arms akimbo.

"He's not exactly forthcoming, and we've had other, more pressing matters on our minds." Joe reached out to pat Ali's belly and grinned. "Ooh, the natives are restless."

Ali placed her hand next to Joe's. "Please tell them to come out. They've outstayed their welcome."

Joe gave her an odd look. "Liam said something like that to Teresa when she asked if he was ready to come home from Israel. That he'd 'outstayed his welcome.' I wonder what that means? That he'd made enemies? Hmm."

"I have an investigator working on it," Carrie said, unapologetically. She poured herself a glass of iced tea and sat down. "Unlike you, I'm unwilling to wait until Liam is feeling chatty."

"Not that I'm surprised." Joe didn't sound pleased.

"So far he hasn't been able to dig up much. The woman who identified him as her son was from a prominent Israeli family."

"Was …?" Ali asked.

"She died in March. He was living with her and her other children up until her death. That's when he moved out and took the security job."

"Our foster father George taught him how to hunt with a rifle," Ali said. "He said that anyone who ate meat should be willing to kill it himself. Not that Liam took to hunting as a sport. That was the extent of it. Aren't most security guards ex-cops or former military?" She looked at Joe. "Now he can throw knives like a circus performer."

Joe's eyes widened with interest. "No kidding. He gave you a demonstration?"

"Something like that." She didn't want to admit he was showing off for Teresa. "If they saw him in action, Barnum and Bailey would snap him up."

Their exchange had ruffled Carrie's feathers. "The investigator didn't say anything about a stint in the army."

Joe turned to Carrie. "If you want to know so badly, why don't you ask Liam?"

"Why don't you?" she tossed back.

"Joe, I—"

That's when Ali's water broke. All she could think as she looked at the mess was, *Thank goodness this didn't happen on Carrie's couch.* The Adirondack chair could be easily wiped off. She did just that. Then stared in horror at the stain on Carrie's linen napkin.

Joe jumped to his feet. "Honey, what are you doing? Leave that to the maid. We have to get you to the hospital. This is so exciting." He helped her into the house. "Where's your overnight case?" He looked at his watch. "Two o'clock. Okay, that's good. We shouldn't have much traffic."

* * *

TERESA AND LIAM PULLED UP to the compound's parking area. The rain had mostly stopped. Just in time. The motorcycle ride had left her so addled with lust she wasn't sure she could stand.

"What are you doing for dinner?" he asked as she took off the helmet and ran her hands through her damp hair.

She was ashamed to admit she'd given the matter no thought. All she'd had for lunch was an energy bar, and she was ravenous. Dinner on her own was usually a salad with a chicken breast or piece of grilled fish. If she got too used to Liam's cooking, she'd have to shop for a new wardrobe.

"I was just going to throw together a salad," she said as he casually lifted her off the motorcycle, his hands spanning her waist. She wobbled as he set her on her feet. "I think there's leftover chicken."

"You burned a lot of calories today. You need real sustenance."

"First, I need a hot shower and a change of clothing. Please don't feel like you have to wait on me."

"Up to you. It's just after four. I was planning to grill some steaks. They're marinating right now. There's one with your name on it if you like." He paused. "You can put it on your salad. It's lean steak. Good protein. I'm not proposing a hot fudge sundae."

"Okay, thanks. But like I said, don't wait on me. Maybe I'll be down when I'm cleaned up."

"You still look good, you know. You worry too much."

She hated it when men said things like that. As if her personal grooming was any of their business, or as if she primped and preened for their benefit.

Back at the cabin, she looked in the mirror at the wet waif with the drawn face and squeezed her eyes shut, engulfed by a hot rush of shame. *God,* how she wished she'd planned her day better. Most of her makeup had washed away, and her hair was a tangled mess. She spent a lot of time blow-drying it straight to tame its natural curls. The coloring and straightening had left it damaged. She considered how freeing it would be to stop doing all that. Why not? She had a feeling Liam would prefer it.

*Why do you care what Liam thinks? What about Kilo?*

Kilo. Liam. They were both impossible. Just because Paul had been ejected from her orbit didn't mean she should hop into bed with one of them. And what if it took? They would hate her life. How would they fit in? She had serious investments, but she doubted Liam would respond well to being a kept man. Kilo at least ran his own business. What would she do while he taught yoga? Stay home with the kids? That was presuming that either man was interested in anything but a fling. Then again, was she really ready to give up the social whirl? Her mother was right; Paul was the perfect fit for that—just not for her.

*How much do you even like your life? You could do volunteer work here as easily as in Seattle.* And now she was back to the real crux of the matter: her so-called life in *her* world was just an elaborate avoidance device, a distraction from the important business of deciding what she really wanted to do. She'd let her entire existence so far—with the exception of the Kilo fiasco—be directed by Carrie. She needed a vocation—some activity that would allow her a modicum of self-respect. She couldn't just wander around Port Townsend forever—leading the locals to speculate about her sanity— wearing out her tennis shoes, reading escapist fiction, and riding her bike into ditches. She was twenty-seven years old. The longer she waited, the fewer options she'd have. If she wanted to go back to school, for instance, she'd need to do it soon. What on earth would she study? She'd done nothing with her Creative Writing degree, nor did she want to. *Oh,* this kind of agonizing soul-searching drove her nuts. *I don't want to think about this!* her id screamed at her.

Then there was the immediate issue. Should she join Liam for dinner?

She *really* wanted to. He was soooo delicious. Couldn't she just fall into his arms? Who would it harm? Why did anyone have to find out? He wouldn't expect her to marry him, wouldn't even want it. *That's not you,* her superego told her. It would be great at first, then she'd be miserable. She'd fall in love for sure. And then, what if he rejected her? Could they both pretend it had never happened? Was it too late? Was she in love with him already?

Superegos and ids. Maybe she should study psychology. She'd treasured her lovely liberal arts degree, with all its elegant, esoteric knowledge that didn't serve any purpose in the real world but help you keep up with the Joneses—if the Joneses were also intellectual snobs. Her education did enhance her inner life. But when you really thought about it, the only practical skill she'd ever learned was typing. Here were Liam and Ali with all these survival skills and no extravagant inheritance to tempt them into navel-gazing and terminal loafing.

After taking a long, hot shower, Teresa towel-dried her hair and pulled it back into a ponytail. Tomorrow she would go to a hairdresser and get the color reversed. The dark roots were showing. She didn't know where to go in Port Townsend, so she'd just choose a place and leave the rest up to fate. Maybe she'd look like hell; then both Liam and Kilo would lose interest. That would simplify things.

Her cell phone rang.

"We have baby girls!"

She had never heard Joe like this, amped up like a crazed fanatic at a revival meeting.

"Congratulations!" she yelled back, vastly relieved to push away the dark thoughts. "How is Ali?"

"She's doing well, though I know it was painful. She looks really happy now. The girls are perfect. Absolutely beautiful."

"Details!" she said. "Eye color?"

"They're identical. *That* was a surprise. Hair color … not sure. Black fuzz right now. Big blue eyes. Only we're told they might still turn brown."

"Weight?"

"One's five pounds, one's five and a half. Not underweight for twins, and they were somewhat early. They're absolutely fine, though."

"I can't wait to meet them. When will you come back to us?"

"Uncertain," he said, more subdued. "Mom hired a nanny, but the nanny expected to live in Seattle, not Port Townsend. I think we should stay here for a bit in any case. Until we see what kind of babies we're dealing with."

"As in, budding Damiens?"

"They don't look like Satan's spawns. But in the movies, Damien is always a cute kid. You never can tell. All joking aside, they might be colicky, or just fussy. If so, I want Ali to have the support she needs. Also, I think we should take care of some security measures in Port Townsend before we return. An alarm system. I hate to think that would be necessary, but otherwise we'll be sitting ducks for the tabloids …."

As he went on, Teresa was only half listening. She was thinking, *Uh-oh, this is one development you hadn't considered. That you would be left alone with Liam for an indefinite period.*

"Teresa?"

"Still here. Maybe I should come back to Seattle."

"Why the heck would you? You'll meet your nieces soon enough. I'll email photographs." A pause. "Is it a problem to be alone with Liam?"

*Oh, that Joe. He's no dummy.* "Why would it be?"

"Mom has this idea—" He cut himself off. "Ali's also a little worried. Says Liam is hard to resist, and that he likes you."

"Well, I hope he *likes* me," Teresa huffed. "Don't worry, either of you. We're both adults." *Teresa, this is Joe you're talking to*, she thought, then added, "Between you and me, it's a bit of a struggle."

"You know I don't want to meddle. You're a big girl now. Liam's cool. Just use protection."

Teresa's laugh was rueful. "How do you protect your heart? Got any heart condoms?"

"If only …" Joe said. "It's over with Paul, right? Live a little. Stop worrying about what other people want for you."

*Mom, you mean*, Teresa thought. "Wow, is this really my brother?" she said. "Please put JJ back on the line."

"I don't know if I'd value Ali as much as I do without the other, uh, prior experiences."

"Shouldn't you be getting back to her?" Teresa was eager to change the subject.

"Sure. If you need to come home, then do, by all means. Only, don't do it for our sakes. I think spending time by yourself is good for you. It's forcing you to do a little soul-searching. That's bound to be uncomfortable."

"Thanks, Bro." Teresa resisted the urge to tell him to can the sermon. She knew that "by yourself" meant "away from Mom." "Give my love to Ali and the twins. And oh, Joe?"

"Yeah?"

"Names!"

"Caryn and Josephine.

"After Mom and you?"

Joe laughed. "Ali insisted. Caryn's middle name is Teresa. Josephine's is Alice."

"Awww. Love and kisses, Bro."

After she hung up, Teresa looked at her watch. Seven thirty already. She was starving. She was also in a panic. She knew she should go tell Liam about the twins. But wouldn't Joe call him next? Her brother hadn't told her to relay the news. Would it be weird if she didn't? And she needed to eat, *now*. That's when she surrendered to the panic. She grabbed her car keys and sped into town, where she found a restaurant with a view of the bay and ordered grilled halibut and a glass of wine. She wished she'd brought a book with her, but what book? Time for something with no romance. A thriller. Or an Agatha Christie mystery. Those were relatively sexless, weren't they? And you could fill a raft with them. After she finished eating, she sat sipping her wine and gazing out at the view. The wine calmed her. Whatever her motivation—cowardice, in this case—she'd been right not to join Liam for dinner. She couldn't let anything happen between them. She just couldn't.

# CHAPTER 10

THE NEXT DAY, TERESA AVAILED herself of the coffee maker in her cabin and ate cottage cheese from her minifridge on a rice cake, thus avoiding yet another meal with Liam. The morning was clear and cool, and she was looking forward to yoga … until she remembered that Liam had promised to be there too. Surely he'd been joking? The entire class was female. She should have warned him.

When she entered the classroom, there he was, a rooster and his brood. Of course he'd had no trouble getting in. Who could say no to Liam? As luck would have it, he had placed his mat in her usual spot, on the left side of the room in the second row. The crowd was far denser in the area surrounding him. As if he were a campfire on a cold night. She unrolled her mat way over on the right side of the room. But really, the room was too small to escape the buzz.

"Who is he?"

"What a hunk!"

"He says he's just visiting—staying with relatives for a while."

Giggles rippled across the room. Liam was smiling and flirting with everyone, young and old, and they were lapping it up. She'd never seen him like this. Silent, sulky Liam.

He was dressed in sweatpants and a T-shirt and using one of the studio mats. She was pretty sure he was winging it. The shapeless clothing did nothing to conceal his splendor. The pants still clung to his firm backside, and his bulging biceps were on full display.

"Isn't he something?" the woman next to her whispered.

Teresa grinned and nodded. She was not going to claim him.

Then Kilo entered, and the giggling subsided, mostly.

"We have a newbie," he said. "Welcome!" Teresa supposed he'd have to acknowledge Liam's presence. He *was* the elephant in the room. More like the fox in the henhouse. "Just a reminder to everyone: if you're uncomfortable in a particular pose, move to a resting position. Some find Downward Dog relaxing. But for the most part, that will be Child's Pose. Or, if you really need a rest, Corpse Pose."

"That's eternal rest," Liam joked. The woman on his left guffawed—there was no better word for it. Like the braying of a donkey.

Kilo shot him a warning glance, and to give Liam credit, he appeared chastened.

As the class got underway, Teresa could *not* find her rhythm. She was too distracted by Liam. To her surprise, despite his lack of experience, he was flexible and a natural. She also couldn't help but notice the attention he gave to the women around him, smiling and kowtowing like a politician. Was it her imagination, or was almost everyone angling in his direction? Not surprisingly, Kilo also seemed off his game. The only woman in the room immune to Liam was Jodi, who Teresa happened to know had a female partner. Jodi just looked annoyed. She also started correcting Kilo when he moved on to the next set of poses without repeating the previous set on the other side. He thanked her without much grace.

After class, Liam stood talking to April, who was separated from her wealthy husband. April was probably thirty years old, with wavy, naturally dark-blonde hair tied into a loose ponytail. She had pouty lips, wide blue eyes, and patrician features. No makeup, yet gorgeous. Teresa couldn't see Liam's face, but April was sending out major signals, playing with her hair, repeatedly touching his arm. It gave Teresa scant satisfaction to note that Liam kept his hands to himself.

"Teresa?"

"Oh, hi, Kilo!" she said, too perky.

He scowled. "Who is that guy, and why is he in my class?"

"Look, I'm so sorry. I'm afraid he's my brother-in-law."

"He's not going to keep coming, is he?" Kilo scratched his head in consternation. His slouchy body language expressed defeat. "He's way too much of a distraction." He laid a hand on her arm. "Lunch? I got a sub for the noon class."

"Why?" she said, turning to look at him. If you could just block Liam out of your mind, Kilo was every bit as gorgeous. Wait … did that even make sense?

"Why lunch or why the sub?" he said with his curiously dry laugh.

"I was told you rarely use subs. Lunch would be nice."

"I need to take it easy this week. Give my muscles a rest. I did a major hike over the holiday weekend. And Jennifer asked for extra hours. Plus, I'd like to have lunch with you."

That was three reasons, she noted. Was the third the most important? *Interesting.* She hadn't thought he was that into her. He'd only proposed coffee that one time. Maybe she'd been wrong. Or maybe it was simply lunch with an old friend.

"Okay, sure. Should I change first?"

"You look wonderful just as you are. We'll go to the natural foods place. They're used to customers in workout clothes." As they headed out the door, she checked to see what Liam was up to. He was still standing with April, but he was staring at her and Kilo, evaluating the situation. Then he smiled, waved goodbye, and turned back to April. Was he telling her they were related by marriage, thus assuring her there was nothing to worry about? She frowned.

"Do you need permission?" Kilo was obviously puzzling over Liam's role in her life.

"No, of course not," she said in too brusque a voice. "Let's go." She led the way, even though she had no idea where they were going. He had to physically turn her around as she headed in the wrong direction.

"Sorry," she said. "He gets my goat sometimes too."

Kilo raised his eyebrows. "As long as that's all he gets."

"Don't be ridiculous. He was raised by wolves." She instantly regretted the snobbish remark.

"If so, they taught him how to wear sheep's clothing pretty effectively." Kilo pulled out a chair for her to sit down.

Teresa tried to concentrate on the chalkboard menu. "He's a puzzle. No one really knows what he was doing during the three years and four months he went missing."

Kilo appeared skeptical. "Really?"

"Everyone thought he was dead—that he'd died in a terrorist attack. When really, he was living in Israel, working as a security guard." She told Kilo what little they knew, that because of his injuries Liam had been misidentified and claimed as someone else's son.

Kilo nodded. "I noticed the scars. He wears them well."

"Yes." Teresa felt the heat rising in her cheeks. Moving right along …. "Kilo, speaking of the last several years, what happened to you after, uh, we parted ways? I thought you'd pursue a ballet career."

He relaxed a little at the conversational shift, as she knew he would. "I dropped out of Cornish to dance professionally. Not ballet. Modern dance. With a multiethnic troupe based in New York City. Perhaps you've heard of the Groban Phillips Company?"

*Only the foremost modern dance company on the East Coast*, she thought.

"Uh, yes, of course. That's amazing. What made you stop?"

"I joined the company at age nineteen as an apprentice. I couldn't afford to quit my main gig as a caterwaiter. After about a year, I was asked to tour with the East Coast company. Five years later, I was burned out. I wasn't a featured dancer and I couldn't see that happening. I followed an … opportunity and moved to London for a bit. But I missed the U.S. I had been taking yoga all along, and it seemed like that might be the way to go. Restorative. I taught in Port Angeles before opening the studio here."

An "opportunity" in London. A British girl? *Hmm*. He'd skated over that one. She was about to ask for more details when the waitress arrived to take their order. Neither of them was a big eater. They decided to split a tuna salad, avocado, and sprouts sandwich.

"Wine?" he asked her.

"Not at lunch. I'm destroyed for the rest of the day."

He grinned. "Two glasses of Pinot Gris," he told the waitress.

"Really, Kilo—"

"This is our first meal together in, what, ten years? Let your hair down a little."

*My hair*, she thought, *symbol of my oppression*. When the wine came, she drank it. After lunch, she planned to visit the hairdresser down the street to do a reverse color. That appointment might require liquid courage.

Kilo was the entertaining companion Teresa recalled, amusing her with tales from the road, including the bad hotel rooms and crazy antics of the dance troupe. Their schedule had been so tight that they rarely got to sightsee and almost never took advantage of the nightlife. Performances were usually in the evenings, and afterward they were too tired. If charged with adrenaline, they went to after-hours clubs, where they enjoyed—strangely enough— dancing. "Showing off," he said, since no one else on the dance floor could hold a candle to them. Several dancers had to be replaced along the way because of injuries, and a few gained too much weight and were fired. That meant "fresh blood." She guessed there had been a lot of incestuous hanky-panky. Kilo was too classy to elaborate, and she didn't push him, didn't think they should go there on such short acquaintance. Their adult selves, she meant. She had been all too well acquainted with eighteen-year-old Kilo.

It was difficult not to fall under his spell. Unlike Liam, he was a talker, which allowed her to relax and listen rather than having to draw him out. Granted, Liam could be funny and loquacious when he was in a good mood and not all broody. One of the qualities that had initially drawn her to Kilo was his perpetually sunny personality. *She* had been raised to excel so she could get into the right universities. Kilo didn't care. He was effortlessly talented as a dancer and had earned his GED after he dropped out of high school to take advantage of the dance scholarship. Male ballet dancers—especially tall, beautiful ones—were always in demand to partner all the women. In fact, everything came a little too easily to Kilo. For her, he'd been the ultimate escape, like a trip to Maui in the middle of the winter of her discontent. And, despite her strict Catholic upbringing, he'd convinced her going all the way was okay. God hadn't smote her—although she wasn't sure what that would have entailed. After Edward had dragged her home following the botched elopement, there had been no adverse consequences other than to her heart. No STDs, no pregnancy. She and Kilo had waited until after her graduation to run away together. The escapade hadn't been well conceived. Neither of them had any money, so they'd used her American Express credit card. That made them easy to track. She'd thought the fact that they had consummated the marriage would force her mother to accept it. She was wrong. It took some doing, but the marriage was annulled.

"Teresa?"

She'd been woolgathering. "Oh, sorry."

"Shall we go?"

"Uh, sure." *Go where?* she thought. She realized he'd paid the bill. "Um, thanks for lunch. I didn't mean for you to pay."

"It's my pleasure." He opened the door for her.

"My car is over by your studio." She pointed.

"The sky-blue Miata. No Beemer or Porsche?"

He was teasing her. "Both," she said in the same spirit. "Left them back in Seattle."

"What are you doing with yourself these days? You never said."

The question vaguely offended her, though she wasn't quite sure why. After all, she *was* the idle rich girl he made her out to be.

"That's a fair question," she said, a little tartly. "I'm not sure. Drifting, I suppose. Looking for answers. Away from my mother."

"Ah." He nodded in understanding. When they reached the studio, he checked his watch. "Class is still in session. Come up to my place?"

"You live upstairs?"

He pointed at an orange tabby in the window. "See the cat? That's Swami."

"Cute."

"He would love to meet you."

He reached for her and pressed his skillful lips to hers, taking her completely by surprise. It was a sweet kiss, soft, and definitely more than friendly. She took an involuntary step backward.

He looked just as startled. "Too soon? It's not as if we haven't—"

"I know," she broke in. "I don't think I can be that … casual."

"Really?" He smiled. "Even now that you're all grown up? We could enjoy an amazing afternoon together. No strings. You'd love my place."

They were climbing the stairs, only their progress was slow, in that they were kissing the entire way. It was as if no time had passed. Somehow he unlocked the door, and they stumbled in. Had she wanted this to happen? He was all hands, making her think of that goddess with all the arms. Maybe because when she came up for air, she was staring at a little statue of that figure.

*He's not Liam*, a voice in the back of her head kept saying.

He was pulling her into the bedroom, and she was only half resisting, when they saw the girl in the bed. *Huh?*

Kilo's hands fell away and the two of them stared at the girl, who appeared to be naked and quite red in the face. You could only see her head, shoulders, and the tops of her bountiful breasts; she clutched a sheet to her chest. Jessica, the receptionist.

"Um, um …" she stammered, "I thought that was why you got a sub. I thought you winked at me when you gave me the key."

"You didn't see me leave for lunch with Teresa?" Kilo was surprisingly calm. That Zen thing again. He might have been a father confronting his daughter over staying out past curfew. "I didn't give you the key so that you could surprise me in my apartment. I told you I wanted you to feed the cat while I was out of town next weekend."

Swami chose this moment to weave between Teresa's legs. "Meow," he said simply, looking up at her. It was a demanding meow, so she reached down to pet him.

"Swami says to keep him out of this," Teresa joked. Kilo's eyes twinkled, and his lips twitched. Somehow they both managed to contain their laughter.

"Meow," Swami said again, this time at Kilo.

"I'd never met your cat. I thought that was some kind of code," Jessica whined.

Kilo tapped his forehead with the heel of his hand. "Ai yi yi," he muttered and picked up Swami, who was purring loudly. "Teresa, I'm sorry about this. Jessica, get dressed. Come on, Teresa." He put down the cat, shut the bedroom door, and gave her a sheepish look.

"It's okay," she said with a laugh. "I hope you won't be too hard on her. It's obvious everyone who comes near you wants to go to bed with you."

"Except for you. I felt your hesitation. Maybe there's more going on with that brother-in-law than you care to admit." He shrugged, surprisingly unperturbed. "Anyway, it's cool. Another time, maybe, when you get your head together." He raised her hand to his lips and kissed it.

"Thanks, Kilo." She gave his hand a little shake then dropped it quickly. "It was good to catch up. I'll see you in class."

"Good. Jessica and I need to have a little chat. I hope she has her clothes on. God, she's barely eighteen." He blew her a kiss as he shut the door.

She stood on the landing for a long moment, trying to regain her equilibrium. What had just happened? Had she invited it? Did Kilo do this kind of thing with other women in the class? Or was she special? Had he carried a torch for her all this time? Unlikely. What if she had just gone with the flow? She'd enjoyed his kisses, but not in a knee-buckling way. If memory served, it would have been an "amazing afternoon." Probably even more amazing now that he'd had years to perfect his technique. *God*, that summer after graduation had been horrendous. They'd sent her away to stay with relatives in Cape Cod, a paradise under any other circumstances. She'd spent the entire summer mooning over Kilo. Her letters received no response, her messages, delivered from a payphone, were never returned. Of course they were left on his mother's answering machine. No cell phones in those days. She doubted that any of her attempts at communication reached him.

And yet, during the entire hour-and-a-half lunchtime conversation, she'd never asked him why he didn't contact her.

It didn't help that the one glass of wine had gone straight to her head.

It was two o'clock when she walked into the beauty shop without an appointment. The sign said WALK-INS WELCOME, and they didn't seem particularly busy. She sat in the reception area and picked up a copy of *People* magazine that looked as if it had been left out in the rain then used as a doormat.

# CHAPTER 11

———◆———

LIAM WAS STILL FUMING OVER the way Kilo had spirited Teresa away to lunch right under his nose. He'd bet the guy was just Teresa's type, similar to Liam physically but more androgynous and so less intimidating. He hated guys like that. Using that "harmless" thing to wheedle their way into a woman's bed. It had taken all his acting skills to assume that breezy air of indifference. What was he supposed to do, something ham-fisted like "remind" her they had lunch plans that didn't exist? What kind of message would that give Teresa? The right one, but that was beside the point. He couldn't let her know how much he cared. Besides, if she and Kilo had something going, didn't that make Liam's life easier? The old Liam would have made a "lunch" date with April on the spot. But when she'd extended that very invitation, he'd pleaded a prior engagement. Not that she wasn't gorgeous. She just wasn't Teresa. Now here he was, chopping wood again. He hoped Joe would never convert the fireplace to gas because this was an excellent way to let off steam. Yet he couldn't stop directing his gaze up the hill and checking his watch. Where the hell was she? Clearly lunch was long over, which meant Teresa was dessert. He ground his teeth.

Throwing the ax into the stump with too much force—it might take the "right-wise king born of all England" to get it out again—he gave up on the woodpile, and on a whim, drove the old pickup Joe had bought at an auction to the Humane Society in Port Angeles.

The truck had way more power than he would have guessed. The local sheriff must have been otherwise occupied; Liam's driving surely deserved a ticket. He set out on his mission like Speed Racer on amphetamines.

* * *

TERESA SHOULD HAVE TAKEN THE ratty magazines and lack of clientele as bad omens. Four hours later, she was headed back to Joe and Ali's place. From Port Angeles, where she'd gone to try to undo the damage the local hairdresser had inflicted on her hair. Now she looked like a concentration camp survivor. *Come on, you silly drama queen*, she admonished herself. She didn't look *that* bad. A bit more hair than that. More like '50s icon Montgomery Clift.

She wished she could just go home and cry in her soup. Except that Liam was there and would most likely laugh his head off—especially since she'd left him in the lurch last night and then departed yoga class in Kilo's company without even returning his goodbye wave.

*What was I supposed to do, interrupt his conversation with April?*

*If you didn't have a crush on him, you would have.*

Back and forth like that. She thought about fleeing to town to get dinner again, but she was going to have to face Liam sooner or later. Might as well get it over with.

She didn't have long to wait. He was at her cabin door, on a ladder.

When he saw her, he did a double take. "What's this?" he said, eyes wide with shock.

"Don't. Just *don't*. I had the day from hell."

He was trying—and failing—to keep a straight face. "Really? Last seen, you were leaving with the handsome yoga instructor. Did he tie you down and shear you like a sheep?"

"Honestly!" She stamped her foot. "You started this."

"*Me*?" The ladder teetered, but he regained his balance and climbed down until he stood beside her.

"You got me thinking about my stupid hair. I was tired of it. Coloring it, straightening it. I just wanted it to stop … oppressing me."

Folding his arms, he gave her an assessing look.

"Julie Andrews in *The Sound of Music*," he concluded. "That's who you look like. Only your hair is darker, of course. Is that your natural color?"

They both laughed. It started with him, and that released the tension for her. There was nothing mean-spirited about his laughter. The reverse-color hadn't worked. It had basically fried her hair. Now it was a steely brown not found in nature.

He tapped his chin thoughtfully. "It will grow out, of course. The color could be better, but the length suits you. You look like Joan of Arc. Jean

Seberg's version. Or a beautiful boy. Nothing wrong with that." He paused, then admitted, "I figured you were with Kilo."

Teresa didn't know how to respond, considering what had nearly happened. "No, that's ancient history."

They were interrupted by a stampede of dogs. That was what it felt like. It was really just two, one very large and one quite small.

"Dogs?" she said in disbelief.

"Guard dogs."

"You cleared this with Joe and Ali?"

"They thought it was a great idea. I found them at the Humane Society in Port Angeles."

Why had he chosen today of all days to go to Port Angeles? Was he keeping tabs on her somehow?

The dogs were making happy noises and wagging their tails furiously.

"I don't think they're going to be very effective guard dogs."

"I don't want them attacking *you*. Or anyone nice. I was assured they could be quite fierce, especially Coogan here." The pint-sized dog, who seemed to already know his name, fell over in front of Liam for a belly rub.

"Coogan?"

"I thought about calling them Mutt and Jeff, but 'Mutt' seemed too disrespectful and 'Jeff' too un-doglike. So I settled on Harry and Coogan, after Clint Eastwood characters."

"Do you know their breeds?"

"Harry has a lot of German Shepherd in him, and something bigger, maybe mastiff. Coogan is a Jack Russell, mostly. Might be some Chihuahua in there. I had to adopt them both because they're best friends."

"How old?" she asked. "Did the shelter know?"

"Somewhere between two and three."

"You're the cutest," she was telling Coogan as she rubbed his back. When Harry nudged her hand with his nose, she gave him a rubdown as well, telling him, "You, *you* are the cutest." She looked up. "What about April?"

"You are definitely the cutest," Liam replied, straight-faced.

"Oh, stop it," she said, but she smiled anyway. "You are being way too nice. You heard about the twins?"

"Yeah, Joe called me last night, filled me in on the details. What a relief. But that set a fire under me." He indicated the camera he'd installed at the top of the ladder. "I'm working on a security system. When I'm done, Fort Knox will have nothing on this place."

"Seems a little extreme for Port Townsend."

"You think so?" He folded up the ladder. "I'm headed back to the house to finish making dinner. There's a chicken in the oven about an hour from being done. I also have asparagus and baked potatoes. Will you join me? No pressure."

"Yes, okay."

Teresa showered to banish the flop sweat of the day, but she didn't bother much with her hair or any cosmetics other than mascara and lip gloss. It all felt too hopeless. Anyway, she shouldn't be dolling herself up for Liam. He was absolutely off limits, despite Joe's assurances. Joe was a guy, after all. He didn't understand that most women her age didn't embark on sexual relationships lightly. Or did they? How would *she* know? She didn't have any close female friends in the area. Her college friends lived on the East Coast, and the few high school friends she'd stayed in touch with were married with children.

She decided jeans and a T-shirt fit the new hairstyle better than a sundress. Now she could seriously pass as a boy. With the exception of the hot-pink polka dot tennis shoes.

"Hey, Terence," Liam said with a smirk. "No, no! Don't be offended. You look cute as heck. You're definitely the cutest." He chuckled. "You and those dogs must have been friends in a past life. They already adore you."

She looked around. "Where are they?"

"Eating dinner in the garage. I'm not letting them in the house."

"That's sad."

"They're outdoor dogs. I have doggy beds set up for them in the garage, and there's a hinged door so they can come and go." Seeing her doleful face, he added, "They are best friends. They won't get lonely. They're here to patrol the area."

"How can you be sure they won't wander beyond the property?"

"Invisible fence."

"Wow, you *have* been busy."

"I had the idea of guard dogs a while back and have been preparing for them. Today I went to Port Angeles on impulse."

*On impulse.* Had he known that was where she had gone? *How silly. How could he know that?*

He started carving the chicken, which had filled the room with a heavenly odor of garlic. "I've been working on the security system for a while now. Maybe you've been too busy to notice."

Now she was embarrassed. *Busy,* she thought. Playing piano. Reading light novels and brooding over Kilo and Liam. She had to be the most frivolous woman alive.

"I like having projects," he went on, as if sensing her thoughts. "I don't begrudge you your down time. If I wanted to read more, I would. I do like reading, just not as much as you." He placed the chicken and baked potatoes on the table next to the al dente asparagus. "I wish I could play the piano. My true passion is tinkering and putting things together. Figuring out how they work"—he grinned—"and think. People, I mean."

They talked a little about books. Predictably, he was more into thrillers. And the movie equivalent. Clint Eastwood, obviously, given the dogs' names. Charles Bronson. Bruce Lee. But, he said, he could be convinced to watch just about anything, French art films, even the occasional romantic comedy. "It's more about learning how a woman's mind works."

"You're talkative tonight," she said.

"And you're kind of quiet." He stood to clear the table. "I have something for you."

After placing the dishes on the counter, he left the room. She quickly rose to put the leftovers away and load the dishwasher. She couldn't let him wait on her all the time.

When he returned, he was carrying a lanyard with two whistles on it. "Thanks for cleaning up," he said.

"Thanks for cooking. It was delicious, as always."

"Simple. That's how I like it."

He hung the lanyard around her neck, somehow managing not to touch her. It was oddly disappointing.

"Let's start with the dog whistle. That's your first line of defense, but only if you're here, of course, and alone. If you're the slightest bit nervous about something while you're on this property, blow on it. If someone is lurking nearby, they won't know you've sounded the alarm."

She picked it up to examine it.

"Don't blow on it now," he warned, "unless you want the dogs to join us for dessert."

She eyed the second whistle. "Does this one summon a flock of specially-trained killer seagulls?"

"Nope. Just me. Though I *am* a specially trained killer." He grinned. "If I'm not around, a good blast from that might be enough to scare off an intruder. Don't worry about false alarms."

*Specially trained killer*, she thought. Clearly he meant to be flippant.

The lanyard was a dud as a fashion accessory. The length allowed the whistles to nestle just below her breasts, which were large enough to keep it hidden as long as her shirt wasn't too tight. She looked up to find him staring. He averted his eyes as color stained his cheeks.

"It's sort of like that medicine bag of yours."

"Huh?" The blush receded.

"The one Ali gave to Joe. It was supposed to keep you safe, right?"

"I hope it's more effective than that," he said with a dismissive wave of his hand.

She absentmindedly fingered the lanyard. "In the case of the medicine bag, you have to believe in it for it to work, I suppose. Why do you think the whistles are necessary?"

"Alternatively, I could just tail you all the time."

The prospect was surprisingly pleasant. "Again, why are you so worried about my safety?"

"The bike accident was already suspicious. And I'm fairly certain the lawn chair was sabotaged."

"Huh." The possibility *had* occurred to her, though on further reflection, it didn't make much sense. "What's the motive?"

Liam shrugged. "I've been wondering that myself. I would say 'to scare you,' but the perpetrator wasn't all that worried that the stunt might go too far and injure or even kill you."

"So, you admit I might have died."

"I never dismissed that possibility." His face was grim.

They both gnawed on that one for a while.

"To me, the 'scare her so she'll leave' motive makes the most sense," he went on, as if the silence hadn't happened. "This person isn't looking to kidnap you and hold you for ransom. He doesn't want your money. Or he's being paid by someone else who wants to scare you though not necessarily to kill you. You know, to be on the safe side, you could just go home to Seattle. I truly doubt you'd be in any danger there—at least from this person or persons."

She threw up her hands in exasperation. "How am I a threat to anyone?"

He didn't hesitate. "That yoga class."

"What?"

"Someone in that yoga class wants you gone. That's my working hypothesis."

"Why?"

The kettle whistled, and he rose from the table and filled the teapot with hot water and several bags of chamomile tea. "Jealousy? Can't think of any other reason, frankly. Kilo wants you, so you are encroaching on someone else's territory. That's why I attended the class. I was mighty relieved to see you return this afternoon."

She wasn't sure she wanted to go there, but she said it aloud anyway, "You were worried I was fooling around with Kilo?"

"More worried you wouldn't make it home alive. When you agreed to have lunch with him—the guy was pretty handsy, by the way—I saw several heads turn in either envy or anger. I think we can rule out April, though."

"Because she's interested in you?" *Interested* was putting it mildly.

"No, because she's not interested in *him*. I doubt she even saw you leave together. I wondered if whoever was responsible for the other attacks was going to set their hounds on you once they got you alone. Human hounds, of course."

"That leaves way too many suspects," she said, accepting the cup of tea.

"I don't suppose you could just stop going to that class? How do you know Kilo, anyway? You didn't just meet, that's clear. 'Ancient history,' you said."

She *really* didn't want to explain. However, if she didn't, the truth was going to out sooner or later, and she'd rather Liam heard it from her.

"We were married," she said finally.

He was too taken aback to respond. He sat, stunned, waiting for more information.

"Right out of high school. He was a dance student at Cornish—we met because I was taking private piano lessons there. A multi-ethnic ballet dancer—my mother's worst nightmare. We ran away together and got as far as a hotel in Redding, California, before my brother Edward found us. The marriage was annulled. They sent me away to relatives in Cape Cod. I never came home at the end of the summer. From there I went straight to Sarah Lawrence."

"Sarah Lawrence? Who's she, an aunt?"

"A fancy-schmancy liberal arts college in New York State."

"You were of legal age, right? How could they force an annulment?"

This was the part that was hardest of all to admit—what a coward she'd been. "I couldn't handle the pressure. My father had died three years earlier, and my mother swore she'd cut me off. Financially, I mean. I didn't expect that. I'm not sure why. Looking back, it makes perfect sense. Even then, I knew no man was worth embarking on a life of poverty for." *Or giving up the free ride*, her conscience added mercilessly.

And then, a year after her botched elopement, her grandmother had died, leaving Teresa a fortune of her own. She could have sought Kilo out—no one could have stopped her. But by then, even she believed the elopement had been a mistake.

Liam was nodding, deep in thought, his expression neutral. "Still have feelings for him, do you?"

"I don't know. Maybe some. He's very charming."

She couldn't read his face. "Well then …." He slapped his thighs and rose to his feet. "Let's take a walk and enjoy the last of the sunlight. I think that's enough serious talk for one evening. You have to be exhausted. I'll take you on a roundabout route to your cabin."

From then on, the conversation mostly consisted of admiring comments about the grounds and the view. As the dogs trailed them at a respectful distance, they came upon three slinky black river otters swimming along the brook that ran through the property.

At the door to her cottage, Liam gave her a friendly pat on the arm, wished her sweet dreams, and left.

Nothing had been decided. Should she keep going to yoga? Absolutely not. She wanted to tell him that, so he wouldn't feel compelled to go himself.

She blew the whistle, and he turned around.

"Just testing?" he asked.

"No. I have something to say."

He waited, his stance studiously relaxed.

"I'm not going to yoga," she declared, "tomorrow or any other day. Not until we figure this out."

"Too bad," he said with an evil grin. "I was enjoying putting Kilo's nose out of joint."

The grin lingered as he turned again to set out for his own cottage.

* * *

ONLY A HEROIC FORCE OF will had allowed Liam to walk away from Teresa. The new haircut looked like a bad wig, but even so, no one seeing her for the first time would deny that his sister-in-law was drop-dead gorgeous. God help him, she just kept getting more vulnerable and appealing. The expensive blonde highlights she'd worn so well had served as a type of costume—an obvious indication of social status and a clear warning to guys like him to keep away. Who knew she'd have the courage to shuck it off? He both hoped and feared she'd done it for him.

*Just keep walking*, he told himself.

# CHAPTER 12

A THICK CLOUD COVER ROLLED in and stayed put during the third week of July, rare for this time of year. It was still in the 70s, with only occasional droplets of rain, so, pleasant enough.

Other than playing piano, Teresa didn't know what to do with herself. With the yoga class, at least she'd had a schedule and therefore some structure to her days. She wasn't convinced anyone in the class was out to get her. Despite what Liam had claimed to observe, she'd always felt welcome there. Perhaps Kilo's attention had wakened some woman's green-eyed monster, but enough to inspire them to hire a hit man to injure or even kill her? That seemed so farfetched.

Nevertheless, she stayed away. She really didn't want to inflict Liam on Kilo again, much as the other women might enjoy it. And Kilo was too much of a temptation in her current state of isolation. She didn't want to do anything foolish.

Carrie O'Connell believed dogs were for hunting and belonged in a barn and that the one purpose of cats was killing mice. Therefore the O'Connell children had been permitted no canine or feline pets. Teresa was allowed a goldfish, which didn't live long enough to finish off one package of food. The boys bonded with the horses at horse camp in Cle Elum, Washington.

Coogan and Harry were hard to resist; even Carrie might soften, given time. The canine odd couple trotted together as if connected by an invisible tether, accompanying her at all times whenever she was outside. At first they trailed behind like nineteenth-century servants, but as she invited them closer for rubdowns, they grew bolder. They were well behaved, not given to crotch diving or face licking. Liam bathed them regularly, and they didn't seem to mind. Teresa couldn't imagine any owner giving them up willingly. Perhaps their original owner had died.

She found a more reliable deck chair and put it on the terrace rather than directly overlooking the ocean. The dogs lay next to her while she read. She'd bought a pile of slim cozy mysteries recommended by a local bookseller and was going through them at the rate of about one a day. After lunch, she'd play the piano for an hour or so while the dogs took to standing on the porch chairs and peering through the window at her. In the afternoons she used the separate workout facility. She had a bad case of cabin fever.

Where did Liam go all day? The property was large, and he had clearly been working on the security system unbeknownst to her, so maybe he was around more than she realized. She didn't always hear him come and go. It was hard to miss the sound of the Harley's engine, but more and more he'd taken to riding his bicycle.

He was even gone in the evenings sometimes, and she didn't hear him come in. For all she knew, he stayed out all night. If so, he returned well before dawn, because most mornings he went to the house to prepare breakfast, and the dogs were fed regularly. When Teresa and Liam did spend time together, usually over meals, he'd ask her about her day and what she was reading, then listen as if she were Garrison Keillor—a good storyteller but not exactly eye candy. Sometimes they'd watch a movie or the PBS NewsHour together, sitting on opposite ends of the couch in the rec room. After watching the news, they'd often discuss politics, and they seemed to be more or less on the same page, though he knew way more about global politics than she did. He never volunteered anything about his own activities except to say that he met his friend Peter at Fort Worden and helped out with various tasks.

Was it her awful hair? Or worse, was he passionately involved with April and only had eyes for her? Teresa was getting used to the shorter cut and learning to style it better. Sometimes she thought it even suited her. She could hardly wait until her natural color reasserted itself. It had to be better than this dull shade of brown.

She decided to try for a color correction, even a few blonde streaks that might help it grow out more gracefully. That required another trip to Port Angeles. She didn't see any danger in that. There was a good chance both her scary brushes with death or injury had been simply accidents; however, if Liam were correct and the two incidents were just someone warning her off yoga class, the fact that it had worked should have appeased them. She couldn't think of a single other logical reason anyone would wish her harm.

Friday morning, after Liam left on his motorcycle for parts unknown, she headed to Port Angeles. Port Angeles was more a place working people lived rather than a retirement or tourist destination, though Sol Duc Hot Springs and Lake Crescent Lodge were within easy driving distance. It did have a flourishing community college and some nice old houses—some Victorians, but mostly Craftsman and cottage-style. You could see that it would like to attract more tourist dollars to replace the dwindling lumber, shipping, and fishing economy. At present you drove through Port Angeles on your way to other places—Hurricane Ridge, Port Townsend, Sequim, the Hoh Rain Forest and the Pacific Coast—or to catch the Black Ball Ferry to Victoria, B.C. Teresa thought it had major potential, and with such a fantastic location, would continue to come into its own, developing a character that would make it increasingly desirable to tourists and retirees. Especially as Port Townsend grew ever more crowded and expensive.

Her first stop was the hairdresser—a pretty, fortyish woman who apologized for the color and volunteered to give her some free blonde streaks. It was a definite improvement, and her mood felt lighter as she found a modest café and ordered clam chowder for lunch. The sky had cleared, so she wandered, starting with West Front Street. On one storefront, a dangling shingle read "Clallam County Music School." She tried the door, which was locked, then saw the FOR SALE sign. She stood at the window, though she couldn't see much, imagining what it might be like to live in this homey town with its easy access to nature and do something useful such as teach piano for a living. Maybe even occasionally perform. Provide scholarships for those who couldn't afford it. Her mother would have a conniption fit. She knew it was impossible, but she still wrote down the realtor's contact information.

On Marine Drive, she picked up a Dungeness crab fresh out of the pot, already cleaned and boiled, and had them pack it in ice for the drive home. Then she bought asparagus and fresh bread at the local market. Maybe her luck would hold and Liam would join *her* for dinner. If she left now, she could swing by the boutique on Water Street where they were holding a skirt for her and still be home by five. Liam typically didn't return to the compound before six. She touched her hair, wondering if he would even notice the small improvement.

With next to no traffic—what a blessed difference from congested Seattle—she arrived back at the compound at precisely five. She was about to drive down the final gravel road leading to the compound when she noticed a car parked along the roadside, a newish black Honda Civic. It couldn't belong to the owners of the other house along the gravel road because then it would be parked there. She let the engine idle as she debated her next move. Should she get out to investigate? Wouldn't that just put her in danger? Should she alert Liam? With no weapon, how would she defend herself? Driving slowly down the road, she peered in her rearview mirror and thought she detected movement in the bushes. If anyone ventured close enough to pass through the invisible fence, the dogs would come running. She checked the parking area to confirm that Liam's motorcycle wasn't there.

The low, husky "woofs" of Harry and the excited yipping of Coogan combined to welcome her home. *They don't seem to sense anything wrong,* she thought as she hugged them and rubbed their backs. She was just being paranoid. She walked the groceries to the house and put the asparagus in the steamer and the bread in the oven to warm. She'd turn on the burner under the asparagus when she saw the whites of Liam's eyes, or when she decided he was a no-show, whatever came first. The crab was ready to go, and all she had to do was melt the butter to dip it in. Her kind of meal prep.

She grabbed the plastic dog-ball launcher and two old tennis balls from the bucket and went out to join the dogs. After a half hour, she launched one of the balls beyond the invisible fence.

Both Harry and Coogan stopped before they reached the fence, sat on their haunches, and whined.

"Sorry, boys. Let's forget about that one."

Neither dog seemed inclined to forget. They barked as if that particular ball contained the secret to doggy bliss. It lay there in plain sight about a hundred feet away, tantalizing them.

"Okay, okay," she said, heading off to retrieve the ball. As she leaned over to pick it up, a man appeared from the bushes, camera poised, taking one picture after another. "Hey!" she said. "What are you doing?" He turned to run, and she took off after him. No danger, just nuisance. A photographer had discovered the location of Ali and Joe's home, unaware that they were out of town. She could hardly be the one he was seeking. Her picture rarely appeared anywhere, except in the society pages of *Seattle* magazine when she attended charity functions. Maybe he thought it was worth taking her photo just in case he could get something for it. Furious, she continued to chase the man as he zigged and zagged among the trees. Until she tripped, falling hard, and got the wind knocked out of her. As she lay there, catching her breath, the dogs appeared at her side and nosed her with worried whimpers. Teresa rose painfully to her feet. A scrape on her shoulder, mud on her jeans, and a dull throbbing on her cheek. More scratches and bruises.

"Oh, you sweet boys!" She hugged each one in turn. "You breached the fence. That must have hurt." She stooped down to switch off the transmitters on their collars, and they all headed back into the compound.

Liam stood next to the door, hands on hips, a scowl on his handsome face. She sighed, bowled over as ever by his fierce beauty. She hadn't heard his motorcycle come in.

"What happened to you?" His anger had to be concern in disguise.

"I'm okay." She didn't sound convincing.

"I'm glad," he said, his voice more level. "Why didn't you alert me?"

"Because"—she sighed—"I didn't think I was in danger. And it turned out I was right. It was just a photographer. Hoping to get a shot of something, maybe just the home. I chased him off."

"What did he look like?"

"Long, lanky, with an awkward, jerky gait. Baseball cap, rail thin. I didn't really see his face because of the camera, but from the way he moved, I'd say older, at least middle-aged. He must be the owner of the Honda Civic I saw earlier."

"Where?"

"Parked on Hastings."

He huffed, "That would have been useful information."

"Didn't you notice him when you came in?" she asked, miffed now, defiant.

"I've been here all afternoon, replacing some of the steps that lead down to the water. The Harley is being serviced." He pointed to the lanyard at her neck. "You should have used the whistle."

*Oh, yeah*. She'd forgotten about the lanyard. "Plus, you've been busy."

He was silent for a moment, his eyes roaming over her as if to assess the damage. "*You* are my priority. *Nothing* is more important than you … your safety." He walked right up to her and gently cupped her cheek. "You're going to have a shiner."

She struggled to control her feelings, suddenly overwhelmed by that deliciously clean, biscuity, leather-tinged, masculine smell of Liam. As he stepped away, she felt bereft and off balance, her foundation ever shifting. Then she touched her own cheek and winced. "I fell when I was chasing the photographer. I must have hit a rock. I also scraped my shoulder." She turned to examine the shallow wound then brushed the grit off the palms of her hands.

"Did someone trip you?"

"No. It was a root."

"I like what you've done with your hair." It was a statement of fact rather than flirtation. *Too bad.*

"Uh, thanks." She forced a smile, unreceptive as he seemed. "I'm going to go clean up. I bought a cooked crab in Port Angeles, and the rest can be prepared quickly. Have dinner with me?"

He hesitated for so long she was afraid he'd turn her down. "Thanks," he said finally and with a discouraging reluctance. "I'll see you back at the house."

# CHAPTER 13

<hr>

STEPPING OUT OF THE SHOWER, Teresa caught sight of her reflection and noted the swollen cheek, the beginnings of a black eye. She'd been foolish to chase the man. What would she have done if she'd caught him? Citizen's arrest? A harsh dressing-down? Bop him over the head with the dog-ball launcher? Any physical retaliation on her part and he could sue. She wrinkled her nose at the sorry image in the mirror. Now it was just red and puffy. By tomorrow, it would be all sorts of gruesome colors.

Knowing any concealment or attempts at beautification were pointless, she left her face alone and put on a tight pale-blue tank top, cream-colored cashmere sweater, and jeans.

At the house, she held a package of frozen peas to her cheek as she switched on the burner to steam the asparagus. Then she set the table, removed the foil-wrapped bread from the oven, and melted the butter. Maybe he didn't like crab. Maybe that was why he'd balked at her invitation. She put down the peas while she set the table.

"That's worse than I thought," he said, making her jump. "Sorry. Didn't mean to startle you."

"That's okay. I was just thinking how foolish it was to chase that guy. There was nothing I could have done. You can't win with those people."

"It's a good thing I wasn't there. I might have killed him."

"That would have been a bit extreme," she said, waiting for him to add "Just kidding." He didn't. He found a bottle of pinot gris in the refrigerator while she seasoned the asparagus and carried the food to the table. "Fortunately, I'm not a celebrity. I doubt he got any pictures of the house, because the dogs would have chased him off. I hope you like crab.”

“Who doesn’t like crab?” Finally, that grin that knocked her socks off. “Although it’s basically a giant sea insect.” He filled their wine glasses.

“Nice image. Thank you for that.”

“I’ve missed Pacific Northwest seafood.” He cracked open a leg and dipped it in melted butter. “Yum. That is wonderful.” He closed his eyes while he chewed.

“Did your Israeli family ever serve crab?”

“No, but they could have. They didn’t keep kosher.” He fixed her with his fathomless blue stare. “What were you doing in Port Angeles?”

She gave him a hard look.

“What?” Liam responded with a confused shrug.

“Why do I have to account for my whereabouts when you just disappear for days on end with no explanation? Maybe I value my privacy too.”

He looked taken aback. “It was an innocent question. I was just making conversation. I don’t think you realize how boring I am. There isn’t that much to it. I stay busy.”

“Sure,” she scoffed. A guy like him tooling around Port Townsend. She had this visual image of Liam strolling down Water Street, fending women off with karate chops like the guy in the ads for Hai Karate cologne.

He laughed. “You don’t believe me.” He popped another piece of crab in his mouth. “This is great, by the way. I used to pick up crab fresh from the pot at the Pike Place Market.”

“Me too. And you thought we had little in common.”

He didn’t respond to that.

“Okay, I tried to improve my Beatles mop-top.” She pointed to her hair. “Then I got this.” She touched her cheek and winced. “I’m just destined to look bad here.”

“Never,” he said without hesitation. “You’ll have to do better than that.”

Her eyes stung with tears. She might have been waiting all her life for such a nice compliment from a man.

“Do you like Port Angeles?” he asked.

“I do. It’s less pretentious than Port Townsend.” Seeing the look he gave her, she added, “Just because I was born to a mother like Carrie doesn’t mean I prefer high society. We weren’t always rich. Maybe I just want to live a normal life.”

He startled her again by breaking into one of his full-throated laughs. “That’s a good one. I don’t hold it against you, but you will never be normal.

Though I'm not sure what 'normal' means. That silver spoon in your mouth is welded there."

She didn't see the point in denying it. Liam's life had been a trial by fire compared to the island in the sun she'd enjoyed.

"I found a music school for sale."

He pricked up his ears. "Tell me more."

"I don't know. I'm looking for a purpose in life. Maybe I could run a music school. And teach piano. Award scholarships in some cases."

His silence spoke of skepticism. Finally, he said, "Would your mother ever sign off on that?"

She wanted to say, *Why would that matter?* But he had a point. "Not at first. It would take some convincing." As if. Her mother would never be on board with her becoming a piano teacher in a working-class town.

"Would you play for me sometime?"

"Now?"

"No time like the present."

They moved to the living room, where he sat on the brocade couch, squirming a bit as if from discomfort, his shock of straight black hair, work clothes, and tall, muscular build out of place in the fussy parlor. *Fussy.* For the first time, she wondered why she'd been so sure Ali and Joe would like a cream and white art deco drawing room out of a Colette novella. That was her fantasy, not theirs. Liam belonged in *The Last of the Mohicans*, not *The Last of Chéri.*

She threw off these uncomfortable reflections and moved to the piano seat. "What would you like to hear? I don't have a huge repertoire, it's true, but you can tell me what you prefer. It has to be classical, though. Much as I enjoy jazz, I can't play it myself."

"Sure. Debussy and Ravel, I guess."

She sat down at the piano and played Debussy's "*La fille aux cheveux de lin*"—The Girl with the Flaxen Hair.

"That was heavenly," he said, eyes closed. "I'm having a religious experience."

She played "*La cathédrale engloutie.*" The Sunken Cathedral.

"Are you trying to seduce me?"

She knew he meant it lightly, but she couldn't help hoping for more. She sat down next to him on the couch, keeping a few feet between them.

When he opened his eyes, they burned into her. "What do you say we go into town tomorrow? I'll take you to dinner."

"That would be nice, as long as you're not worried about being accused of abusing me." She pointed to her puffy cheek.

"You have a point." He leaned forward to examine it more closely. "But I'm no coward. Have you been to Kelpies? If you're okay with a pub."

"Sure," she said, giddy at the prospect.

"Tomorrow is Saturday, and that place is popular, so let's go on the early side. Can we meet there? I promised Peter I'd help him out in the afternoon."

He stood, and taking his cue, she did too.

Then he did something totally unexpected. He reached out to grasp her arms, letting his eyes roam freely over her face and upper body. His expression was neutral. She tried to keep her own face expressionless too, but she probably wasn't succeeding. She recalled the staring contests of childhood. Who would blink first? He did. Or the sensual equivalent. His full lips descended on hers, slowly, as if he were fighting the impulse. Far from resisting, she met him halfway. She had known that feeling before, with Kilo, a very long time ago. The forbidden aspect made it crazy passionate. Burning, reeling, drowning, a hunger neither had acknowledged until now. Though they might have suspected. She had, certainly. His full lips molded blissfully against hers and her entire body followed suit. She couldn't get him close enough. When she began to shrug out of her sweater, he tore himself away.

"That was … unwise." He was breathing hard. "We can't …. We just can't."

*Why not?* she wanted to cry out. *We're adults! What's stopping us?* But she didn't.

"One of us should go back to Seattle," he went on in a quieter voice, regaining control. "And if it's me, who will protect you here?"

"No!" she practically moaned. He was holding her at arm's length again, gripping her more forcefully as she strained to lean into him, seeking more contact with his warm, silky skin.

"Get a grip." He gave her a gentle shake. "I want this too—in the moment. But you and I are not meant to be. If we give in to … whatever this is, there will be misery all around. Your mother will probably disown you."

She broke free and backed away, staggering a little until she found a chair. Her desperation quickly morphed into humiliation. She'd made an utter fool of herself.

"Okay," she said, striving for cool and failing. "I'll go. But the dogs will miss me."

"They won't be the only ones," he ground out.

Darn him, he was being noble. He wanted her too. No point in arguing. She could see that he was adamant. She wasn't convinced it was over, but in any battle, you had to know when to retreat and live to fight another day. All's fair in love and war. With someone like Liam, it seemed that the two were synonymous. Why couldn't she fall for someone easier? Kilo would have been easy. Easy-going, anyway. Not easy to hold on to, if indeed she even wanted that. She also had a sneaking suspicion that she'd quickly tire of his company, that he was too much of a lightweight. There was so much more to Liam than he let on. Not for the first time, she wondered if a more mature version of herself would have accepted that Paul was her destiny. Maybe even her soul mate. She didn't know what that said about the state of her soul. Nothing good.

Rising to her feet was agonizing, almost as if she were extracting herself from quicksand. "I'm going to bed. I'm done." *Not that I expect to sleep*, she added silently.

"Can I walk you to your cabin?"

She gave him a disgusted look. "Definitely not. By now the evil photographer knows his quarry is out of town. I should be safe." She opened the front door to find the dogs wagging their tails so quickly they were just a blur of motion. "Besides, I have canine escorts." She leaned down to greet them. "I'll miss you love bugs."

"When will you leave?"

He just couldn't wait for her to go, could he? "Sometime tomorrow. I have to pack, and I'm too exhausted to do it tonight." She could see that he needed her to be more specific. Who had appointed him her Sir Galahad? "After lunch, okay? Does that meet with your approval?"

"Don't be mad. I need to know that you're safe."

She stopped caressing the dogs and faced him squarely, arms flailing. "I'm not in danger anymore, okay? I'm far from certain I ever was." He remained grimly silent. The danger he was thinking of was himself. "I'll have Joe call you when I arrive safely." She sure as heck didn't want to call him once she was back in Seattle. Out of sight, out of mind. *You wish.* She'd gotten over Kilo, hadn't she? She'd been just as gaga for him, maybe more so.

"Good," Liam said. "Thanks again for the crab."

"Yeah, sure," she practically spit out.

As they all walked toward the cabin, the dogs seemed to sense her neediness and stayed so close that they almost tripped her. At the cabin door, she turned around briefly to find Liam standing vigil. He waved. She didn't wave back.

* * *

LIAM'S BODY WAS IN FULL rebellion. If he didn't get a grip, his legs and cock would lead the way to Teresa's bed. Still, the barrier he'd forged for himself mentally to keep her out of reach held. What had he been thinking, asking her to play for him? He hadn't been thinking, not with the right head. The problem was, she just kept surprising him. Just as he'd convinced himself she was shallow and frivolous, she'd given him a glimpse through music into the depths of her being, shown him her capacity for intense feelings. They were both lost souls, peering into a hazy future in hopes of making the right decisions this time—unlike all those other times.

He closed his eyes and sighed. Another hurdle cleared, maybe the final one, if only she'd go home … and stay there. If she remained here one more day, he was a goner. Once she was safely back in Seattle, he'd find peace. Go on long hikes, exhaust himself with physical labor.

God almighty, the heady moment they'd come together—the subtle combo of vanilla and Teresa that engulfed his senses as he pressed his lips against her hot, smooth skin, the hunger that erupted in him at the feel of her frantic lips, the hardness of her nipples and softness of her full breasts …. He groaned aloud, would have bayed at the moon if it weren't for the dogs or the stillness that would have carried his cries of need to her bedside.

He wanted to hit the whiskey—hard—but that wouldn't blot out the evening, just lower his defenses even more. No. Somehow he'd make it through this night, and tomorrow she'd be gone.

* * *

THE NEXT DAY DID NOT go smoothly. The swelling around Teresa's eye and cheek was worse, and the discoloration had spread. She still applied mascara, a little powder, and some lip gloss, though the expression *putting lipstick on a pig* came to mind.

The more she thought about it, the more convinced she was that she and Liam could work. They liked many of the same movies and food. They both loved the dogs, and he appreciated classical music. She'd been meaning to take up hiking, one of his passions. She just had to get the right boots. As far as other common ground, they'd find it. Liam was a renaissance man. He could do anything. Repair anything. Create anything. Protect anyone and anything.

She loved him. He desired her, but he could learn to love her.

*Stop it*, she told herself. *You aren't going to force him, and his mind is made up. Go home. Enough with the humiliation.*

She heard his motorcycle take off around nine a.m. She dawdled, first working out on the treadmill while listening to her book tape then playing the piano too long. Afterward, she searched in vain for her wallet and cell phone. She felt like she was losing her mind. Had she left them in town? The day before, she'd bought that skirt at the boutique on Water Street; that was the only possibility. She called on the land line and was vastly relieved to discover they were both there. Otherwise packed, she headed out, intending to continue on to Seattle. It broke her heart to leave the dogs, who whimpered and nudged her like they knew something was up. But then, her heart was already in pieces over Liam. It was ten to six by the time she arrived at the boutique, which was just about to close. She considered stopping for dinner but didn't want to drive into the city in the dark. She had no appetite in any case. Maybe she'd spend the night in Kingston rather than catching a late ferry. She was in no hurry to return to Seattle.

The clouds were dark gray, and she expected it to pour at any moment, but she still dragged her heels. As she walked back to her car, she saw a sleek black river otter slink across Water Street and decided to follow its progress. Had it really been swimming in the fountain? That was the only water on the other side of Water Street. If only she could have seen that ….

She walked out onto the dock as it dove into the bay, her eyes brimming with tears. She sat on the dock's edge, willing the tears to stop while she watched the otter swim parallel to the shore toward the marina. It dove and vanished underwater for several minutes at a time, resurfacing once, twice, before disappearing from view.

Why was she letting Liam chase her out of Port Townsend? If she stayed, would he change his mind? Feeling a piece of gravel in her tennis shoe, she set her purse aside so she could empty the shoe. *Patience.* Once she was gone, Liam would realize he couldn't live without her. She found a tissue in her pocket and blew her nose. *There*, she told herself, *dry your tears and get on with it.*

At the first drops of rain, she pulled up the hood on her jacket. Realizing the rain was soaking her jeans, she managed to pull herself together enough to rise to her feet. Heaving a pitiful sigh, she gazed out at the harbor, thinking to catch one last glimpse of the otter.

The dock began to vibrate, and she heard the heavy *thunk* of footfalls. Startled, she looked over her shoulder. A man, head covered by a black hoodie and lower face concealed outlaw-style with a bandana, was running toward her in a terrifying sprint. Skidding to a stop, he delivered a powerful shove to her shoulders.

She flailed then fell—what was it, a twelve-foot drop? It felt like thirty. She landed in a back flop. The shock of ice-cold ocean sucked all the air from her body. As she thrashed about, she struggled to keep her head above water while her increasingly sodden clothing sucked her downward.

Teresa was a strong swimmer, but not under these conditions. The saltwater was not only freezing but nasty. She'd swallowed too much, and some of it had gone down her windpipe, leaving her coughing and retching. She tried to put her panic aside, concentrate on finding a ladder along the dock. As she bobbed to the surface, she couldn't see one. She pulled at her jeans, but sank as she worked at the zipper, and they clung as if glued on.

She wasn't far from shore. Where was the whistle? The lanyard was gone—must have dislodged from her neck in her struggle to stay afloat. There was no point in blowing a whistle now, even if she could figure out how to do that while drowning. Liam hadn't reckoned on her needing him anywhere but on dry land. Besides, he wouldn't be listening for that whistle here.

*Someone* must have seen the man push her. It was Saturday evening, for Pete's sake. That part of the dock was out of view of the street. You could see it from Kelpies' balcony, but the weather wasn't conducive to dining outside. Her stalker had probably seen her powder-blue Miata and seized the opportunity to … what … scare her again or kill her this time?

She heard shouting, and someone jumped in beside her, hooked a steely arm around her chest, and began towing her to shore.

# CHAPTER 14

———•———

TERESA WAS SITTING WITH ALI in the shaded inner courtyard of Carrie's mansion, watching a robin splash around in the fountain until a crow chased it away. The temperature was seventy-five degrees, about average for August, with low humidity and a pleasant breeze. It might as well have been ninety, judging by the way Teresa felt and Ali looked—her normally glowing skin sallow, her cheekbones more prominent than usual. In Ali's case, Teresa totally got it. The twins were keeping her up most nights, despite help from Joe and the nanny. She'd been breastfeeding and pumping, and as she confessed to Teresa, that activity alone felt like a full-time job.

The twins were almost a month old. They didn't cry much, but they were energetic—too energetic. It seemed they hardly slept. At this stage they favored Ali, with their black hair and startlingly blue eyes. It was the nanny's day off, and they were currently sleeping peacefully in their high-end pram designed for twins.

"Enjoy this rare moment of calm," Ali said, slumping into the lawn chair. "I'm starting to think they are changelings. I need eight hours of sleep. Right now, I'm lucky to get four."

Teresa was leaning forward, watching their sweet, pudgy faces, itching to pick them up for a cuddle. No matter that she didn't have to endure their nighttime gurgling and hunger; she wasn't sleeping well either.

In the three weeks since she'd left Port Townsend, she hadn't had a chance to be alone with Ali until now. She'd been staying at her own townhome in Madison Park, and whenever she came over to the Capital Hill house, Joe, the nanny Millie, or Carrie always seemed to be underfoot.

"How is the nanny working out?" Teresa asked. It was Millie's day off.

Ali deliberated before answering. "I guess she's okay. Kind of bossy."

Teresa nodded. "At least she won't be seducing Joe." The statement caused a fit of the giggles. "Seductress" was not a word you'd ever use to describe the poker-faced, jowly, steel-haired nanny.

"I wouldn't be too sad if Mary Poppins came along and got rid of her with a stiff wind," Ali said, wiping her eyes. She looked up. "Too mean? I don't want to seem ungrateful. Carrie's paying her salary."

"She probably isn't too different from Mary Poppins in the original book," Teresa said. "The Disney version is highly romanticized."

"The twins seem to like her well enough, and she's good with them, at least as far as I can tell. She and Joe get along like a house on fire."

"But *you* don't like her."

"She doesn't like *me* much," Ali corrected. "I think she's used to working for well-appointed families, and I don't pass muster."

Teresa looked at her askance. "Are you sure? I don't see that. She just prefers men to women. Some women are like that. You're a new mother, so she's worried you'll mess up."

Ali pretended to snarl at her, "Sure, take *her* side." She was too nice to carry it off.

Teresa smiled. "Definitely not. I'm on your side, all the way. Team Ali, yay!" She pumped her fist in the air.

"Okay, no need for sarcasm. But really, Teresa, thank God you're here. I can't tell you how much it means to me. I just wish you seemed a little happier. Are you missing Port Townsend or … my brother?"

Teresa hesitated before answering. "Maybe I'm just missing the vacation from myself."

"I get that. How did Carrie react to your hair?"

Teresa self-consciously brushed her bangs from her forehead. "The worst haircut since Samson, according to her."

"Her words?"

"No, but close. I might as well have dipped my hair in lye."

Ali threw her head back and laughed, reminding Teresa of Liam. Wiping her eyes, she said, "I wish I could have been there. Your hair is about the same length as mine now. Except that you have that adorable gamine look. I'm just a page boy with Elephantitis."

"You mean Elephantiasis," Teresa said. "Remember, my brother is a doctor with Doctors for Humankind in Africa. I know stuff like that." Ali stared her down. "And you must be aware that you are still heartbreakingly beautiful. You're already dropping that weight."

"If you say so." Ali picked at her tent-like dress. "Dumbo was smaller and cuter than the others, but he was still an elephant. I can't wait to get rid of this pregnant-lady wardrobe. And I'm tired of my breasts hurting all the time." She blew out a sigh. "Enough complaining, and enough about me. Why did you come home, really? No more nonsense about wanting to help me, although you are helpful. Does it concern that final plunge into the bay? Someone *pushed* you, is that right? Why would anyone *do* that?"

"Quick! Alert that TV show, *Unsolved Mysteries*. We'll probably never know. I'm not sold on Liam's theory."

"Jealousy," Ali said, "over that yoga teacher. Joe told me."

Teresa sighed. "Whatever the reason, someone didn't want me in Port Townsend. I got the message. Guess I didn't get it fast enough."

Ali reached over to pat her leg. "This has to be resolved soon because I'm not going back there without you. Especially now that the paparazzi know about our place."

"Liam set up a security system and acquired two amazing guard dogs. You'll be fine."

Ali scowled. "As long as we don't leave the compound."

One of the babies started fussing, and Teresa rushed to pick her up. "I think it's Caryn. She seems to be the one with the most to say."

Ali chuckled. "Caryn has a mole next to her ear."

Teresa checked. "Right. Then this is Josephine."

"She is also quite vocal." Ali reached for the baby, who immediately found her breast and latched on. "So, Liam …."

"He's doing well," Teresa answered too quickly, in a cartoonishly chipper voice.

"There's chemistry, right? You can't fool me."

Teresa threw up her hands in exasperation. "Who wouldn't have chemistry with Liam? Did you hear about his visit to my yoga class? His aura works like that drug … ecstasy. He's a megahit of endorphins in human form. Every straight woman in the class lost fifty points of IQ in his presence."

Ali grinned. "That's been true for as long as I can recall. Liam went through puberty freakishly early. Since then, whenever he was around, no other guy had a chance. All the girls gravitated toward him. If he noticed, he didn't seem to care. His power over the opposite sex meant nothing to him— it was more of a nuisance. He preferred the company of his buddies, and he charmed them too. I'm not sure what dictated his choice of girlfriends. They were all pretty but uncomplicated. You didn't want to be *chosen*, believe me. You weren't treated very well. And nothing lasted. Everyone was disposable."

Teresa picked up a squirming Josephine and nuzzled her neck. "I swear, he's the most complicated man I've ever met."

Ali kissed Caryn's fuzzy head. "Poor Liam. Our crazy foster-child upbringing was harder on him than it was on me." Josephine began to cry. "Here, let's exchange babies. Josie sounds hungry." After the girls were settled in, she said, "Tell me about these so-called 'accidents.' Start with the third one, which was clearly nothing of the kind."

Teresa rocked Caryn in her arms as she spoke. "I would have been gone already if I hadn't left my wallet and phone at a boutique. Then I saw a river otter crossing Water Street and heading toward the bay, and I followed it until I stood at the edge of a dock. The opportunity was too good to resist, I guess. For my attacker, I mean." She paused. "If only he'd realized I was already on my way out of town."

"Could you ID him, do you think?"

Teresa shook her head. "It was raining, and my hood was blocking my peripheral vision. From the glimpse I got before he pushed me, not much registered. He was wearing a hoodie, a kerchief like some old-time bandit, so I didn't see his face at all. He was medium height with a paunch. Might have been the same guy who almost mowed me down while I was biking. I never saw the person who sabotaged the lawn chair—if indeed that's what happened. Liam couldn't be sure."

"Phew." Ali blew out a puff of air. "You had some close calls."

"Joe and I agreed not to tell Mom. Whoever's responsible, I don't think he meant to kill me or even hurt me, although …." She'd almost added, *although any one of those attempts could have been fatal.* Bottom line, she was safe now.

"After you fell into the bay, Liam pulled you out. How did he get there in time?"

"Somehow he knew I was in trouble and jumped in. He must have been close by."

Ali didn't comment. She seemed to be biting her tongue.

"What?"

"Nothing. Go on."

"Liam claims he saw my Miata pass by and came to investigate why I was still in town. Hell of a coincidence." Teresa lapsed into silence.

"So," Ali prompted, "after he fished you out, what then?"

"A crowd had gathered. Naturally they wanted to know what was up. No one had seen the man push me in, so I told them it was a silly accident, that I'd been tracking the progress of a river otter and leaned over too far. By then my teeth were chattering, and Liam just lifted me into his arms like I was a sack of feathers and carried me to my car. He drove me home and drew me a hot bath."

"Liam took you back on his motorcycle?"

"I would have frozen to death or fallen off. No, in my car."

Ali still looked puzzled. "How were you able to drive your car?"

"Huh?"

"Your purse …?"

"Oh," Teresa said. "Liam drove. But I still had my purse. That's the only bright spot in this story. It was sitting next to me on the dock and miraculously didn't follow me in. A kind stranger retrieved it while Liam hovered over me."

Teresa could see that Ali was riveted, but she wasn't about to admit to what had come next. It was Liam's secret as well as hers. "Nothing happened," she lied. "From then on, I was on my own. Liam brought me chicken soup with matzo balls and a snifter of brandy, but he didn't stick around. Well, long enough to ask for a ride into town the next morning to pick up his Harley. I said I'd be happy to do that."

Ali's face fell. "The next morning?"

"I made coffee in my room and ate a stale scone. Then I found him down at the house, took him into town, and dropped him off next to his motorcycle."

Though Teresa suspected Ali wasn't buying her story, her sister-in-law didn't challenge her. "Huh. Where was it parked?"

"On the street near the dock where I was pushed into the bay. Liam must have been tracking me somehow. He never explained. At the compound, he trusted the dogs to watch me. They're great dogs. Super sweet."

"Sounds like it."

"Unless you're a bad guy. Or so Liam claims. All bark and no bite so far. At least with the paparazzo. Fortunately. You don't want to actually hurt those guys. They'd sue you for all you're worth and have the dogs put down."

The twins were lying on their backs again, looking up at the two women with unfocused azure eyes.

Ali smoothed a finger over Josie's plump cheek. "The smiling isn't real yet. It's like a reflex at this age."

Teresa frowned. "Says who?"

"Carrie."

"She's such a buzz kill."

They both laughed.

"You girls seem to be enjoying yourselves."

No child saying "Boo!" earned a more gratifying response. They both nearly bounced out of their seats, and the babies burst into tears.

"Oh, I'm so sorry." Carrie appeared genuinely contrite. "I know it's hard getting them to calm down."

"Don't worry, er, *Mother*," Ali said. "Knowing them, it was just another calm before the storm." Teresa knew her mom was encouraging Ali to call her 'Mother,' but the word seemed to stick in her craw.

Carrie turned to Teresa. "Darling, it was quite a feat, but I got you an appointment with my hairdresser."

Teresa snorted. "I'm not going. What do you hope to accomplish?"

Carrie did not rise to the bait. In a low, soothing, voice, she said, "How do you expect it to grow out gracefully without a little help? She can do something about the … *color*."

"I'm going back to my natural color," Teresa insisted.

Carrie bristled. "Are you sure? If it's like mine, it's mousy brown."

"My hair has more red in it. If it looks really bad, I'll reconsider."

"And in the meantime?"

Teresa shrugged. "Mom, it doesn't look as bad as all that. You'll get used to it." Teresa hated the whine that crept into her voice every time she got into this kind of discussion with her mother.

Realizing that Teresa had dug in her heels, her mother moved on. "Did you know that Paul is back in town? I've asked him to dinner."

"*Mom—*"

"You can be kind to him. He's my friend, too."

"What's for dinner?" Ali asked.

"Filet mignon, ravioli, and Caesar salad."

"Do you have enough steaks for everyone?" Ali asked. "I invited Duncan, Laurie, and her daughter Maddie to come too."

Teresa caught the flicker of annoyance in her mother's eyes. "We'll make do. Rostand can always pick up a few more. They all eat meat?"

Ali didn't answer right away. "I don't know Laurie's daughter very well. I don't think she has any food restrictions. If so, she'll make do. Is the ravioli vegetarian?"

"Spinach."

"Then she'll be fine. Dad would have warned me if she were a vegan or even just avoided red meat. He knows what to expect of us by now."

Carrie rose to her feet. "Ali, do you mind if I borrow Teresa? I have something to show her."

Teresa was standing over the pram, cooing at the babies, who had stopped crying.

Ali put on a brave smile. "I think things are under control. At least for the moment."

Teresa could see her sister-in-law's discomfort. Not surprisingly, Ali hadn't warmed to Carrie. She wished Joe didn't leave her alone so much. Obviously she was itching to get back to their own place in Port Townsend. Teresa knew the feeling. She could flee to her Madison Park townhome, but for Ali, there was no escape from her domineering mother-in-law or Millie, the nanny from hell. First chance she got, Teresa was going to give Joe a piece of her mind for failing to see how disrespectfully the woman treated his wife.

ONCE THEY WERE IN THE kitchen and out of earshot, her mother poured them both glasses of water. "Unless you'd like iced tea? I'd advise against adding sugar. I can see you gained a few pounds in Port Townsend."

No point in arguing. She *had* gained a few pounds. Not that anyone but her mother would notice. "Water's fine." She sat down at the counter.

"How is Liam?"

"Why do you ask?"

"He survived quite an ordeal. I'm wondering about the psychological damage."

Teresa shrugged. Realizing she was showing too much cleavage, she fastened the top button of her silk shirt. She was wearing a skirt because her jeans all felt too tight. "He seemed normal to me. Better than normal. Mature. Responsible."

Her mother gritted her teeth. "If you say so."

Teresa suppressed a sigh. "What did you want to discuss, Mom?"

Carrie got right to the point. "I asked the investigator in Israel to dig a bit deeper."

Teresa managed to stifle the protest that sprang to her lips.

"I was concerned about you two being alone together," Carrie went on. *Obviously,* Teresa thought. Why investigate him otherwise? She wanted to growl like a dog.

"I believe he is a dangerous young man, in many ways."

*Ugh, here it comes.* Teresa folded her arms and worked hard to keep the irritation out of her voice as she asked, "How so?"

"I'm worried that you will waste your best years on a mercenary," she blurted out.

Teresa's jaw dropped. Of all the things she expected to hear, that wasn't one. "A mercenary?" she repeated.

"He attended a program that is mainly meant for Israelis who emigrated to the U.S. when they were young. You live on a kibbutz for a while, study intensive Hebrew, then attend a three-month training camp that prepares you for the army."

Teresa broke in, "But he's not Israeli."

"He was adopted by an extremely wealthy and well-connected Israeli woman who believed he was her son. At least that was the assumption. Her real son must have died in that explosion, and when she identified Liam as him, they believed her. She isn't the type of woman you argue with, I gather."

*You two would probably get along great*, Teresa thought.

"He went through that training but never served in the army," Carrie went on. "After completing the program, he did end up on some secret mission and was gone for a time. No one can explain his absence, and it is said that he was a hired assassin. By all accounts, his skills are extraordinary."

Teresa was seething. "You believe something like that with *nothing* to back it up? Shouldn't Liam have a chance to respond to such serious charges?"

Now her mother had her dander up, though you'd have to know her well to detect it. She was sitting ramrod straight, making a supreme effort to keep her tone reasonable. "I'm not at all sure he'd come clean with us. He is a man of few words, or so I've observed. He's clearly not going to volunteer to regale us with anecdotes about killing Palestinians."

"Oh, please!" Teresa stood and stamped her foot. *That woman can still push my buttons*, she thought. "Buttons she installed," a friend once said. She turned on her heel to go. "I've heard enough."

"Darling," Carrie pleaded, "you have your whole life ahead of you. Don't make a decision that will jeopardize your future happiness."

She turned to scrutinize her mother. "What on earth makes you think I'm in love with Liam? What possible reason do you have to believe that? We lived on the same property, but I rarely saw him. It's true that he was doing his best to keep me safe—"

"What? Why would he need to keep you safe?"

Carrie appeared genuinely mystified. Despite their agreement, was it possible Joe had told her nothing about the "accidents"? She was usually ridiculously well informed. Teresa would have expected her to hire someone to keep tabs on them all in Port Townsend. *Good for her*, Teresa thought. *For once, she left us to our own devices. Probably because she trusts Joe.*

"Why do you think I'm in danger of falling for Liam?"

"I just assumed …. He's a hard man to resist. When he came to dinner that time … I saw some sparks."

Teresa marveled at the sight of her mother sputtering and off balance. She guessed she'd felt the attraction too—Carrie, who she assumed was immune to men. She hadn't dated anyone since Da had died, at least not to Teresa's knowledge.

"Why would he need to keep you safe?" Carrie repeated. She wasn't going to let it go.

"It's nothing …. A man almost drove me off the road while I was biking, and both he and Joe worried that it wasn't just an accident. Really, there's no reason to believe it wasn't. Nothing else like that has happened since," she lied. "An excess of caution."

Strangely, her mother appeared mollified. Teresa breathed a sigh of relief. In the courtyard, the babies were howling. "Mom, I appreciate the info, but I'm going to get back to Ali and the girls."

Her mother stood too. "Remember, Paul will be at dinner tonight. I hope you will be … kind to him."

Teresa nodded. She didn't see the point of arguing anymore. Somewhere along the line, her mother had figured out that Teresa had broken the engagement. The only reason she hadn't brought it up was because she hoped her daughter would reconsider.

"What was that about?" Ali said after they'd managed to calm the babies.

"What do you mean?"

Ali smiled. "I'm pretty sure you stamped your foot."

"Oh, okay, yeah. Mom's worried that I'm falling for Liam."

"We all are, I think."

"It was more than that. Her 'sources' tell her that Liam was trained for the army while he was in Israel and then recruited for some secret mission, possibly as an assassin."

Ali burst out laughing. "Oh, come *on.*"

"Have you ever asked him for details about his time in Israel?" Teresa asked.

"Not really. He's never divulged more than that initial information about his recovery. Have you?"

"No."

They both lapsed into thoughtful silence.

"I guess I'm going to have to be the one," Ali said.

"Do you think he'll tell you the truth?"

"Oh, yeah. I'm afraid he will. If asked pointblank, he's a truth-teller." Ali grimaced. "Obviously I'm not going to do it on the phone. He and I haven't had any in-depth conversations, one-on-one, since our reunion here. You don't just say, 'Listen, I know almost nothing about who you are now, but if you were an assassin, you'd tell me, right?' You kind of have to work up to it." She stood and stretched, breaking into a giant yawn. "Would you mind watching the twins while I nap?"

"Of course not. Have a nice rest."

Left alone with her memories, Teresa couldn't help but travel back to the night she had almost drowned … in Liam's arms.

# CHAPTER 15

———•———

THE FIRST BATH LIAM DREW for Teresa was tepid. Teresa knew hot water would have felt like fire on her numb skin. While she lay in the tub, still clothed except for her jeans, teeth chattering and shivering all over, he left to change out of his own wet clothing. He was back in the blink of an eye. She guessed that she was still in shock. Strange that the bay's freezing water hadn't chilled *him* to the bone. Talk about a man of steel ….

That bath … had to be the most erotic experience ever, despite the trauma of the previous hour. They hadn't spoken at all. Gradually Liam drained the first tubful, adding hot water to raise the temperature. As the warmth began to penetrate, her shivering subsided. Opening her eyes, she found him scorching her with his laser-like gaze. When their eyes met, he looked away. She reached up to touch his face, tracing the lines of worry on his forehead and the faint scars on his cheek. He was inching back, preparing to retreat, when she grabbed his T-shirt and pulled him toward her instead. In an instant, his arms snaked around her, bringing her mouth to his. The soulful, delicious kisses left her dizzy with desire.

His lips and tongue moved on to graze her neck. She strained against him, wanting them to keep moving downward …. But then they stopped.

He pulled away abruptly, features hardening and eyes glittering with renewed determination.

*Oh no, you don't,* she thought. Rising out of the water, she frantically pulled the T-shirt over her head and unhooked her bra. He groaned, shaking his head, still wordless. She stepped out of the tub, wearing only her wet and now transparent pink bikini panties, and confronted this daunting, fully clothed action figure in the flesh. Eyes still locked on his, she pushed down her panties and stepped out of them. He drew in a harsh breath, making no move to take control. *Damn him, he's waiting to see how this plays out*, she thought. *But he's not stopping you.*

She unbuttoned his flannel shirt, confronting yet another barrier, his tight black T-shirt. She pulled that off as well, noting the scars that scored the side of his body. Nothing could dim the splendor of that sculpted chest. He didn't resist and he didn't smile, though the glint in his eye said the situation amused him. Was that good or bad? Would this be nothing but an entertaining episode for him? That was a risk she had to take. She wouldn't stop now.

She pressed her breasts to his bare chest, rubbing against him, aching for him to touch her, her damp skin taking on the rich, clean scent of him. His arms remained at his sides, but he was breathing harder now. She opened the first button of his jeans, looked up into his face. No expression, though his lips were parted and his breathing was labored. The next button, then the next. She pulled down his jeans to find him throbbing and huge. She grasped his erection with her small hand, again daring him to take over, but he didn't. So she took him in her mouth.

This was unfamiliar territory. Face it, she had no idea what she was doing. He didn't seem to mind. He relaxed against her as she tasted and licked and sucked, his hands finding her hair, caressing it ever so lightly. She was bowled over by the whole experience. The delicious taste of him, though it made sense. Sweet and salty, like fresh sea air. The feeling of power it gave her as he struggled not to come. She was definitely enjoying herself.

A little too much? Or was she doing it wrong? Whatever the reason, all too soon he pulled her to her feet. Kicking off his jeans, he lifted her so that she straddled his waist and carried her over to the bed. All the while, they consumed each other with kisses. After he let her fall back onto the bed, he groaned again as if in surrender. Then he moved on top of her, pinning her down.

"This is really what you want?" he said in a firm voice. "Tell me now."

*Tell me you love me*, she wanted to say. *Tell me it will mean something to you, that I am everything to you, that I'm not just another warm, willing body.* What she said was, "Yes."

She wasn't sure what she expected to happen next—not that he would leave the bed. He came back from the bathroom carrying his jeans. *What?* Would he get dressed and leave? Perhaps all he wanted was the ego gratification of hearing her admit to wanting him.

He opened up his wallet. *Ah, a condom.* A man like Liam would naturally have one handy at all times. Keeping his smoldering eyes on hers, he whipped it out of the foil wrapping and slid it on expertly, so fast it was like a magic trick.

Then he was inside her, filling her, and she heard her own involuntary response, weird little breathy cries of pleasure. He kept up his relentless rhythm as his hands roamed sensually over her breasts, her stomach, and her bottom, bringing her nipples to throbbing life. Whenever his exquisite fingers left one part of her body, she gave a little moan of protest. It wasn't long before they both cried out in mindless ecstasy. Finally, they lay together, gasping for breath, limbs tangled and damp.

He groaned again, an expression of frustration this time, and rolled onto his back. "That was so … *wrong*. What are we going to do now?"

He might as well have stabbed her in the heart. "Why is it wrong?" she cried. "We both wanted it, didn't we? I love … loved it." God, she'd almost said, *I love you*. She didn't know much about men, but she did know a premature declaration of love was bound to scare off a guy like this one.

"Did you? I'm glad." She heard childlike vulnerability but also a hardness. Liam was so … *complicated*. So stubborn. She suspected that he loved her too, but he hadn't acknowledged it to himself, and nothing would be decided in this moment. Well, she was in it for the long haul. With a supreme effort, she closed down too. She wouldn't cry, nor would she plead with him. Two could play at that game. She sat up on the bed, took a few calming breaths, then went over to the closet and put on her pink silk robe.

Out of the corner of her eye, she could see him watching her. *Good. Let him wonder.*

"You can go now." Her voice sounded so strange and formal in her own ears, as if she were dismissing a full classroom of children at the end of the school day.

"Teresa"—the word was a caress—"this doesn't change anything. You still have to go home."

"I know that," she snapped.

"We are too different. It can't work. We must never do this again."

"Who are you trying to convince, yourself? Because you don't see me begging for more, do you?"

"Teresa …." He saw through her, understood that she was hurt. "You are … adorable. But I'm your brother-in-law. I'm supposed to protect you, not … ravish you. Joe and Ali would freak. I've betrayed their trust, don't you see? All I can do now is swear it will never happen again."

She remained standing next to the closet, her back turned so Liam couldn't read her expression. She could argue, tell him Joe and Ali had basically given them their blessing, but she was afraid he was using her brother and Ali's theoretical objections as a pretext—that he had other reasons for resisting she didn't want to hear. "I think you'd better go back to your cabin," she said finally, only now composed enough to look him in the eye. She hoped she looked as calm as she sounded.

He looked surprised, as if he'd been braced for an argument. "We're still friends?"

"Sure. *Friends*."

What was he waiting for? Did he want her to shake on it? After a long moment, he stood up to put on his jeans then went to retrieve the rest of his clothes from the bathroom. When he emerged again, he was fully dressed. "My Harley is parked on Water Street. Can I get a ride into town tomorrow when you leave?"

"Of course."

*He that fights and runs away may turn and fight another day*. Who had said that? Some Roman philosopher. Love and war. She had not surrendered. But retreat was in order.

The rest had played out as she'd described it to Ali. Liam knocked on her cabin door an hour later with a tray of chicken soup, crackers, and brandy but fled before she could confront him. The next morning, she ate breakfast by herself in her cabin. Found Liam at the house when she was ready to leave. During the short ride into town, they hardly spoke. When she hesitated next to his bike, he opened the door and said, "Give my love to Ali and the twins."

"Will do." One more awkward moment of silence where there should have been a hug or some gesture of farewell. "All righty, then," she said to fill the void and gave a terse wave. "Later."

"Later." He touched her arm tentatively, as if her skin might burn him. Just before shutting the door, he grinned.

*Hah, you're not fooling anyone*, she silently told him. Once he was well out of earshot, she said aloud, "This is only the beginning, my love."

* * *

PAUL HAD ARRIVED AT SIX for cocktails. Ali wasn't surprised. Though her acquaintance with the man had been brief, she understood that he had four passions: money, power, alcohol, and Teresa, in that order. She'd been overjoyed when Teresa returned earlier than usual before she understood that her sister-in-law had really been fleeing something—an unknown assailant and, she suspected, her brother. At least Teresa was safe here. If you didn't count Paul as a predator. Ali wasn't so sure. He seemed harmless enough, but it had to frost him that Teresa refused to submit to his control.

Ali didn't have a lot of clout in this household, but she could add dinner guests without asking permission. Tonight she had invited her birth father, Duncan, his girlfriend Laurie, and her twenty-five-year-old daughter, Madeleine, who preferred to be called Maddie. Maddie, like her perky mom, was an original, with lovely elfin features, a funky style, and boundless energy. At five feet two inches, she was forced to look mostly upward in this tall group. Both women had golden-brown pixie-cuts with highlights, though Maddie's looked natural. Duncan and Ali hadn't been aware of each other's existence until just under two years ago, but anyone seeing them together now would never know it. Ali bore him no ill will for his absence from her life. Her hope was that Liam would eventually let Duncan in. That couldn't very well happen unless Duncan came to Port Townsend. The mountain would have to go to Muhammad, because Liam seemed to have immediately shot down deep roots in Port Townsend, and he wasn't budging.

Carrie was sneaky. She had put Paul and Teresa together at the end of the table. Ali was seated next to Teresa, so she knew just how awkward that was. When she'd protested her placement, far from Joe, Carrie told her she assumed that Ali would want the twins by her side, and there wasn't room for their bassinet anywhere else. Millie was off duty. Much as she disliked the nanny, Ali would have welcomed her presence in situations such as this one, when she was the one designated to keep them from disrupting everything. Laurie, next to Joe, dominated the conversation, as was her wont. Uncomfortable with silence, she came up with a steady stream of chatter peppered with questions to keep others involved. Her efforts were less annoying than you might think; she was a voracious reader of obscure news items and thus came armed with an endless supply of interesting tidbits. Plus, she didn't just talk *at* you, she tried to engage you. It's just that if you didn't jump in in time, you'd missed your chance, kind of like playing double Dutch with someone who swung the rope at the speed of light. Her daughter Maddie wore a perpetual smile but was far less outgoing than her mother, attempting to deflect the attention away from herself if it happened to land there. The need to conserve his voice had rendered Joe less convivial in public, though he often talked a blue streak when alone with Ali. Carrie, seated on the other side of Paul, was focused on encouraging Paul and Teresa to converse.

No one paid much attention to Ali, which left her free to listen and observe. Every so often, she and Joe exchanged long-suffering glances. Joe's eyes pleaded for patience. Ah, patience. *Someday soon we'll be back in our own world*, they seemed to say, the very words he repeated to her every night before they fell asleep in each other's arms. *I'm so tired that surrendering to the storm is easier than rocking the boat*, she thought, as she rocked the girls in their fancy portable bassinet for two. *The twins certainly lack for nothing. I hope they don't turn into monsters of selfishness. If we're not careful, they will be oh so spoiled.*

Paul had been talking about his recent business ventures in Toronto and how much there was to do in the area by way of entertainment. Ali wasn't sure why Teresa was so dead set against him. He was charming in that clever, self-deprecating prep-school way, his anecdotes amusing and informative and only vaguely self-serving. The hoity-toity version of Laurie. She had always thought that someone like Teresa would ultimately be more comfortable settling down with a Paul than, say, a Liam. Carrie obviously approved of him, which had to be one of the problems. He was handsome enough, a contemporary Leslie Howard. She hadn't liked Leslie much as Ashley Wilkes in *Gone with the Wind*, but you weren't supposed to like that milquetoast character. He'd been far more appealing as the undercover hero saving aristocrats in the French Revolution, the Scarlet Pimpernel. A huge star in his time who died too young in a plane crash, shot down by the Germans in 1943. Who watched that old film anymore aside from her and Joe? They were both big fans of Turner Classic Movies.

"Teresa, will you be returning to Port Townsend?" Duncan said, yanking Ali out of her musings.

"Not anytime soon." Teresa was moving the spinach ravioli around with her fork but not eating much, other than salad.

Teresa worried too much about her weight. Maddie, on the other hand, had a hearty appetite and was neither vegan nor vegetarian. Where did she put it? People used to say that about Ali. During her "salad" days. In the nineteenth century, that meant all you could afford to eat was lettuce. Which had been more or less true of Ali before she married Joe.

"I should think not!" Paul told Teresa. "Not with all those accidents."

Teresa set her fork down and stared at him with wide, accusing eyes. "*All* those accidents?" she repeated. "Whoever told you there was more than one?"

"Why, Carrie, of course," he sputtered, his cheeks turning a shade close to the color of his hair.

"I only know of one accident," Carrie said, looking to Teresa for an explanation.

Teresa's cheeks were almost as red as Paul's, and her clawed hand hovered near her steak knife, as if preparing to plunge it into Paul's heart. He flinched, but otherwise did not react. She stopped clawing and put her elbows on the table, leaning forward, dangerously calm. "Just how many *accidents* do you know about, Paul?"

"Uh, I guess there was only the one. The bike accident?"

She didn't respond immediately, but her eyes continued to rake over him. "You've met Ali's brother, Liam. Mother tells me he was trained in Israel as an assassin. Although I question that information, I know he can be lethal. I've seen him throw knives with impressive accuracy. Ali can attest to that." Seeing that confirmation was required, Ali nodded. She wondered where Teresa was going with this. "If it turns out there is a person behind the *accident*"—Teresa stressed the final T—"he may well end up dead." She paused to let this sink in. "If that happens, and it is revealed that there is yet another person paying that person to do me harm—and I could well have been killed—the identity of that person will certainly be found out. There will be hell to pay. However, if that is the end of it, then the matter will not be pursued." She ostentatiously removed her engagement ring and handed it to him. "Just to be clear, we are done."

Paul cast bleary eyes down at the ring as the ruddy color bleached out of his face.

The rest of the guests had gone silent, even Laurie.

All at once, the babies began to shriek. "Oh dear," Ali said, standing, not knowing whom to comfort first. The distraction had to be a relief for everyone at the dinner party. "Teresa, can you take Josie?" She bounced Caryn, whispering soothing nonsense in her ear. "Let's feed them and put them down. The rest of you, carry on. No dessert for me."

She headed toward the house, trusting Teresa to follow.

Once they were inside and both babies were nursing—Joe had bought Ali a special pillow that kept her breasts in the right position—she said, "Teresa, what was that all about?"

"Oh, that Paul!" Teresa cried, stamping her foot again. "He's definitely the one behind the accidents."

"*What?*"

"Liam believed it had to do with the yoga class, that one of the women wanted me out of Port Townsend so she could have Kilo to herself. That made sense, sort of. Except Kilo and I were not lovers, and he seems to get around. No one has the resources to drive all the women he's ever flirted with out of town. Then Paul refers to 'accidents,' plural, when he couldn't possibly have heard of more than the one. If that, since I only just told Mom about the bike crash." She paused. "Unless he was responsible for them."

Ali wasn't entirely convinced. It seemed too farfetched. Though it made as much sense as anything.

"If I'm right," Teresa went on, "and I'm ninety-nine-point-nine percent sure I am, he'll call off the dogs now—or dog. I think it was just one guy. I never got the feeling it was personal—you know, that my attacker was motivated by hatred or jealousy. It had to be about money. I can't believe Paul realized that he had actually put my life in danger. The guy was just supposed to scare me until I put my tail between my legs and fled for home; instead, he came way too close to killing me. A little more so each time."

Ali grinned as she laid the babies in their side-by-side cradles. "Does this mean you'll come back to Port Townsend with us?"

* * *

Liam should have been exhausted. He had spent the day at Fort Worden helping Peter rebuild a porch. He'd pedaled both ways on his mountain bike, then had thrown sticks and balls to the dogs until they lay down, whining for mercy. Neither the passage of time nor any amount of physical labor could blur the memory of making love to Teresa. For days after, he'd floated on a cloud of exhilaration. Finally, he'd crashed, all too aware that an actual relationship was impossible—could come to no good. He didn't blame Teresa, and he didn't beat himself up for giving in to temptation. In his rush to restore her body heat, he'd been unable to guard against the other type of heat, a fire too poorly banked for far too long. Not that he regretted it. He just hoped that now she'd have the good sense to stay in Seattle.

He'd finally concluded that the quickest way to get over Teresa was to move on. In desperation, he'd headed to Port Angeles to check out the bar scene there. Meeting beautiful women was no problem, and he'd danced with several, even made out with a few, until he grew disgusted with himself. He couldn't silence the voices in his head that compared everyone unfavorably to Teresa. Maybe with the help of heavy drinking … but you couldn't do that and drive. So … last night he'd rented a motel room and headed to the most promising nightspot in Port Angeles, a gastropub touted as attracting the "top babes in town."

Her name was as exotic as she was—Lisette Manegold. She spoke with a vaguely aristocratic East Coast dialect, had an intriguingly imperious air, and was tall and athletic, almost six feet in high-heeled boots. She wore her long, curly black hair loose, tossing it around like a horse's mane. Other than that mildly annoying habit, it was difficult to find fault with her assets. Green eyes, a creamy, sun-kissed complexion, a naturally downturned but generous mouth. Long, toned runner's legs encased in black jeans. He guessed her age at under thirty-five, maybe thirty-two. Older than he was by at least five years. None of Teresa's adorable gawkiness or innocence. A jaded air. That was okay. Like him, she had seen too much.

"Who *are* you?" she said in a whispery, wondering voice as she slid onto the barstool next to him. She fiddled with an antique silver locket at her throat, bringing attention to a semi-transparent blouse that revealed a lacy bra framing full, round breasts. For a moment he was too distracted to answer. Amused by his silence, Lisette ordered tequila shots and handed him one. He drank it down without hesitation, hoping to blot out the little voice telling him, *Watch out.* Finally able to speak, he told her his name, and she asked, "Are you Irish?"

"Half," he replied. "The other half is a wildcard. I was a foster child. My birth father turned up recently, and he's definitely Irish."

"Interesting." Her eyes coasted over him ever so slowly, savoring even the scars as if they were exotic tattoos. "You've been through fire. Lost but found, young but old, finally in your element."

His lips quirked. She was too much. He downed a second shot. "Are you a psychic?"

"I might be," she said with a coy tilt of her head. He didn't stop her as she ran a red painted fingernail along his leg. He was surprised to feel a stir of excitement. Her fingers were elegantly long but her nails were not. Her arms and hands looked strong and capable.

"What brought you to Port Angeles?" Liam asked.

"A man," she sighed, "but he moved on. What about your woman?" Liam's snort of laughter didn't deter her. "The one you're trying to forget," she clarified.

"There is no woman."

"If you say so." She stood. "Walk me to my car?" He signaled for the bartender to close out his tab and signed the slip, leaving a ten for a tip. Lisette gave a little nod to acknowledge his generosity. "You are welcome at my restaurant anytime."

In an astonishing coincidence, Lisette's car was the same model as Teresa's, a 1994 Mazda MX-5 Miata. Teresa's was powder blue, hers was black like her masses of shiny curls. Why did women want Miatas anyway? They weren't highly rated vehicles, and convertibles mussed your hair. They were cute, he guessed. A woman might choose a car for that reason alone, he thought. No way could you compare Teresa and Lisette, but he would have guessed Lisette would have a more rugged vehicle like, say, a Jeep Grand Wagoneer. Was choosing the polar opposite of Teresa really the answer? And yet, here was unexpected common ground. Despite the obvious differences, he might be responding to a photographic negative of Teresa.

Lisette made no move to unlock her car. Instead, she took Liam's hand, pulled him to her, and kissed him. At first he didn't respond, but her lips were insistent, and her firm body and soft breasts felt good pressed against him. The lingering kiss was refreshingly free of the tortured longing he associated with Teresa. But it wasn't an unstoppable force.

He took a step back. Lisette didn't counter his move. Sex with her might feel good, even great, in the moment, but for all he knew, she was the type of woman who'd destroy your possessions and stab your housekeeper if crossed—a cautionary scene from one of his favorite Clint Eastwood movies, *Play Misty for Me*. Without speaking, she broke into a brilliant smile and handed him her business card, which he ostentatiously slipped into the pocket of his motorcycle jacket.

As he drove his Harley back to the hotel, Liam grinned. For the first time since that fateful day Teresa had walked into his life, he could envision a future not necessarily including Lisette, but without Teresa. Sort of. He didn't kid himself that the invisible cord that bound them could be so easily severed. Not until he was certain her safety was no longer threatened. Just in case, he added Lisette as a phone contact. The card said she was the owner of Café Lisette, specializing in Creole cuisine. Not just the manager, then.

# PART II

# CHAPTER 16

———◆———

EARLY SEPTEMBER ON THE PENINSULA was living up to its usual high standards of bright sunny skies, pleasant sea breezes, and cool but comfortable evenings. Teresa was vastly relieved to be back in Port Townsend after all the tense exchanges with her mother. In fact, it was a miracle they'd managed to tie up the most glaring loose ends so quickly—sending Millie the Nanny on her not-so-merry way and casting Paul out of the guest bedroom forever. The first was accomplished after a come-to-Jesus talk with Joe, who hadn't realized the misery inflicted by the dour nanny on the mother of his children. After all, she'd been all affability with him. Of course, for the time being, they had no nanny at all, but Teresa and Ali figured they could make do until a replacement was found.

When Joe, Ali, Teresa, and the babies arrived at noon, Liam was waiting for them with a cold lunch of tuna salad sandwiches, coleslaw, and freshly baked rye bread. He looked as devastatingly handsome as Teresa remembered, his straight, blue-black hair tousled by the wind, his eyes a blazing cobalt-blue, his skin lightly bronzed from all the time spent outdoors. As inscrutable as he was beautiful. *Patience*, Teresa reminded herself. *You're going to have to wear him down gradually.*

First priority was introducing the newcomers to the dogs, who trotted forward side by side, and, observing the strangers' relationship to Teresa, instantly welcomed them into the pack with wagging tails and lolling tongues. Though curious about the twins, Harry and Coogan didn't stick their noses beyond the rim of the bassinet. The babies gurgled and cooed with their usual good humor.

"It's so good to be back!" Ali raised her arms to the clear blue sky and did a few ecstatic twirls while Joe and Liam unloaded the suitcases and the baby gear. "This is hands down my favorite time of year."

Soon they were all seated under umbrellas on the flagstone terrace.

Liam regarded Ali critically. "You're looking good, Alf. Lost most of the bloat, I see."

Teresa couldn't let such a tactless comment go unaddressed. She narrowed her eyes and said in an outraged whisper, "Liam!"

Ali touched her arm. "It's okay, Teresa. I told you, he's a truth teller. I appreciate it, actually. I don't want people mollycoddling me, especially my *darling* brother." This said with the faintest note of sarcasm.

Liam leaned over Ali's chair and caught her in a spontaneous hug. "You look gorgeous. The twins are … Words can't do them justice." As he set her down again, a shadow passed over his face.

"What?" Joe stiffened with concern.

"I'm just wondering when we can expect our first paparazzi invasion," Liam said with an irritated shake of his head.

"Oh, that." Joe waved him away. "We've taken a preemptive strike."

"How so?"

"Our main reason for not coming back sooner was the prospect of lurking photographers," Ali said. "We thought, let's throw them a bone, do an official photo shoot of the new family. I wasn't crazy about being photographed in my current"—her hand made a dismissive sweep down her body—"*form*, but it was for a good cause. *People* magazine only wanted one picture, so Joe's agent Linc also contacted *Country Boy*. They'll do a two-page spread. Once the twins are toddlers, we'll probably have to offer them something else, but maybe they'll leave us alone for a while." She paused. "Or they'll lose interest completely."

Teresa broke in, "You don't really want that, do you? Joe has a huge fan club. He's still writing songs. He might even want to perform again someday."

Joe blew out an indifferent puff of air. "Unlikely," he said and took a giant bite of his sandwich.

Though Teresa didn't believe him for a moment, she let the subject of Joe's waning popularity drop as they all dug into their lunch and the beautiful setting worked its magic on her frayed nerves. The sea breeze was gentle, and the air was crystal clear, giving them a magnificent view of the water and mountains. The seagulls screamed and chattered, and a barge made its way slowly across the horizon.

As Liam collected the plates, he told Teresa, "I'm frankly surprised to see you here. Aren't you afraid of what might happen next?" She tried to meet his challenging stare but had to look away, too disconcerted by the intensity she saw there. She knew he was referring to her attacker. *Not of him,* she thought, *but yes, I'm afraid. Afraid you're going to keep insisting we aren't meant for each other. Afraid you've already moved on.*

"Teresa solved the mystery," Joe said as he collected the remaining plates. "She staged a dramatic reveal at our family dinner party. Mom was *not* pleased."

"Oh?" Liam raised his eyebrows at Teresa.

"It was Paul. He paid someone to ruin Port Townsend for me, so I'd come home."

Liam nodded, unsurprised. "I knew I had a reason to dislike that guy."

Ali snorted. "You would have disliked him no matter what. You don't trust rich people."

Liam turned his implacable gaze on his sister. "You never trusted them either. Until recently." He took off for the kitchen before Ali could reply. She flushed with embarrassment, arousing Teresa's pity.

When Liam returned with more beer, Teresa asked him, "Don't you want to hear what tipped me off?" She wasn't sure how she'd expected him to react, just not with this apparent indifference.

"I'll bite. How did you know?" He glanced over toward the kitchen, as if cleaning up was a bigger priority than satisfying his curiosity.

*He sure can be an arrogant so-and-so,* Teresa thought. She said, "Paul was stupid enough, or drunk enough, to ask me about the *accidents,* plural. When I asked him what he was referring to, he looked all guilty and flustered. He said Mom had told him, but she had only just learned about the *first* accident that afternoon."

"Ah." He gave her a brisk military salute. "Nice work, Nancy Drew."

"Mom is still mad at Teresa," Joe said.

Though stung by Liam's snarky attitude, Teresa went on, "I had to explain, of course, but I couldn't bring myself to expose the full extent of Paul's villainy. I played it down. The bike accident became less of a near miss, and the run-ins with the deck chair and at the harbor were also watered down—so to speak—in the retelling. The drop to the ledge below the lawn chair was reduced to five feet, and the push into the bay was moved closer to shore."

Ali broke in, "Teresa told Carrie she was never in danger of drowning but was able to slog in on her own steam. Carrie agreed that Paul was misguided to go to such extremes, but she blames Teresa for driving him to it. She told us Paul tried to explain what happened. While in Toronto, he confided in his best friend and business partner James that his fiancée was spending too much time away in Port Townsend. James said he had a 'buddy' there who could exert some gentle persuasion for a small sum. The buddy was told not to harm a hair on her head—just scare her a little."

No longer so blasé, Liam bunched his hands into fists, his usual involuntary way of broadcasting suppressed fury. *Is he angry for my sake?* Teresa wondered. *Or because he hates Paul?* She raised a placating palm. "At least Mom agreed that Paul is no longer a desirable candidate for son-in-law. Let's drink to that."

The men raised their beers, the women their herbal iced teas, and clinked glasses.

Ali chuckled to herself.

"What?" Liam said.

"Teresa put the fear of God into Paul. Basically told him you were going to kill the perpetrator if you ever discovered his identity, while implying she knew it was him. She said you'd leave it alone as long as nothing else happened to her."

"She mentioned knives," said Joe, also laughing, "and your history as an assassin."

Dead silence.

"My *what*?" Paling beneath his tan, Liam scanned each face in turn.

"She was on a roll," Joe was quick to add, "so she exaggerated, er, a lot. It was a bit much, I'll admit. She laid it on thick."

Teresa expected a denial from Liam or some explanation, but none came. She was more intrigued than ever. What had he been doing during those months not even the Israeli detectives could account for?

"Liam," she said, "did you get a good look at the guy who pushed me off the dock? I mean, you must have been watching out for me or you wouldn't have shown up so quickly."

"I did, but like you, I never saw his face because of the kerchief and hoodie. He was a middle-aged man with a gut, maybe five feet eight. If I saw him again, I might recognize him, especially if he was running. I had two choices in the moment—pull you out or run after him. No contest, of course. I'm sorry it took me so long to get to you. Once I realized your car had been parked on Water Street for more than five minutes—uh, from my tracking device—I came as soon as I could."

"Why do you think you'd recognize him from his running style?"

"He was fast for a chubby older guy. I think he may have been a pretty good sprinter when he was younger."

"Makes sense," Joe said. "I'm guessing he exceeded his instructions by more than a little." He touched Teresa's arm. "I'm sure Paul never meant for you to get hurt."

"If you say so," Teresa said.

"Where's the nanny?" Liam asked, looking around as if she might pop out at any moment from behind a tree.

"*Millie*," Ali said as if uttering a curse word.

"She wasn't a good fit," Teresa said. "Ali and I are going to team up to care for the twins until Joe can find a new nanny. Hopefully one a little less … how do I say this—"

"Nasty," Ali said. "Don't sugarcoat it. She was terrible to me. Like I was some rube and the most clueless mother, ever."

Joe tugged at the collar of his Polo shirt. "God, I'm sorry, sweetie. She treated me like a king. I had no idea she was being so condescending to you."

Teresa rolled her eyes. "That's putting it mildly. Anyway, it's over. Maybe the next one should be a little younger."

"Not *too* young," Ali said. "I'm insecure enough."

Liam ruffled her hair in an annoying brotherly gesture of affection. "You don't need to be."

"Aww," Teresa said. "That's nice. I agree. Joe adores you."

"I do," Joe declared, giving his wife a tender, lingering kiss. The babies began to cry. "And now, I'm going to clean up. The Terrible Twins have awoken."

"While you're hiring a nanny, can you also get us someone to clean and cook?" Teresa pleaded. "Liam has been doing everything. It's not fair."

Joe scratched his head. "Doesn't a cleaning service come in once a week?"

"Yes," Liam said, "and it's enough. I like cooking."

"I'll give you a budget for the food, if you're serious."

Liam shrugged. "If you'd like."

Teresa wondered what he meant. How had he been supporting himself? He must be hard up by now. Although you didn't want to underestimate Liam. He had many marketable skills. Perhaps he'd accumulated a nest egg of sorts while working as a machinist at Boeing.

"Only," Liam continued, "I have a hiking trip planned for the end of the week. Will you all be okay on your own until I return?"

Joe grinned. "A hiking trip, huh? We'll be fine. We can always get takeout from one of the restaurants in town. Where are you headed?"

"The Royal Basin. It's a three-day trip, nothing too strenuous. I have the permits."

"But … Sunday is our birthday," Ali protested.

"I should be home by then," he said gently, "but you know I'm not one for a big fuss."

Joe's brows flew together. "You don't mind if I make one for Ali, I suppose."

"Joe," Ali said, "you can go with him if you like. I know you want to. It would be a nice break for you."

"And leave you two—I mean four—alone leading up to your birthday?" Joe looked horrified.

The dogs raised their heads and whined.

"You see?" Ali said. "You've offended them! They can totally keep us safe."

"Next time," Liam laughed. "I already have a hiking companion for this trip. We're just getting to know each other. Three might be a crowd."

"Oh?" Joe leaned forward, intrigued.

Liam laughed—suggestively, Teresa thought. *Oh no. It has to be a woman.* There was no mistaking that sinking feeling. The bottom had just dropped out of her world.

# CHAPTER 17

---

Two days later, Ali and Teresa were strolling down Water Street with the twins in their baby carriage. Ali couldn't help but notice that Teresa was far from her usual ebullient self, though she was trying hard to be upbeat.

To avoid some of the foot traffic on Water Street, they veered down Taylor to Washington Street, stopping to admire Haller Fountain, located at the base of the several flights of stairs leading up to the blocks of stately Victorian homes on the bluff, both residences and bed-and-breakfasts.

Ali tilted her head to observe the lovely, mostly naked bronze woman. "She's either Venus or a nymph."

"Venus, that makes sense." Teresa circled the statue for a better look. "With all the women who live in this town without men, someone once told me the culture was Venusian."

"She sure is pretty." Ali smiled. "Kind of reminds me of you." The woman did look remarkably like Teresa before she cut her hair, although her sister-in-law was slimmer.

Teresa gave her an affectionate nudge. "Ha, I wish. But those could definitely be the twins in a couple of years." She indicated the children at the bronze woman's feet, also naked, astride giant fish and blowing water out of seashells. "When they get to be that age, they are definitely going to be frolicking nonstop. And just wait till they are teenagers."

Ali crossed two fingers in front of her face as if warding off evil. "Ugh, I *really* don't want to think about it."

"It was reconstructed only a few years ago."

Startled by the French-accented male voice, they both swiveled about to find an elegantly dressed man whose fine features, thick mop of hair, and closely trimmed beard reminded Ali of the figure to the left of Liberty in Delacroix's painting *Liberty Leading the People*. While in Paris, she'd spent a lot of time at the Louvre.

"Hello," Ali said. "I take it you live here too?"

"Yes, for about ten years. Three years ago, they rebuilt the statue. It had taken much abuse over time."

"I was just telling Teresa that she could have been the model for Venus, or the sea nymph—whoever she is."

"Venus or Galathea. No one is entirely certain. And yes, I see the resemblance." His smile reminded Ali of an animal baring its teeth. A handsome animal. Perhaps his canines were sharper than most.

They shook hands and introduced themselves.

"Reynard Silvestre."

"Ali and Teresa O'Connell. We moved here recently." Ali was intentionally vague. "As you can see, I'm a new mother."

"You are … wives?" His eyes shifted from one to the other.

Ali exchanged a startled glance with Teresa before they burst into laughter. "No, we aren't romantic partners. Not that I wouldn't be proud to be married to Teresa. Her brother is my husband."

"Ah." Ali detected relief in his reaction. From Teresa's blush, Ali thought she might recognize him. Or be attracted. That would be understandable. He was quite handsome in a refined way. Though he might be too old for Teresa. His laugh lines and graying temples put his age at somewhere just shy of forty.

He leaned over to admire and coo at the baby girls, who stared up at him with their disarming blue eyes framed by thick sable lashes. "Wow, they are beautiful." He looked up. "And so like their mother."

"Excuse me," Teresa said, "but aren't you the concert pianist? I have a few of your CDs."

"Yes," he stood a little straighter, "though these days I am mostly composing. I grew weary of all the touring. I have a home studio—"

"For the movies," Teresa broke in. "You composed the score to *One May Night*. It was brilliant."

He preened a little. Ali thought he must not be accustomed to being recognized or acknowledging his accomplishments to a beautiful stranger. No wedding ring that she could see. She admired his style—pressed black jeans, a plain white T-shirt, and a black sports coat. Black Oxfords. At once formal and casual. Very Parisian. She thought he'd get along famously with

Jean-Louis, though the chef's style was more colorful.

Ali decided to act on impulse. "Can you come to dinner this Saturday? My friends Becca and Jean-Louis are coming over from Seattle—North Bend, actually—and Jean-Louis has promised to cook us something wonderful. He is a master chef. You could also bring your ... significant other, naturally."

"I would be delighted." He gave them a rather practiced, closed-lip smile. "There's only me," he added with a careless shrug. "If that's all right."

"Liam said he might be home in time," Teresa told Ali.

Was Teresa worried Liam would be jealous? "I think he planned this hike as an excuse," she said. "Liam doesn't like it when people make a fuss over him."

Teresa turned back to Reynard and smiled. "Yes, please join us."

Ali wrote their address down on one of Reynard's business cards. "Joe and I should really have a calling card made up." She wondered why Teresa hadn't offered him one of her own. She recalled the embossed card her sister-in-law had handed over at their first meeting.

"Do you live with Joe and Ali?" Reynard asked Teresa.

"No, but I'll stay as long as they need me."

"Your ... job permits this?"

Ali was surprised to hear him slip such a personal question into a conversation with virtual strangers. The French didn't discuss work or money casually. It was, well, *gauche*. Perhaps this man had lived in the United States long enough to forget this particular taboo. She felt sorry for Teresa, who often struggled to clarify what she did, or didn't do, for a living. The honest answers, "I don't need to work," "I inherited a fortune," or "I do a lot of volunteer work" weren't Teresa's style.

Teresa was no dummy. With a gracious smile, she replied, simply, "Yes, it does."

Fortunately, Reynard knew better than to push it. They murmured the expected parting pleasantries and he moved on, mounting the Terrace Steps leading to the Uptown area.

Ali waited till he was halfway up the long staircase to comment. "I loved the way he said, 'Wow' with that sexy French accent. Nice-looking guy, right? If you like the Gallic type. Tall, too, for a Frenchman. At least six feet. Someone you might consider?"

Teresa gave her arm a gentle punch. "Don't I get any downtime between engagements or crushes?"

"I assume you mean Liam," Ali said as they continued to stroll down the street.

"You got me." Teresa heaved an anguished sigh. "I can't believe he's already dating someone else."

Ali came to an abrupt stop. "Wait a minute. You two were *dating*?"

"No, no." Teresa waved her arms around. "He did kiss me, though."

Ali looked at her askance.

"Nothing else."

"That's difficult to believe. I've always seen Liam as the kind of guy where once you start kissing him, it's curtains."

"*He* stopped it. Said we were too different. That it could never be."

"Oh. So, what about Reynard the Fox?" Ali brightened. "Does he have a shot? It's a safe bet he's interested."

"He's handsome. I wouldn't call it a *coup de foudre*." She avoided eye contact, all the proof Ali needed that it *had* been that way with Liam. "I certainly respect his work, and as a pianist myself, I'm in awe of his talent. The fact that he lives here is also in his favor."

"*Coup de foudre*," Ali repeated. "Lightning strike. More realistic than 'love at first sight,' don't you think? I don't trust that phenomenon."

Teresa laughed. "Says the woman who fell in love at first sight with a hermit in the woods. He might have been the Unabomber."

Ali chuckled. "It wasn't instantaneous. It didn't take long, for sure. Once he smiled, I was a goner. I'll admit I was intrigued from the start, but the shaggy beard was daunting."

One of the twins started crying, which set off the other one.

"Chain reaction," Ali said, lifting Josephine out of the buggy. "Hungry again. Can you hold Caryn?"

"She won't like having to wait. I wish I could help you feed them."

"You can. I pumped this morning. There's a bottle in the bag."

While the babies were occupied, Teresa said, "I was thinking I'd go back to yoga class, now that I know I'm not risking my neck by attending."

"Only your heart."

Teresa replied with a careless toss of her head, "Maybe not. I'm a one-crush-at-a-time girl. I was tempted by Kilo, but not in any angst-ridden sense. It was purely physical."

"Ouch," Ali said. "That isn't very flattering to Kilo."

"You don't get it." Teresa threw up her hands. "Kilo isn't in love with me, not anymore. I wouldn't be surprised if he's servicing half the class. He was only interested in some afternoon delight."

Ali laid Josie back in the deluxe baby carriage. "Did you go for it?"

Teresa shook her head vehemently. Then she stopped, looking guilty.

"Um, almost. There was already a woman in his bed."

"*What?*"

Teresa laughed. "We got to kissing, and we ended up in his apartment. The pretty blonde receptionist, Jessica, was in his bed. Said she thought that by giving her his key, he was telling her he wanted her. Turns out he only wanted someone to feed his cat while he was away."

"Poor girl."

"Yes," Teresa said, not unsympathetic. "Then Swami the cat appeared, demanding attention. By then we might have all been characters in a seventeenth-century farce."

After they shared a hearty laugh, Teresa went on, "He's a natural flirt. I can see how you'd get your wires crossed with him. He was patient with Jessica, but I doubt she works there anymore." She paused and pointed. "Fawns."

The two dainty animals with their soft, spotted coats ambled gracefully by, followed by their mother.

"They are bold here," Ali said. "I'm surprised they ventured down this far." She turned to Teresa. "Would you have gone through with it?"

"I might have," Teresa admitted, "but I'm glad fate intervened. If I'm thinking clearly, I don't trust myself to sleep around. It's too dangerous, both emotionally and physically."

Was Teresa trying to convince herself? Ali couldn't figure her out. Had Teresa and Liam slept together or not? "How can you be so sure Kilo's not in love with you?"

"It's obvious when you get to know him better. He might have fancied he was in love with me in high school, but he's had a lot of women since then. A *lot*."

"So has Liam."

"I know." Teresa sighed again. "Liam is so … irresistible. He kept me safe. What's sexier than that? It's like that movie *The Bodyguard*."

"Oh, yes! Kevin Costner."

"You've got your own version of Liam," Teresa said. "I never expected Joe to get married and settle down. Not even when he was engaged to Rina. I always assumed it was one of those things where you just start calling someone your fiancée but never set a date."

"I still can't believe it," Ali said as they settled the twins in their infant car seats. "I keep thinking I'm going to wake up and discover it was all a dream."

# CHAPTER 18



BACK AT THE COMPOUND, ALI and Teresa unstrapped the twins while acknowledging a joyous reception from Coogan and Harry. The dogs stayed so close as they approached the main house that they had to dodge their frantically wagging tails.

Joe, almost as excited as the dogs, met them halfway along the path. "I have a surprise for you."

"That's great." Ali gave him a quick kiss. "First I have to change the girls. They were really stinking up the car."

"That's the surprise." He performed a ta-da gesture, arms spread. "Meet Ulla. She'll change the girls."

Ali saw the tall, vibrant Amazon strolling up the path as if it were a runway and gulped. *Uh-oh,* she thought. *She looks like she just stepped off the soccer field and into a Nike commercial. Why would Joe hire someone so young and beautiful? I specifically asked him not to.*

"Nice to meet you, Mrs. O'Connell," Ulla said with a light accent. German or Swedish? It wasn't clear.

Teresa gave Ulla a half-hearted wave of greeting but deliberately hung back. From her bemused expression, her sister-in-law had similar reservations.

Ali asked Joe, "Can I have a moment?" Wearing a tight smile, she led her husband into the other room, where she shut the door behind her and leaned heavily against it. She spoke in an emphatic whisper. "Listen, I appreciate the gesture, but Joe, she's intimidating."

He looked puzzled. "Why?" Then he seemed to understand. "Don't worry," he assured her, drawing her against him in a warm hug. "She's gay. She has a partner—Cindy, I think her name is."

Ali was as wound up as a fishing line. "Okaaay," she said, drawing the word out. "Does she get that there's a trial period?"

"No problem. If you don't like her, we'll show her the door. She came highly recommended through the agency."

"She can't have been at it for long. What is she, twenty?"

"More like thirty. She wears her age well."

*She sure does*, Ali thought as she drew in a few calming breaths. It seemed to help.

Back in the foyer, Ulla had already changed the twins' diapers. Teresa stood by, mouth agape. "She's fast."

"I have another surprise," Joe said as he helped her put away the twins' accessories. "Duncan, Laurie, and Maddie are coming for the weekend. They'll arrive tomorrow, at around the same time as Becca and Jean-Louis."

Ali exhaled in relief. After that first "surprise," she hadn't known what to expect.

Teresa's brow creased with concern. "Wouldn't that be too full a house? We don't want to overwhelm Ali, especially on her birthday."

Ali took Teresa by the arm and propelled her outside. "Don't worry, we'll be fine. My dad, his girlfriend, her daughter Maddie, and my best friend and her husband are never a burden. Besides, the cleaning service is coming tomorrow. I'll have them make up the beds. Jean-Louis is cooking dinner, and he always banishes me from the kitchen. There will be hardly anything extra to do."

"Are you okay with Ulla?" Teresa asked as they sat down in the shade of an umbrella.

Ali's jerky shrug made her annoyance clear. "I'm not stuck with her, right? I can't reject her just because she's too cute. And she's a lesbian, so where's the danger?"

"She looks like that supermodel, Claudia Schiffer. What if she's really bi?"

"Not every nanny tries to seduce the husband," Ali said with an anemic chuckle.

"According to the tabloids, they do," Teresa said in the same quasi-jokey spirit.

But Ali, eager to move on from her own insecurities, was determined to look at the bright side. Now, freed from diaper duty, she could throw herself into a birthday weekend surrounded by all her favorite people. She wished

Liam were coming home earlier, so he could have a longer visit with their father.

Saturday—Ali and Liam's birthday, September twelfth—began with a flurry of activity, as the cleaning service swept through the compound, leaving it looking like a four-star hotel. Every bedroom in the house, plus the remaining guest cottage, would be occupied. They'd given Ulla the bedroom next to the nursery. Though still hoping Liam would show up, Ali knew not to hold her breath. Liam had always loathed birthday celebrations.

Becca and Jean-Louis arrived just after lunch, and Jean-Louis was out the door again as soon as he had put their suitcases in the cottage, insisting he had major food shopping to do before he began his preparations for dinner.

"I agreed to this only because you insisted," Ali said. "And no more cooking after tonight. Otherwise it's just a busman's holiday."

Jean-Louis gave her a big, smacking kiss on the cheek and laughed. "If I didn't love cooking so much, I would not be a chef. This is a special occasion—the day of your birth! I don't cook so much in the restaurants anymore, I supervise. *Là, là,* that is the price of success."

"I'm so glad it's working out," Ali said to Becca.

"Me too. Happy birthday, Ali!" She gave her a huge hug. "With the second restaurant, I thought we might be taking on too much. But Jean-Louis is giving Tom Douglas a run for his money. He has a cookbook coming out this Christmas, did I tell you? It's called *Shriek for Wild Goose.*" At Ali's puzzled look, she added, "Remember how the Cratchit children shrieked for goose in *A Christmas Carol?*"

"I also recall that after Scrooge had his change of heart, he bought them the prize turkey. Goose is pretty greasy."

Becca pouted. "Most people don't know how to cook wild game. This book will change all that."

"I'm glad. I've heard more than one cautionary tale of the goose dinner sliding out of the oven and down the hallway." Ali gave her friend an extra hug. "I've missed you so much."

"I've missed you more. Can I see the babies? I need my fix."

They found Ulla cooing over the twins, who seemed to love the attention. Becca picked up Caryn, who squirmed a little, then nosed around, seeking out a breast. "I think she's hungry." Becca passed the baby to Ali.

"They are *always* hungry," Ali lamented while Caryn sucked and Josie flailed her plump little arms, wanting in on the action. Ulla gave her a bottle. "Do I need to pump some more?" she asked the au pair.

"Yes, when you have a moment," the woman said in her sexy accent.

Once Becca and Ali were outside and seated under an umbrella, Becca whispered, "Why did you hire Heidi Klum?"

"I was thinking more Claudia Schiffer. Joe found her. She's gay, supposedly."

"Well, *that's* a relief," Becca said archly, "though I don't get that vibe. I like to think I have pretty good gaydar. What is she, five eleven?"

"Something like that. Loads of energy. She'll need it. Josie and Caryn are exhausting."

Becca settled into the lawn chair with a relieved exhalation of air. "Ahhh ...."

"You're looking gorgeous, as usual," Ali told her. "Married life suits you." Ali was used to Becca in heels and tight pencil skirts—either that, or gypsy ruffles. Whatever she wore—and her wardrobe was whimsical—she looked great. Today she was wearing white shorts and a low-cut royal-blue T-shirt emblazoned with the name of Jean-Louis' restaurant, La Fête Sauvage. The graphic, created by Ali, depicted a wolf wearing a bib and licking its chops. Becca's olive skin glowed, and her hair was pulled into a chic knot with escaping tendrils that framed her bold features. On her feet were cream-colored espadrilles with gladiator laces and stacked heels.

"Thanks, sweetie, and back atcha." Becca snapped the fabric of her T-shirt. "Love this. Though Jean-Louis doesn't think it's classy enough. He makes a face whenever I wear it. Which is why I wear it: to annoy him."

Ali's shrug was apologetic. "I confess, I had no idea how to make a slavering wolf classy."

They laughed.

Ali gave it a critical once-over. "This one looks scarier than necessary."

"Hmm, why is that? The animals you draw are usually so friendly."

"It depends on my mood. How about if I just draw wolf eyes? Too subtle?"

"Maybe. Not sure wolf eyes are easily distinguishable from other predators'."

Ali wrinkled her nose. "So ... we abandon the wolf idea, which dates back to when you decided not to call the new place Le Loup Vorace because the French words for 'hungry wolf' were too difficult for Americans to pronounce. I'm not sure how to illustrate The Wild Feast."

Becca laughed. "No worries. Or *c'est correct*, as Jean-Louis likes to say. My French is getting totally corrupted by his Québécois." She gave a dismissive wave. "What about Joe's idea that you write a children's book?"

Ali grimaced. "Where's the story? *You* come up with a plot featuring a friendly snail, Mrs. Bigfoot, and a bear in motorcycle leathers."

But Becca was on a roll. "Not me, but how 'bout Teresa? Doesn't she have a degree in Creative Writing?"

"She already told me she has no interest in using her degree."

"Have you mentioned this specific project to her?"

"Well, no …." Ali caught sight of Teresa coming down the hill from her guest cabin and didn't finish her thought. "How's the family? Nathan still on the wagon?"

"Hard to believe, but yes. He hasn't stopped catting around, though. Ma and Pop have been going out of their way to introduce him to nice Jewish girls. Needless to say …." Becca threw up her hands. "I think he had his heart set on you, to be honest."

Ali made a face. "Only because I wasn't interested. What about your sisters?"

The conversation paused while Becca stood to hug Teresa. "Don't let me interrupt," Teresa said, settling in a lawn chair. "I want to hear what's going on with your family too."

"Okay, but I'll keep it brief. Myra still hasn't come out to our parents, though she did confess to me that she's living with a nurse. She's now an ER surgeon at Lenox Hill, and that keeps her so busy no one expects her to take time out for a private life, anyway. Hannah's still working at the public defender's office in Boston. I believe she's dating a handyman, though he does have a degree in English Literature. Not Jewish, naturally. Not very ambitious, Hannah tells me. Too bad for Ma and Pop. I'm the only married lady. And we have no plans to have children—not that I've told them that."

Ali chuckled. "I'm surprised my motherhood experience hasn't changed your mind."

Becca and Teresa joined in on the laughter. "No offense, Ali, but I'm more than ever convinced it's not for me," Becca said, "though I'm sure I'll start envying you once the girls are old enough to take shopping." Leaning back, she drew in a long, luxuriant breath. "Ah, the smell of sea air! I can't tell you how nice it is to be here. We never get away anymore. I do love this place. I hope you don't mind if I move in. I can see Jean-Louis on weekends."

"The more the merrier," Ali said. "Teresa says she's going to be a permanent resident as well."

"Hey, you have a new look," Becca said, noticing Teresa's hair for the first time.

"I'm growing it out," Teresa said, noticeably huffy. Ali hadn't detected any malice in Becca's comment, so she was surprised by her sister-in-law's reaction.

Becca gave her arm a gentle squeeze. "I love the hair, seriously. Heart-shaped faces look fantastic with short hair. And your natural color is a gorgeous dark blonde with auburn highlights. How lucky is that?"

Teresa shook her head. "I didn't mean to overreact. I'm a little sensitive on the subject, that's all. Transitioning from light blonde has been a rocky process. The first attempt had it looking like steel wool. It's been hard on my vanity."

"How's Liam doing?" Becca asked Ali, as if that were a natural transition. Knowing Liam, Becca had to assume something was going on between Liam and Teresa.

"He's staying busy," Ali replied. "His handyman skills are much in demand, not just here but at Fort Worden, where he's befriended the maintenance guy."

"Ah," Becca said. "He's always been good with his hands, or so I hear. Not that I'd know." She giggled, lest anyone miss the sexual inuendo. "That man is not like the rest of us. I do believe he's a selkie."

Ali chuckled. "What … like a merman?"

"Some kind of mythological creature." Becca made a vague fluttery gesture. "Hypnotic, magnetic, what have you. No mortal woman is going to tame him."

Ali clicked her tongue. "Maybe that *was* true. Whatever happened to him in Israel—and we're still hazy on that—has changed him. I think he's in love with Teresa but won't admit it."

Teresa grimaced. "That's why he's off on a camping trip with another woman."

A seagull plopped down next to the table, inching toward the bowl of potato chips.

"God, those things are monsters." Becca shooed it away. "Git along, you beast, git! It's the size of a small dog." The seagull squawked loudly as it flew off.

"They make a surprising variety of sounds," Ali said. "Sometimes I like to listen to them talk to each other. Unless they're screeching. That I can do without."

"It gets a little relentless sometimes," Teresa agreed.

Ali laughed. "I'll take seagulls over Carrie O'Connell any day."

"Amen," her sister-in-law said.

"She can't be that bad," Becca insisted. "Look at how great Teresa and Joe turned out. No parents are perfect."

"At least yours say what they think," Ali said, "even if you don't want to hear it. Carrie prefers to get her way through manipulation. I'd still take Carrie over my foster mom, who was more like a sports coach who wishes she could oust you for not being a team player. It's clear that she loves Teresa. If only she didn't try so hard to control her. And that nanny she forced on me was something else."

"Brunhilda, I think her name was," Teresa said with a laugh.

"She looked more like a Brunhilda than a Millie," Ali said.

"Thank God she's history," Becca said. "How's the charity going—what's it called?"

"Foster Splash Pad, but we shorten it to FOSSP. The goal is to help ex-foster children aging out of the system. It's going well. Joe bought an apartment building on the edge of town as temporary housing. We have counselors on staff to help them define and pursue their goals—whether that means getting a job or applying for a scholarship so they can go to school. One of them is here today; we hired him to help Jean-Louis in the kitchen."

Becca looked worried. "Uh-oh, Jean-Louis likes to choose his own help. The kid better have a thick skin."

"Tiger's a good kid," Ali assured her, "and he's in awe of Jean-Louis. Don't worry; they'll hit it off."

Becca didn't look convinced, but she let the subject drop. "So … back to Liam." She leaned forward to refill her glass from the pitcher of water. Neither Ali nor Teresa responded to the prompt. "Seriously, is everything okay? It must be weird as hell to just have him surface like that after he was supposedly blown to smithereens."

"No kidding," Ali said. "So far we haven't really been alone together. Just the once, for about a half hour. I think he goes out of his way to avoid that, even though I know he loves me and is glad to be in my company. Kind of like a cat who wants to be near you but doesn't want to spend time in your lap."

"Not in *your* lap, anyway," Becca laughed, jutting a thumb at Teresa.

"He's determined to stay out of mine, too," Teresa said.

"He hasn't spilled the beans about those three-plus years in Israel?" Becca asked.

"All we know is, a very rich and well-connected Israeli woman ID'd him as her son, and because his face was so swollen and he was in a coma, the authorities took her word for it. She was someone you didn't argue with, or so they say. When he woke up, it took him a while to get his bearings. He says he just wanted to 'see how it all played out.' And that's what he did. From Carrie, we know that he received combat training, and according to her 'sources,' went on some secret mission as a mercenary, or—get this—an assassin."

"Really?" Becca wrinkled her nose.

"I think she was just being dramatic," Teresa said. "Laying it on thick, because she really wanted me to shun Liam and marry Paul."

"Thank God you didn't," Ali said.

After they filled Becca in on Paul's shenanigans, Becca said, "What a schmuck! Good riddance to bad rubbish."

Ulla appeared at the door of the house. "Excuse me, ma'am?"

"I'm 'ma'am' now?" Ali grumbled under her breath. "Yes, Ulla?"

"Um, could you pump some more?" She made a pumping motion, which made them all giggle.

Becca checked her watch and rose to her feet. "Look at the time. It's already three fifteen. I'm going to take a nap. Knowing Jean-Louis, dinner will be fashionably late, with many courses. I don't want to poop out on everyone."

"Good idea," Teresa said. "Sorry, Ali, I wish I could help." She pumped, but she seemed to be pumping something other than a breast. More laughter.

As Ali followed Ulla into the house, she thought, *Maybe it won't be so bad having this woman around. Now I can take a nap too.*

ALI'S EYES SNAPPED OPEN AT the sound of rummaging in the dresser. "What—?" It was Joe. She propped herself up on her elbows, and the covers fell away to reveal the worn T-shirt she'd been napping in—a threadbare garment Joe had thrown away. *Not very sexy*, she thought, though his expression said otherwise.

"Oh, sweetie, did I wake you? I didn't mean to." Joe gathered her in his arms. "Or maybe I did." He moved in for a soft, lingering kiss.

"What time is it?" Still sleepy and disoriented, Ali caught sight of the wall clock and broke into a wide yawn. "Oh, sorry!" She gave herself a little shake. "Five already. I hate to interrupt this delightful wakeup call, but I think we should go help out Jean-Louis. He's navigating the kitchen for the first time, and Tiger won't be much help with that."

Joe had quickly shed his jeans and crawled in beside her. "He'll just shoo us away. You know, Jean-Louis wasn't happy when I told him we'd hired him an assistant. Then I said we were more interested in his company than perfection, and he saw my point."

"That's good." Ali opened the last button on his shirt and started to pull it off.

Laughing, he rolled away from her and sat up. "First things first." He retrieved a velvet box from the top of the dresser and placed it in her hands. "Something for you to wear tonight. Happy birthday, darlin'."

She held the sapphire pendant up to the light, marveling at its brilliance.

"It's the color of your eyes." He draped it around her neck and when he finished wrestling with the clasp, he led her over to the mirror. "One of the colors. I can't imagine a stone that could capture all of them."

She gasped as she fingered the pendant. "And here I thought I'd never own anything so lovely as those pearls you gave me on our wedding day. Hmm … this outfit doesn't really do it justice." She pulled off the shabby T-shirt, leaving her upper half fully naked except for the necklace. All that remained were her bikini panties.

His grin turned wolfish. "Much better."

Laughing, she gave him a long kiss and took the necklace off. She gazed into his eyes. "You and I are going to get down and dirty, and I can't risk tangling or breaking your beautiful present. Thank you so much, sweetie. You don't need to give me bangles, of course. I love you no matter what."

"I'll remember that next time." He pulled her back onto the bed and gave her another kiss, a longer, deeper one that curled her toes. "Not that it will stop me."

Whatever he referred to—jewels, kisses, what he was doing now—she definitely didn't want him to stop.

# CHAPTER 19

——◆——

AN HOUR LATER, AFTER THEY'D showered, Joe reassured Ali, "I checked on the twins earlier, and all was calm. Or as calm as it gets with those two little dickens."

Ali struggled into her black jeans. Still too tight, but thanks to the stretchy material, comfortable enough. "I'm glad. I'm coming around to the idea of Ulla. It's hard to leave anyone new alone with your babies."

He kissed her on the cheek. "I know. I haven't been spending enough time with them, I realize that. They'll never get around to saying 'Dada.' Maybe they could handle 'Da'—like we called our father."

She stood in her closet and chose a gauzy white blouse to set off the sapphire necklace. "I hope they don't start with 'Ulla.' Kind of rolls off the tongue. How's it going with the new songs?"

"There's one that has promise. The demo is almost done. Just needs a tad more work."

"Why don't *you* sing it? Your speaking voice has gotten a lot clearer."

He brushed her hands away from the buttons of her blouse and opened the top two. "You're too modest. All buttoned up like that, the necklace gets lost."

Ever since pregnancy increased her bra size, Joe had encouraged her to flaunt her new cleavage, but Ali wasn't interested in drawing attention to herself. "Fine." She batted his hands away but left the collar open. "Don't dodge my question. No one does your music better than you."

"Maybe I could record it. I have no interest in another tour. We don't need the money, and that's the only motivation I can imagine. *Hmm*, are you trying to get rid of me?"

"You've found me out." She closed her eyes as he trailed kisses along her neck. "I'm dying to be left alone with Ulla while Liam and Teresa circle each other like horny coyotes."

Wailing erupted from the nursery.

"Duty calls." Ali pulled on her ankle boots and headed for the door. "Or maybe I should say 'doody.' I really appreciate having someone else to change their diapers occasionally. I'll meet you in the kitchen. We need to make sure we can still find all our gadgets and serving dishes once Jean-Louis returns to North Bend."

"It's not like he's going to put anything away. Tiger's the one you'll need to educate." His parting call was, "You realize he's just going to kick us out."

When Ali finally dragged herself away from the twins and was chased from her own kitchen, she found Joe outside, roughhousing with the dogs. "He sent you packing too?" he asked.

She laughed. "Thank goodness. I want nothing to do with meal prep tonight. He's got Tiger running ragged. I'm going to let myself be waited on like the queen herself." Coogan sprang into her lap the moment she sat down. "You little rascal!" she told him. "Doesn't he look as if he's getting away with something?"

Joe smirked. "He is. Liam has trained them not to do things like leap into laps uninvited."

"Funny, I was just talking to Becca and Teresa about Liam and laps," Ali said, seeing how Joe pricked up his ears. "It's nothing. I was comparing him to a wary cat. Anyhow … I feel bad about doing this dinner party without him." Harry laid his heavy head on her knee so she could scratch him behind the ears.

Joe lifted Coogan out of Ali's lap, set him gently on the ground, and rubbed his rump. "I left a message on Liam's cell phone. Reminded him about the dinner, in case he gets back in time. After all, it's his twenty-eighth birthday too. I said that the party would run late." He grimaced. "I should probably have left it alone. He's allergic to crowds. Maybe he'd rather just forget all about your birthday."

Ali frowned. "Or celebrate it with his new woman. This is hardly a 'crowd.' Except for Reynard, he knows everyone."

"Not all that well. Not even us."

They were both silent. "I need to work harder at drawing him out."

Joe slipped his arms around her waist and pulled her to him. "It takes two," he whispered in her ear. "He'll have to meet you halfway."

"I know."

"Did you get him a birthday present?"

Ali reluctantly pulled away. "A watch."

"What make?"

"It's called a Sea Wolf. Duncan said it's the best dive watch. What do you think? Too expensive? Not expensive enough? I didn't want to get him something super-pricey like a Rolex. Not that I'd spend that much of your money. I hope he won't turn it down."

He threaded his fingers through her hair, making her shut her eyes and heave a long, shuddering sigh. "What's mine is yours," he said in a low voice. "And don't worry, we can afford whatever. You're smart not to go too high end, even though Liam appears to appreciate some luxury goods." He paused. "That motorcycle jacket, for instance, which looks like something Jean-Claude Van Damme would kill for. If Liam doesn't want the watch, I'll take it."

"Your birthday isn't until November. Thank God. I have no idea what to get you."

He kissed her tenderly on the head. "You've already given me everything I want in the whole wide world."

*Maybe I* should *have gotten Liam a Rolex*, Ali thought. She recalled the elegant clothing he'd worn at that first dinner at Carrie's. *It's the thought that counts*, she reassured herself, though she only half believed that cliché. She wished she had a better understanding of this new Liam.

Becca appeared, fresh and pretty in a flouncy yellow sundress and white cashmere sweater. "I slept like a baby! Well, not like your babies. Like a proverbial baby. It's so quiet. I am *so* in love with this place."

"Port Townsend?"

"No, your estate." She settled into one of the deck chairs.

"Teresa gets the credit for that," Joe said. "She found it for us."

"She's a marvel," Becca said. "Too bad she can't get out from under Carrie's thumb."

Ali put a finger to her lips. "Shush! She's trying. We're all rooting for her. Speak of the devil …." Ali pointed to Teresa, who was walking down the hill from her cottage.

"I'd kill for that dress," Becca remarked, "but it's begging to be doused with red wine."

In the white, eyelet-lace sundress, Teresa looked like an angel. Her strawberry blonde hair curled fetchingly around her delicate features. *No wonder Liam is crazy about her*, Ali thought. *I just wish he could admit it to himself. Or that it made any kind of sense, given their different backgrounds. On the other hand, if Joe and I can work as a couple, anyone can.*

Joe let out a wolf whistle. "Nice dress. Catch!" He feinted throwing the dogs' slimy tennis ball her way, and she instinctively recoiled, arms raised in a defensive cross. "Fooled you. I'm not going to be the first to besmirch that dress. Can I get you a drink? White wine, I think. Or vodka and tonic."

"I'll have a glass of Cabernet."

Becca laughed. "Ooh, you do live dangerously."

Joe disappeared inside the house.

"Did anyone confirm with Reynard?" Teresa asked.

"He called," Ali replied. "I gave him the code to the main gate and told him to arrive at seven." She shivered. "Too bad it's already cooling down. I hope you have a sweater that works with that dress, Teresa."

"Ha ha." She checked the lawn chair before sitting.

"Don't worry," Becca waved her hand in a breezy fashion, "seagull poop is mostly white."

Joe arrived with a tray of drinks and beer bottles. "Depends on what they've been eating."

Teresa shaded her eyes, looking up the hill. "Someone's arriving. Silver Toyota Camry station wagon?"

Ali stood to get a better look. "Must be Duncan, Laurie, and Maddie." The dogs at her heels, she headed toward the parking area. After giving each one a welcoming hug, she introduced them to the dogs and pointed her father and his girlfriend toward their cabin. "Maddie, are you okay with staying at the house? We're fresh out of cabins."

"Of course. I'll try not to roam about at night, convincing you the house is haunted." Maddie flashed a dazzling smile that made Ali wonder why she hadn't been recruited by Hollywood. Or at least been hired as a commercial spokesperson.

Ali laughed. "It's too new—unless it was built on an ancient burial ground. Besides, the twins have a set of lungs on them that would scare off any ghosts. Join us when you can. The party's already getting underway."

Duncan gave her arm an affectionate squeeze. "Happy birthday, darlin'! Sorry for the delay. Long ferry line this time of year."

Maddie followed Ali down the hill. "I'm sorry. I feel like a party crasher."

"Nonsense. The more the merrier. You are welcome anytime."

After showing Maddie to her room, Ali returned to the terrace and settled into an Adirondack chair. The girl only vaguely resembled her mother, who, though thin, was tall and athletically built. Maddie also had the kind of spectacular breasts that drew everyone's attention, not just men's, and the rest of her was so petite and fine-boned that the effect was almost cartoonish. Had her father been a short, slight man, or was she a throwback to an earlier generation? Also unlike her mother, Maddie was polite, unassuming, and possessed a quiet confidence and charisma. Was it insecurity that made Laurie such a chatterbox? Ali didn't object to her personality on principle—the woman meant well—it was just so darned difficult for Ali to talk with her father with Laurie constantly dominating the conversation. Being Laurie's daughter would be a pain. How had Maddie turned out so well adjusted?

As Ali sipped her sparkling water with lime juice, she wished she could get away with at least one glass of wine. Not until she was done breastfeeding. After the twins were weaned, she wasn't going to miss the swollen breasts, though Joe might. *Men.*

# CHAPTER 20

REYNARD ARRIVED PROMPTLY AT SEVEN, and Ali watched as Joe walked up the hill to greet him. He drove a Mercedes, which seemed about right. He had to be well off. Anyone who wrote movie scores would be handsomely paid, surely. Ali thought about his question to Teresa about her work. Just because he was French, that didn't make him classy. In France, if you were talented and passed the gauntlet of tests and auditions, your education was paid for and you were practically guaranteed a place in your field. At the very least, a pianist could teach in a conservatory. Achieving success at Reynard's level was rare. His English was flawless, but he'd lived here a long time. He hadn't seemed to recognize their names when they met. Port Townsend was a small town, though not like Grover's Corners in *Our Town*. It might still have a rumor mill. Surely people would know that Joe Bob Blade and his wife and twin girls were living on the outskirts. *Don't be silly*, she told herself. *He's French. Why should he know anything about country music? You didn't when you first met Joe. Do you think he attends town forums and gossips about newcomers? Or subscribes to* People *or* Country Boy *magazine?* As far as she knew, they hadn't been written up in the local newspaper. Wouldn't Teresa or Liam have noticed? Why would they, since they didn't have the *Leader* delivered? She vowed to buy a subscription the very next morning. She hated being blindsided.

Reynard was greeting the guests with handshakes rather than three air kisses directed at alternate cheeks, which is how all the French people she knew—French Canadians included—did it. He looked even more dapper than the day before, in what appeared to be an expensively tailored suit with a T-shirt. She knew nothing about men's fashion, but she knew what she liked. He cut a fine figure. When he finally got around to her, he kissed her hand as if she were a grande dame. It was a bit much. Ali didn't like the way Teresa appeared mesmerized as Reynard greeted her, holding her hand too long. *What did you expect?* she thought. *You invited him. Admit it: you really want Teresa to end up with Liam.* But wasn't Reynard a better fit for Teresa? Like her, he was a classical musician, and he was probably in her ballpark, asset-wise. Liam would hate being a kept man. Reynard was the kind of guy Teresa should marry. Though no one would refer to him as a *guy*. Even Carrie might approve.

As the only stranger, Reynard was bombarded with questions. Ali wished she could hear his answers. Joe had switched on the outdoor sound system—choosing a discreet playlist of classical Spanish guitar, probably Segovia or John Williams—and there were at least three conversations overlapping. Ali headed over to where Teresa and Reynard were conversing, even though their body language was already enclosing them in their own privacy bubble. For Liam's sake, she wanted to track their encounter.

As she moved toward them, she was intercepted by Duncan, who enveloped her in yet another bear hug. She didn't mind. She was still thrilled to have found her birth father, and such a nice one at that. "How's my darlin'?" Her dad, with his rangy build, spiky salt-and-pepper hair, and single stud earring, looked more than ever like a dashing older rock star in black jeans and a Hawaiian shirt.

"Better, now that I'm back in Port Townsend."

"I can see why you love it"—he shooed away a fly—"bugs and all."

"I'm a little worried about yellow jackets." She pointed to the traps, half full of carcasses. "Those *should* take care of it. There's always one that evades the traps, and that's all it takes to ruin an al fresco dinner. They go crazy at the smell of meat and fish."

"I see you have pet deer as well." Duncan gestured toward the three deer grazing at the top of the hill next to the cabins.

Ali blew out a disgusted puff of air. "Deer are everywhere. The dogs usually chase them away, but I'm afraid even they are getting used to them. The fruit and vegetable garden had to be totally fenced in. They can leap tall buildings in a single bound. I'd love to expand the garden, but we'd need a taller enclosure—another project for Liam. My parents always gave us that hooey about idle hands being the devil's workshop. He learned the lesson too well."

"Or maybe he just gets bored easily. In that, he takes after me. Now that

I'm retired, I'm trying to figure out what to do with myself. Where *is* Liam, anyway?" Duncan scanned the horizon, as if mentioning his name might summon his long-lost son.

"On an overnight hiking trip … with a woman."

Her father raised his eyebrows. "Not one you approve of, I see."

She shrugged. "Who knows? He didn't identify her. Teresa thinks it's someone he met in yoga class."

Duncan grinned. "*Yoga?*"

"Long story. He only went to one class. He was protecting Teresa."

Duncan stiffened. "Does she need a bodyguard?"

"Not anymore." She started to explain about Paul and the accidents.

"I was at that dinner party, remember? Only … you never explained why Teresa was suddenly so furious at Paul. Now I get it. That guy he paid to wreak havoc is still around, right?"

"Paul must have warned him off. You heard how Teresa put the fear of God into him."

"Jeez." Duncan shuddered. "Was Liam really an assassin?"

"Once again, who knows?"

"What are we speculating about?" Laurie sidled up to Duncan with her daughter in tow. Both women looked as if they'd been posing in a British mod fashion shoot. Maddie was wearing white jeans and flats and a ruffled red blouse decorated with blue flowers. Her mother was chic as ever in black polka-dot palazzo pants and a white chiffon blouse that wafted about in the evening breeze.

Duncan automatically took her hand. "We're talking about Liam. Since he's not here, he's fair game."

Maddie pretended to shiver. "Ooh, Liam. What a dreamboat."

Ali snickered. "If you don't mind bobbing around on stormy seas."

Duncan raised a hand in protest. "I'm not convinced. I'm looking forward to getting to know him. If he ever lets me."

"You and me too." Ali glanced over at Teresa and Reynard, still engrossed in each other. "Will you all excuse me? I'm going to butt into a private conversation."

Duncan held her back. "Wait, is this a new flame for Teresa?"

"I hope not. See you guys in a bit."

Teresa didn't appear to resent the intrusion. "Ali, Reynard says that he and Jean-Louis have already met."

"Yes, I have been to La Fête Sauvage, the new one in Bellevue, and I had a friendly encounter with Jean-Louis. Little knowing we would one day socialize at such a beautiful house." He indicated the grounds.

Ali forced a smile. "We have Teresa to thank for that. She found it for us while we were in Paris."

*Ugh*, she hadn't meant to brag. Bringing up Paris like it was just another of their little getaways.

"I have not been to Paris in years," Reynard admitted. "I spend far too much time alone in my studio. That is the curse of the introvert."

Ali almost did a spit take. This guy was no introvert.

Teresa nodded. "I get it. You like socializing, occasionally, but mostly you prefer your own company. Have you found any likeminded souls in Port Townsend?"

"There are many artists and musicians, mostly older. They come here to retire. Or to escape the big cities. I have friends, but those my age visit only when there is a rare break in their busy lives. I find this an excellent place to work, because it allows me to keep my distractions to a minimum."

Teresa glowed in his presence. Ali wondered how much she'd had to drink. *Stop that, Teresa's a big girl*, she told herself. Once again, she longed for just one glass of wine. She wasn't a big fan of multi-course meals. She got too hungry and ate too many appetizers, leaving no room for the main course.

Reynard was talking about the movie he was currently scoring, an intellectual thriller by some director whose name she was supposed to recognize. She seized on a lull in the conversation to ask about his background. "When did you come to the United States?"

"I won a scholarship to Curtis, the music conservatory where Samuel Barber and Gian Carlo Menotti studied, along with many other masters. Then I spent time in Hollywood, though I was impatient to leave. Once I had met enough people, I fled. I followed a wo— I somehow ended up here." *Woman*, he'd almost said. "I love it. It is not too cold and not too hot. The people are discreet—they sense when to keep their distance." He gazed around the estate with undisguised curiosity.

Fortunately for him, Teresa volunteered the information. "Joe is a musician too. A country music singer."

Reynard was practically drooling for details. "It's a long story," Ali said, "but his health forced him to stop touring. Now he mostly composes for other singers."

"I hope he is not sick?"

"He's fine," Ali told him. "The problem was with his vocal cords, not his general health."

As Reynard scanned the property, she fancied she could read his thoughts: *He must have done very well indeed.*

Jean-Louis made a grand entrance with his usual over-the-top, bon-vivant enthusiasm—lofting a tray of hors d'oeuvres that he described in French. They had all studied the language. Joe was the least fluent, though Ali's French was no great shakes, either. She heard *foie gras*, oysters (*huîtres*) and wild mushrooms (*champignons sauvages*). As her guests savored the delicacies, they showered Jean-Louis with compliments.

Well-deserved ones. After three of the rich morsels, Ali was already full. More bottles of wine were produced from the wine cellar Teresa and Joe had stocked together—no point in consulting Ali. Next came crab cakes, green beans with slivered almonds, then Roast Magret Duck Breasts with black truffles and new potatoes. Salads came after, as was the European way, then the cheese course. By then Ali was just pretending to eat, taking a small taste here and there. There was only one particularly pesky yellow jacket, heroically dispatched by Duncan with a rolled-up *Newsweek*.

They switched on the gas firepit and heat lamps to ward off the evening chill. Ali produced a pile of large, colorful shawls picked up at one of the boutiques in town, and everyone wrapped them around their shoulders, including the men. She smiled at the sight.

"How are you holding up?" Becca asked Ali. "You've been hanging back. I've noticed."

Ali smiled reassuringly at her friend. "You know how I enjoy being a fly on the wall. It looks as if Teresa and Reynard are hitting it off."

Becca appeared puzzled. "Isn't that good?"

"I don't want Liam to get hurt."

"Liam?" Becca made a disgusted sound. "Don't worry about that boy. If he was so crazy about Teresa, why did he go hiking with another woman? Not to mention that, if you're looking for someone to go on backpacking trips, you wouldn't choose Teresa. Do they have *anything* in common?"

"What does that matter?" Ali huffed. "No one would point to Joe and me as natural soul mates. What about you and Jean-Louis? Sometimes people can be really different but just ... fit together. You know, opposites attract. I feel as if Teresa and Liam were meant to be."

Head tilted, Becca observed Reynard and Teresa. "Hmm, sure that's not wishful thinking?"

Ali sighed. "Maybe."

They looked up to see Jean-Louis, face florid from exertion and several glasses of wine. "What are you two ladies plotting? *Là, là*, come with us into the drawing room. Reynard is going to entertain us on the *pianoforte*."

*Hoo boy*, Ali thought. *There is no better way to woo Teresa.*

The group assembled in the rarely used, mostly cream-colored drawing room, with its art deco style. The floors were tiled, and Teresa had managed to find them lamps and sculptures with the distinctive geometric patterns and pleasing curves of the Belle Époque. *Great Gatsby, watch out.* Ali still wasn't sure how she felt about the elegant, museum-like room. She didn't like being reminded of those long winter months in Paris.

"A Bösendorfer!" Reynard rhapsodized when he caught sight of the piano, flashing his feral smile. "With such a magnificent instrument, one of you must play."

Teresa didn't step forward, and Ali didn't want Joe or she to be the ones to out her. She gave Joe a pointed look and saw that he understood. If Teresa admitted she played the piano, then she too would get roped into performing, and she clearly wasn't in the mood.

"We all play, some of us only a little," Joe said. Ali admired his discretion. "As a musician myself, I hoped to attract other musicians to my home."

"Yes, I understand." Reynard sat and executed a few rapid scales. "Wonderful. The tone is exquisite." He began with a slow piece Ali recognized as a Brahms intermezzo. Then, ignoring the scattered applause, launched into a spectacular showpiece.

With the final notes still vibrating in the air, Ali caught sight of Teresa's slack jaw.

Becca regarded Teresa with wide eyes. "What was that?"

"Chopin's *Étude Number One*," Teresa answered without thinking. "It's a bitch to play."

Reynard's eyebrows flew up. "You have played it?"

She froze, color blossoming in her cheeks. "No," she said with too much vigor.

He gave her his shark-toothed grin. "But you *do* play. Will you perform for us now?"

"Not tonight," she said in a tight voice. "It's unkind of you to invite comparisons. Will you treat us to one more?"

"Of course."

He played the first movement of Ravel's "*Le Tombeau de Couperin*," one of Ali's all-time favorite pieces. She couldn't help but fall—just a bit— under Reynard's spell. She watched as Teresa inched closer until she stood at his side, eyes riveted on his fingers. It was almost as technically showy as the

Chopin and totally captivating. Ali could hear Joe's teasing voice in her head: *So says Ravel's Number One Fan.*

The other faces in the room were equally rapt. *Uh-oh.* There was a new face, not so rapt. Not at all. He stood next to the door, body rigid and features set in stone.

*Liam.*

As if sensing his presence, Teresa looked over her shoulder and their eyes locked. Ali expected Liam to leave, but he stood his ground.

Reynard slowly lifted his fingers from the keys and rose to his feet.

Liam led the applause.

"*Bravissimo!*" Jean-Louis called out, surging forward to shake Reynard's hand.

"Liam!" Joe gave him a light slap on the back. "We're so delighted you could make it. Have you had dinner? There's boatloads of food left." The two men disappeared into the kitchen.

Teresa shot a helpless look at Ali, whose heart was breaking for her brother. She didn't for a moment believe he had fallen hard for the woman on the camping trip. She was just a distraction.

As the others swarmed around Reynard in the living room, Ali joined Joe and Liam in the kitchen. Liam had shaken off his initial reaction—shock, anger, jealousy?—and was digging into a large helping of roast duck with green beans as if it were the first hot food he'd had in months. Or had she imagined his displeasure at the scene in the drawing room?

"Did you have a good trip?" She gave him an awkward hug from behind.

"Fantastic." He leaned into her. "And this is fantastic too." He pointed at his clean plate. "Tell Jean-Louis we're holding him captive and forcing him to cook for us from now on."

Ali smiled. "I don't think Becca would take much forcing."

Jean-Louis swung around the corner. "I heard that. It's okay, I'll just open another restaurant here."

"I'll finance it," Joe said.

"*Prends garde, mon ami,* I might be serious," Jean-Louis said, shaking a finger at him.

"I might be too," Joe replied with a comic waggle of his eyebrows.

"*Please,*" Liam narrowed his eyes. "Maybe *I'll* finance the restaurant."

His voice was so deadpan that they all stared at him, dumbstruck. Ali resisted the urge to say, "You're kidding, right?" It was clear that both Joe and Jean-Louis wanted to say the same thing. The question "Could you, really?" would also be rude.

The awkward silence was cut short by the inopportune entrance of Ulla. "Oh, hello!" she said brightly. "I don't believe we've met."

Liam's eyes glittered. "No, we haven't." With a friendly grin, he came forward to take her hand, holding it too long. "I'm Liam. You are …?"

"Ulla," she cooed, suspiciously flirtatious.

"The new nanny," Ali explained in a flat voice. She didn't appreciate the supposedly gay nanny flirting with her brother. Liam was even more irresistible than she realized.

"Ah," Liam said, amused by Ali's reaction.

Teresa entered, registering the sight of Liam holding Ulla's hand.

Jean-Louis, sensing weirdness afoot, announced, "I hope you have all had time to regain your appetites. Dessert will be served … on the terrace. Everyone, out of the kitchen. *Aweille!*"

Ulla stood by expectantly, awaiting an invitation.

"Ulla, is everything okay?" Ali began to lead her away toward the nursery.

"Oh, yes. The babies are asleep."

"Good. You're doing a wonderful job. Let's go take a look. Can I bring you a plate of food?"

Ulla explained that she was a vegetarian, so Ali filled a plate with green beans, potatoes, and salad. "When you're done, come join us for dessert," she said before she could stop herself. She had no experience managing household help. She'd meant to say, "Enjoy," and leave it at that.

Once they were all assembled on the terrace, Jean-Louis burst forth, holding aloft the birthday cake, an elaborate dacquoise made with meringue, ground nuts, berries, and cream. Ali groaned aloud as Joe led them all in the birthday song, accompanying the group on his guitar.

Funny that Reynard had not urged Joe to perform. He obviously didn't realize that her husband was a classically trained guitarist and every bit as talented as Reynard himself. Reynard was used to hogging the spotlight, she guessed, rather uncharitably.

Becca and Teresa gave her their gifts first: Becca, a colorful skirt with a stretch waist, and Teresa, a blouse that happened to go perfectly with the skirt. Duncan's gift was an antique charm bracelet that included a tiny guitar, a diver with mask and fins, and a mermaid, earning him a huge hug. Finally she drew their attention to the sapphire necklace Joe had given her, and they all oohed and awed.

Ali handed Liam her present for him. "It's a Zodiac Sea Wolf Dive Watch. From both Duncan and me—and Joe, of course. Duncan says it's the best dive watch around." As Liam examined the watch, she added, "You don't have to be a diver. The point is that it's durable and waterproof."

Liam slipped the watch on his wrist. "It's the nicest gift, ever. Thanks, Alf." He looked up at Joe, then Duncan. "You too, Joe, and … Dad."

For a precarious moment, Duncan's eyes welled with tears. He recovered quickly and patted Liam on the shoulder.

To her surprise, her brother handed her a small package wrapped in tissue paper. It contained a carving of a beautiful girl with long hair and large eyes. Her arms were outstretched, and she was barefoot and dressed in a simple, calf-length shift that seemed to flow around her. "It's carved from olive wood. I found her in the market in Jerusalem. She reminded me of you."

Now Ali was tearing up. "You bought her for me?"

"For myself, originally. To remind me of you."

The touching scene was brief. If Ali had hoped Ulla would turn down the opportunity to join them, she'd underestimated the woman, who had changed into a low-necked silk blouse and pencil skirt.

"Who is *that*?" Duncan nodded at Ulla.

"Our new nanny."

His brow furrowed. "Did you hire her?"

"No. It was Joe."

Duncan scowled. "Shame on him. From Millie to Ulla—gorgon to siren."

Ali smiled at the images he evoked. Snakes for hair would not have made the woman any more frightening, at least to her. "All the Hestia au pairs must have been taken."

Duncan's brow furrowed. "Huh? My knowledge of Greek mythology begins and ends with Hollywood B-movies."

"Goddess of hearth and home. A virgin. Too boring for Hollywood. But no worries, Ulla is gay. Or so I'm told."

He cocked his head. "Joe believes that? I'm not getting that vibe."

"Neither am I."

Her dad gave her a sideways hug. "You have nothing to worry about with Joe."

She hugged him back. "I know. But Jeez, why is she all over Liam? Excuse me, I want to monitor this."

She went over to where Ulla was talking to Joe and Liam. She and Teresa exchanged looks, and her sister-in-law approached. "Uh, Ulla," Teresa said, "Joe says you have a partner—*Cindy*." She stressed the name. "Since you'll be living here for a while, won't she miss you?"

Ulla smiled sweetly, not bothered by the question, though Teresa had obviously meant to put the brakes on her flirting. "Cindy is in Germany for a few months. She has an au pair job there. This position will keep me occupied. And so pleasantly. I am *so* happy. The twins are *so* beautiful."

*I'm* so *glad* was on Ali's lips, but she stopped herself in time. How the heck was she going to navigate these shallow rapids? Ulla was more than competent, and she could definitely make Ali's life easier. If only Ali could get past the nagging feeling of *wrongness*.

# CHAPTER 21

———◆———

Teresa rolled over in bed and groaned.

She wasn't sure how much wine she'd drunk the night before, not more than three glasses. She'd eaten enough that she'd never felt more than tipsy. Still, the feeling she had now was akin to a hangover. *Regret*, that was it.

She had only just met Reynard, and yet she was already drawn to him. Especially after his sensitive performance had warmed her insides like a shot of brandy. His long fingers rippled effortlessly over the keyboard with an ease that would always elude her. So why had she felt so bereft when she caught sight of Liam at the back of the room, scowling?

Teresa was attracted to both men, for entirely different reasons. If only she could smush them together into one perfect specimen. Reynard appealed to her better instincts: her love of culture, her appreciation for sophistication and intellectual brilliance. He was undoubtedly good-looking in a refined way—not drop-dead handsome like Liam, of course, and at least ten years older. He was ethereal; Liam was elemental. You could float off into the heavens with Reynard. He'd flatter you, cajole you into doing his bidding, tickle your senses and play you like that piano. Maybe if Liam hadn't already rooted himself in her psyche like some invasive weed. She longed to be carried off into his lair, where she would be safe—at least from outside forces. Satisfied in some deep, animalistic sense.

*Will you listen to yourself?* she thought. *In the end, they are both just men. This type of romantic musing isn't fair to either one of them.*

For the first time since her return, Teresa considered retreating to Seattle. Despite her mother's presence—why did she need to "guide" her every

158 "

move?—her existence there was so much simpler. For a while now, she'd been skimming the surface of life with no deep, aching desires to contend with. Now, whoever she chose, she would wonder what might have been.

*What makes you think it's your choice? It's obvious Reynard is a much better match. Let the Ullas of this world contend with the Liams. Liam is too much man for you. He will burn over you like a wildfire. Not to mention that you overestimated your hold on him. He's already moved on.*

She groaned again. Ten minutes to six. Was anyone else up? She wanted to talk to Ali and Becca, get their take on the evening. But the husbands would be underfoot, and like most of their gender, they wouldn't have a clue. They wouldn't understand how she was being ripped apart.

Could Liam return from two nights with another woman and still be hurt by her? Fleeting as it was, she had caught the look of pain on his face, which instantly ruined the evening for her. Then he had turned his potent charm on that Valkyrie …. Why would Teresa worry about hurting someone like that? A man who always had a condom or two handy and could slip it on almost undetected, the way she applied fresh lip gloss. She wished she could slap some sense into herself.

*Coffee. Must have coffee. And human contact.* She was sick of her own company.

She showered and dressed simply in jeans, tennis shoes, a pink tank top, and an off-white fleece jacket, then made her way down the hill to the house. The dogs joined her almost immediately, after first demanding their tribute. She gave them each a quick rubdown. Already she felt better. Doggy therapy was the best.

In the kitchen, Ali sat alone at the counter in her fuzzy pink bathrobe. Her stoop-shouldered posture was not what you'd expect from the belle of the ball on the day after. Teresa hoped that her own private drama hadn't spoiled what was meant to be her sister-in-law's special day—not that Teresa had been the one to invite Reynard.

"Morning, Ali!" Teresa helped herself to coffee. "Did you sleep okay?"

She obviously hadn't. "Oh, you know." Ali gave a careless wave of her hand.

"Yeah, me too." Teresa took the stool next to hers.

"Last night was weird," Ali said. "In some ways it was great. But in others—"

"Yeah, I know." Teresa took another long sip. "Let's go outside, shall we? Someone might come in."

"Good idea. Should I get dressed first?"

"If you'd rather, although we're all friends and family here. And by the time you're changed, we might not be alone anymore."

"Good point." Ali followed her outside. They settled in the Adirondack chairs farthest from the door.

"So," Teresa began, "was Liam's entrance as weird as I thought?"

Ali didn't hesitate. "Uh-huh. He wasn't happy to see you hovering over Reynard."

"But he had just returned from—"

"I know, sharing, uh, gorp with another woman," Ali finished for her. "It's odd, all right. Then he and Ulla locked eyes like horny teenagers at a school dance."

"Also quite surreal," Teresa agreed.

"I'm past due for a talk with my dear brother." Ali appeared more flustered than the occasion merited. "I have no idea who he is anymore. I could swear he was falling in love with you."

Teresa didn't reply right away. "Something like love, perhaps. I don't trust it, not at all. Reynard, I understand. He's more from my world."

"I hate to say it," Ali said, "but you'd be *much* better off with someone like that." She cleared her throat. "On the other hand … maybe I'm partial, but I think whoever ends up with Liam will be lucky as hell. I would say who 'catches' him, but he won't be caught. It will have to be absolutely right. Like it was for me and Joe. No games. And I'm not talking about sharing the same likes and dislikes. Do you know what I mean?"

Teresa didn't know, not really. She did see that what Joe and Ali had was special, though Joe could be maddening—the way he'd hired Ulla without consulting Ali, for instance. He left her alone too much, even when she really needed his support. But those complaints were minor in the greater scheme of things. Because no one doubted for a minute how much Joe loved Ali, or vice versa.

"Liam is a puzzle," Teresa said finally. "I trust you when you say he's a catch … I mean, a prize. No, I don't mean that either. A good guy. A treasure."

"I hope someday you do understand, before it's too—"

"Mornin'!" Joe's cheerful voice rang out. "What a great time last night, right? And we're going to have an even better time today."

"We?" Ali cupped her ear as if she hadn't heard him correctly. "You're not going to sequester yourself in your studio?"

"No! I have house guests. I chartered a boat for whale watching." He struck a mock-heroic pose, coffee raised in triumph, waiting for her praise.

"That's great, sweetie." Ali popped up for a quick kiss on the lips.

Joe gazed up the hill toward the cabins. "I hope Liam will come too."

Ali caressed his cheek. "Don't count on it. I'm going to get dressed." After giving Teresa's outfit a critical once-over, she said, "You should be fine. When Becca shows up, tell her to put on something practical. It might be cold out on the water."

Try as she might, Teresa couldn't picture Becca in practical clothing.

For everyone but Teresa and Ali, the whale-watching trip was a success. Liam slipped away from the compound without sharing his plans, but the rest of them formed a little tour group—Becca and Jean-Louis, Duncan, Laurie, and Maddie. The captain surpassed even Laurie in loquaciousness, going on and on about orcas and their history in the area, plus all the other sea creatures they might see and how that varied from season to season. They could have dressed any way they liked, because the main viewing area was enclosed in glass, with only the outer perimeter for those who wished to venture into the cold wind and ocean spray. Teresa, slightly queasy and lulled into a near-trance by the vast expanse of roiling ocean, tuned most of the commentary out. Coffee and pastries were served, and sandwiches were available. It seemed like hours, but the orcas eventually showed up, first forming a flotilla of black fins, then breaching the water several times, the beautiful black and white bodies rising in energetic arcs and blowholes spurting, more than earning the cries of rapture from their human audience.

Teresa wasn't feeling the joy without Liam, and she could see that Ali was also missing her brother, wishing he were more interested in entering into the spirit of the close-knit group of family and friends. She pictured him coming home to only Ulla and the twins .... *Stop it*, she told her overactive imagination. *Just because Ulla enjoys a little attention from a handsome guy, that doesn't mean she's after him. Or even that she isn't gay.*

They returned at dinnertime. Joe made a side trip for fresh oysters and presided over an oyster fry at the grill. Liam didn't apologize for skipping the boat trip.

Ali and Becca spent much of the evening apart from the others, head-to-head. They were best friends who saw each other far too infrequently.

"You okay?" Ali asked Teresa as they cleared the dishes.

"Oh, yeah. Just tired, I guess. The charter was a great idea. It will be a breeze getting your guests to visit again. Now, getting them to go home ...."

"I want them to visit as much as possible. As you well know, Joe leaves me alone a lot. My conversations with the twins are a tad one-sided, and I don't really want to get to know Ulla any better."

"How did they do today? Did you worry about leaving them with the Amazon queen?"

"Sure, but Ulla came highly recommended. They seem as jolly as ever. Too bad I still wish I could fire her."

Teresa's laugh was rueful. "I totally understand. Hang in there and try to enjoy the extra time for yourself."

Ali gave her hand a squeeze. "I've seen Liam sneaking peeks at you."

*Dream on*, Teresa thought.

"Becca and Jean-Louis are leaving early tomorrow," Ali went on. "They are so busy these days. Liam said he'd take a walk with me tomorrow afternoon. How would you feel about running into us? It's a small town ...."

Teresa narrowed her eyes. "What are you plotting?"

"No plotting, honest. Just trying to normalize things. You two haven't said a word to each other all evening. We should dial down the awkwardness for when we have the place to ourselves again."

"When are Duncan and his crew leaving?"

"They'll be here all week. Tomorrow they're driving out to Lake Crescent to have lunch at the lodge and hike to Marymere Falls."

"You should tag along," Teresa said, seeing the longing in Ali's eyes as she stared at her father's new clan. "You love Lake Crescent."

"Not with them," Ali said in a low voice. "With Duncan, sure. I can only take so much of Laurie. Maddie seems great."

Teresa nodded in regretful understanding. "Like me and my mother, somewhat. Laurie has a strong personality. She needed more than one child to expend all that energy."

Ali regarded her skeptically. "How many children would have gotten you off the hook with Carrie? Five wasn't enough?"

"Four boys and *one* girl. With Mom's need to manipulate, she'd have needed three, maybe four girls. Controlling boys is way harder. A girl is eager to please. You can really whip her into shape. And for Catholic girls, guilt is mother's milk."

The sparkle in Ali's otherworldly blue eyes made Teresa wonder if she'd revealed too much about her resentment toward her mother.

"So," Ali prodded, "are you going to 'run into' us?"

Teresa hesitated, then shook her head. "No. I'm going to let you and Liam have your alone time."

Ali's brow furrowed. "Are you sure? I'm meeting up with him at three. We talked about strolling around Uptown, above the bluff, then heading down to Water Street at four for happy hour. If you're somewhere in the vicinity of Kelpies, you could stumble upon us."

"He'd know it was a setup," Teresa insisted. "He's not dense."

"When it comes to you, he is. He seems to think you're ready to marry Reynard."

"Yeah, sure. After only two encounters?"

But Ali could see right through her. "During Reynard's performance, you looked like a goner."

THE NEXT DAY WAS A Monday. Teresa was tempted to seek out another yoga class, merely for something to do. She was sadly lacking in inner calm. There had to be another studio in town. What about a bike ride? But no, she wasn't quite ready to take that giant psychological leap.

In the morning, she hung out with Joe and Ali, reading *Newsweek* and watching the new parents interact with Josie and Caryn, who were lying on a blanket in the playpen they'd set up on the porch. Ulla had the morning off but would return after lunch.

Teresa left the house shortly after Ali and parked near Manresa Castle, built as a grand residence then taken over by the Jesuits before being converted to a hotel. It was located up the hill from downtown Port Townsend. She didn't want to chance running into Ali and Liam.

Whenever you ventured far enough beyond the tourist attractions and B&Bs, you arrived at the areas where the working class lived. Closer to the papermill, the houses were cheaper construction and only dated back a few decades. Here the sulfurous stink of the mill was ever present, not just occasionally wafting on the breeze. Teresa guessed the neighbors didn't even smell it anymore.

Reynard's phone call after lunch had confused Teresa more than ever. She'd agreed to meet him for dinner the following Friday at his place. That meant she'd get to see where he lived. It also meant she'd be on his private turf, subject to unspoken rules. Would he expect sex so soon? If so, did that make him a creep or a normal guy? Reynard had a buttoned-up, almost fussy demeanor that reminded her of Paul, who'd been largely harmless in the first few months they dated. So much so that she'd started to wonder if he was even attracted to her. Paul had finally gotten around to making a clumsy pass. Their sexual encounters had been almost uninspiring enough to get a PG rating in today's Hollywood. Clearly he'd been a monk compared to Kilo. Practice had not made perfect. That was okay with her. After Kilo, ecstasy and anguish were inextricably linked in her mind. Paul was physically fit, clean, nattily dressed, and good-looking in an Irish American way. Rich and successful. Sex wasn't exactly unappetizing. More like the kind of meals served at Carrie's fundraisers—a little bland but palatable. One of their mutual friends had called them Barbie and Ken, but Teresa's first thought had been, *Not Ken. Alan.* The redhaired boyfriend of Barbie's friend Midge. Teresa was no Barbie, but she wasn't a secret Midge either.

Then Liam had come along and reminded her of what she'd given up.

A Frenchman like Reynard would surely know how to please a woman. But the memory of Liam's lovemaking was still fresh; Teresa needed time to warm up to the idea of someone else. In the French films she'd seen, sex was treated so casually it almost seemed beside the point. As in, of course you would sleep together as quickly and as elaborately as possible, even if you were twelve years old and your first lover was your twenty-five-year-old teacher. On the other hand, if you drew broad conclusions about American men based on the movies of, say, Woody Allen, chances are you would be surprised by the reality.

Why hadn't Teresa insisted their first real date be at a restaurant?

She chided herself for overthinking things. More to the point: was she excited? Yes, though not as much as she should be.

She rounded a corner and stopped at the sight of the pickup truck parked there. Old, yellow, and rusty, with dirty license plates that might have been worked over with a sledgehammer. Was it the same vehicle that had almost run her bike off the road? Sure looked like it. Had the numbers on the plates been purposely obscured before? They were legible now. She repeated the letters and numbers to herself enough times to commit them to memory, also taking note of the signs at the cross streets. Worried that the owner would show up, she hurried on.

# CHAPTER 22

———◆———

ALI ROLLED INTO FORT WARDEN at precisely three o'clock and saw Liam on the porch of the commanding officer's mansion whose sign read "Col. Norbert S. Byrne." He was sitting on the front porch next to an older man with crinkled blue eyes and a grizzled beard—balding but with a scraggly ponytail. She parked the silver BMW and walked over.

"Peter, meet my sister, Ali."

Ali shook his hand.

"Two peas in a pod," Peter said. "You got the same eyes. Blue as the night sky, a little eerie."

Ali laughed. "Uh, thanks. What do you and my brother do all day?"

"I don't know what *he* does the rest of the time, but here he helps me fix things. It's almost a joke. Any task I come up with, he can do. Doesn't matter how tricky."

"You pay him?"

Peter was struck dumb.

Liam seemed appalled by the suggestion. "No. There's no charge. It's fun."

Ali had no response for that. Why would Liam, who must need the money, work for free?

"Come on." He stood and placed a hand at the small of her back. "We're going for a walk, right? Peter, see you later."

The man took a swig of beer but stayed seated on the porch. "Alrighty then."

"What was that all about?" Ali asked when they were out of earshot.

165

"Peter's a friend." He looked at her car, then his motorcycle. "Shall we just walk around Fort Worden?"

"Didn't you want to end up at Kelpies?"

"I love that place, but not necessarily. I like walking the beach more than the streets. It's a lot more private."

"Are you going to tell me your secrets?" Ali joked, then wished she hadn't said it. It was exactly what she wanted.

Liam went on as if he hadn't heard her. "Peter's the head maintenance guy here, and he's in a little over his head. I enjoy helping him out."

They walked together in an uneasy silence along the sidewalk leading to the beach. "We haven't had much chance to be alone," she said finally. "It must be as weird for you as it is for me—being together again back in the States after everything that's happened."

He draped a muscled arm around her shoulder and gave it a gentle squeeze. "Worse for you than for me. I'm sorry I left you alone like that. It's just that … it took me months to regain my footing. I was in a really weird position. This woman had claimed me as her son. She was also taking amazing care of me. You'd have loved her—the mother we'd always wished for. Not someone holding her nose while she did the charitable work of raising us. I had every luxury. And after that explosion, I was kind of shredded." He absentmindedly touched the scars on his face.

"Do they bother you?"

"What?"

"The scars."

He shook his head and laughed. "Nah. I'm still a handsome devil. And even if I weren't, I wouldn't care. I'm not interested in women looking for perfection, money, or"—he made a face—"*breeding*." He clearly meant the word as the worst insult.

That described Joe's entire family. Reynard too.

"You don't like Joe?" Ali asked, holding her breath.

He looked startled. "Did I say that? No, Joe's great."

*Ah, we're talking about Reynard*, she thought.

"You said 'she *was* great,' " Ali said quietly.

"Huh?"

"The Israeli woman who misidentified you."

A shadow passed over his face. "She died."

"When?"

"A month before Teresa found me. After her death, I was at loose ends. She'd had cancer for quite some time but never told anyone until close to the end. The rest of my, uh, family, wasn't quite as welcoming, even after…." He didn't finish the sentence.

Should Ali ask him point blank? No. She wanted him to tell the story at his own pace.

When the silence grew too oppressive, she took the plunge. "Were you really an assassin?"

He burst out laughing. "God, some people," he practically spit out. "No. I could be," he added with a waggle of the eyebrows. "I've got the skills. If the person were evil enough. If they threatened someone I cared about, yeah." The look he gave her was laser sharp. "But I wouldn't get caught."

She tittered uncomfortably. "Now you're scaring me."

"I always scared you a little, didn't I?" he said, not without regret.

"Yes. You wouldn't let me grow up."

"By 'grow up,' do you mean join the Sexual Revolution? Are you sorry you didn't get to sow your wild oats while you were in high school? I know how guys think—only too well. It wasn't easy to watch you cast your pearls before swine at the UW." He scowled at the memory.

*Pearls before swine.* He had a point.

"What if I'd been drawn to someone nice in high school? Would you still have stopped it?"

He picked up a flat rock and skipped it, watching it stutter expertly out to sea. "I don't know. Guys that age are out of control, even the ostensibly nice ones." He picked up another rock and launched it like a grenade. It wasn't clear when it landed, if ever. "You know, that protective instinct wasn't entirely rational." The grim expression melted away, replaced by a smug smile. "In the end, you found someone real nice. Thanks in no small part to me."

Did he mean the ill-conceived ritual of her hike into uncharted woods that brought her to Joe or the years of unwanted protection against anyone who positioned himself as a potential boyfriend? Both, maybe.

She smiled. "In a roundabout way."

He didn't smile back. "Do you think Joe would have fallen for you as hard if you'd indulged yourself the way I did ever since I hit puberty? You see how well that worked out for me."

That was interesting. So he regretted his wild youth? Come to think of it, he hadn't exactly reveled in his relationships. Treated his girlfriends more like grim necessities, sort of like soldiers with their K-Rations.

Her relative innocence might have worked in her favor with Joe. She liked to think that what had made a novelty was her kindness and indifference to fame and wealth. She knew what Liam thought.

"What about you and Teresa?"

Squatting, he chose two rocks to skip. Once again, they appeared to skip into infinity. Finally, he said, "There is no 'me and Teresa.' "

"There could be."

He picked up a piece of driftwood as if considering its possibilities. Sculpture, weapon? It was shaped like a gun. Aiming it at a seagull, he said, "Bang." He let out a long breath and faced Ali. "I envy you. You seem not to realize how much background and breeding matter to a woman like Carrie."

Ali scoffed, "Joe never talks about his ancestors, but I'd bet they included more than one shanty Irishman."

"Teresa was all set to marry Paul."

Ali frowned. "The fat cat with major snob appeal turned out to be a skunk of the first order."

Liam hurled the driftwood out to sea and brushed off his hands. "Still …. We don't know what we come from. Duncan is a mensch, but he's also from a large, lower-middle-class family and didn't go to college. Our *mother*"—he blew out a disgusted breath—"is a giant question mark. We know nothing about her background or ethnicity. What we *do* know isn't good. At the time she abandoned us, she was a druggie. She had no maturity, willpower, or maternal instincts. If she developed those qualities later on, she hasn't bothered to let us know. Don't you worry that the twins might turn out like her?"

Ali shrugged. "Every family has at least one rotten apple, or one with a lot of worm holes. Besides, her own mom might have made Carrie look like mother of the year."

He gave her a long, measuring look. "Do you think we're mixed race?"

"Probably. Would that matter?"

"Not to me, certainly. To Carrie, undoubtably."

Ali couldn't help the huffiness in her tone. "Carrie is not the boss of me. Joe makes sure of that. Teresa would insulate you too."

Liam's classic features were set in a stubborn scowl. "When it comes to her mother, Teresa is sadly lacking a spine. When you marry a woman, her family is part of the deal."

Ali had run out of patience. "What happened in Israel?" she blurted out.

They faced each other, frozen, as the waves battered the shore and the seagulls screeched all around them. Ali hadn't meant to arrive at the point of no return. But here they were.

"I already told you." His tone was harsher than expected.

"Not much you haven't. I'm your sister. I have a right to know. I love you. If you're still hurting, tell me. Why couldn't you get word to me somehow?"

She tried not to cower under his unsettling gaze.

"You knew I was alive," he said.

Her breath caught in her throat. "I did," she managed to say, "but after too much time passed, I thought it might be wishful thinking."

"Sometimes it's hard to tell the difference." His eyes tracked a passing barge. "Between the voices and wishful thinking, I mean."

She waited for him to elaborate.

"I sent you the toy soldier."

"Yes, and I appreciated it. Why not include a note? 'Hey, Alf, I'm alive! I might be gone awhile. XOXO."

He picked up a piece of sea glass, examined it, then dropped it again. "I thought you'd get that I'd contact you when I could. And, if I'd continued on the course I was on, having a past of my own would have been a hindrance."

"What was that? What course were you on?"

"My, uh, mother had a significant … mission for me," he explained carefully. "That was why she sent me in for that training. She also wanted me to have survival skills, and if I was going to stay in Israel, as she hoped, I'd need a profession. A scary-looking security guard is always in demand there."

She pushed further. "What mission?"

He gazed out to sea, lost in grim reflection, his mouth set in a firm line. "Her daughter had been kidnapped. She was being held for ransom in a Hamas terrorist camp, but my 'mother's' spies had told her that her daughter no longer wished to come home. They said she had Stockholm Syndrome. That's when—"

"I know. When you fall for one of your captors."

Avoiding her eyes, he stated in a flat voice, "I got her back."

She waited for more details.

He gave a slow shake of his head. "You don't want to know."

"Did you kill anyone?"

He closed his eyes and took a deep, slow breath. Then he stuck his hands in the pockets of his motorcycle jacket, assuming a nonchalant air. "A few people. They deserved to die. They shot at me first," he was quick to add.

They were both silent as they tracked a new barge on the horizon. Ali spoke first. "Was she grateful?"

He hesitated. "My mother? Yeah, definitely. The daughter? Not then.

Getting her home wasn't easy. And she didn't appreciate my shooting her … *husband*. Though he was clearly a murderous devil. The wounds might not have been fatal. I aimed for his arms and legs. Might have hit an artery."

She gulped. "Did you have help?"

He thrust his hands deeper in the pockets of his leather jacket, pulling it tight around him as if to ward off the cold. "That would have been even riskier."

The wind was picking up. Ali shivered, not just from the cold. "Why did you do that for her—the woman who claimed to be your mother, I mean?"

"Because," he paused, "by then she *was* my mother. It felt real."

Ali found herself smiling just a little.

Liam's full lips curved upward as well. "Why the smile?"

"When we were considering names for the twins, I looked up the meaning of 'Liam.' It means 'fierce guardsman.' That's you, certainly. Did our birth mother hope that by giving you that name you'd be strong enough to deal with fortune's slings and arrows?"

"What about your name?" he asked.

"Mary Alice …. Mary seems to mean either 'sea of sorrow and bitterness,' 'rebel,' 'wished-for child' or 'lady of the sea.' Alice means 'noble one.' "

Liam shook his head. "From what we know of our mother—what Duncan told me about his one night with her—she was a beautiful party animal. Doesn't sound like the kind of person who would carefully consider the names of her children."

Ali broke into a devilish grin. "Now, 'Lord' …."

He blew out a disgusted breath. "Let's forget about my middle name. It's the kind of pretentious name ignorant people give their children."

Ali smacked her lips. "Liam Lord Ryan." She drew the names out as if announcing him at a grand ball. "Has a ring to it, don't you think? If your last name were Byron, that would be cool, because you've been a bit of a rake in your time. Lord Byron was quite dashing, maybe not so much as you." She gave him an affectionate shove. "It actually means 'loaf-keeper.' She would have chosen Earl or Prince or even Jesus if she was looking for grandeur."

"I do like to bake bread," Liam said, as if giving the matter serious thought. "I bet she just pulled names out of a hat."

Ali kicked at the remains of a small crab.

"Joe hired a PI to track her down," Liam went on. Seeing Ali's confusion, he touched the arm of her jacket and said in a gentler voice, "You didn't know? The trail is ice cold. No trace of her since she lost custody after leaving us in the car when we were five. She could be dead, or homeless, or living in another country. We might never know."

"Maybe that's for the best." Ali could just imagine what depths their mother might have sunk to since then.

Now they both stood in silence, shuffling their feet, hands in pockets.

"Ali," Liam said finally, "did I tell you what you needed to know?"

She wanted to say, *Why did I have to drag it out of you?* Instead, she asked, "Was your hearing affected by the explosion?"

"Eh? Speak louder."

"Was your—"

"Just pulling your chain." His laugh was more carefree than usual. "At first. I hear ringing in my ears sometimes."

"Do you need to get back to Peter?"

"Yeah, we still have something to finish up."

She tugged on the sleeve of his jacket. "One more thing." He gave her a wary look. "There's no tracking device, is there? For Teresa, I mean."

Liam grinned. "Nope. So far I just kind of *sense* her, you know?" She nodded. "When she's in imminent danger. I don't get much advance notice. What worries me is, someday I might be too far away to arrive in time."

*Ha*, Ali thought. *You have no intention of letting her move on.*

They had just arrived at Ali's car. They hugged, and she watched him stride away, back toward the commanding officers' mansions.


As usual, the dogs gave her a joyful reception and stayed close by her side until she reached the front door. Harry was running in circles, and Coogan was dancing on his hind legs. "Hey, big and little dudes," she told them, "you'd think I was Liam or Teresa. It's only me." She hoped her brother wouldn't be too miffed when he discovered she let them into the rec room when he wasn't around.

She wandered into the parlor, where Teresa was seated at the piano, staring at a sheet of notepaper.

"You missed quite the conversation," Ali said, sitting in one of the stiff armchairs covered in cream-colored floral chenille fabric. Such a beautiful room, this off-white, art deco parlor of subtle textures and beveled mirrors. Too bad Ali kept picturing it covered in plastic. Not a place for dogs or children, certainly.

"I've been busy," Teresa said. It was then that Ali noticed her hand was shaking.

"What happened?" Ali asked in a soft voice, her brain leaping to worst-case scenarios. Her brother? Joe?

Teresa gave her a startled look. "What …? Everyone is fine. It's just that I think I found the, uh, bad guy."

Ali relaxed a little. "The man who attacked you?"

"Not the man himself. His truck." She handed over the scrap of notepaper with the license plate number and cross streets. "He might live in the house where it was parked. It's a ramshackle rambler with peeling yellow paint."

"He might have been visiting someone," Ali said, "and Paul must have warned him off, but just in case … can I give this to Liam?"

"Sure." Teresa smiled and stood up. "Did you ask Liam about the dreams?"

Ali made a helpless gesture. "Hah! One revelation at a time. I did get him to open up about Israel. Those dreams—the ones where the phantom threatens me and Liam pulls it away before it can strike—I haven't had them in a while. Joe and I believe they stem from that period between being taken from our mother at age five and going to live with George and Emily at eight. Those years are just … hazy. A few vague memories of a harried foster mother with a revolving door of boyfriends. Perhaps Liam has blocked them out too. But I can't know that until I ask."

Teresa disappeared into the kitchen for a minute and returned with two glasses of water, handing one to Ali. "Maybe you don't want to know."

"Maybe I don't." Ali sipped her water, trying not to let her mind wander into that dark territory.

"Now, about Israel …." Teresa sat down opposite Ali and leaned forward, eyes bright with anticipation.

Ali told her about the mission and its outcome. When she was done, Teresa gasped, as if she'd been holding her breath all the while. "So he *was* an assassin of sorts."

"He didn't kill those men because he was paid to. He was defending himself." Ali didn't want to think what her brother was capable of.

"Of course," Teresa said. "Poor guy. That's a helluva favor to ask of anyone, especially someone you're calling your son." She stood and looked out the window. "Where's Liam now?"

"Still at Fort Worden. I hope he'll make an effort to connect with Duncan before he returns to Seattle."

Retrieving their empty glasses, Teresa headed toward the kitchen. "If he doesn't, there will be other opportunities. Closeness can't be rushed. Especially between men."

# CHAPTER 23

———◆———

Teresa thought of what Ali had told her about Liam, how he'd been convinced to risk his life for a supposed sister who didn't want to be rescued—all for the sake of a woman who wasn't really his mother but thought she was. Was claiming Liam as a son better than accepting that her real son was dead? Unless the woman was totally off her rocker, she must have realized her mistake once Liam recovered. He was so American, spoke not a word of Hebrew then. She thought of *The Return of Martin Guerre*, a French movie she'd seen in the '80s. A soldier, having returned to his village in the aftermath of war, claims to be Martin Guerre and takes the man's place as a husband. They'd remade the film a few years back with Richard Gere and set it during the Civil War, but Teresa hadn't seen it. She already knew it had an unhappy ending, and she avoided films and books that made her cry.

Hearing the roar of Liam's motorcycle and the silence that followed when he turned off the engine, she longed to go to him. If only they could return to the budding friendship that had been cut short by that first kiss and the amazing, mesmerizing, heartbreaking encounter after her near drowning. She touched her lips and closed her eyes, trying to summon back the sensations that had flooded her. Then she recalled her upcoming date with Reynard and told herself to get a grip.

Through the window of her cabin, she watched Liam walk down the hill. Duncan met him partway, and they stood facing each other, stiff and awkward, for several minutes. Teresa couldn't see Duncan's face, but Liam's head was cocked; he was listening. Finally, he nodded and smiled. They still hadn't shaken hands or made any physical contact. Keeping a few feet apart, they walked back up the hill together.

*It's a start*, she thought. *Ali will be relieved.*

AS THE WEEK WORE ON, Teresa noted a new ease between Duncan and Liam. She wondered what they talked about and wished she were the one walking alongside Liam. That Wednesday, Duncan accompanied Liam to Fort Worden while Joe remained sequestered in his studio, saying he was on a roll with a particular song. Duncan and his party planned to depart the following day, so on Thursday, the three men did a day hike together.

Liam didn't wear his motorcycle jacket on hikes. Though usually meticulous about storing his things in his own cabin, he'd left the jacket hanging on a hook in the mudroom. Teresa couldn't resist slipping it on and reveling in the rich, clean smell of leather and Liam. She put her hands in the pockets … and drew out a business card. *Uh-oh.* Her jacket-nuzzling had been innocent up until that moment. Now she was snooping. The card was for a woman named Lisette Manegold, who owned and managed a restaurant in Port Angeles. Café Lisette. Burning with shame and disappointment, Teresa slipped the card back into the pocket and returned the coat to its hook. She had *not* wished to know the name of Liam's lover, *nor* had she wanted the woman's existence confirmed.

"Teresa?" Ali called from the kitchen. Teresa did her best to greet Laurie and Maddie as if nothing had happened, and they all bundled into the car in search of lunch. With Laurie there, Teresa's preoccupied silence went unnoticed, except by Ali. Sitting next to her in the driver's seat, her sister-in-law shot her a worried look.

With the men busy bonding, Teresa and Ali had done their utmost to entertain the mother and daughter. First they'd taken them to a movie at the Rose, which had been restored and reimagined as a movie theater just a few years ago to showcase its retro charm—tin-tile ceilings, newly revealed murals, art-deco stained glass and the like. They'd also visited tourist attractions such as the Rothschild House and the Jefferson Museum of Art & History—places that held little interest for the men, although Teresa thought they'd all enjoy the museum. Visiting Victorian houses preserved along with their original furnishings was more of a girl thing. Women liked to imagine how other women had lived, and the Rothschild family was fascinating. The youngest daughter had never married, choosing instead to care for her mother and become a librarian—the spinster stereotype. Seeing how pretty she looked in the old photos, Teresa felt a pang of pity. What if Teresa had been forced to devote herself to Carrie's welfare till the end of her days? That had been the fate of many a youngest daughter back then.

Once settled in at the café, they finally coaxed Maddie into talking about herself.

"I'm between gigs—*acting* gigs, that is." She might have been confessing to slopping pigs for a living. With less embarrassment, she went on, "I'm also a caterwaiter, which takes up the slack, especially in the summer. Now that I'm a member of Equity—that's the actors' union—it's harder to get summer-stock work. They have to pay you a living wage, or sort of. LORT D theaters aren't required to pay as much because of smaller box office receipts, and that's mostly where I get hired. As a waiter, I've been doing tons of weddings this summer and have another long weekend coming up, starting with a wedding on Saturday. That's why we're returning Friday. I'm sorry about that; I know you were counting on Duncan to stay through the weekend. I guess I could find my way back by bus? Maybe I should do that." She paused to take a breath. "Oh, sorry—too much information." She blushed.

"Don't be silly, darling," Laurie said. "You're allowed to talk, aren't you? And don't worry about us having to leave early. We looked into your going home some other way, and the trip would take an entire day. Duncan and I can come out again on our own another time."

Teresa stole a glance at Ali, impressively neutral. Her sister-in-law missed the times before Duncan and Laurie became attached at the hip and she could have her birth father to herself. Now she was also competing with Liam for her father's attention—much as she rejoiced in their new closeness.

"What does LORT stand for?" Teresa asked.

"League of Resident Theatres," Maddie said. "I'm not sure I fully understand the system. LORT A-plus theaters are eligible for the Tony Awards—they pay the highest salaries. Then there's A, B, B-plus, C, and D. Anyway, most of my experience is at non-Equity houses, which means they don't have to follow the LORT rules. Pay is low, sometimes non-existent, though they usually put you up in some rathole or with a local patron. I have an agent now, fortunately. I get the occasional print work—real girl stuff, since I'm hardly model material."

"You're lovely," Teresa protested.

"Thanks, but too short and curvy."

Teresa thought curves like that were probably every man's dream. Never mind if they made you ineligible to model. Maddie's waist had to be nineteen inches.

The waitress arrived with their food. After she was gone, Ali said, "I used to do a lot of caterwaitering. I didn't mind the work at all. Once you put on that black-and-white uniform, you're invisible. You can observe human nature at its most uncensored."

"You mean when people have been drinking," Maddie chuckled. "There's certainly a lot of that at weddings. I use what I observe onstage."

"Straight acting or musical theater?" Ali asked as she hailed the waitress. "I could use more salad dressing."

"She's a triple threat," Laurie burst in. "She can act, sing, *and* dance. I loved her in *Annie Get Your Gun*. But she also has a legit voice."

Maddie's jaw tightened. Like Carrie, Laurie had the annoying habit of answering questions for her daughter with explanations that were embarrassing or not entirely on the mark. "She means I do more than belt," Maddie explained. "Belting is singing in chest voice—in a speaking range. Most dancers are belters. I was classically trained, which teaches you to blend your chest and head voices so there's no break." Seeing their general confusion, she added, "Man, I'm getting way too technical. Please, that's enough about me and my so-called career. Honestly, I'm on the verge of hanging it up. I'm not cut out for the uncertainty. And I'm getting long in the tooth. Stage work isn't much of a living, and soon they won't even consider me for television or movies. I'll just be too old."

"How old are you?" Teresa asked, wishing her chicken wasn't so dry.

"Twenty-five."

They all laughed.

Ali's brow was furrowed. "Really? Washed up at twenty-five?"

Laurie launched into extravagant praise for her daughter, which Maddie did her best to curtail but failed. How she'd graduated early from NYU's Tisch School of the Arts, having been admitted at age sixteen. The callbacks for movies and commercials. Her roles in Shakespeare plays. Maddie finally looked at her mother and said, "Enough already" in a voice that commanded silence. "End of subject. It's not a glamorous life if you never get your big break. Even then. You are boring them silly."

Laurie looked offended and Maddie, chagrined, though both recovered quickly. Teresa's own mother wouldn't have sung her praises like that, at least regarding her piano playing. She was only proud of her education and social accomplishments, which lately had been few and far between.

Maddie broke the silence. "Mom, I'm sorry. I owe the rest of you an apology too. I'm not sure what came over me. I know you mean well, Mom. Does anyone want to share a dessert?"

Laurie appeared mollified, and she and Maddie agreed to split a piece of chocolate decadence. Teresa ordered coffee and Ali a decaf, but they both gazed longingly at the cake when it arrived. Duncan's girlfriend and her daughter seemed blessed with hummingbird metabolisms.

Afterward Teresa took everyone to her favorite boutique, noticing how Maddie and Laurie lost interest in their finds after checking the price tags.

"But … you always look so chic," she told them.

"Goodwill and consignment stores," Maddie confessed.

"I remember those days only too well," said Ali.

Teresa hadn't realized how much Laurie and Maddie struggled financially. Hoping she wasn't overstepping, she hung back to surreptitiously buy the items they'd been admiring. Considering the amount spent, the saleswoman volunteered to deliver them to the house herself after closing.

Outside, the rain was falling in sheets, so they headed for home. Ali worried the men would get struck by lightning. "Don't worry. Liam will rescue them," Laurie said. "He's like Superman. Or James Bond. I swear, I wouldn't put anything past that man. If ever there was a person who can rescue himself and everyone else, it's him."

Ali laughed. "No doubt. I didn't appreciate him enough when we were kids."

After the other women retired to their rooms, Ali asked Teresa what had upset her earlier. Silently, Teresa led her to the mudroom. "Look in the pocket of Liam's coat," she said. "I wasn't snooping, I promise. Truth to tell, I was feeling it up."

"Perfectly understandable," Ali said. "I keep meaning to ask Liam where he got it. It looks like it cost a zillion dollars."

"It did, unless it's a knockoff, which I truly doubt."

Ali reached inside and pulled out the calling card. "Oh." She shot Teresa a look of sympathy. "Lisette is the woman he hiked with?"

"I'm assuming."

"Maybe now you can give Reynard a fair chance?"

"I'll try," was all Teresa could say.

Ali gave her a hug. "I'm going to take a nap. You should too. You look tired."

Tired didn't begin to describe the way Teresa felt. It didn't help that the cloud cover was low and oppressive, and a hard rain was falling. As she raised her hood and slogged up the hill to her cabin, she gave herself a pep talk. *You can't have Liam, you silly, silly woman. He's like chocolate decadence. If you did have him, you'd lose all control and probably be desperately unhappy. Then he'd leave you for a piece of white chocolate ganache drip cake.*

God, she should have ordered dessert. Hadn't she read somewhere that too much self-denial could backfire?

THAT EVENING AT DINNER, TERESA marveled at Maddie's patience with her mother. At least, unlike Teresa, when she reached her limit, she spoke up. Odd that Duncan didn't seem to mind Laurie's need to dominate every conversation. True, like Joe and Liam, he was a man of few words. Ali claimed that Joe could talk a blue streak when they were alone. Though Joe was five years older, Teresa recalled how, as a boy of eleven or twelve, he'd chatted up strangers. Fame had put the kibosh on the talking-to-strangers business, although he still did it if they didn't recognize him. If they did, he was gracious but careful not to encourage them. He'd never liked talking about himself, or, oddly, being the center of attention. Performing had been a business and a pleasure, and the adulation had never gone to his head. Now, sadly, his capricious vocal cords forced him to choose even his spoken words more carefully.

Though he could turn on the charm when necessary, Liam was, at heart, a loner with an instinctive mistrust of strangers. Teresa supposed that if she'd experienced similar life events, she'd be warier too. The "accidents" Paul engineered had thrown her for a loop. She'd never have guessed he'd stoop so low.

The clouds had passed, and the evening was clear and cool. They lit the tiki lights and turned on the heat lamps and firepit so only light jackets or sweaters sufficed. The meal was simple—barbecued halibut steaks with blueberry sauce served alongside asparagus with sweet potato fries. Bread, a cheese plate, and fresh berries. Ulla kept materializing on the sidelines at different locations, reminding Teresa of those pop-up cutouts rookie police officers used to train their shooting skills on cop shows. The nanny was angling for an invitation. Teresa couldn't help but notice how often Liam would go over to talk to her. Only once did he fetch Ali, which meant Ulla had no valid excuse to hover. Not even he invited Ulla to join them, perhaps knowing it would annoy his sister. Teresa watched his body language as he talked to the au pair. He didn't touch her casually or lean in too close, and though he smiled politely, he didn't laugh at anything she said. Ulla batted her long eyelashes at him, a simpering smile glued on her face. In her stacked sandals, she was close to Liam's height, and Teresa had to admit they made a striking couple. No doubt Ulla, unlike Teresa, could keep up on any hike. Lisette hiked. Was she an amazon like Ulla?

"What's up?" Ali said, startling her. "You're quiet tonight."

Teresa gave a frustrated shrug. "Between the men's hiking adventures and Laurie's baffling repertoire of trivia, there's really no need for my insignificant input."

"Ouch." Ali winced. "Duncan claims she calms down once she feels comfortable. Not that I've noticed."

"I bought her and Maddie some of the clothes they were coveting. Was I wrong? Now I don't know when to give them the stuff."

Ali laid a hand on her arm. "That was kind of you. Do you think they'll be embarrassed?"

"Frankly, yes. It seemed like a good idea at the time."

"Oh well, don't make a big deal of it. Wait till they're about to leave so they only have time for a simple thank you." She stood closer to the heat lamp. "Chilly out here tonight."

"Have you noticed how Ulla keeps appearing? She reminds me of myself when I was little and my parents were having a party. I lurked at the sidelines, wondering what I was missing. Now I know. Absolutely nothing."

Ali assumed an expression of mock-hurt. "You don't think our company is more pleasant than that? Unlike your parents, our position in society isn't at stake. I'm sure Carrie was busy vying for social dominance even then."

"You said it, I didn't." Teresa gestured toward Liam and Duncan, chatting like old buddies. "That's a promising development, don't you think?"

Ali nodded enthusiastically. "I love it. I can't wait to get the skinny from Duncan. Maybe Liam opened up even more to him about his past."

"But not *your* past. The missing years. You'll still need to take that up with him privately."

"I know." Ali hugged herself. "Brrr! Let's take the party inside." A commotion on the hill caught her attention. The dogs, sleeping on the terrace side by side, lifted their heads, then made a mad dash in that direction. "More deer," she explained, as Teresa searched for the source of the disturbance.

Ali made a face. "I'm surprised they still venture inside the compound, since they end up with the dogs nipping at their heels every time."

"They're slow learners, I guess." Teresa's gaze shifted to Liam, who was talking to Ulla again, seemingly oblivious to her welcoming body language. "I'm not one to talk."

"So, hot date tomorrow night?"

"I'm a little worried. It's at Reynard's house. What if he pounces?"

"Then you leave," Ali said with a broad shrug. "Simple as that. He's too classy to force himself on you."

"You think? Sometimes the 'classiest' men are the worst."

Ali widened her eyes in exasperation. "Then don't go. Most women would be panting over a guy like Reynard."

"I might be, if it weren't for Liam."

"Oh, Teresa." Ali gave her a sideways hug. "Don't wait for Liam. I see him flirting with Ulla, and then there's Lisette, or April—whoever he took on that backpacking trip …. I'd like nothing better than to see you two together. You would be so good for him. But would he be good for you?" She shrugged. "I don't know. He's dangerous, and I don't mean in the assassin sense."

"Don't worry about me. I don't shatter easily. I'm not made of glass."

Ali let that one pass, though her eyes expressed doubt. Switching off the heat lamp next to her, she told the group, "Let's go inside, okay? It's freezing out here, and I felt a drop of rain."

They brought in the plates, extinguished the torches, and turned off all the heat lamps. Ali put on the tea kettle and the espresso machine, asking everyone for their preferences. That was when Teresa realized she'd left her sunhat on the terrace and went to retrieve it.

She opened the door and turned to stone. Liam and Ulla were kissing. The image seared across her brain, inflicting an almost physical pain. Leaving behind her hat, she tiptoed back inside. Though in shock, she closed the door silently. She doubted Liam or Ulla had noticed her.

"What's wrong?" Ali's eyes widened. "You look like you had the scare of your life."

"Something like that," she mumbled. "Liam and … and … Ulla. Kissing."

"Oh no!" Ali clapped a hand over her mouth. "Really? Shame on them both! I knew I couldn't trust Ulla."

"It's not Joe," Teresa said mournfully. "Liam is free to do as he likes."

But Ali wouldn't be placated. Her cheeks were splotchy, and her hands bunched into fists like she was itching to punch someone. "Joe didn't bring her here to seduce my brother or lurk at the edges of my social gatherings."

Joe must have heard his name. "Uh-oh. What did I do now?"

Ali turned her fury on him. "Ulla is seducing my brother!" she said in a low, lethal voice.

Joe raked a hand through his thick chestnut-brown hair. "Yikes. Really? Are you sure it isn't the other way around?"

For a long moment, they all just stood there in helpless frustration.

Joe broke the silence. "I'd let her go, but she might claim Liam was trifling with her affections."

Ali pursed her lips. "What is this, a nineteenth-century novel? That woman doesn't have an innocent bone in her body."

"Calm down, sweetie. I didn't say I *wouldn't* let her go. I just can't do it this instant. I'd like to get Liam's take on what happened." He scratched his head. "What was he thinking? What about the woman he took hiking?"

Duncan stepped forward. He was alone for once, with Laurie and Maddie in the other room. "He didn't take a girl hiking. He took Kilo."

They all stared at Duncan in disbelief.

"Said something about 'keeping your friends close and your enemies closer.'" Duncan turned to Ali. "Don't mention it to him. And don't assume he's done anything wrong without hearing his side first. He's a sensible man." He cleared his throat. "Usually."

Teresa had had enough. She stormed off through the side door toward her cottage. Darn it, she was going on that dinner date tomorrow with a new attitude. She was *done* with Liam.

Fury kept her tossing and turning for hours. When she did finally sleep, she dreamed of being tied up and forced to witness that kiss again and again. Which made sense. Her sheets had her in a stranglehold—wrapped up like a mummy. She was also figuratively tied up in knots. Her subconscious wasn't going to let her forget Liam's … not *betrayal*, much as it felt like one. He had made her no promises. Call it *callous behavior*.

Come morning, she was all the more determined to move on.

* * *

LIAM TRIED TO CLEAR HIS head as he trudged up the hill to his cabin, rolling his shoulders to release the tension. It wasn't a full moon. Was Mercury in retrograde? One of his high school girlfriends had been into astrology, and some of that BS had stayed with him. Lately everyone but Duncan had been acting weird, as if afraid of ruffling his feathers. Tiptoeing around. Had they all been replaced by pod people? Had Teresa said something? He didn't think so. He had only himself to blame. He'd been withdrawing more than he should, purposely letting Teresa believe he had something going on with another woman. She'd started it. First Kilo, now Reynard. He had to admit, Ulla had surprised the hell out of him. No one was treating her kindly, so he'd tried, in his own way, to act decently, and look how that turned out? *No good deed goes unpunished, as the saying goes.*

Lately, even more than usual, Liam had been contemplating what a relief it would be to move out, find his own place. What was keeping him here, other than the dogs? Did Teresa really still need his protection or was he following an old script, the way he had with his sister? Once Ali turned sixteen, he should have allowed her to make her own decisions when it came to boys, consequences be damned. After all, he'd lost his cherry with an eighteen-year-old college student at the age of nine, soon after his body made that disconcerting, premature leap into adulthood. If he wasn't going to claim Teresa, how could he blame her for moving on, even if she made the most maddening, head-scratching choices? Just as Liam had managed to defang Kilo to his satisfaction, yet another wolf was sniffing at her heels. If you could call that snooty French fop a wolf. More like a fox. His name *was* the French word for fox.

*Damn it*, he needed to blow off steam. You didn't bike or jog in the dark here with so few streetlights. Even with a headlamp. Using the gym would disturb the others. He'd have to settle for pushups. A half hour later, he was still grunting away.

# CHAPTER 24

———•———

Teresa stopped by the house just long enough to say goodbye to Duncan, Laurie, and Maddie, who were predictably overwhelmed by her generosity. Turning down Ali's offer to take her into town for coffee, she filled a travel mug instead. No one had confronted Liam or Ulla, blissfully unaware of the havoc they had wrought.

Teresa had a ten o'clock hair appointment in Port Angeles. The bad dye job was history, and her hair had finally grown out enough that she could give it some style. She was quite satisfied with the resulting wavy, dark strawberry-blonde pixie cut. The shorter cut required little maintenance and didn't blow in her eyes when she walked in the wind. After strolling along the waterfront for half an hour, she realized it was time for lunch and wandered back to West First Street. And there it was: Café Lisette.

Teresa scanned the menu posted on the window then peered through the glass. At noon, the place was almost full, but there was a small unoccupied table toward the back. Just a quick cup of soup …. Cajun food was heavy, and Teresa preferred a light lunch. Lisette probably wouldn't even be around. As she entered, she squared her shoulders, trying not to skulk like a spy on her first secret mission. She wished she'd brought a magazine to hide behind. A fiftyish waiter with a bald crown and a broad smile brought her a menu, and she ordered the appetizer-size gumbo. As she waited, she noticed a statuesque woman with luxuriant raven hair standing next to the bar. She was wearing a pencil skirt and silk shell, revealing sleekly muscled calves and arms. Could *this* be Lisette? Her heart sank. This woman could probably run a marathon, climb a mountain, or kayak all the way to Victoria. As if sensing prying eyes,

183

she looked up to survey the room, confirming Teresa's fears that she was a stunner. Sparkling green eyes and a sensual mouth. Confidence to burn. Everything Teresa was not. When the waiter brought her order, she asked for the check, sneaking in the question, "By the way, is there a Lisette?"

"That's her next to the cash register." Fortunately, he didn't point.

Teresa handed him her credit card and ate the gumbo quickly, joylessly, and without really tasting it. When he brought the slip for her to sign, she scrawled her signature and filled in a tip and made a beeline for the door, feeling thoroughly chastised for being such a snoop. Could the fates be *any* more obvious? Liam was not for her.

On the way back to her car, she dropped by the music school, still for sale or rent. In the grim mood she was in, she told herself to get real—the school was just another castle in the air.

Back at the compound, she noted with relief that Liam's motorcycle was gone. She didn't want to run into him before she left for Reynard's at six thirty.

Choosing from her extensive wardrobe of sundresses, she put on a fitted, retro, pastel-pink number, '50s style with a wide ribbon decorating the bodice. It was dressier than the others and gave her an air of innocence. She had to admit that the shorter hair and slightly fuller cheeks from the few pounds she'd put on suited her, though the platinum-blonde chignon and rail-thin silhouette had been a type of armor. She felt disconcertingly vulnerable—like a virgin, and not in the Madonna "your love makes me want to be deflowered all over again" sense.

Reynard's home was an impeccably restored Victorian on the bluff overlooking the bay, just above the fountain where they'd met. She thought she recalled it being a B&B several years back. The Captain's Retreat, or some such name. When he greeted her at the door, his cheek kisses gave her a whiff of his subtle, heady French cologne. Whatever it was, it smelled good on him, and she relaxed a little. He was wearing a crisp white shirt, open at the collar, designer jeans, and short boots. Perfect for a photo shoot for *Vogue Hommes International*. The men she normally dated favored the preppy Polo shirts and khaki slacks of the casual golfer or the bespoke suits of the successful business executive. Teresa supposed this was what the well-dressed creative man wore, especially if he was French. He looked quite delectable. Had he taken special care with his appearance just for her?

As soon as she crossed the threshold, Reynard gave her a large glass of red wine. She was so nervous, she downed half of it in one gulp.

The Victorian-era décor was in too pristine a condition to be genuine or even refurbished. Pricey reproductions. Victorian style had itself been eclectic, borrowing from different periods. Ornate as it was—rich brocades and mahogany furniture and bookcases with carved embellishments of cupids and flowers and animal feet and heads—it all went together. And it was masculine, somehow. It could have been the interior of a nineteenth-century men's club.

Reynard flashed her a beguiling though hungry smile. "What are you thinking? You seem a little … off balance. Do I make you uncomfortable?"

He did, but what she said was, "I'm just in awe of your place. It looks like the set of a Merchant Ivory movie. I'm expecting your valet to enter any minute."

His booming laugh would have suited Mephistopheles. "No servants, only a cleaning service that comes once a week. Any domestic help I'd hire would not last long. I am difficult to please."

*Hmm*, she thought. *That doesn't sound promising*.

"I cooked dinner myself. You may be surprised to learn I am also my own—how do you say it?—handyman. These tasks relax me and bring new music into my head."

"And no one else would do it right," she joked.

"That's true," he said, unsmiling. "Are you hungry?"

"Yes. I tend to eat on the early side, unfashionable though that is."

In truth, she'd downed that first glass of wine too quickly and needed something in her stomach to soak it up.

Taking her hand, Reynard led her into the dining room, where she admired the long mahogany table with lion's-claw feet. "You own some beautiful pieces," she said as he pulled out the chair at the end of the table for her to sit. She pictured them eating at opposite ends, like aristocrats in movies, but he sat next to her. He used cloth placemats rather than a tablecloth, burgundy colored. So he could be practical.

"As something of a germaphobe, I prefer reproductions to antiques. I don't buy used books, either, unless they are very old."

Personally, she didn't worry about germs, but his confession didn't put her off.

The intricate dishes appeared quite labor intensive, starting with the appetizer of deviled eggs with crab. The main course was Veal Cordon Bleu—little coils of meat laced with cheese and coated with a light breading. She didn't dig in immediately, thinking a moment of admiration was in order.

Reynard misread her hesitation. "Do you not eat veal? I should have asked. That is remiss of me."

"No, I do, though rarely, I admit. I am just taking the time to appreciate your little works of art. They are quite beautiful. And these sauteed beets are delicious."

"Thank you." He took a dainty bite and savored it. "I studied to be a chef—it was my second-choice career. After I decided I didn't like being a teacher. I didn't know if I could support myself as a concert pianist. So few succeed."

"Yes, I know. My mother wouldn't even let me consider it."

"So you did study piano seriously?"

"Yes," she admitted. "I used to be somewhat proficient. Now I'm just a dilettante."

"A harsh word. I would never use it to describe you. I think you have a true passion for classical music."

"You haven't heard me play," she reminded him.

"I saw you listen. Will you honor me tonight?"

"Not if you give me too much wine." She raised her glass to him. "I don't play when I'm tipsy. For other people, anyway."

She couldn't read his smile. "Next time I will ask you to play first." He promptly refilled her glass.

*Uh-oh*, she thought. "It's a very nice wine," she said, leaving the glass alone for now. *Pace yourself, Teresa.*

He passed her the bottle. The label read E. Guigal Côte-Rôtie La Mouline 1990.

"Wasn't that named the number-one red wine of the year at some point?" Teresa asked him.

He raised his glass to her. "*Chapeau*. Number two in 1994. We are drinking it a little early."

She tasted the wine again. She generally preferred white wine, but she had to admit, this red was delicious. She was duly impressed by the trappings of his existence. Life with Reynard would be oh so hedonistic. Was that so terrible?

"Ever been married?" After the words escaped her mouth, she realized they were out of the blue and possibly rude at this early juncture. But really, she needed to know.

Reynard didn't gasp or recoil at her audacity, just blinked a few times before answering. "Twice. The first was to a costume designer, and our careers kept separating us. The second was a mistake. I was tired of solitude and allowed that to influence my decision."

*Hmm*, she thought. *He's making himself sound remarkably blameless.*

*On the other hand, he's not disrespecting the women either.*

"You?" He took a large bite and chewed while awaiting her reply.

"I eloped with my high school sweetheart. The marriage was quickly annulled by my mother."

"How old were you?"

"Eighteen."

"Your mother? Where was your father?"

"He died when I was thirteen."

"*Desolé*," he said. "You didn't fight this … action?"

What if she had? She didn't want to admit to her cowardly capitulation. "I suppose, deep down, I knew it wouldn't work. He was an aspiring dancer. I couldn't see myself living in a drafty garret like Mimi in *La Bohème*."

"Especially not like her," he joked. "Given her terrible health."

"What was your childhood like?" she asked. "You didn't say where you grew up. Paris?"

"Lyon. My childhood was … short."

*Like Clint Eastwood's convict character says in* Escape from Alcatraz, Teresa thought. Hopefully not *that* bad. Dare she probe further? Did he intend his answer to open the door to more discussion or slam it firmly shut in her face?

"So … not idyllic," she translated.

"I had no siblings. My father was a locomotive engineer and rarely home. My mother was in poor health. I left home at seventeen."

*Darn.* She should have let that door stay shut. Now she felt sorry for him.

Reynard pushed his plate aside and stood. That was when she noticed a second bottle of that delicious award-winning Syrah breathing on the mahogany sideboard. He picked up his empty glass and the open bottle. "Bring your glass," he said as they moved to the parlor, which was dominated by a Steinway concert grand piano. "I have other pianos." He gave a careless wave of his hand. "Some prefer a Pleyel or a Fazioli. I do have a Pleyel in my studio, but for the late Romantics, I prefer this instrument." He sat down and pounded out the splashy opening of the Grieg *Piano Concerto in A minor*. He gestured for her to join him on the bench. "Did you ever play those two-piano versions of concerti?"

She slid in next to him. Was it the wine or his playing? She felt more than a little dazed. "Yes. This one, in fact."

He raised his eyebrows. "Oh?"

Before she could chicken out, she plunged into the same selection. She didn't sound anywhere near as accomplished as he had, though she managed to hit most of the notes. It was a snippet she often used as a warm-up.

"Nice." He turned to kiss her. A light kiss on the lips that made her absurdly happy. She hadn't felt this way since her teacher had offered extravagant praise after her senior recital in high school.

Gazing into her eyes with soulful solemnity, Reynard framed her face with his long fingers and kissed her again. Caught up in the entirety of him—his scent, the exotic surroundings, his exquisitely European image—she kissed him back.

Teresa was almost sold. Almost. Part of her understood that a man like this would never take her seriously if she surrendered so easily. And yet, the cynic in her suspected his interest had more to do with acquiring a trophy than finding a nice girlfriend. A pretty, slim, chicly dressed, independently wealthy socialite. Didn't every guy who came from nothing want one? Not Liam. *Forget Liam.*

Reynard had lots of money. Or was he spending more than he made? He was clearly a perfectionist. Maybe he wanted an entrée to her social circle.

He was kissing her on the neck, running his hand down the front of her dress. The straps had both fallen off her shoulders, and the bodice was slipping. She pulled it back up. Why couldn't she just lose herself in the moment? If she had sex with him, that didn't make them common-law spouses. But it did mean they'd be tied together forever in some vague psychological sense. She had only made love to two men since Kilo—Paul and Liam. Liam …. She flushed at the memory. No *good* sexual encounter would ever be casual for her. She wasn't made that way.

Reynard writhed over her as they lay beneath the piano, his kisses ravenous. She wasn't repelled. He certainly had it over Paul. However, although tipsy from the wine, Teresa was clear-headed and not in any danger of becoming drunk with desire. She made a sudden movement that caught him by surprise, freeing her. Breathing hard, she crawled over to her purse and found her car keys.

She rose unsteadily to her feet and started walking backward toward the door. "Thank you for a lovely evening. You are amazing, and so is your home. I'll see myself out."

As she drove away from Reynard's majestic mansion, she couldn't help but ask herself, what was a man so handsome, gifted, and charming doing alone? He'd been divorced twice. Too fussy? Too much of a curmudgeon? Was he controlling? They'd only touched upon their respective romantic histories, which in her experience was unusual for a first date.

She had done her share of dating. She rarely went on third dates, because men seemed to believe that was the magic number for sex. If not truly interested, she threw in the towel after the second date. By the time she'd met Paul, Kilo was a footnote in her life story, and she'd thought the recipe for happiness was a good, appropriate man who didn't make her heart beat faster. Until experiencing Liam, she'd assumed no one could compare to Kilo. The yoga teacher and former dancer had done her no favors by working his sexual magic on her. He'd never explained how an eighteen-year-old had acquired such a thorough knowledge of a woman's body. Now she believed that Liam was the be-all and end-all. Compared to him, every man would come up short. Then there was the uncomfortable truth that despite Paul's respectable veneer, he had turned out to be a total creep.

*Shame on you*, she thought. She'd known that Reynard's invitation to dine at his home carried the implication of an overnighter. As the evening progressed, his intentions had become crystal clear. The twenty-first century was just around the corner, and most women would have gone with the flow. Teresa, on the other hand, couldn't help but see a lack of respect in his rush to bed her. At least with Kilo, she had a history. She had to admit that she'd been more tempted than she'd expected to be. She'd overestimated her ability to hold Reynard off. She thought about Liam and his plain cooking that suited her so well. He didn't do fancy concoctions like Veal Cordon Bleu or care which wines were touted by *Wine Spectator* magazine. Didn't both men reveal themselves through their cooking? Liam was a premium, juicy New York steak, and Reynard was a tightly wound, fussy Veal Cordon Bleu. Despite her upbringing, she was a simple girl. Could she thrive on so rich a daily diet?

If she let herself fall for Reynard, she might never pick herself up again.

*Liam*—she groaned aloud as her car headed slowly down the gravel road leading to the compound—that wasn't healthy either. Okay, so he'd hiked with Kilo—what was *that* all about?—not a woman, reviving her hope that he might have real feelings for her. Then he'd gone and ruined it all by kissing Ulla. Now that she'd seen Lisette, she was convinced Liam had slept with her too. They were too perfect for each other. Why would he hesitate, given the opportunity? He carried condoms in his wallet, ready for sex at a moment's notice.

When she arrived at the parking area next to the garage where the dogs slept, she turned off the engine but remained in the driver's seat. Soon the dogs were sniffing at the door, tails wagging hard and tongues lolling. They knew better than to bark. She opened the door and received their ecstatic greetings.

"Now, that's true love," she told them. Not that she wanted a man who would lavish her with affection, even die to protect her, for such scant returns—mediocre food, a bed in the garage, and the occasional gift of her company.

There was no sign that anyone was awake. Even when guests were present, the lights were out by ten thirty or eleven. The digital clock in her car read twelve o'clock. "Just when you were about to turn back into a pumpkin," she told the car and laughed in spite of herself, a nervous, thready sound. She searched in vain for Liam's motorcycle.

*God only knows where he goes*, she thought. *You'd always wonder, and it would drive you around the bend.*

# CHAPTER 25

<br>

The next morning, Ali watched Teresa as she plodded down the hill from her cabin, looking as if she carried the weight of the world on her shoulders. She was accompanied by Harry and Coogan. Sensing her weariness, they leaned against her legs as if to support her in a literal sense. Ali greeted her with a heartfelt hug.

Teresa hugged her back. "What was that for?"

"You looked like you needed it." Ali observed her sister-in-law with concern. Her dejected body language didn't bode well for her future with Reynard. Poor Teresa. Liam's roving eye was a trial not just for her, but for everyone. They still hadn't decided what to do about Ulla. Joe wouldn't consider letting her go until they knew the full story, and he wasn't going to prod a confession out of Liam. Far from seeking Ulla out, Liam was giving her a wide berth, so it wasn't as if they were in a relationship. Ali hated that the woman was dividing her family. Too bad she was so good with the twins.

With no clouds and a light sea breeze, Ali and Teresa could bask in the sun while they breakfasted on the terrace.

Ali took a sip of her tea and made a face. "I'll be sooo glad when I can drink coffee again. The twins are too energetic already. I don't want to risk stimulating them further with my breast milk."

"How long are you supposed to breastfeed?" Teresa asked.

"Oh, until they're three," Ali joked. "But seriously, it depends on who you listen to. I think it's okay to introduce formula now as a supplement, but the longer you can give them breast milk, the better the babies' immunity. Me? I'm going to call it quits at six months. By then they can start on solid food. So … wanna talk about last night? If not, I understand."

"Where is Liam today?" Teresa sounded grumpy. "Did he even come home last night?"

"Oh," Ali put down her mug, "the date was that bad? So bad that we're going to worry about Liam's whereabouts instead? Actually, he went on a camping trip … by himself."

Teresa heaved an exasperated sigh. "By himself? If you say so. Okay, let's talk about Reynard." She paused to sip her coffee. "It wasn't bad. In fact, it was kind of a fantasy date, if your fantasy is being a coddled Victorian woman willing to surrender all control to her man." The dogs started barking and dashed up the hill to greet the motorcycle. "Liam's home," she said in a flat voice.

Despite the carefully neutral tone, Ali couldn't help but notice the way her sister-in-law's entire being energized at the sight of her brother.

"Fantasy date for a masochist who's into acting out scenes from erotic Victorian postcards," Ali translated. "Go on."

Teresa described his mansion and the fussy, immaculate décor. "He cooked Veal Cordon Bleu. He was trained as a chef—his backup career if music didn't pan out."

"Interesting," Ali said.

"He served a very expensive wine … and made sure I was impressed with its quality. Then he plied me with it."

Ali made a wry face. "Uh-oh. Or should I say, 'Ah yes!' "

"Fine, joke all you want. I was tempted. He's quite the ladies' man. Only I wonder where all the ladies have gone."

" 'Long time passing …' " Ali croaked in her thin little voice.

" 'Where have all the flowers gone.' I remember that song. We sang it around the campfire at Camp Nor'wester."

"Camp Nor'wester," Ali laughed. "That would have been so cool! Isn't that the camp on Lopez Island that Paul Allen bought?"

"Yes," Teresa said. "He bought the entire Sperry Peninsula."

"Emily and George never sprang for sleepaway camp," Ali said. She bit back a snarky gibe at rich people and their playgrounds. Sometimes she forgot she was now one of them. "But don't stop now. Liam might appear at any moment, and I want to hear the skinny."

"Hate to disappoint you, but there is no skinny … or bare skin, anyway. I hightailed it home. I'll admit I was pretty worked up for a minute there. It was a struggle. My point is, why is Reynard single? You'd think he could have any woman he wants."

"Did you ask him? Maybe he's holding out for the right one."

"After two divorces, I'd proceed with caution too. The first ended because it was long distance and the second because he married out of loneliness."

"Huh. What else did you discuss?"

"Food, wine, music. General topics. His terrible childhood."

Ali leaned forward. "What?"

"Absent father, ailing mother, left home at seventeen."

Ali clicked her tongue. "Poor guy. Unloved with a lot to prove." *Jeez*, she thought, *that applies to Liam too. And Kilo. So what?* She'd bet Paul had a coddled childhood, and look how he turned out?

"It does seem that way," Teresa said. "He played the piano, then I played a little bit."

"Ah," Ali nodded, "musicians' foreplay. I have to admit, I got a little woody after I heard him play the piano here."

"Me too," Joe joked.

They all laughed. Ali looked at him askance. "How long have you been standing there?"

"Not long enough. I missed the recap." He took a seat in the sun. "Thumbs up or thumbs down? Or was he all thumbs?"

Teresa smiled, appreciating his light tone. "None of the above. I escaped with my virtue. This time. There might be a rematch. I haven't decided. I tend to give it at least two dates, because men usually wait until the third to pounce. Not in this case. He definitely pounced. Which makes me think he doesn't respect me or that his MO is just to seduce and abandon."

Joe raised a hand to stop her. "I wouldn't assume that. I sensed genuine interest. Maybe you're too irresistible. He couldn't help himself." He paused. "And you're funny with your 'seduce and abandon' thing. We do live in more permissive times, in case you haven't noticed. 'Seduction' implies an unwilling partner. He's a guy, though a fancy one. He naturally put everything he had into persuading you to stay the night. Can't fault him for that. Maybe he was too eager to clinch the deal."

Teresa pursed her lips. " 'Clinch the deal'? Men really think like that? I expect men *not* to assume I'm just going to fall into bed with them, willy-nilly."

Joe chortled. "You said 'willy'!"

"What are you, six?" Teresa gave his leg a playful slap. "Grow up!"

Ali loved watching the siblings tease each other. They needed to spend more time together. "What if we all go to lunch at Kelpies?" she suggested. "Liam too. The subject of Reynard will be verboten."

Teresa looked skeptical. "Do you think he'll agree? He's been avoiding me."

"I'll convince him," Ali said, jaw set in determination. "You'll have to learn to get along." She hit the flat arm of the Adirondack chair for emphasis.

"Damn straight!" Joe said, echoing her gesture then leaning in for a long kiss.


ALI WALKED UP THE HILL toward Liam, waving. "Hey, Bro! How's it hanging?"

He folded his arms, waiting, clearly wondering what she was going to ask of him. Something he wouldn't want to do, his stance said.

She was panting from exertion as she came up to him. An awkward moment passed before he relented and gave her a hug. "Mornin', Alf. What's up?"

She shaded her eyes against the sun. "How about lunch with your sister and brother-in-law? Kelpies?"

He narrowed his eyes. "Just the two of you?"

"Uh, no. Teresa too." If Ali hadn't been so winded, she would have held her breath.

"Okay," he said, much to her surprise. "What time?"

"Let's arrive early so we can get a place on the balcony. But first, I've been meaning to give you this." She handed over the piece of notepaper where Teresa had written the license plate number and street address. "Teresa was walking down by the papermill and ran across what she is fairly sure is the truck that almost ran her down. I'm surprised she didn't mention it to you."

If he'd been a Doberman, his ears would have pricked up. "I haven't spoken to Teresa in a while." His tone was flat, but his midnight-blue eyes glinted dangerously.

"I noticed," she said, taken aback by the sudden transformation. "She thinks he might live there. She described the house to me, but I don't recall the details. You'll have to ask her."

"Where is she?" came the gruff command.

"Down on the terrace."

"Let's go." He headed down the hill so quickly Ali couldn't keep up. She'd never known a man with keener protective instincts. When she arrived at the flagstone terrace, once again out of breath—she really needed to start running again in addition to her daily gym workout—Liam was already deep in discussion with Teresa.

"You're sure this is the truck?" he said. He might have been interrogating a stranger.

"The rear bumper had that same damage. If I saw the guy and the truck together, then I'd be sure, even though I've never gotten a look at his face."

"I know how he runs," Liam said. "I'd recognize him from that alone."

Joe was still sitting in the sun, observing Liam and Teresa with obvious curiosity.

"Sweetie," Ali said, "can we leave early for lunch? I want to make sure we get a place on the balcony."

"How early do mean?" Joe asked.

"Not until noon," Liam replied, "but we could get there early so we're first in line."

Joe nodded. "Let's leave at ten after eleven. I'll drive."

Liam checked his watch. "You grab a table. I'll meet you there. I have an errand to run first. Later." He walked back up the hill at a fast clip. *A man with a mission*, Ali thought.

Teresa and Ali watched him go. Ali caught her sister-in-law's sigh. "He's so … *manly*," Teresa said.

Ali laughed. "It's those broad shoulders and long legs. And the way his straight black hair flops over his forehead."

"And those dreamy blue eyes," Joe added in a falsetto voice behind them.

"Darn it, Joe!" Teresa said. "Don't make fun of me."

Joe ruffled her hair. "You make it so easy. Anyway, I think that's a good sign." He jutted his beautiful cleft chin in Liam's direction. "His interest, I mean. If he didn't care about you, he wouldn't react that way."

Lost in thought, Teresa didn't reply.

At eleven thirty-five, they were driving at a crawl down Water Street, trolling for a parking spot. The one they found was several blocks from the historic building that housed the pub.

"Typical Saturday," Joe remarked. He took Ali's arm and Teresa walked behind them.

They ascended the long flights of stairs leading to the hallway on the top floor, where they waited for the doors to open. They had been seated on the balcony for twenty minutes when Liam finally arrived. Something was up. Ali saw him rubbing his knuckles and said, "Are those bruises?"

He'd never looked more like his teenage self, in trouble over some after-school scuffle. "Yeah."

"Did you get in a fight?" Ali whispered after the waitress delivered their drinks.

"I stopped by the house where Teresa saw the truck," he admitted, sipping the beer Ali had ordered for him.

"And …?" She braced herself.

"I decked the guy. Told him we were onto him, knew who he'd been working for." He paused. "He tried to shoot me."

Ali felt like she'd been gut-punched. Joe and Teresa appeared dumbstruck. Liam might have been describing an annoying trip to the licensing bureau.

"I rang the doorbell, then stood well back so I could confront him from a distance. He obviously doesn't get many invited guests, 'cause he was holding a gun. Dropped it when my knife grazed his arm. He took off, and I took off after him. When he realized he couldn't outrun me, he threw a punch, so I clocked him in the jaw. Lights out." Liam wasn't bragging, just stating the facts.

"Did anyone see you?" Joe asked, somehow managing to convey both admiration and horror.

"Don't think so." As Liam scanned the menu, he chuckled, a sinister sound. "I scared the pants off him."

"You're sure you had the right guy?" Joe asked.

"Oh yeah. I could tell from the way he ran."

"You just left him there, unconscious?" Joe said. "What if he's dead?"

They were all speaking in hushed voices.

"He's not dead," Liam said as if the very notion was ridiculous. The waitress approached, forty-something, dyed blonde hair, skin sun-roughened. "Hey, Cindy. I'll have a cheeseburger, as rare as your conscience will let you make it."

She giggled and simpered. Liam had that effect on women. The rest of them had ordered already.

After she left, he continued, "I waited until he came to. He stood up and brushed himself off. Then he saw I was still there and ran back inside. Slammed the door." Liam glanced at each one of them, taking in their shocked faces. "What?" He gave a careless shrug. "The guy deserves much worse. I had to make sure he would stay far, far away from Teresa."

Joe nodded a little too emphatically. "Sure, I get it. You did the right thing."

The waitress arrived with their orders. It took a while for the atmosphere to normalize.

"How's the songwriting going?" Liam asked Joe.

Joe told him about his latest phone meeting with his agent Linc, how he'd had a few bites on the demo he'd sent out but was considering keeping it for his own album. Liam kept asking questions, steering the conversation away from himself as was his wont.

"Why don't you ever tell us what *you're* up to?" Ali asked, already regretting her querulous tone. "I, for one, would like to know. Other than punishing career criminals, that is." She grinned.

"Nothing much." Liam raked a hand threw his hair. "Still helping out Peter at Fort Worden. Reading a John Grisham novel."

"Which one?" Joe asked.

"*The Street Lawyer.*"

"Good?"

"Yeah. He's dependable."

"Can I borrow it when you're done?"

"Of course."

Ali still couldn't believe Liam had so casually knocked a guy out. Until the police came by late in the afternoon and took him away.

# CHAPTER 26

JOE LEFT TO PICK UP Liam at the police station around seven p.m. A neighbor of the man who had attacked Teresa had peeked through the drapes and witnessed the entire dust-up between Liam and Sam Grody, including Grody's brandishing the gun and Liam's knocking it out of his hand with a knife. Also the scuffle that followed.

The problem was, Sam Grody was dead. Someone had shot him in the head with his own gun. So far, no clues as to the culprit.

Liam was technically a person of interest, but Joe assured Ali he wasn't a serious suspect. After lunch he'd followed them home on his motorcycle, and they could all vouch for the fact that he spent the entire afternoon working on a table he was building out of an old door. Whenever Liam was working, the dogs stayed close by—he was definitely their favorite, with Teresa a close second—and you could hear the whirring and grinding of power tools throughout the afternoon.

Ali and Teresa were roasting a garlic-rubbed chicken for dinner, along with biscuits, mashed potatoes, asparagus, and a simple green salad on the side. They wanted Liam to feel cherished with comfort food after his ordeal, especially if there was any chance he'd be charged with assault.

"Have you heard from Reynard?" Ali asked.

"Yes, the next morning. He said all the right things. That he was sorry he rushed me, that I was special, worth waiting for, blah, blah, blah."

*Hardly a ringing endorsement*, Ali thought as she set the dining room table, it being too cold to eat outside. "All those things are true," she said.

Teresa appeared restless and irritable, worry lines etched on her forehead, as she handed Ali the cloth napkins. "I won't lie to you. Reynard's got skills when it comes to seduction. These are our prime years, sexually."

They wandered back into the kitchen. As she filled water glasses, Ali thought of her own limited experiences before Joe. She'd been ready to give up on sex by the time they met. Her first boyfriend Trip had no idea what he was doing or any interest in learning. She'd had high hopes for Luis, who had seemed hungry for her. He had some skills but lacked the patience or finesse to make her have an orgasm. And he'd turned out to be macho and possessive. She shuddered to think what might have happened if Liam hadn't been around to scare him off. Looking up, she saw that Teresa was waiting for her to respond. "And men reach their prime at seventeen. That always seemed unbalanced to me." After placing the water glasses on the table, she said, "I think I told you this already, but Liam went through puberty freakishly early. At age eight, he could have passed for fifteen. It must have been awful for him." Checking on the chicken, she said, "Almost done. We can take it out to rest in ten minutes or so. I think the guys'll be home soon."

Teresa perched on one of the kitchen stools, her posture rigid. "Liam was so … cold-blooded. When I gave him the license plate number and cross streets, I didn't expect him to leap into action."

Ali gave a little snort of laughter. "You didn't? If you really knew him, you'd have expected exactly that. I did."

"You're saying I basically loaded the gun and handed it to him."

"In Liam's case, it's more like, primed him for action. *He* was the loaded gun, with his mad knife skills. I think he missed his calling as a circus performer. Or a Hollywood action hero. He makes Arnold Schwarzenegger look wimpy." She placed a glass of water in front of Teresa. "Are you going to see him again? Reynard, I mean."

Teresa gave Ali a hangdog look. "I suppose so. On neutral ground. I'm not going back to his nest—excuse me, lair, den, I mean *house*. If he wants to 'date' me, he can take me to a restaurant or a movie theater. I don't want the evening's end to be a foregone conclusion."

Ali failed to suppress a smile. Teresa's crush on Liam was definitely not working in Reynard's favor. "Ah. You hoped against hope he wouldn't 'pounce,' but you were pretty sure he would. And he assumed that was your understanding when he made the date."

"Bingo," Teresa said, lowering her eyes in shame.

"Can you set some rules now? Tell him, 'We can get together again, but you must understand in advance, nothing will happen.' "

"Hah!" Teresa rolled her eyes. "Did you ever do that?"

"No," she replied, "but I'm an oddity when it comes to dating. My first boyfriend took two months to make a move. Luis—I won't call him a boyfriend—basically attacked me before we even left the dorm room. Even after Joe wrote that song about meeting me, he seemed to think he was doing me a favor by keeping his hands to himself. Jake"—she sighed—"I'm not sure even he knew what his endgame was. Other than to stick it to Joe. Our three dates before Joe resurfaced were hard on my ego. I felt like he was only going through the motions—that he wasn't really attracted to me. Unless he's gay. Is that possible?"

Teresa burst into startled laughter. "Are you kidding? No. Definitely not. I hope Joe and Jake find a way to bury the hatchet. I miss him. He has this wry sense of humor, and his charm is legendary, though different than Joe's. In James Bondian terms, Jake is Roger Moore and Joe is Sean Connery."

Now Ali was laughing. "Pete, the gay busboy at La Fête Sauvage, told us he'd only watch the James Bond films with Roger Moore."

"Well," Teresa said, "Roger Moore was elegant and ridiculously handsome, but he wasn't gay. He had four wives and three children."

"Okay, I can see marrying a woman once if you're gay—especially men of Roger Moore's generation—but not four times. Then … Jake just didn't find me attractive. I can accept that."

"That is weird, I'll grant you," Teresa said, "although the only women I've seen Jake with, other than you, were on the flashy side. Not flashy in the Rina Bakersfield mode," she explained, referring to Joe's former girlfriend, a country music diva who modeled herself after Dolly Parton. "I guess I mean trashy. You were a good girl. So it might just be that he didn't know what to do with you."

"I wasn't his type," Ali translated. She wanted to add, *And you're pretty sure Reynard isn't yours. So why give him another chance?* But she knew the answer. Teresa was doing whatever she could to distract herself from Liam. Only, it wasn't working.

For a time, neither of them spoke. Finally, Ali cleared her throat and said, "Liam was pretty heroic today, even if his methods were more caveman than the law allows. Could you possibly give him another chance? There's some pretty compelling evidence that he cares for you."

"What about Ulla?"

Ali made a face. "I don't think he's been seeking her out, do you? Just the opposite. That was—I don't know—an aberration. A moment of weakness. Nothing serious."

"If you'd seen Joe kissing her, would you feel the same way?"

Ali looked away. "Of course not."

"I rest my case."

By eight that evening, they all sat around the living room table, eating dinner. The general mood was subdued, with the exception of Liam, who ate heartily. "I'm not a suspect, and the police aren't going to press charges for assault. It's straightforward self-defense, though you could I argue I provoked the guy. Sam Grody has an extensive police record." He helped himself to more chicken. "This is great, by the way. Just what the doctor ordered. Assault and battery, breaking and entering, attempted murder. He lived alone. No one will miss him."

*Who put the nickel in you?* Ali thought. Her brother was positively voluble.

"Do they have any real suspects?" Joe asked.

"If so, they didn't tell me. I'm not their favorite person. They think I'm at worst a vigilante, at best a troublemaker. Can't say as I blame them." He took a large bite of chicken and chewed with relish.

As Joe and Liam theorized about who might have offed Sam Grody, Ali observed how Liam appeared to be avoiding eye contact with Teresa. Otherwise he might have caught the longing she hid so ineptly. His extraordinary efforts to pretend she wasn't present—other than a neutral comment here and there—just confirmed for Ali what she'd expected all along. That her brother was desperately in love with Teresa and would rather jump off a cliff than acknowledge his painful vulnerability.

One week later, as Joe and Ali were futzing around in the kitchen, the phone rang. After the initial "Hello," Joe was silent but didn't hang up. His expression turned stony, and he regarded the receiver as if it exuded a bad smell. "My brother-in-law was not *arrested*, or even a person of interest," he fibbed. "Sam Grody was threatening our family. After Liam confronted the man verbally, he attacked my brother-in-law physically. Liam defended himself in the least harmful way possible. Now Grody is dead. No one thinks Liam is responsible. *No one*. He was with us when the man was shot. That's all I have to say about it." Joe slammed down the receiver, then stared at the phone long and hard as if contemplating throwing it against the wall.

He turned to Ali, and his face softened. "Sorry. That was the press. The *Seattle Times*, actually. The reporter had read a tabloid story online about Liam. At least he had the decency to attempt to get his facts straight. I shouldn't have been so hard on him."

Ali gulped. "Oh boy, here it comes. We'd better look for the story online."

There was a computer in the small downstairs office Ali used, and it didn't take long to find the story on a country music gossip website connected with *Country Music Scoop* magazine. The photos popped out at them first: Liam with his shirt off, chopping wood, Teresa yelling at the photographer, Joe and Ali kissing on the terrace, the twins in the stroller beside them. The caption indicated that more photos would be appearing in the print version.

"How did they get these?" Ali was close to tears.

"Telephoto lens," Joe said through gritted teeth.

The headline read: THE FAMILY WOES OF JOE BOB BLADE.

Joe Bob Blade, his promising career as a country and pop icon sidelined by vocal nodules and fatherhood, has gathered family around him in his new life as a gentleman farmer in Port Townsend, Washington. Sources indicate he didn't realize that his new brother-in-law was a ticking time bomb. Supposedly killed in a terrorist attack in Israel, Liam Ryan turned up alive over three years later and moved in with his twin sister Ali and her new husband Joe. Joe and Ali met while he was recovering from surgery at his agent's cabin in the woods—a meeting that inspired Joe's number-one hit, "Babe in the Woods," which soon crossed over to the Pop Charts and won a Grammy. Fate brought them back together two years later, and they eventually married and had identical twin daughters who are just over ten weeks old.

Ali's brother Liam is almost more beautiful than she is. A black-haired, blue-eyed god. We'd pay to see him light up a big screen any day. But apparently he could give Sean Penn a run for his money in the temperament department. According to an inside source, he is a loose cannon with a mysterious past. Supposedly trained as an assassin in Israel, he is quite the fierce warrior. Now he is suspected of shooting a local drug dealer. Rumor has it the man threatened his sister-in-law, Teresa O'Connell, also residing at the family compound under Joe's generous patronage. Are the siblings, related by marriage, an item? Teresa is an eyeful herself, though not in Liam's class. The two would make a striking couple. Who can resist Liam? Unless, of course, he is convicted of murder. Does the ex-mercenary have an eye on Teresa's family money? It's unlikely that Teresa and Joe's high-society matron mother would approve.

"Ooh," Ali seethed, "I could just … just …." Sitting next to Joe at the computer, she put her head in her hands.

"It's mean-spirited on so many levels," Joe agreed, his own voice tight with frustration. "Somehow it manages to insult us all. *Gentleman* farmer. Where are the crops? Are they referring to the rather sad-looking vegetable garden? A rancher, maybe. With my herd of deer."

Ali ground out, "Who is the inside source? Ulla?"

"Hold on." Joe rubbed her shoulders and gave her a reassuring hug. "It could be, but there's no proof. A waitress might have overheard us, and there are others who know our business. Paul, for instance, though he'd have some nerve contributing to a story like this. He'd want to stay as far out of it as possible, lest it come back to bite him."

"Did Ulla sign a confidentiality agreement?" Ali asked.

"Yes, though I don't know how to enforce that without inciting further ugliness. The trouble with these gossipy articles, posts—whatever you call it online—is that trying to refute them just adds fuel to the fire. I gave the *Seattle Times* an official quote. I'm going to leave it at that. The story will blow over. I just wish we could make this innuendo-laden piece of dreck go away. Unfortunately, none of it is precisely false, other than the claim that Liam is a suspect and the gentleman-farmer BS. I could make them issue a retraction with regard to Liam, but then I'd have to engage—which is what they want. Time will absolve him quickly enough."

Realizing that she'd been slumped over in the chair, Ali squared her shoulders. "What can we do, then?"

"Remain calm, for one," Joe drew in a deep breath, "and alert Liam and Teresa to this before it blindsides them too."

At that precise moment, they heard Teresa's voice call out, "Anybody home?"

"Here," Ali yelled back, "in the den at the end of the hall."

When she saw their faces, Teresa frowned. "Uh-oh. What now?"

Ali stood and offered Teresa her chair. "I think you'd better sit down." Joe rolled the desk chair away so his sister could view the screen.

As she read, Teresa turned tomato red. "Ugly, *so* ugly. And the photos. I hate to think what else they have. Can we sue?"

"I'm still a celebrity." Joe gave a disheartened shrug. "I can't opt out of that. I could try suing, of course, but it's not worth the energy. It's out there. The internet is forever."

"Who's the 'inside source'?" Teresa spat out. "Ulla?"

Ulla must have sensed a negative energy in the air because she appeared at the door, all innocence. "I heard my name, and you all sound upset. Has something happened?"

Without speaking, Joe invited her to read the screen. She paled. "Do you believe it is I who spoke to them?" she said, hurt. "I would never do such a terrible thing."

It was difficult not to believe her, Ali thought. If Ulla was lying, she was an awfully good actress. On the other hand, the article hadn't mentioned her, and that was weird. With all the other nastiness, surely the reporter would have found a way to implicate the beautiful au pair, perhaps as part of a love triangle. Unless she'd contributed to the story. However, Joe appeared mollified, and she wouldn't accuse the woman without proof.

"It's okay, Ulla," Joe said. "We don't think you're part of this. How are the twins doing?"

"They're sleeping soundly. I was just going to ask if you could spare me for an hour or so. A friend asked me to join her for dinner."

"Yes, that's fine," Joe said, distracted. He was already scrolling down to make sure they hadn't missed anything.

When they were sure the au pair had left the house, Ali said, "They didn't mention Ulla in the article."

"I noticed," Teresa said.

"You think that's significant?" Joe asked. After giving it some thought, he added, "I suppose it is. But we have no proof. And firing people these days isn't easy. Given the present circumstances, it might drive her to 'tell all'— whatever that constitutes, in that we have no idea what happened between her and Liam. Or the tabloids might conclude the firing indicated that she has some sordid role in the household other than childcare."

Liam was the last one to pop his head in. "I saw Ulla leave, and I received a phone call from the *Seattle Times*. How did they get my number?" His jaw was set, and his body seemed poised for action.

Joe offered him the desk chair. "Someone has a friend at the police station, I guess. Happy reading. You might want to count to ten first."

Looking vexed, Liam sat down in the chair and rolled up to the computer screen.

Ali pointed to the wall clock. "It's after five. I'm uncorking a bottle of wine. And I'm going to have a glass. One glass isn't going to spoil my breast milk," she said in response to the worry in Joe's eyes. "We all need it."

Having finished reading, Liam said, "I'll need something stronger."

"I'll have whatever you're having," Joe said, following him into the kitchen. "Do you know how to make a Long Island Iced Tea?"

* * *

DINNER WAS A RANDOM AFFAIR of leftovers. No one spoke much, other than to express their helplessness. Liam left first. Teresa heard the dogs greet him and figured he'd sought their comfort. She could use a little of that. The thought that her mother was reading the article delivered a fresh surge of rage and frustration. It was only a matter of time before someone pointed it out to her. Perhaps a preemptive strike was in order. She'd have to raise the possibility with Joe sooner rather than later. But right now, she wanted to be alone with her thoughts. The article had been mostly accurate when it came to her and Liam, certainly with regard to Carrie's reaction. She thought of her dinner date tomorrow night with Reynard, who'd been in Los Angeles on business. They would be going to a restaurant. Did they dare? Surely the gossip wouldn't have spread all over town yet. She hadn't seen anything in the Port Townsend *Leader*. It would surely have appeared in the Community Record.

Dining at Reynard's house would be safer, technically. On the other hand, the Belle Monde Brasserie was an intimate, expensive restaurant located south of the main tourist area. The reservation was in his name, and their acquaintance, relationship—whatever it was—wasn't known outside the household. Unless that "inside source" struck again. She'd take the chance. This date would be the deciding factor. Should she go forward or throw in the towel?

She was crazy about Liam—she didn't think the word "love" should be used unless it was returned—but she believed that without Liam in the picture, she could have fallen for Reynard. It was just that Liam had come along first. A relationship with him was out of the question, even more so now. Everyone would assume he was after her money. And *something* had happened between him and Ulla or Lisette, maybe both, even if it hadn't been serious.

# CHAPTER 27

———◆———

Reynard picked Teresa up in his Mercedes. She was relieved to see that Liam's motorcycle was gone.

"Nice car," she said as she slid into the buttery soft leather of the seat and admired the walnut wood details.

"It's a C-forty-three." His appreciative once-over flooded her with warmth. "You look lovely as ever. What a beautiful dress."

"Thanks." She had bought it at Neiman Marcus last year, a silk-blend, spaghetti-strap number by an obscure designer who called herself Miomolani. It clung to her body down to her thighs with a few inches of flouncy hem that fell just above her knees. Tiny red flowers on a light-pink background. Cream-colored stacked sandals not fit to walk farther than a block or two in. She wasn't sure why she had taken such care with her appearance. *Perhaps it's because Reynard does*, she thought, admiring his black suit jacket and crisp, open-collar striped shirt. His clothing was made of the finest fabrics, and everything was exquisitely tailored. Did he ever dress down? She pictured Liam as he had appeared at that first dinner at her mother's, which now seemed a very long time ago. In his European-style casual wear, he could hold his own against Reynard. And she'd like to see Reynard rock a muddy T-shirt and torn jeans. Liam would even look masculine in drag. *Stop it*, she told herself. *Forget about Liam. It's not fair to Reynard.*

When they reached Hastings, the car sped up to ninety miles per hour. Her gasp and death grip on the car door grab handle made him slow down. "Sorry. I couldn't resist. This car loves to go fast."

*So does its owner*, she thought. "I can see that," she said in a schoolmarmish voice.

"I'll be a good boy now." He shot her an impish, sharp-toothed smile.

*God, I hope so.*

"Your family has had a rough week."

*He's not beating around the bush.* "You heard."

"Liam only came in at the end of the dinner party, but I did get a sense he was somewhat … untamed."

"He is a tad overprotective, but his heart is in the right place." *The rest of him too*, she thought.

Reynard didn't reply immediately. "Did he kill the man, do you think?"

"Definitely not. He worked in the garage the entire afternoon. We can all vouch for him. Besides, he had no reason to kill him. He'd already scared him half to death."

"That impresses you." A statement, not a question.

"Yes, a little. He's an impressive person in many ways."

"I'll take your word for it. I would have used the word 'brutish.' "

When they arrived at the restaurant, the maître d' greeted them enthusiastically, as did the waiter. No one appeared to regard them as anything other than well-appointed customers. The waiter pulled out a chair for Teresa. She'd never been to the Belle Monde Brasserie. It was surprisingly formal for a restaurant on the Peninsula. The menu was in French. "We can bring you an English menu if you'd like," the waiter said.

"We both speak French," Reynard told him curtly. Teresa bristled. *No need to be rude*, she thought. Though the waiter did seem a little dense. Reynard had a pronounced French accent. Perhaps he'd offered the English menu for her benefit.

When the waiter returned, Reynard ordered escargot for two and cassoulet. Teresa was about to protest, then thought better of it. She would have preferred lighter fare. "They are both specialties of the house," he explained, and she nodded uncertainly.

Next came an involved discussion with the sommelier. Teresa didn't bother to chime in, even though she was no dummy when it came to wine. She didn't mind letting him choose. Her main expertise was in California wines rather than French, which Reynard obviously preferred—no surprise.

"The finer establishments stock their cellars with special vintages you can't obtain elsewhere," he explained, somewhat pompously and wholly unnecessarily. Teresa was no stranger to navigating a wine list.

As they sipped their admittedly delicious wine and savored their escargot, he asked, "Other than your unfortunate early marriage, have there been other, uh, serious relationships?"

Teresa swallowed a mouthful of snail and replied, "I was engaged until recently."

Her answer startled him into silence. Was he waiting for an explanation?

"Why did you, uh, break it off?"

She smiled. "You're assuming I called it quits."

"Didn't you?"

"Yes, for a number of reasons. He was my mother's choice."

Reynard's laugh was a terse, "ha-ha." "That's reason enough."

"And you?" she asked cheerily. "Other than the two divorces you mentioned?"

"Do you think worse of me?"

"I was surprised to find you available. I'm sure you have your choice of women."

"I am used to women offering themselves to me," he said, as if such behavior was shameful. "You are … twenty-five?"

"Twenty-seven."

The question, which seemed apropos of nothing, made her ask in turn, "And you?"

Lips pursed as if mildly offended, he replied, "Thirty-nine."

That sounded about right. But thirty-nine was the Jack Benny's "forever age," and she wouldn't put it past Reynard to shave off a few years.

The waiter served the cassoulet, a smaller helping than she'd expected. Plenty of food, of course, though less than restaurants usually served on the Peninsula. She thought about La Fête Sauvage and wondered whether the concept would fly here. Obtaining wild game would not be a problem.

"Do you like it?" He sounded less confident now, and rightly so, considering he'd robbed her of any say in the matter.

"Yes, it's wonderful."

"This man you were engaged to …. For how long?"

She had to think about it. "A year? Thereabouts."

"Why such a long engagement? He agreed to this delay?"

"He had no choice. I'm not sure why anyone needs to get married these days in any case. Unless you want children."

"You don't? Want children, I mean."

*Hmm*, she thought, *maybe. Just not with Paul.* "I don't know," was what she told him.

"At twenty-seven, you will have to decide soon."

"Tonight?" She meant it as a joke, but she heard the snark in her own voice and bit her lip. Why was he pushing her about children?

"Of course not," he said, with a chuckle that sounded like a cough.

The waiter brought the salad course next, then the cheese plate. She was more than sated, but she nibbled on the salad and tried a tiny sliver of each of the cheeses. Reynard had a hearty appetite for such a slim man, so she assumed he was athletic. Maybe he played soccer with the other expats in the area. She couldn't picture him in hiking boots and a backpack.

"Do you like to hike?" she asked.

"Yes," he said, much to her surprise. "Not backpacking. I am too fond of cleanliness and a good night's sleep. I also enjoy kayaking. You?"

"I'm a walker, not a hiker, but I could be convinced. I have kayaked before, a few times. Perhaps now that I'm here—"

"You are planning to stay?" he broke in.

She hesitated before answering. "I'm at a strange juncture in my life. In Seattle I was always helping my mother with her causes. Here I'm free, but I need an anchor, something to give me purpose. I thought I could teach piano, perhaps run a music school. I saw one in Port Angeles that's for sale."

She hadn't meant to confess all this. She hadn't even known the dream was serious. Until now. She saw that his mouth had formed a moue of distaste or disapproval.

"You don't really want to teach, do you? If the student is gifted, then yes, but so few are, and in Port Angeles you are unlikely to find talent worth your energy." He paused. "Have you ever taught?"

"Well … no." In light of that fact, her plan sounded like the height of stupidity. She didn't appreciate having that pointed out.

"I'm sorry," he said quickly. "I have offended you. It's only that I am practical. I did have to teach when I was younger. I found it extremely frustrating. You may well be different. I do think you should try teaching first before you buy a school."

"You're right, of course." She sighed. She hated to admit it. "As someone who was not allowed to study piano seriously, I imagine there are others out there who would appreciate the opportunity. Especially since I can afford to provide scholarships." The truth was, she could teach everyone for free without breaking a sweat, but she wasn't going to tell him that.

"Of course." Taking her hand, he rubbed the palm in a way that was embarrassingly intimate. The waiter arrived, and she pulled her hand away.

The intrusion clearly annoyed Reynard. "Yes?" he snapped.

The waiter recoiled. "Excuse me, *monsieur.* Will there be anything else?"

"No," was Reynard's curt reply. "The check, please."

She hoped he was a decent tipper. Or was he one of those men who liked to find the service wanting on the slightest pretext and punish the waiter accordingly? That wasn't her business. If she ever came back to this restaurant, she'd tip lavishly.

Much to her dismay, he drove them back to his house before asking, "Will you join me for a nightcap?"

The dinner had left her ill at ease, and she was uncertain how to respond.

He leaned over and kissed her, encircling her waist and running his fingers up her back until they found bare skin. She shuddered.

"Come in," he said in a silky voice.

"Please take me home." She put a hand on his chest to hold him off. "I don't like to be rushed."

He looked annoyed, also startled when she opened the car door and got out. "Good night, and thank you for dinner." She called Liam on her cell phone. He answered immediately.

"Come get me?" she pleaded. "I'm just above the fountain."

"Right away."

Liam's Harley zoomed up at the same moment Reynard's Mercedes rolled forward to retrieve her. She hiked up her skirt to climb on as he handed her a helmet and his leather jacket, the cashmere sweater being totally inadequate for a late-September evening on a motorcycle.

"You know the drill," he said in a chipper voice.

She wrapped her arms around his wonderfully solid chest and didn't look back.


WHEN THEY REACHED THE COMPOUND, Teresa released Liam with some reluctance to dismount the Harley, return his jacket, and smooth the hem of her dress. At least she knew she didn't want to see Reynard again. The relief of that clarity washed over her.

"You were on a date."

"So what?" She sounded defiant.

"With that French poodle."

The snarky remark made her laugh. "If he's a poodle, then you're a Doberman."

"Fair enough." His eyes roamed over her with a disconcerting and not unwelcome hunger. How many women had he looked at that way—dozens, hundreds? She didn't care. "You look … stunning," he said.

She gave in to the gravitational pull of him, and he responded immediately.

They were kissing, tasting, hands roaming, bodies striving for ever-closer contact. The straps of her dress slid from her shoulders, and if the dress hadn't been so tight, she would have shrugged it off. She felt him pulling at the zipper, willing him to succeed. Her fingers raked the hard muscles of his stomach, feeling the light dusting of black hair she already knew was there.

The dogs arrived, barking joyfully, startling them out of their frenzy. They reluctantly pulled apart, and she rearranged her clothing.

"Nothing has changed," he said, breathing hard.

"I'll tell you what has changed." She grabbed him by the shirt. "I love you. I don't care what anyone thinks. We can make it work."

"You're … delusional. Of course I want you, more than want, *crave* you …." His breathing was ragged. "The fact remains, your mother would do everything in her power to pull us apart."

"She can disinherit me for all I care. My investments are not in her control. Besides, I don't need so much anymore."

"How much did that dress cost?" He rearranged one of the straps on her shoulder.

She shielded the dress with her hands, as if defending the affronted garment from attack. "Not as much as you think, and I haven't bought a designer dress in over a year."

"You love me so much you date other men." Bitterness leaked from his words.

"I tried to like Reynard. You keep insisting you're not an option."

She had him there. The dogs were sitting, watching them attentively, heads following their exchange as if refereeing a prize fight.

"What if your mother disowns you?"

"She won't."

"Don't be so sure."

"I'm her only daughter." She took a step toward him.

"Don't." He held up a hand, palm out, to stop her. "I have no willpower when it comes to you. We've been together once, and the memory is still fresh. I might just haul you off to my cabin right now. And although I think you'd let me, you'd regret it."

"I wouldn't." She stamped her foot.

"You would," he insisted in a harsh voice. "You talk a good game, but when it comes right down to it, you'd never marry someone like—"

They swiveled about at the sound of footsteps and saw Joe ambling toward them. "What's up?" he said, trying too hard to appear casual. "I was just coming back from the studio, and I heard voices." After ostentatiously checking his watch, he turned to Teresa. "You're home earlier than I expected. It's only ten."

"Liam rescued me."

She couldn't see Joe's face clearly in the dim outdoor lighting, but she noted how his body stiffened. "Did that jerk try to force you?"

"Nothing so dramatic. It might have come to that, I suppose. I didn't stick around long enough to find out. More likely it just would have been a wrestling match with a sore loser. He'd have given up, eventually."

The mask-like faces of the men told her they believed otherwise.

"How did you get there so quickly?" she asked Liam.

"I was at Kelpies," he replied, "and I drive fast."

Watched over by Joe, they retreated to their separate cabins. Teresa knew her brother didn't disapprove, just wanted to give her breathing space after her disastrous "date." Her heart was still thumping in her chest, as if to say, "I'll just go get Liam; feel free to stay here!" She heated water in the coffee maker for tea. Why was Liam being so stubborn? She didn't want anyone else, was convinced she never would. Yes, her mother would have a fit, but what else was new? She'd eventually come to realize there was much more to Liam than his brute strength and combat skills.

*Like what?* the devil on her shoulder responded. *She'll grow to respect him as a handyman and protector? Stop caring that his only degree is from a junior college?*

# CHAPTER 28

———•———

Joe and Ali were breakfasting alone on the terrace, the dogs lying at their feet and the twins gabbling in their bassinet stroller. Ali was starting to believe Joe's contention that they had a secret language.

"What are we going to do once it's too cold to eat out here, even with the heat lamps?" Ali said, sipping her tea. "The dogs will miss us."

"I don't know why Liam insists on banishing them from the house," Joe said. "They're well trained. We can keep them off the furniture and out of the bedroom."

Caryn began fussing, and Joe picked her up. "What is it, little sweetums?" he said in his baby-talk voice. "You need some attention? You need Mommy?"

Ali sighed. "She wants you." She resumed their conversation. "Liam's mighty stubborn. So, what happened last night? You promised to explain in the morning."

Joe frowned. "The second date did not go well."

"Good," Ali chuckled. "I wasn't looking forward to having Reynard in the family. Talented as he is."

"Me neither. I have a bad feeling about the guy."

"So …" Ali prompted, "Liam and Teresa?"

"Something was going on. I didn't get there soon enough to be sure. There was a definite crackling in the air. All the pheromones, you know." He sipped his coffee. "The dogs intervened first, fortunately."

"Why 'fortunately'?"

"Don't get huffy. Liam isn't ready to admit Teresa is worth the trouble."

"*The trouble*," she repeated.

"It was one thing for Mom to welcome you into the family. You're beautiful and were—before I got to you—relatively innocent, she knew that from her investigator. She'd already braced herself to accept Rina as a daughter-in-law, and rich, talented, and famous as Rina is, she's the type of woman who sets Mom's teeth on edge." There was a mischievous gleam in Joe's eyes. Ali knew he sort of enjoyed ruffling Carrie's feathers. "Mom holds men to different standards."

Liam appeared out of nowhere, like one of the stealthy American Indians he so admired. "Caught the tail end of that conversation. Something about Carrie and her standards."

Joe gestured toward the house. "Help yourself to coffee first. The subject of my mother requires liquid fortitude, and it's too early for Bloody Marys."

"Who says?" Liam headed into the kitchen and returned with a giant mug of coffee. Ali wondered if he'd poured a swig of whiskey into it. Not that she suspected her brother of being a morning tippler, but these were trying times.

As if reading her mind, he told her, "I don't drink in the morning."

"Of course not," she said, too emphatically.

"Carrie and her standards …" Liam reminded Joe.

"She expects whomever Teresa chooses to be rich, from the 'right' kind of family, and overeducated." Joe was counting the qualities on his fingers.

"Well, I'm rich enough, even for her." Liam might have been confessing to a weakness for potato chips.

As he no doubt intended, the casual remark rendered both Ali and Joe speechless.

Liam grinned. "Don't look so shocked. My Israeli 'mother' deposited a large sum of money for me in a Swiss bank account." He paused. "That was part of the reason I'd worn out my welcome. The rest of the 'family' didn't take kindly to sharing their fortune." He added quickly, "There was plenty left. I didn't steal anyone's inheritance. And I earned it, believe me."

Joe finally found his voice, though it was huskier. "How much are we talking?"

"Two million or thereabouts. I know it's not in your family's ballpark, but I don't have to go job hunting anytime soon."

Ali whistled and broke into a delighted smile. "That might bring Carrie around."

"Don't bet on it," Joe told her, "but it will help." To Liam, he said, "When were you planning to tell Teresa?"

Liam shrugged. "Why should I tell her at all?"

"Because sooner or later, you're going to accept the fact that the two of you belong together. And Teresa's worried Carrie will think you're a gold digger."

Liam downed the rest of his coffee with a scowl. "Listen, there is no 'me and Teresa.' I'm not about to face the gauntlet of her family. She and I are too different. They would never accept me."

Joe gave him a sidelong look. "Who is this 'they' you refer to? Ali and I are totally on board. Edward and Jake barely talk to us as it is. David has his own problems; he'd be the last person to throw stones. Carrie appears to be scrutinizing our relationship for cracks every time she visits. We've done without her approval. You can, too."

Liam had taken up a fighting stance, minus the raised fists, reminding Ali of the teenage rebel she'd known and loved. "Teresa's been blowing hot and cold. She might want me in her bed, and she likes to throw that word 'love' around, but I don't believe she'd marry a guy like me. Not when all is said and done."

Josephine started to wail, and Ali rushed to pick her up. As she rocked the fussy baby, she said, "What on earth gave you that idea? She'd *totally* marry you. If you'd given her any hope, she never would have considered Reynard."

"Don't be a fool, Liam," Joe said. "I'll tell you what Teresa's problem is. She's not worried about your creds or even what Carrie thinks of you. She's just worried that you can't keep your johnson in your pants."

"Why would she—?" He cut himself off, and they all looked up the hill to where the dogs had raced to welcome Teresa. As she walked slowly toward them, no one spoke.

"Coffee," she said, bleary-eyed, and headed, zombie-like, into the kitchen.

When she reappeared minutes later, Ali asked, "Better?"

"In a moment." She sipped her coffee. "What are we talking about?" She peered at each one of them in turn. "Me, I guess."

"In part," Ali said. "Liam was just telling us a fun fact about himself, weren't you, my dearest bro?"

Liam glared at her.

"He's not hurting for cash," Joe said, "so you can rest easy that he's not after your money."

Shock froze Teresa's features. "I neither thought nor cared—"

Liam stood up abruptly. "Well, I'm off to Fort Worden. If the police or the tabloids call, tell them I sailed off into the sunset, never to be seen again."

"Don't you do it!" Ali called after him as he strode up the hill.

Teresa waited until he was well out of hearing range. "How much are we talking?"

"Two million, at least," Joe replied, "in a Swiss bank account. His Israeli mother gave it to him before she died. Payment for services rendered, I gather."

Teresa took a large gulp of coffee. "That explains the motorcycle jacket."

Ali was surprised by her low-key reaction. "Aren't you pleased?"

"It doesn't change anything." Teresa's tone was peevish. "He still kissed Ulla and probably slept with April and Lisette and God knows who else."

"We need girl time," Ali said after she finished feeding Josephine and placed her back in the bassinet. "Ulla has the morning off. Let's take the twins and head downtown for lunch and shopping. I've lost a few more pounds, and I want to celebrate by buying something that fits."

"Aren't you worried about the paparazzi?"

"No. They're more interested in Liam right now. According to that article, you and I are the less attractive members of this family, remember?"

They both laughed. It was nice to be able to joke about it, Ali thought. *Finally.*

"ABOUT LAST NIGHT ..." ALI BEGAN after they'd finished unloading the twins' gear from the car. They headed north down Water Street.

"Shall we eat at the Marina?" Teresa hedged. "The restaurant at the end has a nice deck."

"Teresa ...."

"Okay, okay." Teresa drew in a deep breath and blew it out slowly. "We made love. I mean Liam and me, not Reynard. Not last night. After he rescued me from the bay. I'm sorry I lied, but he didn't want you to know, said he was supposed to be protecting me, not ravishing me. It was ... all-consuming. He's like a drug."

"Like in the Huey Lewis song," Ali joked, unsurprised by her confession.

Teresa squeezed her eyes shut. "More like heroin. He could have done anything he wanted with me."

Ali squeezed her arm. "I know that feeling. At least you didn't get pregnant."

"No," she sounded bitter, "he used protection."

"Um, that is bad how?" Ali's brow furrowed.

"It's just that he seemed awfully prepared, and he couldn't have been anticipating having sex with me. That condom had to have some other woman's name on it."

The twins were babbling away. "Have you caught any actual words yet? They are definitely smiling now."

"They are little love bugs!" Ali made kissy faces for their amusement and was rewarded with delighted gurgles. "No words yet. I'm just worried they're going to begin with 'Ulla.' "

Teresa narrowed her eyes at Ali. "Let's not talk about her. Please. I'm in a pretty good mood, and I don't want to spoil it."

"Are you sad about things not working out with Reynard?"

"More like relieved. The Liam versus Reynard thing was tearing me apart. Fortunately Reynard revealed his true colors."

"How so?" Ali pointed to a bird perched on the mast of a nearby yacht. "Kingfisher?"

"Could be. I think they have crests like that. But I'm not sure I'd know a kingfisher from a jay."

Ali shook her head. "That's not a jay. Okay, what did he do?"

"First, he was rude to the waiter."

"Bad start," Ali agreed.

"Then he kissed up to the sommelier and ordered the most expensive wine on the menu."

"Some women would be impressed. Not you, I gather."

"I don't like snobs," Teresa declared. "Then he ordered for me without asking permission."

"Oh, the male chauvinist pig!" Ali partly joked. "Some women wouldn't mind. I can see he was terrible at reading you."

"To top it all off, he totally denigrated my dream of starting a music school in Port Angeles. Told me I'd hate teaching."

"Have you ever taught?"

"No."

"Hmm."

"Okay, so he might be right. It might be an impractical dream. It's just that he didn't have to be such a know-it-all jerk about it."

Ali gave a little bark of laughter. "Hah! Tell me how you really feel."

"Then he drove us to his house and attacked me in the car."

"He was just trying to get you to come in." Ali raised her hands in protest. "Don't look at me like that. I'm playing devil's advocate. If he hadn't already turned you off with his arrogant behavior, it might have been a different story, right? Or if Liam didn't loom so large in your head."

"I suppose. Anyway, I got out of the car and called Liam on my cell phone. I swear, he came to my rescue in about ten seconds flat."

Eyes wide, Ali stopped in her tracks. "How? Is Liam really Superman in disguise?"

Teresa cocked her head, considering the question. "I think so. He said he was at Kelpies. I still would have expected him to take at least ten minutes. All those stairs in Kelpies' building, then the hill …."

As they strolled together in silence, the babbling of the twins seemed to grow louder. Ali cupped an ear as though listening attentively. "Do you think they understand each other? Joe believes they have a secret language. I don't remember anything like that with Liam. Could be an identical-twin thing."

"Liam's always been on the quiet side, then?"

"Guess so."

They both laughed.

"I told him I loved him."

"Oh. How did he react to that?"

"He said I was delusional. That it would never work, no matter how much he wanted me. 'Craved' me, in fact. His exact word."

Ali wrinkled her nose. "That silly boy. When will he ever learn? He loves you, I know it. He's just so darn stubborn."

"I'm almost ready to give up. I think he's serious. He doesn't want the aggravation. Thanks a lot, Mom."

"You know, your mom was pretty great to me at first." Ali smiled wryly at the memory. "Without her, Joe and I might never have gotten together. I'm not sure why she's had such a bee in her bonnet lately. But I am sure of one thing: Carrie loves you and wants the best for you, even if she's misguided as to what that might be."

" I know," Teresa said. "It's a mother-daughter thing. I am her precious baby. She just can't bear to see me with the 'wrong' person. Wrong by her definition, of course."

"She needs to get a life beyond her social circle. She needs a Liam."

They both laughed until their eyes watered.

Teresa wiped away a tear with the back of her hand. "Oh, that's a good one! I would give a lot to see that."

The kingfisher had returned, and Ali observed it closely so she could sketch it later. An idea occurred to her. "Teresa, would you ever consider a writing project?"

Teresa looked so alarmed that you'd think she'd been asked to join a gang of thieves. "What?"

"I know you majored in Creative Writing. I have an entire sketchpad of rain forest creatures. Joe thinks they would work in a children's book."

"Ali, it's a nice thought, but I'm not—"

"Don't say no, not yet. That sketchpad is full, and I'd like you to take it back to your cabin, live with it for a while, see if a story occurs to you. It would give you something to think about other than Liam."

Teresa scratched her head, clearly wanting to turn Ali down flat. "What is the audience?"

"I don't know. From preschool to preteen. Teenagers are too cynical."

Teresa stared out to sea, as if the answer might be sailing in. "All right. But don't get your hopes up. I've never done anything with that degree. I don't think I've picked up a pen except to write a check or sign a credit card slip since I graduated. The novel I wrote for my thesis was completely lame. A piece of my sorry life disguised as a novel."

Ali suppressed a sigh. So much for that idea. She adored Teresa, but whoever wrote the children's book would need to have a passion for literature in miniature. Teresa's protests rang true. If she didn't think writing was fun, she wasn't going to have the patience to come up with the kind of goofy tales Ali's drawings would require.

# CHAPTER 29

---◆---

Back at the compound, Ali entered by the terrace door and froze. What had happened to Ulla? She had shrunk five inches at least, aged ten years, and dyed her hair brown.

*Oh*, it wasn't Ulla.

"Who's that?" Teresa whispered.

The woman turned around to greet them. "I'm May Allen." She extended a hand to shake. "The new nanny?"

Ali and Teresa exchanged broad smiles as they each shook the woman's hand. "Music to my ears," Ali said. "You are so *very* welcome here. Allow me to introduce you to your charges, Caryn and Josephine."

May leaned over the carriage and cooed at the babies, who gurgled and smiled at her.

Ali sniffed the air and made a face. "I'm afraid they're in dire need of changing."

In a baby-friendly voice, May told the girls, "I can smell that. We'll get you fixed up right away, little angels. Joe already gave me a tour. He asked me to direct you to his studio when you got back."

"Thanks so much, May," Ali said as they turned to go. "And again, welcome to our home!"

Once they were clear of the nanny, Teresa said, "Hallelujah!" and pumped her fist in the air.

"Amen! God does answer prayers after all. Actually, I am living proof of that already. Ulla was just a minor glitch in a pretty amazing run of good luck. Still, she was turning out to be a thorn in my side."

"And mine."

They knocked on the studio door, and Joe ushered them in, flashing his cheesiest grin. "You met the new nanny, I see."

Teresa shut the door behind her. "We were just reaffirming our belief in miracles. What happened?"

"That Ulla," Joe muttered. "What a piece of work."

Ali and Teresa sat down on the couch. "Go on," Ali said.

"She came into the studio right after you left. I thought she had the morning off and figured there'd been some emergency. She collapsed on the couch and told me her girlfriend had broken up with her. Then she started crying."

Ali looked down at the couch cushions as if they might have cooties, but she didn't budge.

"I never know what to do when a woman cries," Joe went on. "No man does. I patted her on the back. Then she fell into my arms. She was all over me, like an octopus. I had to pry her off."

Ali jumped up and started pacing. "That … *hussy!*"

Joe shook his head in disgust. "Did she really think I'd go for it? I shoved her away, and she fell back on the couch. Then I fired her."

Reality finally sinking in, Teresa scrambled to her feet and burst out with, "You're my hero!" She gave Joe a huge hug.

"You need to have a talk with Liam," he told her. "I'm guessing that kiss you witnessed was entirely one-sided. He never ratted on her, maybe because he thought she was good with the twins and he didn't want to make waves. And he must not have known someone had seen them."

"That makes total sense." Ali came over to kiss Joe on the cheek. "Anyhow, it's behind us now. I like May a lot."

"I do too," Joe said. "She comes highly recommended."

*Ulla came highly recommended too*, Ali thought. "That hire was fast … lightning-fast," she said.

"Oh that." Joe waved his hand dismissively. "I had her lined up, was already paying her, in fact. She lives in town. I was just waiting for the right moment to let Ulla go. Then she made it easy for me."

"May Allen looks like a normal person," Teresa said. "That's the best part. No more seductresses or ogresses. I hope you've learned your lesson."

"What?" Joe threw up his hands. "How was I supposed to know she was bisexual?"

Teresa gave him a look of reproach. "Everyone else suspected it."

"Okay, I'm sorry. I meant well. She looked strong and capable, and the twins liked her."

"They are super easygoing," Teresa said. "I think they'd like anyone."

"Liam's around, by the way"—Joe gestured up the hill—"if you want to question him. At least he was a half hour ago. In the garage, working on some furniture project. You can congratulate him. There's this TV show called *Shipmates* that's in the pre-production phase. It's a dating show that takes place on a cruise ship. They want Liam."

Teresa left the studio steaming mad.

"That was mean," Ali said after she had kissed him thoroughly.

He tousled her hair. "Oh, lighten up. Teresa can take a little teasing. It's not like Liam's going to do the show, though he did think it was pretty funny."

"You're not joking?"

"Nope. Hollywood has come calling. Don't think it will be the last time."

* * *

TERESA HAD LOST HER HEAD of steam by the time she reached the garage. She did not want to scare Liam off by plowing into him like a runaway truck. She was, however, determined to have it out with him. If he didn't want her, she was going to find her own place in Sequim or Port Angeles. Then she could dip a toe in the music school idea. Or write Ali's children's book. Liam's befuddling presence made any movement forward impossible. Freed from his spell, she'd surely be able to see her way through this cloudbank in her existence.

She was done with suffering over the impossible man.

The dogs detected her first, heralding her presence with excited whines and an audible *swish* of tails whipping through the air. Liam leaned through the open door as if prepared to discourage an interruption. His silky blue-black hair stuck out in all directions like a crow's ruffled feathers. From his smudged face and clothing, you'd think he'd been rolling in the dust. He'd never looked more adorable.

Teresa relished the rugged whole of him—the well-worn jeans that clung to his long legs and the Kelpies T-shirt that hugged the bulging muscles of his chest and shoulders. You couldn't pay enough for publicity like that. She hoped the pub appreciated it.

"I'm kind of in the middle of something," he said while she petted the wriggling dogs.

"Can you take a break?" It was more command than request. *Cool it*, she warned herself.

He paused, recalculating. "Sure, I could stretch my legs."

She stepped into the garage and peered around, noting the worn wooden door he was transforming into a faux-antique dining table, complete with artistic details such as scrolls and clawed feet. Heading over to the utility sink, Liam washed his face and hands and raked his fingers through his hair. Now he looked as if he'd just returned from a swim—she tried to shut out the image of his naked magnificence emerging from a river.

They ventured up the hill and through the gate, the dogs following close behind.

"I hear you're going to be on a dating show," she ventured.

"What?" His laughter incited a "yip!" and a "ruff!" from the dogs. "Hey boys, shh." Eyes still merry, he went on, "That Joe …. No, not my thing. But they did offer. I suppose I should be flattered."

"You heard about Ulla." Teresa kept her eyes on the path ahead.

"Uh, yeah. No surprise."

"Because she came on to you first."

He stopped walking. "How did you—?

"I saw you both." She faced him, confused. "I thought *you* were the one—"

"Yeah," he broke in, slashing his hand in the air. "No, I had zero interest in her. I didn't say anything because I didn't want to rock the boat. Now I wish I had."

"So do I," Teresa grumbled.

"You know, I haven't been with anyone but you since I arrived here," he said as if the comment should come as no surprise.

Her breath caught in her throat. "Really? I … I assumed there were dozens. You certainly haven't lacked for opportunities. April—"

Liam reached out an arm to steady her, his touch electrifying. His blue eyes darkened and a smile traced his lips. "That was just to make you jealous. April isn't my type. And she's still married … or was at the time. I don't do that. I like other men too much to impinge on their terrain."

"What about the condom?"

He looked taken aback. "What about it?"

"You were awfully prepared."

He burst into one of those full-throated laughs that curled her toes. "I've had that condom in my wallet for a long, long time. Some German brand I bought in Israel. I was worried it was so old it might break. If I'd had more than one …. With you I could just keep going all—" He cut himself off, suddenly wary.

The silence stretched.

"We've wasted a lot of time," she said, her words bolder than their shaky delivery would indicate.

"Yes," he said, surprisingly gentle, "but Carrie's still a problem."

She felt a surge of hope. "Not a deal breaker?"

A smile tugged at his lips. "Maybe not." He moved in closer until they were almost touching. The dogs whined. "Back, you two!" Liam told them. "I love you guys, but … go home."

At the command, they looked at each other as if to say, *Jeez, what did we do?* before trotting back toward the garage.

"Did we hurt their feelings?" Teresa asked.

"We can make it up to them later." He pulled her into his arms. His full lips descended on hers and her body softened against his hard muscles. Adrenaline coursed through her as she felt the frantic thumping of his heart. "I do love you," he said in a low, almost pained voice, his hot breath ruffling her hair. "I think I fell in love with you the first moment we met. In Israel. You're gonna marry me?"

In breathless wonder, she asked, "Is that a proposal?"

He chuckled. "Is that a yes?"

"Yes!"

He pulled back as if to re-set the picture. "Then it is." With a wolfish grin, he took hold of her hand and began to lead her toward the cabins.

She hung back coquettishly. "You mean … we're not waiting for our wedding night?"

"Seems kind of pointless, don't you think?" He smoothed away an errant curl, his fingers lingering on her hot cheek. "Although maybe *I* should hold out. Otherwise, you might get cold feet. I'm counting on you to make an honest man of me."

Grinning from ear to ear, he scooped her up into his arms and draped her over his shoulder, his large hand cupping her bottom.

She laughed helplessly, her small fists battering his back with little impact. He gave her a gentle spanking, and she cried out his name in protest.

He kept chuckling to himself as she watched the garage retreat into the distance. His cabin was unlocked, and he kicked the door open. Once inside, he set her down as if she were as delicate as a piece of puff pastry, cradling her head as he lowered her onto the bed. Eyes smoldering with naked longing, he sat down beside her and ran a large hand up and down her clothed body.

"Is this really happening?" he said.

She laughed, giddy with relief and desire. "Hey, that's my line."

He looked around, on the alert, as if attuned to possible danger.

"Do you hear something?" she asked.

He cocked his head. "I thought you did." His hand had stopped its exploration and was resting beside him on the bed.

She couldn't bear the silence and said in a thready voice, "Are you waiting for me to make the first move? I made an utter fool of myself that last time."

Expression grave, he said, "I wouldn't say that."

She averted her gaze, preferring to stare at the wall. "I'm sure I was totally inept. I just wanted to break the ice. I'd never done anything like that before. We were at an impasse."

He caressed her cheek and gently turned her face toward him so she had to confront his deep blue gaze. "You succeeded. I knew you weren't … an expert, but believe me, it was mind-blowing. I've never …" he didn't finish. He rubbed his hands together as if warming them. "Okay, then, you want the full treatment?" His dry laugh, a little devilish, sent a fresh thrill through her.

"Are you going to *ravish* me?" She grinned. "Because to that I say, bring it on."

"Now you're making fun of me." His scowl was unconvincing.

"Oh no, 'ravish' is my new favorite word." She started to unbutton his shirt, then stopped.

"What?" he said with a lazy smile, still gazing into her eyes.

"You take the lead." She flopped back on the bed.

He grinned at her theatrics. "Okay, just this once." He reached for her pink cashmere cardigan. "But I'm warning you … this might take some time. You're gonna have to be patient." He unbuttoned the sweater as if disarming a bomb. "I'm not going to be responsible for destroying this expensive garment." She reached for the mother-of-pearl buttons, intending to rip them off. "Back!" he ordered. "Behave. You gave me the reins, remember?"

Liam's hands trembled slightly …. So he was nervous too. For a time she was content to observe him from beneath heavy lids, her heart fluttering like a trapped bird, her brain struggling to accept the reality that he loved her enough to defy her mother. Her hot gaze blazed over every inch of his achingly beautiful face—the sharp cheekbones, the slightly aquiline nose, the deep-set cobalt-blue eyes, the generous, slightly parted lips, the smooth, honey-colored skin, lightly scored with scars on one side. The shock of straight blue-black hair that reached the base of his powerful neck. He was almost too beautiful to be believed, and he was all hers.

He appeared to be moving underwater, heedless of her hungry eyes, drugged by passion. Finally she moaned in frustration, and his eyes came back into focus.

"Music to my ears," he whispered. She breathed in the heady scent of biscuits, leather, and soap. "That's right, wait for it," he whispered again. He finished unbuttoning the sweater and carefully peeled it off her arms. After folding it with a shopkeeper's expertise, he laid it on the nightstand. Grasping the hem of her tank top in both hands, he slowly rolled it up, stopping just short of her breasts. She heard herself whine. Another dry chuckle emerged as his mouth descended. Pulling up her bra with his teeth, he growled and blew on her already stiff nipples then drew one into his mouth, suckling and nibbling. His fingers crept into her jeans, which he had stealthily unzipped, and brushed lightly over her sex.

"Liam, *please* ..." she begged.

"You want more?" he whispered. She nodded, frantically, and he gripped the sides of her jeans and eased them off her hips and down her legs, leaving her pink-lace panties in place. He loomed alongside her as his fingers played at the edges of her sex, toying with the trimmed nest of curls, deftly darting in and out. Then he found her nub and brushed over it once before returning to circle it with maddening delicacy. As her excitement reached a tipping point, the light pressure stopped. "Not yet, sweetheart," he cooed.

Her eyes flew open in protest in time to see the heat in his as they raked over her body. Then he crawled downward to enter her with his tongue, moving with surer, more deliberate force and sending indescribable pleasure pulsing through her. She'd abandoned all dignity, panting like a puppy and arching against his mouth.

He sat back on his haunches.

"Liam, damn you!" she cried out in frustration. His chuckle of satisfaction made her realize how ridiculous she sounded, and she laughed, covering her face with her hands in helpless embarrassment.

He pressed her arms back down on the bed and released her, pointing at her eyes then his body, bidding her pay attention.

He shrugged out of his flannel shirt by rotating his shoulders back and forth, allowing it to slither down his arms like a snake shedding its skin. She couldn't help grinning at the show he was staging for her benefit. Next he drew his T-shirt upward along his chest, making his muscles ripple. He circled it around his head like a lasso and tossed it clear across the room. Who knew Liam had this playful side? All the while his expression was deadpan, though his eyes sparkled with amusement. He unbuckled his belt, pulled it out of the loops, and whipped it against the bed with a loud, "Hi-yah!"

Seeing her helpless with laughter and lust, he pretended to pout. "What's so funny?" But his own serious façade was cracking.

"Nothing," she said, her voice huskier than ever. "You're enjoying this too much, that's all."

"Oh yeah." He stood and pulled off his jeans, revealing that he wore no underwear and was more than ready for her. He reached into the nightstand drawer for a condom, deftly rolling it onto his beautiful cock with deliberate slowness, in full view of her wide eyes. "Anticipation is everything. That's today's lesson."

She pouted. "I need lessons?"

"We can all learn new tricks," he laughed, sliding his smooth, hard body along the length of hers. "You're teaching me a thing or two."

She was still grinning like an idiot, though he couldn't see it. He was too busy worshipping her breasts.

"I am your slave," he said in a muffled, patently vulnerable voice. She wasn't sure how to reply, didn't want to ruin the moment.

"Oh!" she cried out as he filled her slowly, moving with sinuous grace, seemingly lost in his own world of pleasure, though he could hardly miss her ecstatic response. She was floating off on a wave of the most intense sensation she'd ever felt.

When she could speak again, she whispered, "The slave is the master."

He fell against her, spent, then rolled over and lay next to her on the bed, breathing heavily. "Hegel," he said. "You think I don't know my German philosophy?"

Her laugh was a long, merry peal of giddy happiness. "Um, I was thinking Sting. You know, The Police? Take your pick."

# CHAPTER 30



"LET ME GET THIS STRAIGHT," Joe said. "Teresa and Liam want to *elope*?"

Joe and Ali were tending to the twins in the rec room while May Allen did laundry. Side by side on the couch, each cradled and soothed a fussy baby.

Joe's consternation fed Ali's own anxiety. "You think it's a mistake."

"Mom would go through the roof. She's been so weird lately. Our family is already screwed up enough. Much as she and Teresa lock horns, they do love each other."

"Does Carrie have to find out? They could get married twice, like we talked about doing."

"Yeah, but we had a real wedding the first time. Mom was invited and attended, even if she did look ready to run screaming into the bay. Thank God she gave up on the church wedding idea. Or thank Liam. All the hullabaloo over his return diverted the attention from us."

"The twins also provided a convenient diversion," Ali said.

Caryn burped a copious amount of milk on Joe's shoulder. Not all of it was absorbed by the towel.

"Oh, yuck," Joe muttered as he laid a squirming Caryn in the bassinet. "Phew! It stinks. I'm gonna go change. I'll be back in a second."

"If you think that's bad, you can change the next poopy diaper!" Ali called after him.

When he returned a few minutes later in a fresh shirt, he said, "Back to the wedding. No secret ceremonies. Mom would find out, and she'd never forgive Teresa."

As Ali attempted to lay Josie beside Caryn, the baby grabbed her ponytail. Joe had to pry the tiny fingers open, but they still came away with a few strands. "Ouch," Ali said without raising her voice. "Josie has an iron grip. You know, Carrie might not forgive Teresa anyway."

Together again, the babies launched into a stream of gibberish.

Joe sighed. "What's their hurry, anyway? Since they don't need a license to—"

"Yes, I know," Ali broke in. "They spend so much time in Liam's cottage that I've been giving it a wide berth. Maybe they'll consider a small family wedding at the compound."

Joe petted Caryn's downy head, and she babbled in response. "What did you say?" he asked the baby. "That you love your mommy and daddy very much. What was that?" He cupped his ear. "And you'd like a sapphire necklace like Mommy's when you turn ten."

Ali gave a helpless shrug. "Who wouldn't?"

"Hey, I didn't tell you, I got an email from David. He's coming home, hopefully for good. We could plan the wedding accordingly. I doubt Edward would show, but we should invite him. Jake … let's put him on the guest list too. I'd like to keep that door open. He and Teresa used to be close. Odds are good that he'll skip it. I haven't heard from him in ages."

Rocking the bassinet, Ali smiled at the sleepy babies who gazed up at her with bright blue eyes so like her own. She spoke in a low, soothing voice. "Aren't we getting ahead of ourselves? If only everyone could put aside their grievances for Teresa's sake."

Joe made a derisive sound. "The 'family' has been on life support for years. Da's death threw us all into a tailspin. Partly because he died before we could convince him to let us find our own way in the world. It's as if we're all still trying to fulfill his life plan for us. Or in my case, trying to prove that I didn't make the mistake of my life by not staying with classical guitar. I could have a cushy job right now teaching in a university and touring with classical guitar societies. Maybe if Da had acknowledged Jake's writing success … but no, instead he crowned him heir to the family business. David, rather than taking a lucrative surgery residency, chose to escape to the jungle, and Edward has basically joined a sanctioned cult where he's expected to shun all worldly things. So we're all following an old playbook. Da could be great, but he and Mom never considered anyone's wishes but their own. Still, you gotta feel sorry for Mom. Two of her sons shun their siblings and another— me—married against her wishes and has his dirty laundry regularly aired by the tabloids. Even if David does decide it's time to toe the line, it won't make up for Teresa. Mom can't get over the fact that her only daughter came so close to marrying Dream Date then did an about-face and ran off with the Dud."

Ali was about to tell Joe off when he amended, "*I* don't think Liam's the Dud! I'm giving Mom's perspective."

But Ali wasn't angry. "Liam has *great* taste in clothing," she joked. "And his hygiene is excellent."

Reacting to their animated voices, Caryn began to wail. Josephine joined in.

"Oh, Jeez. I didn't mean to upset them," Joe said.

It took several minutes to restore order. "Phew!" Joe exclaimed, wiping his brow. "Will you talk to Liam, or should I?"

"I'd like to. Is he working at home today?"

"Try the garage. If he's not there, his cabin."

Ali made a wry face. "If he's in the cabin, our talk will have to wait."

Having heard the ruckus, May Allen the nanny joined them.

"I'm afraid Josie needs changing," Ali said.

Joe added, "Caryn too."

The nanny smiled sweetly. "They like to do everything together." There was always laughter in her voice.

ALI STOPPED TO GREET THE dogs on her way to the garage, where the door was open.

"Hey, Bro. What are you making now?"

"Still a table." He took a step back as if to get a different perspective. "What, you can't tell?"

She uttered an uncomfortable "hah," knowing the job was going slowly due to frequent visits to his steamy love nest. "Of course I can tell. I was just making awkward conversation. Where will this one go?"

"The common room of the new FOSSP residence on the edge of town."

"Can you take a breather?"

He didn't hesitate. "Of course." He pointed to two wooden chairs he'd also built. "Have a seat." He sat down next to her and shifted around experimentally. "They need cushions. What's on your mind?"

"Do you guys really plan to elope?"

His laugh was bitter. "Are you afraid Carrie will have our marriage annulled if we do?"

"You might be pleasantly surprised if you give her half a chance." Ali told him the story of her initial lunch with Joe's mother, where she had discovered Carrie knew what was going on with Joe and Jake and had been quite reasonable about it. "She can be … difficult, I know. What if we hold a simple ceremony here? David—the only brother Joe is currently in touch with—is coming back to the States and will be visiting us on October thirteenth. We could do it on the fifteenth. See? No wait at all." Her cheeks flamed. "Not that you're waiting."

Now they were both blushing. Ali was charmed by this new Liam. *Tamed by love.*

Pretending concern over the hardware attaching a leg, he said, "I'll ask Teresa. I suppose it doesn't matter if Carrie boycotts the ceremony. At least this would be a path toward peaceful coexistence. She's going to have to learn to tolerate me eventually if she wants any kind of future relationship with Teresa."

"That's right." Ali stood but didn't make a move to go.

"Is there more?" He sat down again, more receptive this time.

Tempted to chicken out, Ali hesitated before sitting again. "Something I've been meaning to ask you. It's not that I'm worried what you might think—it's that I might not like the answer."

He leaned forward, hands resting on his powerful thighs. "I'm intrigued. Shoot."

"Those few years after they took us away from our mother are … hazy for me. Until George and Emily took us in. If asked to describe that first foster mom, I'd be at a total loss. But for a while now I've been having this recurring dream." She paused. "Not much lately, it's true."

In the tense silence, he said, "I'm listening."

"I'm asleep, and a figure rises up next to my bed. I know he wants to hurt me, but I can't make out his features. Not enough to identify him, though I know it's a man. Then you appear and whisk him away. It's as if the devil himself reached up from hell and sucked the guy down with a Dustbuster."

Liam smiled briefly at the absurd image then became dead serious. "I've tried to shut those years out too—with less success than you."

"Joe and I believe I was molested, maybe worse." Breathing shallow, she waited for his dreaded response.

"Our first foster mother was a nervous wreck. Any false move on our part, and she walloped us. There was an endless stream of boyfriends—or were they johns?. The social workers who checked up on us were clueless. One of Frida's boyfriends sneaked into your room."

Ali's mouth grew dry. "Did he—?"

"No"—he cut her off with a chopping gesture—"I stopped him."

"But you were only eight."

"I was a strong eight-year-old, and it was one month shy of our ninth birthday. As you know, my hormones went into overdrive way early. The night of the day it happened was unusually hot for August, maybe even in the nineties. We spent the day at Matthews Beach. Does that ring a bell?"

The memory began to take shape. "Yeah. The teenage lifeguard flirted with you. And we bought ice cream from Jolly Joe. I always got a fudgesicle. It was so hot … it broke all the records." She looked up at him. "What did you do?"

"I almost killed him."

Her brother's capacity for violence always caught her unawares. "With your hands or a weapon?"

"With my hands. But *he* had a weapon—a combat knife engraved with his name. That proved I was defending you. He had a prior conviction for statutory rape, so his intentions were clear."

Ali couldn't believe her ears. "If they knew you were justified, why did they arrest you that night?"

"They didn't, though they did take me in for interrogation, and I ended up sleeping over. Later on, I spent a few days in juvenile detention after mouthing off to one of the officers."

For Ali, the memories flooded back. "I was asleep, and when I woke up, that guy—wasn't his name Trey?—was looming over me. He put a finger to his lips, though I was too terrified to make a sound. Then he showed me his knife and ripped the front of my nightgown—"

"You don't have to work at recalling this," Liam rushed to say.

She held up a hand. "It's okay. I think it will help. He had these beady little eyes …. He was panting and stank of stale cigarettes, whisky, and rot. My heart thundered in my chest, and I thought I was going to faint. He groped my breasts … then you burst in. How did you know?"

"My room was next to yours. I heard footsteps, then the sound of your door opening and closing."

"I could have been on my way to the bathroom."

He held up a finger. "These footsteps were heavier."

She stood and walked over to the dogs, who were sitting patiently, as if absorbed in the story themselves. She lifted Coogan onto her lap and stroked him, which was the signal to Harry to lean against her leg so she could pet him with her other hand. She smiled up at Liam. "You'd make a good detective. Or a bodyguard."

"Thanks, but I'll stick to protecting the people I love." He cleared his throat. "I'll spare you the details of what I did to that guy. The detective assigned to the case contacted me months later to say he'd been killed by a fellow inmate in prison."

"Joe will be glad to know he met a bad end. He wondered if you'd been … assaulted too. He said beautiful boys are just as vulnerable."

Liam was slow to respond. "Was Joe sexually abused?"

"When he was an altar boy, there was a priest. Joe was already on guard because word had gotten around. Before the man could make his move, Joe told his parents."

Liam's eyes wandered around the room. "Okay, yes. I worried about you because several of Frida's male visitors had tried it on with me. I figured it was only a matter of time before one of them decided you were an easier target."

"'Tried it on'?" Ali repeated fretfully.

"Don't worry. No one got past groping. Even before my crazy growth spurt, I figured out how to defend myself. Once they learned their pigeon had a hawk's talons, they backed off. Part of the reason no one hung around for long. Frida was a looker, for a junkie."

Did knowing the truth make Ali feel worse or better? *Better*, she thought. *Now maybe my subconscious can stop trying to solve the puzzle with that scary dream.*

"It wasn't easy to find us foster parents after that," Liam went on. "Thank God George and Emily came along. They weren't models of parental affection, but they meant well."

"Yeah," Ali said. "I appreciate now how lucky we were. Despite all the babysitting and volunteer work."

"Yes. Ugh. On the other hand, I picked up a boatload of useful skills." He pointed to the table and chairs, and they both laughed. "I do feel guilty, you know, that I can't mourn them. It *is* sad that they died in the prime of life. It's just that … when you start going down that road—dwelling on your regrets—where do you stop? We didn't choose any of the crap that happened to us as children or teenagers. I believe in living for today."

"And you're still helping people."

He smiled. "So are you. Maybe that's thanks to George and Emily. Tough love sometimes works, I guess, though I can't see doing that to my own children."

"Do you think you'll have any?"

He grinned. "It'll be fun trying."

She touched his hand. "I totally get why you were so protective."

He hung his head. "Oh, *that*. I'm sorry, Alf. I'm afraid you didn't get to date much."

She pouted comically. "I didn't get to date at all. And when you stopped scaring off my admirers, I couldn't tell the creeps from the good guys."

"All teenage boys are creeps," he sneered. "And a lot of guys never grow out of it. Guess I should have kept it up through college."

Her hands flew to her cheeks in mock horror. "I'm *so* glad you didn't."

He squatted down next to her to stroke the dogs, who were making happy noises and wagging their tails. "My own relationships, if you can call them that, were nothing to write home about."

"You broke a lot of hearts."

"Yeah, I suppose. I only went for women with experience. I tried, in my own way, not to inflict too much hurt. The first woman who, uh, initiated me was a predator herself. Remember that lifeguard?" He held up a hand. "Never mind. I was pretty stoked at the time. Certainly couldn't see the harm. I was just an overgrown kid with an out-of-control libido."

"Being experienced doesn't make you immune to heartbreak, you know."

He winced. "I know that now. I wish I could make amends, but it's not like AA. You don't contact women you hurt and apologize for ruining their lives. Not sure it would be appreciated."

Their shared laughter startled the dogs, who became restless, milling about the garage.

"Hey, guys, you can go!" Liam said. They took off at a run up the hill.

"You couldn't help it," she told him. "Women can't keep their hands off you. You were—*are*—so beautiful."

"You too," he said.

"Not as beautiful as you, according to the tabloids."

He stood to give her ponytail a playful tug. "Beautiful enough."

They exchanged a long hug.

"Thanks, Ali, for everything. For bringing me home. Letting me stay here. I can't imagine—"

"Thank *you*," she interrupted him. "It means so much to have you back." She walked to the edge of the garage. "Uh, Liam, there was more to it, right?"

Crouching next to the table, he looked up. "Huh?"

"That night I was attacked, you just *knew*, right?"

"Uh, yeah," he admitted grudgingly. "I could kind of ... *sense* things when it came to you."

"And now you can do it with Teresa."

He regarded her solemnly. "You and I have always had that connection.

Like how I knew you were in danger in the forest. And how I sensed the attack at Jean-Louis's restaurant."

Ali came over to give his arm an affectionate squeeze. "See you at dinner?"

Smiling, he turned his attention back to the table. "I'll talk to Teresa. An intimate wedding here sounds perfect."

# CHAPTER 31

———•———

"WHEN DOES CARRIE ARRIVE?" ALI asked Teresa. The wedding dress having just been delivered, Teresa was trying it on to make sure the alterations worked. The white-lace dress reminded Ali of a Barbie Doll gown from the sixties. Though Ali hadn't been allowed to own Barbies, she would ogle them in toy departments. The well-loved doll she had coveted had been for sale at a secondhand store. Like this one, her dress had been long and form-fitting with a five-inch flouncy hem at the bottom. A mermaid dress, appropriate for a wedding with an ocean view.

"David's driving Mom," Teresa said, pivoting to look at her backside in the mirror. "Tomorrow morning. I don't have an ETA. This dress isn't too Morticia Addams?"

Now that she mentioned it …. "Um, a little. But Morticia—all the Morticias, even the original cartoon one—were gorgeous. And it's white, not black. Don't worry, it's perfect!"

Teresa's expression told Ali she wasn't convinced. "It's too tight around the thighs. I'm going to be waddling down the aisle like a penguin." She slapped herself on the bottom. "Do I look fat?"

Ali gasped and clapped a hand to her mouth. "You should never ask questions like that … of anyone! Especially when you're talking to a matronly mother. But no, absolutely not. You look like a million bucks. And you won't have to waddle, just take small steps."

"I've gained five pounds," Teresa moaned. "And you're almost the same weight you were when we first met, so I don't want to hear anything about 'matronly.' Did your dress arrive yet?"

"Yes, two days ago." She retrieved it from the closet. *I love it*, she thought, not wanting to say it aloud and make Teresa feel worse. She'd chosen a filmy chiffon number cut on the bias, sapphire blue to match the necklace Joe had given her. Both dresses were purchased from a boutique in Seattle's Wallingford neighborhood. The wedding dresses ran in the two-thousand-dollar range, too low-end to suit Carrie but way more high-end than the four-hundred-dollar dress Ali had worn to her own wedding. Though she was pretty sure she'd never wear that dress again, she couldn't quite bring herself to give it away. She imagined that was true of every wedding dress. At least one that cost four hundred dollars was less wasteful.

"*Your* dress is perfect," Teresa said, while still staring balefully at her own backside. "I don't suppose I can return this, now that it's been altered."

"Why would you want to?"

"It's just … neither fish nor fowl. It's not expensive or chic enough to please Mom, and it's not comfortable enough to please me." She plopped down on the bed. "It's a stupid compromise dress. Arghhh!"

"We'll find something else, then," Ali said, sitting next to her and rubbing her back. "You can dye this one black and wear it on Halloween."

They dissolved into helpless laughter, collapsing on the bed, side-by-side. Teresa finally wiped her eyes and said, "A two-thousand-dollar Halloween costume. Now, *that's* excess." She turned her head and added, "Am I on the verge of a nervous collapse?"

"I think this wedding will drive us both around the bend."

"Was it a mistake not to do a Church wedding?"

"Because you're so Catholic?" Ali raised her eyebrows.

"Because it would be throwing Mom a bone. And because if the weather doesn't hold, we're going to be screwed. What was I thinking? An outdoor wedding in October …."

"The forecast is for partly cloudy and seventy degrees," Ali said. "It'll be okay, you'll see. Joe has a contingency plan. If it comes to that, he'll cover us all with a canopy." She slid off the bed and readjusted her skewed ponytail. "Ya know, even if you're rich, Catholic priests aren't laissez-faire when it comes to letting non-Catholics marry in their church. I wanted to do it to please Joe and Carrie, but the priest had a long row of hoops for me to jump through. I couldn't face it."

Still prostrate on the bed, Teresa slapped a hand to her forehead. "I know. Liam is even less likely to jump through those hoops."

"Hey!" Ali did a clumsy soft shoe to lighten the mood. "Jean-Louis will officiate. He did a great job with Joe and me. We are thoroughly married."

Teresa smiled and propped herself up on one elbow. "Yes, you are." Her brow furrowed. "Are he and Becca really okay with staying at Manresa Castle?"

"It was their idea. They're worried about getting caught up in the family drama. Now they have a place to escape between events. Besides, it's a beautiful hotel. You get the Victorian ambiance without having to break bread with your fellow guests. Carrie and Rostand will be staying there too, and David opted to keep his mother company, even though he'd rather stay here. Joe's agent Linc will stay with family in Port Angeles. I wish Jake and Edward hadn't begged off but … oh well. Jake didn't even offer an excuse."

Heaving a tragic sigh, Teresa rolled over onto her stomach. "Release me, will you?" Ali unzipped the dress and pulled it down as Teresa wriggled out. On her feet once again, she said, "I'm frankly surprised at Jake. He and I have always been close. Well, not so much lately." They were silent as they both stared at the dress, now draped over a chair. Their thoughts had turned inward, giddiness forgotten.

Ali said, "None of your friends are attending. Are you sure that's all right?"

Teresa picked up the dress and hung it back in the closet. "I have many so-called friends in Seattle but few genuine ones. I thought they were real friends once—when we had common goals. A few emailed me when news got around, and I told them 'small family wedding' so they wouldn't expect invites. They would never understand a groom like Liam. Or they would make false assumptions."

Ali nodded. "As in, you were motivated by lust, not love. I get it. I, of all people, get it."

"I know you do."

"What about your college buddies?"

"It's too much to ask of my East Coast friends to come all this way and take so much time off their demanding jobs. Besides, we've drifted apart."

"Is it weird that Kilo is attending?" Seeing Teresa's troubled expression, Ali wished she hadn't raised the subject. "None of my beeswax. I just thought … with such a small group—"

Teresa silenced her with a light touch and an imploring glance. Covering the wedding dress with the plastic dry cleaner bag, she put it back in Ali's closet and slid the door shut, as if she couldn't stand to look at it one more minute.

Finally, she said, "You mean, speaking of lust?" She stepped back into her sundress and zipped it up the back. "I don't know. He and Liam have bonded somehow. That shouldn't surprise me. There's some common ground. They are both too gifted with beauty, grace, and skills in a world that prizes other things in men—things like money, power, and prestige. Didn't you tell me Liam has always had close male friends? He inspires loyalty. And it supports my theory that Kilo loves playing the field and isn't interested in settling down. Every woman wants to believe she's special when a guy hits on her. I wonder how often that's really true."

"I think there's a good argument that you meant more to Kilo than a fling."

"Aw, you're good for a girl's ego, sis."

*Moving right along*, Ali thought. She had no experience with men like Kilo and therefore no business judging them. "Speaking of Liam's friends, what about Peter, the groundskeeper from Fort Worden? Has Liam heard back from him?"

Teresa sat back down on the bed, restless fingers clasped in her lap. "He's too shy. No amount of reassurance would change his mind."

Ali gazed longingly at the bed then plopped down next to Teresa. Why was she so exhausted? It was morning, she'd slept okay, and all she'd been doing was watching Teresa try on her dress. You'd think they'd been hiking on Hurricane Ridge.

Teresa stared out the window at a passing barge. "I can't wait for this wedding to be over."

Ali gave her a startled look. "I was just thinking that. I didn't want to say it aloud, didn't want to spoil your day."

" 'My day,' " Teresa repeated, using air quotes. "As if a wedding is some kind of lifetime achievement for a woman. I never saw it that way. That's why I didn't mind eloping with Kilo."

"I'm with you," Ali said. "Weddings are necessary rituals, I suppose, but in all that caterwaitering I did, I rarely saw a bride and groom who couldn't wait to sneak out."

"Maybe if you have lots of close friends and a tight-knit, loving family."

They both laughed, less hysterically this time. "How many of those are there, do you think?" Ali said.

CARRIE AND DAVID ARRIVED AT lunchtime the following day, her cook and general factotum Rostand trailing behind in a show of deference that harkened back to another era. The rehearsal dinner would take place at the Manresa Hotel. As for the wedding dinner, it was being catered by a seafood restaurant in town. Ali and Joe wouldn't hear of Jean-Louis exhausting himself as both chef and officiant. Rostand had promised to help, and they'd hired more FOSSP kids to work as domestics for a generous salary that included free rooms in the only other house located along the gravel drive leading to the compound—a large but nondescript white saltbox colonial purchased to preserve the O'Connell clan's privacy.

Rostand would oversee the FOSSP kids. With that wonderful man around, nothing could go wrong.

Joe and Liam were building an archway in the center of the field next to the porch and arranging folding chairs to face the ocean. There'd be only sixteen attendees, including Rostand and May Allen—eight chairs on each side of the aisle. This time they'd hired a professional photographer with the understanding that they would be the ones to decide where the photos would run, though they expected interest to be minimal. The only member of their family who seemed to be newsworthy now was Liam, and possibly Teresa, the lucky woman who'd captured his heart.

Carrie gave Ali a glacial hug that made Ali think of Hans Christian Andersen's Snow Queen, but as if to counter his mother's coolness, David went overboard, drawing her in for a bone-crushing embrace. Joe hugged Carrie until she squirmed, and the greeting he gave David included hearty backslapping.

"It's been too long, D.O."

"Yeah," David replied in his resonant, bass-baritone voice. "I can't believe how much has happened. You have *two* babies!" He walked over to where May was standing, rocking the bassinet, and leaned down to get a look at the twin girls. "Are you sure they belong to you? I think you had Ali cloned. Look at those bright blue eyes."

Joe's reproving look didn't convince. "They looked like me when they were born. They're over three months old now. Their hair is curly, like mine."

"They talking yet?"

"Joe thinks so," Ali said. "They seem to understand each other."

David nodded. "Twin talk. You and Jake did that. What about you and your brother, Ali?"

"There's no one around to tell us how it was when we were babies." Seeing their chastened expressions, she was quick to add, "Please don't waste your pity on Liam and me. We were the lucky ones, and look at us now."

As soon as she said it, she wished she could take it back. To her own ears, it came off like, *Yep, we won the jackpot—we bagged rich, beautiful spouses.*

Carrie hung back, as if hoping they'd forget her presence. Ali had no idea what tack to take. Then Joe went over to his mother and said in a cheerful voice meant to infect her with his enthusiasm, "Mom, I'm taking you and David on a tour of the compound. Follow me."

Ali resisted the urge to say, "Do you want to borrow some rubber boots?" because she had an awful feeling Carrie was going to ruin her fancy sandals in the mud. Instead, Ali joined May and the girls in the parlor.

Not long after, Teresa dashed into the parlor, casting about the room. She was clad in jeans and a T-shirt. "Did I miss them?" she said, breathing heavily. "I saw Mom's Cadillac." Teresa was officially sharing Liam's cottage now.

Caryn was breastfeeding. "Joe's giving them a tour," Ali said from her chair.

"What do you think of David?" Teresa picked up Josephine, who was flailing her arms, reaching for her, and sat down next to Ali.

"Another fine O'Connell boy." Ali had been prepared for David to tower over them all—he was six-foot-five, after all—but she hadn't expected to find him quite so imposing. It was a manly-man's face, not a boy idol's, like Joe's, or a newscaster's, like Jake's. He didn't have Joe's and Jake's soulful gold-flecked brown eyes. Instead his deep-set eyes were bright green, his cheekbones jagged, and his lips thinner, though still shapely and sensual. The hooked nose that kept Joe's face from being too pretty gave David a dashing, piratical air. The shaggy red beard and bristly dark-auburn hair didn't help, as if he hadn't had access to a barber in a while. Carrie would certainly have tried to drag him to one. Joe told Ali none of Carrie's sons heeded their mother's advice, which was why she clung so tightly to her daughter Teresa. David would make an even better Paul Bunyan than Liam. Liam had the height and impressive musculature, but he was too beautiful. Each of the O'Connell boys she'd met had that devastating smile, and David's, like Joe's, expressed an irresistible warmth.

Pointing to her charge, Teresa said, "Swap babies? I think Josephine is jealous."

May helped them switch the girls, and Josephine immediately found Ali's breast.

"David's a big sweetie," Ali said, "though I can't help but think of Red Beard the Pirate."

Teresa laughed. "Like in *Scooby-Doo*? He must have grown out his beard again. He's a little fierce looking at first glance. Larger than life. I think that's why he smiles so much. He looks a lot better clean-shaven. I'm not sure what the facial hair is all about. Mom is already stressed to the max."

"He's very tall," Ali said, "and no one else in your family has that hair.

Come to think of it, yours has red in it now that you've gone back to your natural color."

Teresa's hair, which curled fetchingly below her ears, was a dark strawberry blonde with lighter streaks from the sun.

"Edward's hair is auburn too," Teresa said, "and he's tall, though not so tall as David. Six-three. Da was also six five, and there are other tall, redheaded relatives on his side of the family. David inherited those genes with a vengeance. He's the only one with green eyes. Edward's are blue, like mine."

"That's unusual, isn't it? Your dad was brown-eyed, and your mom has blue eyes. So, how did David end up with green?" Ali wished she'd never mentioned it. Was David the product of an affair?

Teresa laughed. "Whoa! Don't go jumping to conclusions. David's got Da's cleft chin and height, no question. Green eyes are a combination of brown and blue. There are six genes involved in eye color."

"How do you know that?" Ali asked.

"I got good grades in high school biology. Don't think we didn't ask that question ourselves."

"Why did David come home?"

Teresa gave a helpless little shrug. "You'll have to ask Joe. David's job was never easy. Imagine being a doctor in a place where disease is rampant, they don't trust doctors, and you can't get the medications and supplies you need. My best guess is, it all got to be too much."

# CHAPTER 32

———•———

Teresa's wedding day began with a clap of thunder.

"Oh no!" she groaned, clinging to Liam in bed. "Please tell me that wasn't what I think it was."

Liam reached over and pulled at the blind, which slid up to reveal a water-dappled window and sheets of rain. "Um, I could tell you it's a beautiful day, but you'd learn the truth soon enough."

He gave her a long, lingering kiss that normally would have distracted her. Not this time.

She sat up abruptly, the covers falling to her waist. "What are we going to do?"

Liam's eyes roamed hungrily over her bare breasts. "I know what I wanna do …."

She swatted his hand away. "No, Liam, please, I have to think." She stood up, grabbed the silk kimono from the bedside chair, and started to pace.

He rolled onto his back with a long-suffering sigh. "Look … maybe it will stop. The wedding isn't until one. And Joe and I have a contingency plan."

"You don't understand. It will ruin the photos. Even if I can stay out of the rain, the humidity will mess up my hair and makeup."

"You look fantastic right now. What's to mess up?" He gave her a lazy grin.

"You are maddening." She just couldn't get angry, not with him so gloriously naked in a pose worthy of a *Playgirl* magazine centerfold. She started toward the bed then stopped herself. Instead she headed for the dresser, pulling out jeans, a sweatshirt, and tennis shoes. As she dressed, she said, "I'm going to the house to talk to Ali."

"Okay ...." He slid the covers down slowly.

"Stop it, you can't lure me back in." Laughing, she covered her eyes with her hands, parting two fingers to peep through.

He pulled the covers back up and folded his hands behind his head. "Your call. I guess tonight will be all the sweeter. Maybe Ali will knock some sense into you. Whatever happens, we're getting married today. Bad weather isn't going to change that."

* * *

ALI WAS STANDING AT THE stove, an apron covering her T-shirt dress, when Teresa burst in, rain jacket dripping. David, Carrie, and Rostand were due to arrive at eight thirty, and Ali was busy frying bacon. She could have followed Joe's advice and asked the aspiring-cook intern Tiger to come over and whip up a quiche or soufflé—above her paygrade—but why bother? A gourmet breakfast was unlikely to improve Carrie's mood, and besides, Tiger had a part-time sous-chef job at a restaurant in town that kept him out late, and she didn't want to run him ragged. She'd scramble a dozen eggs when she saw the whites of their eyes. Speaking of whites, Carrie probably would prefer an egg-white omelet, and did a woman so thin ever eat bacon? The bacon … was there enough for all the men? A man David's size could probably devour a package on his own. She groaned.

"Oh, sorry!" Teresa said. "I didn't mean to drip on your nice clean kitchen floor." She grabbed some paper towels and started wiping up the small puddle.

Ali dismissed the apology with a careless wave of her hand. "No problem. Drip away. There are so many other things on my mind right now." She took a closer look at her sister-in-law, who might have been shot through a downspout. "Oh sweetie, don't look so forlorn. I hope your wedding day isn't ruined. Rain is one thing, but we don't want anyone struck by lightning."

"It's God's punishment," Teresa said, half-serious. "A sign that we should have gone for a Church wedding."

"Pooh," Ali declared, hands on hips. "God should be happy you're tying the knot at all. The Supreme Being has to take what he or she can get these days. Joe's outside setting up the canopy. He says the rain isn't supposed to stop, so we might as well proceed with Plan B."

Eyes closed, Teresa was taking slow breaths, summoning inner strength. "Okay, okay. I'll try to re-set my expectations." She opened her eyes and licked her lips. "Yum. Bacon. When's breakfast?

"Your mom and brother are coming over in about fifteen minutes. That should give you time for a shower. Use our bathroom."

Fifteen minutes later, almost to the minute, the doorbell rang. Ali took off her apron to greet Carrie, David, and Rostand, who smiled broadly and promptly took over for her in the kitchen without being asked. She wanted to kiss him.

"I see the weather's not cooperating," Carrie said wryly.

"Mom," David warned, "let's not make things worse."

"Sorry," Carrie sniffed. "It's a shame, that's all."

Joe stepped into view, his jacket and Stetson safari hat dripping. "Come on, Mom, lighten up. Your only daughter is getting married. Give it time. You're gonna love Liam. Did we tell you about his Swiss bank account?"

* * *

WHEN TERESA SHOWED UP, TWENTY minutes into breakfast, the four of them were seated around the kitchen table. Teresa's hair was still damp, and she was wearing one of Ali's maternity sundresses—her jeans being too wet and muddy. It definitely qualified as what Becca's mother Leah called a *schmatta*. Ali was too small for it now too, but she'd mostly been wearing jeans lately and hadn't updated her wardrobe.

"How are you going to style *that*?" her mother moaned, pointing at Teresa's hair, though she was taking in her overall appearance in horror, as if her daughter had received a Mennonite makeover. Teresa almost explained the dress, but decided her mom needed to lighten up.

"It will look fine, Mom." Teresa leaned over to kiss her cheek. "I've figured out how to blow-dry it."

"Who's doing your makeup?"

"Um, me? I didn't hire a makeup artist."

"Whyever not?" Her mother was so tense, Teresa was afraid she might shatter. Not for the first time, she questioned her decision to marry quickly. Her mother clearly believed that her only daughter would regret settling for such a low-key ceremony. "Joe, please pass the coffee urn," Carrie said with an air of defeat.

Joe did her one better and filled her mug. Teresa didn't think more caffeine was going to help matters. If only they could slip her a shot of whiskey so she'd mellow out. She helped herself to coffee, eggs, and two strips of bacon.

Carrie's eyes widened at this small act of defiance. "What will you wear?" she asked, dread in her voice.

She almost said, *Hot pants, a bustier, and combat boots*, but decided to behave. "Ali and I picked up a dress in Port Angeles. It's one of a kind. Only … the designer isn't well known."

Carrie didn't respond. She just stared, aghast, at her changeling daughter.

Fortunately Ali chose that moment to intervene. "Come on, Teresa, let's get you ready. Everything but the dress."

Once they were alone in Ali and Joe's bedroom, Teresa wilted. "I was hoping she'd get into the spirit of the thing."

Ali sprayed Teresa's hair with a mister. "She will. She's here, isn't she? And I see signs that she's making an effort."

Teresa stood in front of the bathroom mirror to blow out her own hair. They didn't try to speak over the roar of the dryer. After she was done, she turned to face Ali. "What do you think?"

Ali's smile was reassuringly radiant. "Lovely! Soft and fluffy. You look like an angel."

Teresa grimaced. "Or maybe a cherub. It's not the most feminine look. Mom's right."

"Just you wait. In full makeup, you'll look plenty feminine. And the new dress is perfect. Even your mother will like it."

THE RAIN CONTINUED. WHEN TERESA saw Joe's handiwork, she almost gasped. He'd festooned the long, plain-beige canopy tent with filmy fabric, ferns, moss, and flowers. The fantasy bower might have been straight out of the movie *Ferngully*, only the Hoh Rain Forest in place of the Brazilian one. Joe and Liam had been clearing an area on the other side of the house for a hot tub and had raided the yard clippings for embellishments. Outdoor carpeting would keep them off the wet grass.

"Oh, Joe, it's so beautiful," Teresa sobbed, throwing her arms around her brother's neck.

"Teresa, your mascara!" Ali warned her.

"It's smudge-proof," Teresa explained as she surveyed the stormy scene with trepidation, as if the journey to the bower required crawling along a fraying rope bridge. "How am I going to get there without being soaked?"

"I found an oversized umbrella," Ali said. "I'll hold it over you like you're an East Indian princess and we'll make a mad dash. Just don't change into your shoes until you're under the shelter. And let's wait for everyone else to gather first."

* * *

IN THE END, IT ALL worked out.

The bridal bower was open on both sides to reveal, past the wedding arch, the dramatically stormy waters of the Strait of Juan de Fuca.

Teresa's dress, a classic cream-colored sheath of silk and chiffon, was indeed perfect. She simply floated in it. Wanting to please his soon-to-be mother-in-law, Liam wore a traditional tux borrowed from Joe rather than rented. They were the same height, and given Joe's broad shoulders and the comfortable cut of the suit, it also worked on Liam's more muscular build. In fact, it might have been made for him.

Joe accompanied the wedding procession on his acoustic guitar, playing Bach's *Jesu, Joy of Man's Desiring*.

Rather than writing their own vows, Liam and Teresa had simplified the traditional Catholic wedding vows. Their decision to do without a videographer was probably for the best. As the matron of honor standing right next to Teresa, Ali had no trouble hearing her, but she imagined everyone else had to strain their ears. Her voice, as usual, was a little rough at the edges— like Joe's but much softer. The contrast with Liam's booming baritone didn't help, though he caught on quickly to the disparity and modulated it to the point where you could barely hear him either. He cut a dashing figure, and Ali beamed to see him so happy and confident. Jean-Louis officiated with his customary flamboyance, though he toned it down when he realized his two leads were barely audible. Liam's best man, their father Duncan, stood beside him, bursting with pride. She wondered who had lent him the navy-blue three-piece suit, easily a size too large. Never mind; he looked grand. David gave Teresa away.

There was an unintentionally humorous moment when Jean-Louis addressed Liam as "Liam Lord Ryan." Teresa looked startled. Was it possible he'd never told her his middle name? Then it was her turn: "Teresa Flora O'Connell." That was a new one to Ali and apparently also to Liam, whose eyes widened and lips twitched. With such a brief engagement, she imagined other revelations would surface in their future. She could only hope none of them were deal breakers.

After the vows, Maddie sang Gershwin's "Our Love is Here to Stay," accompanied by Joe. Ali had expected her to be an accomplished singer, but not to this degree. Joe had told her she'd be impressed. He wasn't kidding. Ali also believed every word she sang. Why wasn't she a Broadway star?

The twins, in the back with the nanny, waited until the song was over before breaking into a chorus of screams. Their timing struck everyone as hilarious. Coogan and Harry, sitting on their haunches next to the twins' bassinet, exchanged glances, as if embarrassed by their humans' loss of control. But they didn't bark. Ali couldn't believe how well Liam had trained them.

Ali rushed to calm the twins down, and she and May each picked up a baby and returned to the house to attend to their needs. As she fed Josephine, Ali thought back to the rehearsal dinner, held at Manresa Castle the night before. The "castle" was the former residence of a wealthy merchant. Its next incarnation had been as a Jesuit Seminary. Ali wasn't sure when they had added all the bathrooms. It was just far enough from downtown that it could easily be overlooked in favor of the B&Bs, but she and Joe had stayed there when they were doing some preliminary work on their house, and it had been quite pleasant. With its period-appropriate décor—some Victorian antiques and some reproductions—the place had loads of atmosphere.

That afternoon, Carrie and Joe had gone for a walk aimed at clearing the air. Joe didn't tend to be long on details. In his usual succinct fashion, he told Ali how he'd driven home the fact that Carrie's entire future relationship with Teresa and any children she and Liam might have hinged on her being on her best behavior at this wedding. All the wishing in the world was not going to make Teresa relent and seek out a less unscrupulous version of Paul.

At the dinner, Ali marveled over the change in David's appearance. His red beard was now just a light dusting of stubble, revealing a strong cleft chin like Joe's. His hair was clipped in a fashionable brush cut; its coarse texture made it impervious to the elements. How she envied him. Her own hair, straight as blades of grass, only behaved when it was perfectly blow-dried.

"Wow!" she said aloud when she first saw her neatly groomed brother-in-law. David and Carrie responded to her shocked reaction with puzzled stares, making her cheeks burn. "You look … amazing," she told David. "It's quite a transformation—the hair and beard, I mean."

"Thank goodness," Carrie said, only mildly snippy. "Joe and David could regress to the caveman era with little effort. As children, they were happiest when wallowing in the mud."

After Joe's lecture, Carrie behaved more congenially to one and all, even if Ali sensed that her heart wasn't in it. She was surprised and a little dismayed to see Kilo hit on Maddie. She could have smacked herself for seating them together. However unconsciously, Maddie oozed sex appeal— she couldn't help it with that body. Kilo was almost as irresistible as Liam. They were a natural couple, with Kilo being a former professional modern dancer with a prestigious company and Maddie an actress/singer/dancer. Although they weren't by any means falling-down drunk, they did imbibe enough that their attraction became obvious, especially in a party of fifteen. They stood too close together and laughed too much. Thank goodness there hadn't been any dancing because she hated to think where *that* might have led. The thought made her recall—wryly—the Hasidic wedding where she had been a caterwaiter. Only the men danced. For women, dancing was thought to be a leap onto the road to ruin. Maybe they were right.

At least there was no sneaking off, and they left separately—partly due to Laurie's vigilance. Although she still wasn't Ali's favorite person, Laurie had used a firm hand when one was needed.

As Ali laid Josephine back in her cradle, she heard a warning knock and looked up to see her father. As always, she was struck by the resemblance to Liam—eyes, cheekbones, and slightly beaky nose. Liam should really consider an earring.

"The door was open. I didn't mean to disturb you."

"Hey, Dad! No disturbance at all. Nice wedding, huh? Sounds like the storm is getting worse."

In silence, they listened to the thrum of rain on the roof.

"God is applauding," Ali said finally.

Duncan chuckled. "As well he should. Joe just floors me. How he rescued the day."

"He's something, right?" Ali couldn't stop grinning. "I'm so happy, I can't help waiting for the other shoe to drop."

Duncan put a finger to his lips. "Shh … don't tempt fate. When life goes your way, enjoy it full tilt. It's not always going to be so wonderful. Maybe you and Liam got all your suffering over with in advance."

Ali kissed his cheek. "What a nice thought."

# EPILOGUE

Liam and Teresa lay in each other's arms, listening to the rain pelt the roof of the cabin.

"Happy, darling?" Liam smoothed back her strawberry-blonde curls to kiss her neck, where he breathed in the essence of vanilla rising from her skin, now an intoxicating blend of both their bodies' scents. For him, the word was "ecstatic," and he hoped she felt the same. He wasn't entirely comfortable admitting it to himself. In his mind Teresa had all the power. He was besotted, head-over-heels, whipped, every crazy-in-love cliché. He'd sat at that café in Jerusalem thinking it was just another day, never suspecting that this amazing woman was about to burst into his life and change everything. He hoped he wasn't overwhelming her with his perpetual randiness.

She slid down to kiss each of his nipples in turn. "What do you think?"

Ordering his cock to stop taking the lead, he gently pushed her away. "I want to hear you say it."

"I love you madly, Liam Lord Ryan. No woman could be happier."

He cursed the day his so-called "mother" had saddled him with such a ridiculous middle name. Nothing to do but be a good sport and hope the ribbing would subside soon. He pretended to pout, and with a sidelong look, said, "Sarcasm noted."

"Only a hint," she said. "I meant every word—I *do* love you madly—but it *is* weird that you make me say it so often."

Stung, he hesitated before replying, "I can't help it. I'm insecure. When it comes to you."

She kissed his nose. "I should be the insecure one. You think 'Flora' is such a great middle name?"

He wrinkled his nose. "Why 'Flora'?"

"The possessed girl in *Turn of the Screw*."

He blinked. He wouldn't put it past Carrie.

"Just kidding. My father's mother."

She was kissing his navel, moving downward. He laughed at the mischievous gleam in her eyes. "All right, then. Proceed."

"Wait a minute." She sat up suddenly. "Is that barking? What are the dogs doing outside in weather like this?"

Liam detected no undercurrent of warning in the dogs' yelps and yips. Coogan and Harry were roughhousing. "Well, it's dogs' weather outside," he said, feasting his eyes on her. "Isn't that what the French say when it's raining? *Il fait un temps de chien*."

"I think that means the weather has gone to the dogs." Teresa slipped into her silk bathrobe. "Not quite the same thing."

"Where are you going?" Liam grabbed her hand, tugging her gently back to the bed.

She freed her hand and checked her watch. "To see what the barking is about. Besides, everyone's expecting us at dinner. Rostand is cooking up a surprise. Then we have to pack for our honeymoon."

His stomach lurched. *Hold the phone,* he thought. *Honeymoon? We've never discussed a honeymoon.*

She opened the door to two wet dogs, tails wagging. Teresa shielded her face as they simultaneously shook themselves, spraying water everywhere. Standing between them was Joe, his raingear impressive enough for a commercial fisherman. "I thought you might need some advance warning," he said, water dripping off his oilskin hat. "I guessed you were, uh, busy. We have a roaring fire going at the house, and everyone is salivating over the champagne. We can't start the party without the guests of honor." Pointing at Liam, he said in a falsetto voice, "Put some clothes on, you big lug!"

Liam folded his arms across his chest. "Not until Teresa explains about the honeymoon."

Joe stared at Teresa in disbelief. "You haven't told him yet?"

Liam's nostrils flared. "Wait. Don't I get a say in this?" What was Teresa up to now? Something that cost a gazillion dollars, no doubt. He didn't need a friggin' honeymoon. There was no place he'd rather be than here.

Guilty as hell, Teresa stared down at her pretty feet with their pink-lacquered toenails. "I rented us a villa in Provence," she confessed, avoiding his eyes. "We're leaving tomorrow afternoon."

He kept his voice calm. "Where in Provence?"

"I'm sorry," she burst out. "I meant it as a surprise. Something a little more exciting than having two-pound Maine lobsters for dinner."

"Really?" He raised his eyebrows. "Lobster?"

Joe laughed. "Only the best for my sister and her new husband. As for the honeymoon, I told her she should consult you. She insisted on the surprise. Ali thought you'd detest Parisian snobbery, that you'd appreciate France more outside the big city. The villa Teresa chose has a saltwater swimming pool and three outdoor seating areas. Ménerbes is famous for its charm."

Teresa chirped, "*A Year in Provence* took place there."

Liam gave it about two seconds' thought, realizing it was a done deal. He did *not* wish to start his marriage off with an argument. If this was what Teresa really wanted, he was all in. He hopped out of bed. "Sounds great."

Joe covered his eyes. "Whoa! A little modesty, please. Just in case someone is out there with a telephoto lens. You've already given me a run for the money in the celebrity department." To Teresa, he added, "See you in half an hour? After that, we're opening the champagne without you. It's *Dom Perignon*." He waggled his brows.

Teresa took a moment to love up each of the dogs, even though it left her silk bathrobe damp. Liam appreciated her devotion to those scruffy animals, much as it bugged him that everyone treated them like family members rather than working dogs.

When the door closed behind Joe, Liam said casually, "Provence, huh?"

"We don't have to go," she said, head hanging. He didn't buy her chastened act.

He pulled her back down on the bed. "I can never say no to you."

She laid a delicate hand on his bare chest to hold him at bay. "Really?"

"For at least a month or two," he amended. "Then … watch out. You'll never get your way again."

She rolled him onto his back. "We'll just see about that."

*Photo by Claudia Meyer-Newman*

**Cat Treadgold** has been a publisher and editor, a classical singer, an Equity actress, a coordinator in Newsweek's External Relations Department, a secretary at Siemens AG, a voice teacher at Shoreline Community College, a receptionist at a major recording studio, a cater-waiter with Glorious Foods, a restaurant hostess, and a coat-check girl at a fancy New York nightclub.

Cat has an AB *cum laude* in German Literature from Princeton University, a Master of Music in Vocal Performance from the University of Washington, and a certificate in Technical Writing and Editing from the University of Washington.

She was once semi-fluent in French, German, and Italian and occasionally attempts to revive those languages.

Thank goodness she's good with computers (for a digital immigrant) and learned to touch type in high school.

Two of her unpublished novels, including this one, made it to the finals in their categories (mystery and romance) in the Pacific Northwest Writers Association Annual Contest.

Three of her one-hour adaptations of operas (original translations and dialogue) were performed by Shoreline students while she was a teacher there.

She and her husband Jeff reside in Washington during its drier months and Arizona during its cooler ones.

Cat loves to hike and walk, ride her bike, hula hoop, play golf, listen to audiobooks, cook dishes with lots of leftovers, play piano (she used to be good at it), and play accordion (she will never be good at it). She sings in the occasional concert with Ladies Musical Club, but never in the shower. Her favorite classical composers are Ravel, Debussy, and Brahms. She prefers pop music from the '60s and '70s, particularly Steely Dan and the Rolling Stones.

One hot, humid summer in Ohio, while playing a Shawnee Indian in an outdoor drama during the week and Anne in the musical *Shenandoah* on the weekends, she became certified in stage fighting. That skill later helped her win the role of a broadsword-wielding Maid Marion in a Theater for Young Audiences musical titled *Maid Marion (and Robin Too)*. She always wanted to sing the role of Carmen, but only did it in Seattle Opera previews. She has played Edwin Drood in *The Mystery of Edwin Drood*, Maria in *The Sound of Music*, Julie Jordan in *Carousel,* Cherubino in *The Marriage of Figaro*, Prince Orlofsky in *Die Fledermaus*, Maddalena in *Rigoletto*, Julius Caesar in Handel's *Julius Caesar in Egypt*, and Rosina in *The Barber of Seville*. Along with other fun gigs (including a few at Port Townsend's UpStage), her opera quartet (The Operatic Four Players) performed regularly on Friday nights for about a year at an Italian restaurant. For three years, she toured with NOISE (Northwest Opera in Schools Etcetera).

Videos of her vocal performances can be found on the Cattread channel (www.youtube.com/@cattread),

For more information, go to www.CatTreadgold.com.